Praise for Chri

"Christi Caldwell writes a gorgeous book!"
—Sarah MacLean, *New York Times* and *USA Today* bestselling author

"*Along Came a Lady* is exactly what I needed to read right now. Edwina and Rafe's love story is ribboned with subtleties about gender roles and class expectations that make this novel both thoughtful and delightful all at once."

—Jodi Picoult, #1 *New York Times* bestselling author of *The Book of Two Ways* on *Along Came a Lady*

"Christi Caldwell's crisp, sparkling writing is infused with emotion, passion, and a belief in the healing power of love. This is terrific Regency romance!"

—Amanda Quick, *New York Times* bestselling author on *Along Came a Lady*

"Emotional, funny, and filled with passion—everything I want in a romance."

—Lorraine Heath, *New York Times* bestselling author of *The Duchess Hunt* on *Along Came a Lady*

"In addition to a strong plot, this story boasts actualized characters whose personal demons are clear and credible. The chemistry between the protagonists is seductive and palpable, with their family history of hatred played against their personal similarities and growing attraction to create an atmospheric and captivating romance."

—*Publishers Weekly* on *The Hellion*

The Heiress at Sea

OTHER TITLES BY CHRISTI CALDWELL

The Duke Alone

Wantons of Waverton

Someone Wanton His Way Comes
The Importance of Being Wanton
A Wanton for All Seasons

Lost Lords of London

In Bed with the Earl
In the Dark with the Duke
Undressed with the Marquess

Sinful Brides

The Rogue's Wager
The Scoundrel's Honor
The Lady's Guard
The Heiress's Deception

Wicked Wallflowers

The Hellion
The Vixen
The Governess
The Bluestocking
The Spitfire

All the Duke's Sins

It Had to Be the Duke (novella)
Along Came a Lady
One for My Baron (novella)
Desperately Seeking a Duchess

Scandalous Affairs

A Groom of Her Own
Taming of the Beast
My Fair Marchioness
It Happened One Winter

Heart of a Duke

For Love of the Duke
More Than a Duke
The Love of a Rogue
Loved by a Duke
To Love a Lord
The Heart of a Scoundrel
To Wed His Christmas Lady
To Trust a Rogue
The Lure of a Rake
To Woo a Widow
To Redeem a Rake
One Winter with a Baron
To Enchant a Wicked Duke
Beguiled by a Baron
To Tempt a Scoundrel
To Hold a Lady's Secret
To Catch a Viscount
Defying the Duke
To Marry Her Marquess
Devil and the Debutante
Devil by Daylight

The Heart of a Scandal

In Need of a Knight (A Prequel Novella)
Schooling the Duke
A Lady's Guide to a Gentleman's Heart

A Matchmaker for a Marquess
His Duchess for a Day
Five Days With a Duke

Lords of Honor

Seduced by a Lady's Heart
Captivated by a Lady's Charm
Rescued by a Lady's Love
Tempted by a Lady's Smile
Courting Poppy Tidemore

Scandalous Seasons

Forever Betrothed, Never the Bride
Never Courted, Suddenly Wed
Always Proper, Suddenly Scandalous
Always a Rogue, Forever Her Love
A Marquess for Christmas
Once a Wallflower, At Last His Love

The Theodosia Sword

Only For His Lady
Only For Her Honor
Only For Their Love

Danby

Winning a Lady's Heart
A Season of Hope

The Brethren

The Spy Who Seduced Her
The Lady Who Loved Him
The Rogue Who Rescued Her

The Heiress at Sea

CHRISTI CALDWELL

Text copyright © 2023 by Christi Caldwell Incorporated
All rights reserved.

Published by Montlake, Seattle

www.apub.com

Amazon, the Amazon logo, and Montlake are trademarks of Amazon.com, Inc., or its affiliates.

ISBN-13: 9781662503818 (paperback)
ISBN-13: 9781662503825 (digital)

Front cover design and photography by Juliana Kolesova
Back cover design by Ray Lundgren
Cover image: © hideto999 / Shutterstock;
© ENRIQUE ALAEZ PEREZ / Shutterstock

Printed in the United States of America

To my special readers part of Christi Caldwell's Corner!
Thank you for all the smiles and talk about my books,
characters, and worlds. With your posts, comments, and
discussions, you definitely make the day brighter and fill
my author-heart. I am so very grateful for each of you!
Nathan and Cassia's book is for you!

Chapter 1

Since he'd been a boy, Lord Nathaniel Ellsby, the fourth Marquess of Winfield, had delighted in subverting his father's wishes. Any opportunity to disappoint or keep him waiting, Nathaniel had grasped.

This time, stopped outside the Duke of Roxburghe's offices, however, was no deliberate ploy on his part.

"A letter has arrived for you, my lord," his family's butler murmured, handing over the missive.

Accepting the note, Nathaniel examined the official seal of the Crown. He slid his finger under the crimson wax and unfolded the page.

He proceeded to read the handful of lines there.

It was time.

"When you're able to join us," his father shouted from inside his office, his displeasure reaching out into the corridor, "please do so, Nathaniel."

After folding the letter along the neat crease, Nathaniel tucked it back inside his jacket, then waited several more moments before strolling inside. "Mother," he greeted, crossing over to kiss her on the cheek.

"Nathaniel! My boy!"

The duke rolled his eyes at that display of affection.

"Do sit! There is so much to talk about," his mother said, guiding him to the chair opposite the duke.

Silence fell over the room as father and son engaged in a long, unspoken battle of wills.

Nathaniel hadn't been born the heir. Rather, he'd been born as the spare, along with a line of four other spares behind him.

In his mind, there'd been absolutely no expectation that he would one day be duke. It had surprised even his father, who'd been wholly disinterested in the lot of children he'd gotten on Nathaniel's mother. The only child he'd seen had been his heir.

His other babes were just babes, an extension of the title—emergency children there in the event the worst ever befell the ducal line.

But there'd not been any idea that such an emergency would ever befall him.

After all, bad things didn't happen to powerful, wealthy men of influence.

The paternal disinterest hadn't bothered Nathaniel. Rather, it had been a boon.

He'd never envied his brother the attention he'd gotten from the duke. Just the opposite, really. He'd been grateful Marcus, older by a year, had received all the duke's attention. It had spared Nathaniel the misery of his father's company, and it had allowed him the freedom to do that which a nobleman's heir was not allowed: whatever he wanted.

It was why, when he'd finished school and sought a naval commission from the vice admiral, he'd been free to do so without intervention or even an iota of interest from the man who'd sired him. When all the other lords of his ilk were strutting around London, drinking and bedding women, he'd gone to sea. He'd resolved to make something of himself . . . besides being just the spare.

It was why, after Nathaniel had learned all he could from the navy, sold his commissions, and established himself as a shipping magnate, his father hadn't so much as batted an eye. After all, to do so, he'd have had to be interested in *Nathaniel*.

It was why he'd not had to discuss or debate his decision to pursue the scandalous venture of being a wartime privateer.

These were the freedoms and luxuries afforded the ducal spare. Such gifts were not so extended to ducal heirs.

This discovery had become increasingly clear since the unexpected passing of his elder brother, dead too soon by a fall from his horse.

Since that moment, all expectations had transferred to Nathaniel.

The duke broke the silence first.

He slammed his fist on the immaculate surface of his mahogany desk, the crystal inkstand jumping. "I have been patient with you, boy. I've been tolerant. Indulged your little pastime. But it is long overdue that you get on with your duty to me."

"A duty to you which, of course, supersedes my service to king and country," Nathaniel drawled.

His father, a man who was never crossed, would also never expect sarcasm. "Bloody right it does. At least you know *that* much," he blustered. "Furthermore, you've not served king, Crown, and country for some years now."

Leave it to his contrary father to happen to know *that* detail about him.

The duke looked to his wife, hovering just at Nathaniel's shoulder. "Your son is being stubborn, just like you."

Just like *her*?

The duchess's greatest challenge to her husband's ways had been to love her children far more affectionately than the duke deemed fit and proper. Children, in the duke's opinion, should be raised by nannies, governesses, and the staff—not by his lady wife.

She fluttered there, like a pale, uncertain butterfly. "Nathaniel is a good boy."

"A *good* boy?" The duke snorted. "If he were a *good* boy, he'd do his damned duties, seeing to his responsibilities instead of making my life difficult."

His mother made nonsensical soothing noises, placating the blustery duke the same way she'd tended to all her sons.

Nathaniel narrowed his gaze on his sire, searching for a hint of himself in that face. With the duke's bulbous nose flaring and his dark-eyed gaze rheumy from age, Nathaniel luckily found none.

Nathaniel had blond hair where his father's was dark. He possessed blue eyes where the duke's were brown. Aside from the obstinate line of an intractable jaw and a like towering height of six feet four inches, that was where all similarities between father and son ended.

Though there was one even more important difference between the two—Nathaniel didn't give ten damns about the old duke. That indifference and absolute lack of connection to his sire had been a gift handed down from the man who'd sired him.

His Grace dropped his meaty paws upon the desk once more and leaned forward, putting Nathaniel more in mind of the duke's prized hounds. "I've indulged you enough," he said, spittle forming at the corners of his fleshy lips. "I've let you play at being a pirate—"

"Privateer," Nathaniel interrupted in frosty tones to rival those of the coldhearted lord across from him.

The duke remained unvexed. "I've even allowed you to buy yourself a shipping company." He thumped his fist once more, this time harder. "But I'll be damned if I . . ."

As his father rattled on about his latest grievance, Nathaniel curled his hands sharply in his lap. For most noblemen, it would be enough that behind Nathaniel were Laurence, Sebastian, Eric, and Jamie—four equally capable sons. While the duke continued his lecture, Nathaniel stared at a point over the top of his head. He'd once had five brothers in total. The eldest, Marcus, however, was gone, as was the memory of him. Though in truth, as the heir, Marcus had been shut away by the duke and tasked with learning his future responsibilities early enough that he'd never been there—not truly. The fact that Marcus had been more stranger than sibling hurt still, and it served as another needless reminder of why Nathaniel so resented the man who'd helped give him life.

He cut into the duke's fiery speech. "If anything should happen to me, Laurence, Sebastian, Eric, and Jamie would *each* do an admirable job in the role of future duke."

"Sebastian and Eric are fighting that cur's forces, and Jamie is just a boy."

That left the rogue amongst them. "Laurence—"

His father slammed his palm down. "*You* are my heir."

Nathaniel kicked back in his seat and dropped his booted foot across his opposite knee. "Ah, yes, and it would be unpardonable to interact in any way with your younger sons."

Another man might have taken offense and sworn his affection and allegiance to the four spares.

Intractable and unfeeling, the duke proved as indifferent as he'd always been. "You are done, Nathaniel. I will speak to Prinny myself," his father vowed.

He'd do it, too. Yes, the duke had four sons behind Nathaniel who were just as capable of taking on his responsibilities, but to him, the next heir was the only heir. And as the duke was the best friend of the Mad King, his son, the prince regent, would honor the duke's connection to the Crown.

His father jabbed a finger Nathaniel's way. "You are *going* to marry the Duke of Talbert's girl." He cast a glance at his wife. "What is her name?"

"An—"

"It doesn't matter." The duke cut off that detail, refocusing his attention on Nathaniel. "It's your godmother and godfather's daughter—"

"Of *course* it doesn't matter," Nathaniel interrupted in tight tones. "Why should the name of the woman you're attempting to force me to wed be of any relevance?"

The duke gave his first approving nod of their meeting. "Exactly. Talbert expects his daughter will marry a duke."

Only further solidifying their fortune and connections.

"Not on my part," Nathaniel snapped. After all, he'd solidified his own fortune.

"The gel is getting on in years, boy, and you need to be getting the next duke after you on her."

"Angela," the duchess whispered to Nathaniel. "The girl's name is Angela."

There was nothing the Duke of Roxburghe couldn't or, more, *wouldn't* do in the name of protecting the Roxburghe title, and that included determining everything that went into *continuing* that line. Reasoning with the mercenary duke was as impossible as conversing with the now-demented king.

"And if I don't?" Nathaniel asked quietly. An understanding had existed between Lady Angela and Nathaniel's late brother. That responsibility had shifted to Nathaniel upon Marcus's death. "What if I decline to marry the lady?"

"We honor our obligations." Yes, they did. Perhaps there was something more they had in common, after all. That realization left him chilled.

As if he sensed Nathaniel's weakening, the duke managed what Nathaniel expected was as close as he could muster to a smile on unforgiving lips that'd known far more scowls in life. "You may have sold your commission and built a fortune, but I am the one with the power and connections to put it all to an end. If you don't make this match, you will never set foot upon your beloved boat again."

Nathaniel ground his teeth. "Ship."

"You're all done." His father wagged a fleshy finger at him. "There'll be no more of your fun until you get yourself married and secure an heir."

Fun. Red rage, visceral and real, slipped through his heated veins. Even if the duke knew the truth, that the missions Nathaniel ran were about not just growing his fortune but intercepting French ships headed for various battles, it wouldn't matter. At every turn the duke would diminish what Nathaniel had accomplished. And yet, Nathaniel could not tell him of the work he did in the name of the war effort. If he came right out and informed his father that he'd received directives to intercept a French squadron and gather their war plans in the Adriatic campaign, the duke would ask what that mission had to do with his title.

"You get me an heir on the girl, and you're free to go on playing pirates," the duke was saying, bringing Nathaniel back from his musings. He arched a bushy black brow that'd always put Nathaniel in mind of a caterpillar. "That is a ducal order. If not, I go to Prinny."

With that statement from the duke, the *discussion* was at an end.

In other words, Nathaniel didn't have the four days he'd anticipated. It meant he had to round up as many of his crew as he could and cut their leave short.

Nathaniel stood. "Your Grace," he clipped out, and steeling his jaw, he stalked off.

The delicate tread of a softer football echoed behind him, and Nathaniel made himself slow his steps. Where he had been free to escape and bury himself in his shipping ventures, and to flee aboard his ship, the *Flying Dragon*, his mother had not been granted that same reprieve from the oppressive hand of her ducal husband.

He made himself stop. "Mother," he said when she reached him.

She went up on tiptoe, and he leaned down, allowing her to kiss his cheek.

Slipping her arm through his, she joined him on his walk to the foyer. "That went well, did it not?" she chirped in her usual singsong voice.

Nathaniel cast her a sideways glance. Long an optimist and still capable of cheer and smiling, despite the medieval man she'd been betrothed and then bound to, she'd retained her sunny disposition. Nathaniel had never been able to wrap his mind around how. "If you mean 'well' in that His Grace will have exactly what he wants"—as always—"and my business shuttered, then . . . yes. It went prodigiously well."

His mother laughed softly, then lightly gripped his arm. And with that gesture, she silently asked for him to stop.

Nathaniel complied.

Because she was the one and only person for whom he had a hint of weakness. Because he pitied her. Because he felt bad that she should be so trapped when Nathaniel went about freely. Or . . . had gone about freely. A muscle twitched at the corner of his eye. All that freedom of movement was about to end.

"Your father . . . He has not been the same since Marcus." Tears formed in her eyes, and the sight of her grief ravaged him. His mother never cried, and as such, he was unaccustomed to the emotion.

He removed a kerchief from his jacket, and she accepted it, dabbing at her cheeks. "Losing his son has shown him his own fallibility."

"It showed him that five sons aren't enough? That he needs a grandson, too, to shore up the ducal line?" Nathaniel asked flatly.

She nodded. "There is some truth to that."

There was *only* truth to that. He'd not debate his mother, however.

"And . . . as for Angela"—he tensed—"she is heartbroken at losing your brother. It was understood they would wed, and after mourning him as she did, she's far past an age most girls are when they have their first Season."

Nathaniel's cravat grew increasingly tight; panic threatened to choke him. Fortunately, his mother steered them away from talks of that expected marriage.

"Your father . . . He cares about you, Nathaniel."

He snorted. "You cannot possibly believe that."

A frown formed on her lips and brought her brows dipping down. "He loves you as he is able. Just as he loves me. He can be cantankerous and has a different way of showing it, but there is no doubt about it: he does."

"Different," as in "nonexistent." Not for the first time, Nathaniel felt more than a touch of regret for his mother, who, for some reason, loved the miserable boor of a man she'd married and had convinced herself that he felt some of that same regard for her.

"And marriage to Lady Angela will not be such a bad thing," his mother put forward with her usual cheerful optimism.

Nathaniel stared at her incredulously. Did she *truly* believe that? Had she given such similar assurances to herself when her father, Nathaniel's grandfather—another equally powerful, overbearing duke—had arranged a match between her and Nathaniel's father?

"When do you leave?" his mother asked, proving she knew him in ways his father never had and never would.

Nathaniel tensed. He wasn't due to sail for a number of days. That timeline now needed to be moved up. "I did not say—"

"Come," she scoffed. "Do you truly believe I think you'll let your father have the last say on all this?"

He remained stonily silent.

"Very well." The duchess smoothed her palms along the front of Nathaniel's jacket and patted him affectionately. "I know you think you will always *want* a life at sea, my boy. But you won't. Someday, after you wed, you are going to find there is, in fact, a reason to remain on land, and you'll be ever so happy to trade in your sea legs for land ones."

He stared at her confusedly.

His mother laughed softly and patted him once more. "Your wife, Nathaniel. Your wife."

Surely she didn't expect he'd go and fall in love with the woman handpicked by the duke, his sole reason being the connection to be gained by their union? And at that, a woman who was still in love with his brother's ghost?

Actually, the duchess likely could convince herself of as much.

"I will eventually marry," he said quietly, needing to disabuse his mother of whatever delusions she had for him and his return. "I will do as Father requires and cement those connections." Because he knew if he didn't, ultimately his father would see his business ruined. "And he'll get his all-important ducal heir, but only so that I can return to the sea, Mother."

Because the sea was his home. The crew he'd assembled, who'd become like family, were men who relied upon him, and to whom he owed his real fealty. "But I've no intention of being landlocked, or of shifting my responsibilities to being the next duke." He flexed his jaw. "Not when I expect Father will outlive all of us, just out of sheer obstinacy and for the love he carries for the Roxburghe title." It was the one and only thing in the miserable bastard's life he did, in fact, love.

A mysterious-looking smile hovered on her lips. "Yes, I expect that is what you think, Nathaniel. You will see."

The only thing he saw was the work in front of him and the calming peace of a ship rolling softly under his feet when the waters were calm, and then the thrill of danger when they rocked the vessel violently about. That was all Nathaniel wanted or loved.

And the last thing he'd ever have a want or need of was some woman who would expect to tie him down and keep him ashore.

Chapter 2

London, England

With a leather sabretache she'd pilfered from her elder brother's belongings and modified for her frame now slung over her shoulder, Lady Cassia McQuoid made her way along the north bank of the River Thames.

No one stared. In fact, no one paid her notice one way or the other.

After half a Season being stared at by everyone, it was a welcome way to find herself.

Undetected.

Unnoted.

Free.

A light breeze cut through the coal-smoke fog hanging over the city, bringing the stench of sewage mixed with the sulphury smell of the North Sea. That gust teased the wool, shovel-shaped hat Cassia had also availed herself of—the article having been one of the more cherished heirlooms her siblings had all coveted.

Pausing at the corner of Preston's Road, Cassia adjusted her hat. She took care to keep her plaited braid tucked inside and hidden before continuing forward.

Nay, she wasn't free. Not just yet. But she was close.

There was still the matter of boarding the boat her elder brother Arran was to sail on with his best friend, Captain Jeremy Tremaine, and then remaining undetected until they sailed away from London.

How difficult could that be?

Nay, going unnoticed should prove simple.

In all of Cassia's two and one-quarter London Seasons, there had never been so much as an unkind word written about her in the gossip pages.

Neither, however, had there been kind ones.

More, *nothing* had been said about her. At least, not *specifically*.

Not when her parents had dragged her along to meet their new neighbor, the Duke of Aragon, and attempted to marry her off to the brooding, mysterious gentleman. Ultimately, the gossips had noted and not been kind to Cassia's parents for those very public, grasping attempts. After all, one only *privately* grasped a duke.

Nor did Polite Society say so much as a peep about Cassia when her younger sister Myrtle, who'd not even had her Come Out and a London Season, had instead married the same duke.

No, the papers had heaped praise upon Myrtle for being so very witty and charming and interesting as to have snagged the once reclusive Duke of Aragon.

Which—at that point—had been peculiar praise, as not a single member of Society had so much as met Myrtle. Though in fairness, they'd not had to meet her. All they'd needed to know was that Myrtle was now the Duchess of Aragon.

And it was that, right there, that accounted for Cassia's current plans.

Not the duchess part.

Cassia had no interest in being a duchess.

She'd be dreadfully bad at the whole "almost royalty" business.

Nor, for that matter, did she find Society had erred in their generous and bright opinion of Myrtle. They hadn't.

Even at eighteen, Myrtle was clever and spirited and sunny, and had a keen wit.

And then there was Cassia.

Possessed of just as much spirit as the Lord gave any soul, and of average—if she was being generous with her own self—wit.

In short, Cassia was something unforgivable in the world of Polite Society: just an ordinary, unremarkable girl. She wasn't a Diamond and she wasn't flirty. She didn't have any womanly wiles. She was simply . . . *herself*. There was nothing to distinguish her amongst all the other young ladies and misses.

Unmarried at one and twenty, and well into her third Season without so much as a suitor, Cassia did not harbor any misunderstandings as to the reason for her unwedded state.

Nor was she one given to self-pity or disparagement. Rather, her understanding came from a place of actual fact. Her sister was clever. Bookish. Her parents had believed in Myrtle so very much that they'd sent her away to a boarding school to further broaden her intellect and feed her love of learning, and . . . and . . . antiquities, and whatever else it was they'd had Myrtle and other students sent there to study.

Whereas Cassia? Her greatest skills: Painting. Needlepoint. Singing. Playing the pianoforte. Arranging flowers and rooms. Cassia possessed *ladylike* talents—the same ones perfected by every lady, and certainly not enough to recommend her. A skill set that didn't require that she leave home, like Myrtle. But oh, how she wished to broaden her horizons with new sights and adventures. She'd lived a dull, ordinary life. It was, however, only just now she'd realized as much.

She wanted to know what it was to feel the ocean breeze upon her face, as her brother had regaled their family with tales of. Or to sail so far out that one lost the sounds of the gulls and seabirds and instead heard the squeals of dolphins, only to then reach distant lands where wharves brimmed with actual sunshine and people from all corners of the world. With the support of their parents, Arran, who'd partnered with Jeremy in his trade ventures, had *seen* that world. Even Myrtle had left home. Whereas her younger sister had learned about those fantastical lands from books, Cassia was determined to experience it all for herself. Her family wouldn't have supported her in that dream, because they didn't believe her capable or deserving of it. As such, she had been forced to take matters into her own hands.

Otherwise, for the rest of her days, she would have found herself confined to a London ballroom and parlor, never experiencing anything outside those rigid, unbending, and unforgiving walls, where tedium reigned and souls withered.

Pulling her cap lower over her brow, she made her way through the wharves.

Her heart thundered, and she stole furtive glances about as she walked.

Despite having bound her breasts and dressed herself in garments she'd filched from her younger brother, she expected someone would surely see. That someone would recognize her as the fraud she was, and cries of horror would go up. And she'd be dragged off until her parents were summoned and brought 'round to collect her. Only . . . there were no cries. Rather, the men and boys—of all ages, from the very young to the very old—remained engrossed in their own specific tasks and chores along the wharf.

With three docks sandwiched between Bridge Road and High Street, the area fairly vibrated from the bustling activity.

Cassia paused briefly to take in the sight before her. The scent of the salty sea air filled her nostrils, while cries and shouts of men at work carried around the wharf. It was, in short, everything Arran's best friend, Captain Jeremy Tremaine, had regaled Cassia's family with for years and years.

Jeremy had been as much a presence in her family's household as an extra sibling in the noisy, eccentric McQuoid clan.

She knew him so well, in fact, that she could say definitively that her plan would have been met with nothing but resistance.

It was why, even now, she found herself searching for his ship, the *Waltzing Dragon*.

Cassia caught her lower lip between her teeth and worried at that flesh. Did boats carry their names painted upon them?

They must.

Otherwise, how else was a person to know the difference between any of them? They were all enormously soaring wood vessels with matching white sails. Hardly anything marked them apart. Nay, only a deliberately painted, clever name would ever help a person tell one from another.

She supposed she should have asked as much during Jeremy's visit last week, when she'd hatched her scheme. After all, she'd come up with the idea during dinner, and there'd still been dessert for her to ask that necessary question.

At the time, however, she'd let her mind wander with just how she'd implement her plan and what she'd need to wear to disguise herself and how she'd find those garments and whether a woman in trousers looked the same as a man did in trousers and . . . well, there'd been so many of those important issues she'd not put proper thought into other, equally important ones . . . like how to tell which ship her brother and Jeremy sailed upon.

Or what she would do if her sack filled with books and charcoal and pencils for recording her adventures became too heavy.

And it had, since she'd made the long walk from the hired hackney that had brought her to the shipyards, become outrageously heavy.

Grunting, Cassia staggered slightly under the weight. The muscles in her shoulder screamed under the strain she'd placed on them, and . . . well, she'd never even known she had muscles there. Perspiration dotted her brow and trickled down into her eyes. She blinked several times to drive back the sting.

That was something else she did not know about: human muscles. Cassia paused to shift the bag onto her opposite shoulder; even as she did, she added a mental note to her list to find Captain Jeremy's surgeon so that she might put questions to him about the human body. That was decidedly something else she wished to know about. And she knew Captain Jeremy Tremaine had a doctor aboard his ship because of the story he'd imparted about the time his ship had been wrecked. Yes, the surgeon's presence would provide Cassia with an opportunity to expand even further on her knowledge.

Even more enlivened to continue her Edification of Worldly Matters, as she'd titled her studies, Cassia did a sweep once more of the wharf. Craning her neck back as she walked, she took in the magnificent sight of the towering ships around her. They were—

She encountered a solid, unforgiving rock wall in her path.

Cassia grunted as she collided headfirst with the immovable granite. The sack slipped from her grip as she went flying, soaring back, landing hard on her buttocks.

Pain instantly radiated and burnt all the way up her back, and she groaned in misery. A lady did not rub her buttocks. A lady did not even so much as say—or, for that matter, *think*—the word "buttocks." Her mother and governesses had reminded her of those details as a child. But if ever there came a time to do both—rub and curse—this was decidedly that moment.

"Oi, ye got yer demned head in the clouds, boy," a voice barked from above her, and she crept her eyes up.

Only, it . . . wasn't a wall she'd collided with but, rather, a man.

He was a giant, clearly seven feet, at least. His chest was as big as the barrels being lugged aboard the ships by smaller men.

Attired in a black-and-red-plaid shirt and a pair of snug trousers that displayed bulging muscles, he was single-handedly the biggest and most unique-looking fellow she'd ever laid eyes on. His enormous bald head was so bright it nearly gleamed, like he polished it the way her family servants did the silver.

"Something wrong with yer blasted ears, too, lad?" he called over the din of the bustling wharf activity, and Cassia gulped hard. He jabbed a beefy finger down at her. "Ye got yer head in the clouds, then ye should be flying, not sailing."

Flying?

"Pegasus is really just a legend, you know." She felt inclined to educate the glowering ogre. "Although"—she wrinkled her nose—"I do suppose you're referring to the hot air balloons," she amended as understanding dawned and she thought about those colorful, egg-shaped spheres she'd witnessed take flight in London some years ago.

"Yes." Cassia struggled to her feet, and as she spoke, she dusted her palms together. "I suppose I should have considered flying. Alas, the flight would likely prove less . . ."

Eyes entirely too small for the sailor's enormous head bulged. "Are ye makin' loight of me?" he thundered.

Cassia—and the dozen or so seagulls that'd been picking their way along the pier—jumped. Those grey-white birds squawked, flapping their wings wildly, and took hasty, frightened flight.

"No?" she managed to squeak out, and Cassia really did wish she'd the ability to fly, after all.

"Is that a question?" he barked, taking a warning step toward her, and she backed up into a hard surface.

Cassia startled as hands closed over her shoulders, and she glanced back at the person who held her.

"Have a care," the kindly-eyed gentleman said, and Cassia crept her gaze back a fraction to the inches between her and the waters lapping against the dock. She'd not even known she had come so close to tumbling into the River Thames.

His smile slipped, and the man turned a scowl on the Mountain Man. "What's the meaning of this, Shorty?"

Shorty? *That* was the man's name? Why, the choice was as ridiculous as if England had been called "Land of the Sun."

"Ran hisself roight at me," the giant growled, and Cassia took a reflexive step backward, but her rescuer gave the shoulder he still held a light, reassuring squeeze.

The tall man, possibly in his early thirties with dark hair that had begun to prematurely silver at the temple, scowled at the Mountain Man. "You have work to see to before sailing, and that doesn't include wasting your time bullying a mere lad, Shorty," he admonished in the same tones Cassia's younger siblings' governess adopted when scolding the troublesome children.

And unlike the McQuoid children, who could not be tamed, a blush broke out on this bear of a man's cheeks—big bright, circular splotches of red. "Aye, aye," he muttered, and then with a last quick scowl for Cassia's benefit, he took himself off in the opposite direction.

She followed his swift retreat, never more grateful to be away from a person and relieved she'd not have to face him again. "Thank you so much," she said, dipping her voice into those deeper tones she'd been paying extra close attention to every time her brother-in-law and brothers spoke, practicing in private and, at last, putting them to use. "I'm grateful for your assistance."

The gentleman touched the corner of his brow. "Think nothing of it," he said, going and gathering up her sack, scooping it as easily as if he hefted a pillow and not a weighted bag filled with sketch pads.

He handed it over, and Cassia took that offering, grunting as she sagged under its weight.

The gentleman's pleasant mouth tipped slightly at the corners as if he were fighting a smile. "I gather this is your first time," he ventured.

Cassia wrestled her sack onto her opposite shoulder. "I . . . yes." She troubled at her lower lip. "Do I look very green?"

This time, the gentleman allowed a smile to fully form, and it was a warm, gentle one. "You definitely have the look."

"And what look is that?"

"Like you're a peer's son off for his first adventure, queasy before you've even set foot on the ship."

"Oh." She balked at how very close this stranger had come to the mark. That was, with the not-so-insignificant difference being that she was no peer's son, but one's daughter. And here Cassia had believed that all the time she'd spent reading from the sailing books she'd pilfered from her brother's room would allow her to easily slip in amongst Jeremy's crew.

"It gets easier, and the men less frightening, too," he promised.

The men less frightening. Which suggested . . . there were men even surlier than Mr. Shorty about.

Cassia swallowed. Or attempted to. She choked around the knot of unease that had formed in her throat.

Oh, stop, she silently chided. Jeremy wouldn't hire men like Mr. Shorty. Why, it'd be more likely he'd an entire crew made up of men like Cassia's kindly rescuer.

"Hayes!" someone bellowed from afar, and the gentleman looked in the direction of that summons.

"Duty calls," he said. He gave Cassia a reassuring pat on her shoulder, and she sagged under that solid thump.

Another grin played on Mr. Hayes's lips, and then he left.

But when he did, she'd be on her own, and amidst a crowd of angry-looking men with even angrier eyes, he'd been the first kind one to meet, and the moment he was gone, until she found Jeremy's ship, she would be well and truly alone once more and . . .

Quickening her steps, Cassia hurried after him, her shorter legs and the added weight of her bag making it impossible to catch his longer strides. "Mr. Hayes?" she called after him.

The gentleman stopped and turned back, waiting for her to catch up to him.

Panting lightly from her efforts, Cassia struggled to get a proper breath in. "I was wondering if you might help me locate my boat."

His eyes twinkled warmly. "Your ship?"

Cassia stared quizzically at him. That was what she'd said. Hadn't she? She searched her mind for the reason for his confusion.

"What is the name?"

"My name?" she blurted. Her mind drew a momentary blank.

"Your ship," he said gently, and a wave of relief hit her.

"Dragon," she said on a rush. "That is, the—"

His eyes flared with surprise.

She took an eager step forward. "You know of it?"

"Very much so." His eyes twinkled. "I am the quartermaster."

She didn't have an inkling as to what a quartermaster was or did, but there was a sound of importance to it, and she had to say something. "Indeed!" she exclaimed, her voice climbing an octave, and she instantly felt her face go warm.

Mr. Hayes gave no indication, however, that he'd identified her as anything but the lad she pretended to be, with her breasts strapped uncomfortably down, passing for a youth. For if he had, he'd have at best offered to help her with her hefty sack and, at worst, dragged her to Jeremy, who'd in turn drag her straight back to her family's Mayfair townhouse. Instead, he swept his right arm in a light arc forward. "Come along. I will show you to the ship and below deck, where you'll be sleeping."

"Thank you ever so much," she said, deepening her voice a touch more, as she'd practiced since she'd crafted her plan.

And as Cassia followed beside the gentleman, now her escort, the earlier trepidation receded and she felt the same forbidden thrill that had followed her from the moment she'd crafted her plan to last night, when she'd been unable to sleep from the excitement of the adventure to come, and out of fear that, with her love of sleep, she'd in fact miss arising in time to make it to sail with Arran and Jeremy.

"Which is it?" she asked, unable to keep the excitement from creeping into her voice.

"There she is." Mr. Hayes pointed his finger on a slight diagonal, and she followed it to—

Cassia gasped.

The boat soared several hundred feet into the sky. Even had her family's townhouse been plucked from its foundation and set on this shore, it would have still been dwarfed in size by the mighty vessel.

"Beautiful, is she not?" He spoke with the same pride he might have possessed had he been the owner of that great big boat.

"She is." Sheer reverence made her reply come as nothing more than a breathily exhaled whisper. Since she'd cooked up her plan to see the world and expand her knowledge of it, she'd imagined any number of times just what the vessel she'd be sailing on would look like. Nothing, absolutely nothing, could have prepared her for the sight of it. Set against the backdrop of the inky black in early-dawn hours, the sails stood out, as stark as the white clouds that peppered the still night sky. What looked like hundreds of ropes twisted and twined like a spider's web that men of all ages and sizes scrambled and scurried upon as effortlessly as if they strolled the perimeter of a ballroom.

If possible, the closer each stride brought her to the boat, the greater that vessel soared in size. Long, and far narrower than she'd ever imagined, there was a sleekness to the boat.

"She instills awe in everyone who sees her," Mr. Hayes explained with another one of his friendly smiles.

As they approached, the bustle of activity around that area grew, with men and boys swarming like busy ants, going about a familiar routine—back and forth, men streaming up a plank and others coming back down. She'd never set foot upon anything other than a horse or carriage—and the earth, of course—in the whole of her life, but even she could see these men were masters at their jobs.

Mr. Hayes reached the wood slatting that served as a gangplank onto the boat. He cupped his hands and shouted, "Permission to come aboard." When an answering cry went up, the kindly gentleman motioned for her to follow. "This way, lad."

Cassia took a step forward, setting a foot on the boards, and then froze; the plank shifted and swayed with the rise and fall of the boat, and she along with it.

Her entire stomach lurched, and Cassia planted her feet firmly, fighting to keep her balance.

Only, the weight of her bag bore her backward, and she gasped, staggering, fighting to stand. And then, miracle of miracles, she retained her footing.

Swallowing hard, she glanced over the side at the space between the boat and the wharf. The dark waters lapping against the side of the vessel churned and slapped in a violent tug. Unlike most young misses of her acquaintance, she did know how to swim. She had that going for her. And yet swimming in her family's loch in Scotland was entirely different from being plunged into the inky-black waters of the Thames.

More than halfway up, Mr. Hayes seemed to have realized she'd not followed.

He glanced back and then, with a frown, jogged. "Come along," he called, and she gave another heave of her bag and forced herself to keep moving.

They reached the main deck, and the same level of buzz of activity that filled the wharves played out aboard the vessel.

Men lugged lines of ropes. She lifted her gaze skyward and took in up close the sight of those men scaling the masts. *My God, they must be higher than fifty feet in the air—*

"I'll show you to your hammock in the crew quarters. Then get you scrubbing down the ship."

"Hayes!" The bellow Cassia had heard before came a second time, its proximity making it boom like a shot of thunder, and she jumped.

"Aye, aye. I'm coming, Fox," he called back. Mr. Hayes signaled to one of the deckhands, and a child an inch or so smaller than herself hurried over.

"Will you see to . . . ?" The gentleman paused and looked questioningly at her.

She could not allow herself to be discovered just yet. Yes, Jeremy was like another brother to her, but neither was she foolish enough to believe he'd allow her to flee her family and the London Season.

"Cassius." She supplied that fake name, holding her breath, all but bracing for Jeremy or one of his men to shout, "Liar! You are Arran McQuoid's sister *Cassia*!"

And yet a moment later, when the gentleman left and the boy, Timothy, was showing her to her temporary quarters, Cassia was seized by another thrill of triumph.

She'd done it.

She'd slipped away from her family and boarded Jeremy's boat.

After they set sail and were well away from the English shore, she'd share everything with both Jeremy and her brother, who was accompanying the gentleman on this latest voyage, and then she'd begin her study of the sea.

Chapter 3

Three days out of port with a smaller crew, and one comprised of many new sailors, and everything had gone smoothly—as it invariably did when the *Flying Dragon* set sail.

But then, sailing was something Nathaniel understood, an endeavor he excelled at. And in a world where noblemen's spare sons were expected to live a life in the military, or of the cloth, or worse, some indolent existence based on nothing more than one's pleasures, Nathaniel had established a real purpose in life. He did meaningful work and, in doing so, provided other men—ones who'd not had the same advantages Nathaniel had been born with—options that allowed them to escape a lifetime of drudgery.

Where nearly all noblemen lived off the comforts that came from the titles they'd come to by nothing more than the sheer luck of their blood, Nathaniel had sold his commission and, with it, built something of his own.

At that moment, he stood at the wheel of his ship with his sailing master, Lieutenant Alexander Albion, at his side. As the other man ran through the navigation charts and maps for this voyage, Nathaniel sucked in a deep breath, letting the crisp salt air fill his nostrils and flood his lungs.

The bright orange sun had long begun its ascent into the morning sky and now hung upon the horizon. The blue waters gleamed a titian hue.

All around, the crew carried on with their assigned roles as they pulled farther out to sea. Even as Nathaniel listened to Albion, he privately marveled at the considerable number of differing accents he heard among the men calling out to one another across the deck. With this many new sailors, he was still learning all their voices.

From the corner of his eye, he caught the approach of Nicholas Hayes, his quartermaster, the second son of a marquess. Like Nathaniel, Hayes was also a forgotten spare, and they had gotten on well from the moment they'd gone away to Eton. That friendship had continued into their Oxford days before ultimately being cemented when, after their service in the navy, Nathaniel had established his shipping enterprise and Hayes stepped in to serve as his number two.

Albion and Hayes exchanged brief greetings, before Hayes turned his attention fully on Nathaniel. "We've got a problem, Captain."

He tensed.

It was the first time in the whole of his almost ten years of sailing the other man had uttered those words. Hayes had never been unable to handle the problems which had arisen.

"What is it?" Nathaniel asked tersely.

They'd a mission to see to, one that the Royal Navy's plans in the Adriatic hinged on. Unless it pertained to those plans, it was irrelevant.

"It's . . . the new deckhand . . . Cassius."

The other man twisted his cap in a display of unease Nathaniel didn't recall witnessing in all the years they'd set sail together. "And?" he asked impatiently.

"You see, the repairs weren't completed because of our early departure. As such, I instructed him to apply fresh paint to the interior walls. And . . . and . . ." Color splotched the other man's cheeks.

"And?" he prodded for a second time.

"And . . ." Hayes dropped his voice to a whisper. "He painted them."

Nathaniel stared confusedly at his quartermaster. "Weren't those the instructions?"

"Yes."

When it became apparent the other man didn't intend to elaborate, Nathaniel prodded him. "And you . . . find his work problematic?"

Hayes cleared his throat. "I . . . suspect you might?" There was a slight upward tilt of a question there.

It was also the first time in all their years together the other man had come to Nathaniel with something as inconsequential as a deckhand's performance. "Hayes, I trust you are entirely capable of seeing to the matter. If you think it should be painted again, then have him paint it."

"I had him paint it twice." Hayes shot his fingers up. "This would be his third attempt. The other lads aren't being too kind about—"

"I'm not running a nursery," Nathaniel clipped out.

"Uh . . . yes . . . no, of course. I know that," the other man rushed to assure him. "I just thought I should mention—"

"You don't have to mention it. If there's conflict between the crew, deal with it. But the ribbing of new crew members is suddenly something you're concerned with?"

"The lad almost cried."

Nathaniel closed his eyes. *Bloody hell.* The last thing he cared to tolerate were tears, and the absolute last place for those pathetic drops was on a damned ship—especially his damned ship. "Then give him a damned kerchief and tell him to build a skin, Hayes."

"I did." His friend paused. "Not in those exact words, necessarily. And I should also mention, he's been asking to speak to the captain." He added that last part under his breath.

Albion guffawed with laughter, and Nathaniel shot him an annoyed look that instantly quelled the man's mirth. "What did you say?"

"I said . . . the boy continues to ask when he might speak to the captain. Several times now. He's said it is a matter of some urgency."

"I trust you can help the boy with whatever concern he—"

"I assured him of that, Captain," Hayes interrupted. "He's growing . . . agitated. Almost yelling and such. He said it was private and that it was for your ears only and that he knows you'd absolutely be willing to speak with him."

"I'm not."

"I said as much, too, but . . ." Hayes coughed into his fist. "He insisted I was wrong and asked to speak to you immediately."

"And taking orders from new deckhands is now something you do?" Nathaniel drawled.

At his side, Albion attempted to stifle a grin.

Hayes's cheeks flushed. "No. Yes . . . Well, it is just . . ." He cursed. "It is just that he's not like other deckhands. He issues commands like he's a captain, but in a polite way . . ."

This time Albion didn't bother to quell his bellow of laughter.

"And he seems to really think you'd want to talk to him—"

"I don't," Nathaniel said over his quartermaster's interruption. "Tell him to paint it a third time, and if he doesn't do it right, then a fourth and fifth, and I don't care if he has to paint the goddamned walls a thousand times over, tell him to get it right. And if there's something wrong with the paint, then figure out what that is and fix it."

Hayes swallowed noisily. "Yes, Captain. Of course." He dropped a bow.

Dealing with green deckhands wasn't a responsibility he took on. Nathaniel's focus belonged solely on the mission and the details surrounding the upcoming confrontation with the French. He didn't have the damned time to go about coddling a lad just finding his sea legs.

"Deal with whatever concern it is he has," he ordered the quartermaster. Failure to do so wouldn't properly prepare the boy for the correct order of rank and succession upon the ship.

From the corner of his eye, Nathaniel caught a glimpse of the deck-hand Oliver rushing over to Billy, a fellow deckhand scrubbing down the railings.

The boys exchanged a handful of words, and then with his cleaning rag in hand, Billy quit his post and followed after the older, taller deckhand.

Nathaniel's frown deepened. *What in hell is this?* Members of his crew leaving their jobs? Nathaniel ran a tight ship and didn't tolerate men who didn't follow orders. If a captain let his sailors be lax, then both the mission and the crew were in jeopardy. This was what came from hiring a skeleton crew, and yet his father and the demands he'd made of Nathaniel had left him no other choice. "Where is he?"

"Just below deck. As I said"—the other man looked like he'd downed a mug of seawater—"I had him . . . painting the corridor walls."

"Albion, man the wheel," Nathaniel ordered, and his second-in-command's shoulders sagged with a palpable relief. "Hayes, you come with me."

Both men spoke. "As you wish, Captain."

"As I wish," Nathaniel muttered. "If that were, in fact, the case, I'd be navigating the ship, and whatever damned nonsense going on between my blasted deckhands would be settled by my quartermaster."

Albion erupted into another round of laughter.

Bright splotches of red filled Hayes's cheeks, and Nathaniel stalked off. There was no place on either his ship or his mission for things to be amiss. There was even less of a place for it in this particular one, which the duke had marked as Nathaniel's absolute last if he did not fulfill his obligations and responsibilities as damned ducal heir.

Determined to put an end to whatever games were afoot, Nathaniel headed in search of his suddenly insubordinate deckhands, and to meet the newest one responsible for all his troubles thus far.

They were laughing.

Or mayhap a better word for it would be "sniggering."

It had begun with two of the deckhands, who'd hurried past when she'd begun her work, only to double back to take in her efforts.

From there, her audience had only grown . . . and also grown bolder in their meanness.

"Gor, methinks ye need some pinks in there, lad," one of her detractors called over, and Cassia flared her nostrils as his mockery met with more raucous mirth.

Lad.

Lad.

It was all she could do to keep from boxing the little fellow's ears and pointing out that she likely had five or so years on him.

"You may rest assured, dear sir," she said, keeping her voice deep and even and her gaze on her strokes. "If I were in possession of a greater selection of paints, then I'd take your suggestion into consideration. As it is, I am working with less than stellar options when it comes to paint, and I've been forced to blend together different colors to make new ones."

She silently tacked that on to the rapidly growing list of things she really needed to speak with Jeremy about when he came 'round. "If your captain ever bothers to visit, I will tell him as much."

One of the sailors sniggered nastily—in fairness, was there anything less than a snigger that wasn't nasty? "He's yer captain, too." He paused. "That is, as long as yer on this ship."

"Which isn't likely for long," another fellow declared, his pronouncement met with hoots and whistles as the boys all clapped their hands and stomped their feet in a rolling, happy noise.

One of the boys stuck his head over her shoulder, and his warm, tepid breath slapped her cheek. "He's tossed men overboard for less, and Oi sure think ye've enough offenses on yer list where ye'll find yerself suffering the same fate."

Despite herself, and despite the fact she personally knew the captain, that she'd played dress-up with his trousers and tricorn hat when she was a girl, the mean boy's threat sent dread tripping along her spine.

Do not rise to the bait . . .

Do not take it . . .

You have a family full of troublesome children who love nothing more than to get under your last frayed nerve . . . Why, these miserable little buggers had absolutely nothing on the McQuoids.

Sure enough, as she refused to give in to their gibing, the little boy drew back and returned to the still-growing gang of youths mocking her.

Since she'd made her Come Out, she'd gone unnoticed. She'd been invisible to the gentlemen looking for brides. But neither had she been an object of scorn and mockery. When presented with the unkindness of Jeremy's crew, Cassia rather found herself preferring the former state.

In fairness, she could admit their censure wasn't *completely* unwarranted.

It wasn't her finest work.

She was usually infinitely good at painting.

It was one of the skills Cassia did possess in abundance.

She knew how to paint and draw everything from the wild fields of Scotland to the bowls of fruit faithfully set out every morn at her family's breakfast table.

Yes, along with sewing and needlework, painting was one of her finest skills.

At least her governesses and parents had said as much. Often they'd spoken those words with pride and wonderment, and well, she'd always felt proud, because it was a rare day when Cassia was commended for absolutely anything.

And yet, as she stared at the white wall, she could not fathom that her latest work was so very bad that even kindly Mr. Hayes should fault her efforts.

In fairness, he'd seemed uncomfortable doing so. By the strain at the corners of his warm eyes and the way he'd wrung his hands together, he'd not wanted to disparage her work. Nor was he deliberately cruel and mocking, as the deckhands had been when they'd seen her painting.

But . . . they were surely expecting miracles of her. The paint collection from which she had to choose was certainly not vast. Why, even Sir Joshua Reynolds would have been hard-pressed to compose a *mediocre* work with that selection before him.

And it certainly did not help that the boat was pitching and swaying, and her stomach along with it, and—

Not for the first time, Cassia slid her eyes shut and prayed for the sensation to pass. Prayed for her stomach to settle so that the bile in her throat would retreat. She swallowed it back several times and drew in slow, steadying breaths.

"Gone all green, 'e 'as," one of the boys in her audience announced loudly.

"Oi know," another little one piped in. "But then 'e can add some greens to whatever work o' art 'e starts next."

More laughter went up, echoing around the too-narrow, crowded corridor.

Cassia forced herself to ignore the miserable buggers behind her and their crude talk, and not just because they were harshly mocking her.

She hated casting up the contents of her stomach. Not that anyone truly liked it.

Ever since she was a girl of four who'd fallen ill and emptied the contents of her stomach on Arran's feet, she'd lived in fear of the day when she'd again experience that horrible feeling. And now, since boarding Jeremy's ship, she'd felt it unceasingly, and yes . . . well . . . they couldn't fault her for struggling with the task they'd assigned her when she not only felt quite ill but also didn't have much to work with.

The subject options for an artist were limited when the materials *themselves* were limited.

She froze.

Of course.

Why had she not thought of it?

Inspired for the first time since Hayes had pointed her to the art supplies and handed out her assignment, Cassia set to work. She let her arm fly, surrendering herself to those always-soothing strokes, and as she did, dipping her brush and returning to her work, even the queasy sensation in her belly receded somewhat.

Cassia painted, throwing herself fully and completely into her rendering, until the boys' mockery faded to a dull hum in her ears. And then . . . even they fell silent. With awe?

Why, she'd silenced her detractors. Pride and an ever-growing confidence in her skill lent her an added enthusiasm.

And this was not so very bad, after all.

This was quite . . . lovely.

In fact, this was how she'd even imagined herself spending her days aboard Jeremy's boat. It was why she'd packed her sketch pads. When she'd thought of her days of sea travel and exploration, however, it had always included thoughts of her above deck and not banished below.

Not that she was banished, per se.

The moment she revealed her presence on board to Jeremy, he'd surely allow her free rein of his boat and the freedom to wander about and take in the sights of the ocean. Until that moment, however, Cassia was relegated to painting the walls. Not that this was so very terrible, after all.

She—

"Oh, my God." That horrified whisper split the quiet, and she gasped, her hand jumping and leaving an errant stroke across her work. "What in hell are you *doing*?"

Another detractor.

By the surly, gravelly tone of his voice, a grown man this time.

Different from that of Jeremy's friend, Mr. Hayes.

He really did need to go about providing his crew with some edification on their manners. From boys to grown men aboard the *Waltzing Dragon*, they were all atrocious, and it was all she could do to keep from telling each of them precisely what she thought of them.

"Did you hear me, lad?" the man bellowed.

Cassia frowned at that accidental mark he'd startled her into making upon the country scene she'd begun. Her tree had been perfect. The sky was a soft pink and blue with a perfect cherub painted onto a puffy-looking cloud, and annoyance filled her at his having caused her to commit that error on an otherwise perfect canvas. "You really should not go about using the Lord's name in vain, you know. It is both bad form *and* a sin." Cassia turned to deliver the rest of a deserved scolding.

Every thought went clear out of her head.

She swallowed hard.

Oh, God.

It was just because the corridor was so narrow and the ceiling so low. That was all that accounted for the sheer breadth and size of the man dwarfing the corridor.

And yet, Cassia recognized the lie there.

She knew she merely sought to reassure herself. She knew she wanted to believe the enormously tall man glaring blackly at her was still human, and not this . . . towering figure he, in fact, was.

At five inches past five feet, she wasn't so short that she struggled to look a person in the eye when she spoke. With this man, however, she found herself having to crane her neck back to get a better look. He possessed broad shoulders and a heavy, square jaw; his muscles strained the snug-fitting fawn breeches on his corded legs.

The planes of his cheeks were sharp slashes, as though in crafting him, the Lord had taken care not to omit a single bit of anger from his person.

She shivered.

Even his eyes were a shade to rival the darkest sapphires; they were nearly black.

Why, she'd never known eyes could be black.

The stranger sharpened his gaze on her face, narrowing his eyes so that his sooty black lashes swept down and all but swallowed those menacing irises.

She attempted to swallow once more, but the once reflexive movement had become a chore. *Think of pups and paintings. Anything* but the fury teeming from this man. A fury which she gave thanks was directed at the crew of nasty boys who'd been bullying her. Cassia reminded herself of that reassuring detail.

"Is something wrong with your ears?" he snapped.

And just like that, Cassia found her voice. "I assure you, they hear quite well," she said archly when the young boys still failed to answer. Yes, they'd been miserable buggers, but she'd not see them bullied by this one.

The man's eyes thinned all the more. On her . . . ?

If this surly crew member was going to be a cur to the boys around her, she'd have him take them to task for the real violations they'd committed. "I'll have you know, sir, they also dole out rather rude opinions unkindly, too . . ."

The boy Oliver scratched at his brow. "Oi . . . don't think 'e's alroight in the 'ead, Captain."

Captain?

Cassia tipped her head sideways. "There are two captains?" Because that was an unexpected detail. When the audience gawked at her, she bristled. How was she to know? This was only her first time aboard a sailing vessel. "It's just, I would expect it gets very confusing if there are two captains," she said defensively. Or mayhap not. "Unless you require two captains so that—"

"Go," the menacing stranger said through his teeth, that gravelly order more ominous than had he thundered it.

As one the boys clicked their heels and scurried off, and proving a coward, relief swept through Cassia as she started after the children.

"Not. You."

That curt command brought Cassia to an abrupt stop. Still hopeful that she wasn't the one left to face the towering captain's wrath, she glanced around the now empty hall. "Not me?"

"Not. You," he rumbled.

And here she'd thought only storms and angry dogs capable of that deep, resonant, and more than slightly terrifying sound.

Oh, drat and dash.

Alas, as her governess had oft said, "Charm them all with a smile."

Mustering her courage, Cassia donned a smile and faced the foreboding gentleman. "Captain . . . ?" She stared at him, pausing deliberately so that he might supply his name.

He stared darkly back at her. "Captain Ellsby."

"Captain Surly-Breeches" suited him better. "I was wondering if you might fetch the other captain, as there is something I desperately need to speak with him about." She had quite a few things to say to Jeremy about this one.

"The *other* captain?" he repeated in that slow, bearish way.

She nodded. *"Jeremy,"* she clarified. After all, what if there were even more than two captains aboard a boat? Jeremy would be far safer to speak with first than her brother traveling with him. Arran would be beyond livid. Jeremy, however, would manage to calm down her—

"You think *Jeremy* is a captain?"

Jeremy . . . wasn't? The bottom dropped out of her stomach once more. "He isn't?"

"He's the cook."

She gawked at him. "The . . . *cook?*" All these years, it'd been a lie? Why? Why had he lied? Except . . . "Of course," she whispered to herself. "It makes complete sense." Lying about his rank aboard the sailing vessel had been the only way his stern father, the Earl of Westmorland, would have countenanced his sailing. Cassia jammed her fingertips against her temples. What else had been a lie?

Understanding dawned in the captain's eyes. "You were hired by Jeremy."

It wasn't a question, and she felt as dazed as when she'd caught a pall-mall ball to the head and come to on the court to discover a sea of McQuoids staring back at her. She blinked just as slowly. "Hired by Jeremy?" A nervous giggle slipped from her lips that she disguised as a cough. "You might say that."

"I just did," he said bluntly, and not taking his gaze from her, he shouted, "Oliver?"

Almost instantly, a tiny, waiflike boy appeared. "Aye, Captain?"

"Fetch Jeremy," he ordered, and the child clicked his heels together and dashed off, leaving her and Captain Surly-Breeches alone.

A surly captain who was Jeremy's superior, and also . . . her brother's superior? Which meant that Jeremy was decidedly *not* responsible for the vessel. And what, exactly, did that mean for her and her place aboard the boat, and—

The rapid rise and fall of approaching footsteps cut into the swirl of questions in her mind.

A moment later, a short fellow with an impressively gleaming head, bald of all strands but for two tufts of white curls on either side, approached. Dread threatened to swallow her whole. "Who is this?" she blurted.

Both men ignored her.

"You wished to see me, Captain?" the shorter, older of the pair asked, pushing his round, wire-rimmed spectacles back on his nose.

"You hired this deckhand, Jeremy?"

This was Jeremy? Cassia's heart thumped at a sickeningly slow beat. *Oh, dear.*

"He is not my Jeremy," she whispered. "My family's Jeremy is tall and young and—" *Handsome.* Except, she was supposed to be a man, and men didn't call other men handsome. How did men refer to other men? "He is not . . . ugly."

This Other Jeremy turned a scowl on Cassia.

Oh, God. Could she muck up any of this more than she had?

"Not that I mean any offense," she said, her throat as dry as her mouth. And the words felt thick on her tongue, and to her ears as they left her lips, they sounded just as heavy. "You're just not . . . *the* Jeremy."

"And who, exactly, is your Jeremy?" Captain Surly-Breeches pressed.

Nay, not just any captain. This was not Captain Jeremy Tremaine. Rather, the bad-tempered man before her was the captain of this vessel.

The vessel she'd mistaken for Jeremy's, which meant her elder brother was also not aboard. *At least you won't have to face Arran's wrath.* No, instead, she'd have to face the wrath of a furious stranger. Panicky laughter built in her chest.

No. This was all a mistake! Of course. Her brother and Jeremy had gathered what she'd done and were merely seeking to scare her, to teach her a lesson.

Those assurances didn't help.

"What is the name of your vessel?" She managed to squeeze out that question between her frantic breathing.

By the deepening glower on the captain's sun-bronzed skin, he wasn't one who took well to being challenged.

"The *Flying Dragon*, and I am Nathaniel Ellsby, her captain."

Her heartbeat thudded to a slow, sickening stop. "That is . . . different from the *Waltzing Dragon*."

"*Waltzing Dragon*? That's a bloody foolish name for a ship," the Other Jeremy, Cook Jeremy, was saying. His words, however, droned on in her buzzing ears, every other one coming in and out of focus.

The *Waltzing Dragon* was decidedly different from the *Flying Dragon*. Which would also mean she'd landed herself on a boat filled with strangers. At that, ones who were angry-eyed, and who'd been not at all friendly. Her heart knocked wildly against her rib cage. She, a lone female without so much as a chaperone or a companion, had landed herself aboard the wrong boat. There was no angry Arran, just this furious stranger.

No. Not just a furious stranger. She looked to Not-Her-Jeremy and the captain.

Cassia's eyes slid shut.

Ruined.

She would be completely ruined. But then, was there really anything other than *complete* ruination?

And her ruin would come only if she survived. *If.*

Her stomach churned, and not for the first time, it threatened to revolt. And this nausea, unlike all the times before, had nothing to do with the swaying boat and absolutely everything to do with the peril she found herself in.

Why . . . ? Why had she come up with this scheme?

Except, no, that wasn't right. She knew precisely why she'd set out. To see the world. To see and experience something, anything other than the monotony of a tedious world she already knew, and one she'd remained invisible to. It had all sounded so exciting and glamorous when she'd crafted the plan in her head. She'd told herself Arran and Jeremy would keep her secret and protect her reputation. She'd let herself believe that no one would ever discover the adventure she'd gone on, and that even if they did, it wouldn't matter because she'd already accepted she wasn't going to marry and was destined to be an old-maid spinster. She had come to peace with that reality.

Or . . . she'd *thought* she had.

Only now, when fully confronted with the *actual* reality, with what she'd done and what her fate and future would be, were it discovered— *when* it was discovered—she realized she'd deluded herself.

She shook her head sharply. "Mm-mm," she said to herself, and even through muffled ears, she caught the cessation of whatever it was one of the two very tall, very angry-looking fellows had been saying. Digging her fingers into her temples, Cassia began to pace.

The better question was not why she had done this, but how she could have made this mistake.

With every step, and with every thought churning in her brain, terror and panic lent her strides a greater speed.

Myrtle, her younger-by-several-years sister—and married sister, at that—wouldn't have made this mistake. A panicky sound built in her chest, commingling with a laugh.

Nay, Myrtle had been left behind last Christmas, forgotten at the townhouse, and not only had she bested two thieves intending to steal their family's antiquities but she'd also snagged a duke for a husband. Her younger sister had never made such a tragic blunder, mixing up something so simple and also so essential as the blasted name of Jeremy's boat.

Then there was Cassia. "Stupid, stupid Cassia," she whispered as she went, as unable to stymie her self-ramblings as she was to stop her frantic pacing. Only, she wasn't . . . Cassia. She especially couldn't be Cassia here. Her lower lip wobbled. "Stupid, stupid . . . Ca-ca"—*not* Cassia—*"Cassiussss."* She whipped around and found two sets of equally horrified—and worse, equally harsh—eyes locked on her.

"He's mad, he is," the smaller man breathed.

She dimly registered the monster of a man with long blond locks pulled back in a queue saying something to Not-Her-Jeremy, and the shorter, older, seemingly relieved fellow with his bald pate dropping a bow and rushing off.

And, well, she quite understood how the fellow felt.

Desperate to run.

To flee.

Only, Cassia needed to flee not this corridor but the whole ship.

She was sinking, swimming, drowning underwater.

She needed to get herself back to land. And then it hit her.

Cassia stopped abruptly as sound came whirring back into normal focus in her ears.

"Lad . . . ?" The captain clapped his hands sharply. "Lad . . . ? What is your family name?"

Her family name. God, how she missed them all. "McQuoid," she whispered. "I am . . . a McQuoid."

A flash of recognition lit his eyes. "Your family is of the *ton*."

He knew of them. Of course he would. He was as refined in his speech as she was in hers. She hesitated, and then nodded.

Why, of course. Why had she not thought of it? If he believed she was a young man of the peerage, wholly out of place here, he'd see that she could not remain. She nodded frantically. "My father is the Earl of Abington." Purpose pushed back the dread, and concentrating on that more steadying sentiment, Cassia stormed over. "I have to leave," she said. Even deepening her voice as she'd practiced, fear lent it a crack. "Now. Y-you have to turn the boat around." And then in the way of the McQuoids, Cassia did that which she and every McQuoid who'd come before her, and every McQuoid certain to follow her, would do: she rambled. "I've made a terrible mistake, a very, very bad one. You see, I was invited to take passage on another boat. My brother's friend's boat, and his name is Jeremy, Captain Jeremy Tremaine, and Jeremy isn't a cook, like your Jeremy. And he'll be expecting me"—no, he wouldn't, but better to let this man think someone out there was looking for her—"so if we can really . . . get going"—Cassia pointed behind her— "back the other way, that is. I'd be most appreciative."

The captain stared at her for a long while, so long she wondered whether something was wrong with *his* ears. "Ship."

Ship...?

Cassia cocked her head. That was what he'd say? Why was he saying that? "Yes, yes. That is what I said. I boarded the wrong boat, and I really need you to turn yours back around." And as he continued to just stare, Cassia proceeded to explain just how vital it was.

Just, whatever you do, do not mention you are a female...

Chapter 4

Over the course of his life, as a duke's son turned naval officer and then privateer, Nathaniel had encountered all manner of people.

Be it from the ballrooms and halls of Polite Society to the floors of his ship, those he did cross paths with or work alongside proved remarkably predictable in the way they carried and conducted themselves.

The lords and ladies of the *ton* were measured and cool and not given to shows of emotion. And in that reserved way, they were more similar to, than different from, the men who made up Nathaniel's crew of rough, worldly mariners and whose legs, like Nathaniel's, proved steadier at sea than on land.

Even the young boys he'd sprung from the cells of Newgate, who'd managed to escape the noose and swapped out that life of crime for a new beginning, proved cynical and laconic.

The ones who were not jaded by life were surly, equally terse men.

Not a single person in Nathaniel's past, present, or, he prayed, future rambled or yammered the way this boy did, stuck in that place between child and man where his voice still cracked when he spoke.

Not his mother.

Not the lusty women whose beds he shared when he visited a harbor.

And he was filled with a sudden urge to rub at his temples the way the boy continued to do.

He looked over as Hayes arrived.

The other man stared wide-eyed at Cassius. "I'd wager he's giving himself a headache."

"Undoubtedly," Nathaniel muttered, continuing to eye the new member of his crew with a rapidly growing horror that rivaled the boy's. "Because he's giving me a bloody megrim."

Hayes chuckled, and both Nathaniel and the boy glared at the quartermaster.

"You really cannot b-blame me . . . ," the accidental deckhand stammered.

Oh, Nathaniel blamed the lad for a lot. A lot, indeed. Calling his ship a "boat." Distracting the crew. Pulling Nathaniel away from his duties, even now.

The list really did and would and could go on as long as one of this boy's ramblings, and there was no greater grievance in Nathaniel's mind than a person who gabbled.

Suddenly, the young man's lower lip quavered.

Nathaniel recoiled. *Good God.* He'd been wrong. So wrong. There was something vastly worse than a person's blathering.

"Do not," he said sharply.

"Do not *what*?" Cassius whispered.

"Cry."

The wide, luminous eyes went all the wider; Cassius's tears glittered and glimmered, and Nathaniel shrank back.

And then, horror of his greatest horrors, more tears glimmered, and a single one slid down the dandy's high, pale, too-smooth cheeks.

"Don't," Nathaniel repeated a second time.

With a sniffle the accidental deckhand dashed the back of a hand across his nose. "I cannot help it."

The hell he couldn't. "You can." He fixed a glare on him. "You just aren't trying."

The young lad gave another little sniff. "Well, I'm not trying *now-now*." *Now-now?* "But I have t-tried b-before, a-and it's—" Cassius's large mouth, softer than his unblemished skin and unworked hands, quivered, and then the deckhand erupted into a blubbering mess.

Desperate, Nathaniel looked to his number two.

Hayes shot his palms up and shook his head.

"Your job is to do what I tell you," Nathaniel muttered.

Hayes grinned. "Not this. This one is all you, Captain."

Nathaniel flashed a vulgar gesture, and the lad slapped a hand over his mouth, stifling a gasp. "Did you just t-turn a c-crude finger on me?"

Did he—?

The lad crooked his middle finger up and waggled it. "Because I'll have you know my brothers taught me what that means and—"

"Your brothers should have also done you a favor and taught you not to go weeping like a woman at the slightest provocation," he added under his breath.

The deckhand's tears faded, and an annoyed frown turned his mouth down. Angling his hands on his hips, the boy came forward. "Without provocation? Without provo—"

"That's what I said. Isn't it, Hayes?" He directed that at his quartermaster, not even looking at the other man.

Folding his arms at his chest, Hayes nodded. "It's what he said."

"Provocation?" Cassius finished, ignoring the both of them. "I'll have you know I've—"

"Boarded the wrong *boat*?" Hayes ventured, ignoring the glare Nathaniel tossed his way.

The boy jabbed a finger in the quartermaster's direction. "Precisely. Mr. Hayes understands."

"Quartermaster Hayes," Nathaniel corrected. "He is the quartermaster."

That pronouncement managed the seemingly impossible—it silenced the chatterbox.

For a moment.

"Quartermaster Hayes?" Cassius McQuoid echoed. "*That* is what you call when you need him?"

Nathaniel opened his mouth to confirm he'd just said as much but couldn't manage to sneak in even a breath before the boy continued.

"I expect there is some better term or title to call out."

"There isn't," he said tightly.

"But if there are some sailory problems that arise . . . ," the lad went on.

"Sailory problems?" Nathaniel mouthed.

At his side, he caught the twitch of Hayes's lips.

"Quartermaster Hayes, get here now." The lad cupped his hands around his mouth and deepened his voice, and added—Nathaniel narrowed his eyes—"The jib is plunging." The lad did a surprisingly accurate impression of . . . Nathaniel.

Hayes let out a sharp bark of amusement that not even Nathaniel's glare could manage to quell this time.

"See?" Cassius McQuoid said, gesturing to Nathaniel's entirely-too-amused quartermaster. "He gets it."

Nathaniel couldn't even make his mouth move to get words out, which was fine, as the deckhand had plenty for both of them.

"I think you should give him a new title. In fact, until we return to England, I can help y—"

"No."

"You," the boy finished over his curt interruption, "create an entirely new system of how to refer to your crew to help make communication easier with them."

Nathaniel stood frozen, his mind spinning, and if he'd been the sort given to levity, he'd have laughed his damned head off at the thought of this jabberpot doling out lessons on "making communication easier."

Alas, he'd a problem on his hands, and a mighty one at that. Had his parents sent this problem into Nathaniel's lap, there couldn't have been a more effective tool to make him at least consider returning to London.

It was a thought.

But not a serious one.

There was no way he was ending his mission. He'd French plans to intercept and funds to shore up to last his men long enough for him to fulfill the duke's demands of him. Either way, he'd not cut a voyage short before, and he'd never not succeeded, and he'd no intention of failing now. Not because of a pale English lad who could really benefit from some time in the sun and some hair on his chest.

There was no way Nathaniel was turning his ship about.

And yet . . .

"Captain?"

"I'm thinking," he muttered to Hayes.

Nathaniel also couldn't have the lad underfoot. If he sent this boy to freely mingle with the crew again, they'd eventually eat him alive faster than a swarm of sharks converging on a bucket of fresh chum just tossed out to sea. As it was, McQuoid had already made a pain of himself. There wasn't a single crew member who had the inclination or patience to deal with an untried son of some nobleman—even less so the motley crew he'd been forced to hastily assemble. With the exception of him and Hayes, the rest of the men on board this ship were a rough sort from the streets and prisons of London. There was also the fact that not a single member of Nathaniel's crew deserved the punishment of having Cassius McQuoid about.

"I'm assigning you to my cabin," he finally said. Even as he made the offer, he saw the implicit peril in doing so. There were problems, either way. However, it was better to not have his men distracted, and this was the surest way. That lofty position would also signal that the boy had Nathaniel's protection.

Relief lit Cassius's eyes. "I am ever so grateful. I trust your chambers are surprisingly lovely. More elegant than the other space I've been occupying."

"Quarters," he said tightly. "They are not 'chambers.' They are not 'rooms.' They are *quarters*."

"Quarters, then," Cassius corrected himself. "Well, I thank you for your benevolence, Captain. It is most generous of you."

Thanked him for his generosity . . . ?

And then it hit him.

Apparently, the same time it did Hayes.

His quartermaster strangled on a laugh, and Nathaniel glowered at the man who'd been one of his closest friends in the world, glad one of them could find amusement in this mess. When the other man had managed to get his mirth under control, Nathaniel looked at the pampered boy/man before him.

"To clean, McQuoid," Nathaniel snapped. "You're to tidy my quarters."

The lad's soft jaw went slack. "Like a . . . servant?" he ventured as if he'd been handed a riddle to solve.

Hayes lost it. *Again.*

Ignoring the quartermaster's explosion of hilarity, Cassius bristled. "I most certainly will not."

That managed to kill Hayes's humor.

Nathaniel narrowed his eyes on the insolent boy across from him.

"Hayes." With palpable relief, Hayes took that one word—his name—for the pardon it was. Dropping a bow, he rushed off.

The moment Nathaniel and his accidental deckhand were alone, he peered at the lad before him. Cassius McQuoid had called him out in front of his crew. It had been the first—and only—time in the whole of his career running ships. In his haughty tones and lack of deference, Cassius had proven precisely what he and Hayes had taken him for: a high-in-the-step nobleman's son, or by-blow, with an inflated sense of his self-worth. And there was nothing more essential than disabusing those types of the illusion that they held any power—both lads and men.

The lad shifted under Nathaniel's scrutiny but didn't so much as lower his insolent gaze. Nay, rather, the boy tipped his chin up a fraction and glared back.

"I've whipped men for gainsaying my orders," Nathaniel said coolly. His words or his tone managed to penetrate the brash lad's thick head.

McQuoid paled.

Nathaniel took a step closer. "And do you know why that is?"

The boy shook his head jerkily.

Nathaniel stopped a pace away. "Because any time a man challenges the captain of a vessel, it raises the risk of mutiny." Even from a loyal crew.

Something, however, in the fear radiating from the boy's eyes hit Nathaniel in a place he'd not known existed within him. Pity filled him. It was an unexpected softening. And the last place softening was needed was here.

Nathaniel opened his mouth, prepared to gentle his tone and words, and then stopped. He sniffed at the air. "What the hell is that?"

McQuoid tipped his nose up and mimicked Nathaniel's gesture. "C-captain?" The boy's voice broke.

Nathaniel smelled the air again. "You stink like—"

The young man gasped. "I do *not* stink. It is an apple fragrance, and it is quite—"

The deckhand must have seen something in Nathaniel's narrowed eyes, because wisely, he fell silent.

Apple fragrance. Nathaniel recoiled. *Good God.* Not only had he been saddled with some lord's rebellious son, he'd landed a *dandy* in training, at that.

Getting back to the matter at hand, Nathaniel gave his new cabin boy a stern look and launched into his lecture. "You landed yourself in a situation—"

"You could say that," McQuoid muttered.

"I just did," he clipped out. So much for an *uninterrupted* lecture.

"No. I know. It was a *rhetorical* statement."

Nathaniel stared dumbly at the young man opposite him. Good God, the young man was mad.

"As in an artificial extravagance to highlight some point or—"

"I bloody well know what the word 'rhetorical' means," he thundered, and the boy jumped.

But he'd hand it to the lad—under that snap in Nathaniel's composure that would have seen any one of his crew stammering and begging apologies, McQuoid didn't dissolve into another of those blubbering messes. Rather, he turned an annoyed frown on Nathaniel.

On *him*?

"How am I to know whether or not you know what the word means? I've only just met you, and given our limited exchange, you appear to do a good deal of unintelligible grunting and bite your words like you might chew your food, which really does slow your cadence."

"Slow my cadence?"

The lad nodded. "You also have a tendency of repeating yourself."

"Are you giving out elocution lessons, Governess?"

Bright crimson splotches formed perfect circles in the gaunt lad's sharp cheeks. "I'm not a governess. I'm not even a girl. But if you are asking for lessons, however, on the proper ways in which to conduct yourself, I—"

"I was being sarcastic."

"Oh." The boy paused, wrinkling his pert, freckled nose. "I'll have you know the McQuoids are quite a forthright family."

The McQuoids. He knew of the name. But good God, the lad had painted an image of a lot of people just like the boy before him. Nathaniel couldn't repress a shudder.

49

"And we are as direct in our humor as we are in our speech. As such, we tend to not notice when a person is being droll."

Nathaniel kept his features in a solemn mask. "That is indeed important information I'll be sure to store away for all my future dealings with the McQuoids."

"It is a good general rule when dealing with all people," Cassius elucidated like the elocution instructor Nathaniel had mocked him as.

The boy was not a fast learner, then. Why did Nathaniel not find himself surprised?

"If a person doesn't really know another person, then one cannot distinguish if a question is really a question or an—"

Nathaniel cut off the remainder of that lesson. "I was being sarcastic." What mad Shakespearean farce had he landed himself in?

"Again?"

He nodded.

The lad bristled. "Well, then. It is rather rude, and there is no call for rudeness."

"I will work on that," he drawled.

"Thank . . . *you* . . ." That nose wrinkled up again. "You are being sarcastic."

"There is some hope for you, after all."

Cassius beamed. "Thank you."

And despite himself, despite the absurdity of the situation Nathaniel now found himself in and the bothersome boy he was trying to figure out how to keep from driving him mad or his crew to mutiny, a laugh exploded past Nathaniel's lips.

"You're laughing at me," his stowaway muttered.

"Absolutely, I am. You'll be responsible for my quarters. Making the beds, cleaning the room, emptying the chamber—"

Cassius's already impossibly big eyes threatened to bulge right from his face. "I will *not*."

"Emptying the chamber pot," he finished over that objection.

"Can you not do your business . . . elsewhere?" The boy stomped his foot as he spoke. He actually stomped a fine leather boot like a peer only accustomed to having his way. Which he likely was.

"My business?" Nathaniel drawled.

"Yes, as in your . . . your . . ."

"Shite?"

If embarrassment could set a person ablaze, then Nathaniel's ship would have been a burning pile of tinder lost to the seas for the redness of Cassius's cheeks.

"It is not my problem that you boarded the wrong ship," he said, all out of patience for the pompous prig. "You did that all on your own. As such, you're going to earn your keep like every other boy and man on this vessel. Failure to do so will see you in the hulk."

"The *hulk*?"

And by the emphasis the boy placed on that word, Nathaniel didn't know whether he knew what a hulk was. Nor, however, did he care. He'd figure it all out fast enough.

He proceeded to fire off the remainder of his expectations for Cassius. "You can begin by cleaning my quarters and then applying fresh paint to my walls." He finished that list. "I'm not looking for bowls of fruit, baskets of flowers. Country scenes. Am I clear?"

"Abundantly so. I've never been fond of painting baskets of flowers anyway."

"That's reassuring," Nathaniel said caustically, and then he brought his brows together, darkening a glare on the lad, who'd already brought him too much trouble. "This is a sea vessel. It's a ship. A *ship*," he repeated for good measure, and not because, as the boy had noted, he'd a tendency of parroting words. He didn't. "It's not the pleasure boat you thought you were getting yourself on. You'll finish out the journey."

Just then the ship rolled to the right. Nathaniel planted his feet firmly to keep himself from sliding, even as the young man went stumbling.

He shot an arm out, catching the very green-in-the-face young man by his small shoulder.

The boy's lower lip began to tremble all over again.

Nathaniel released him. "And you won't cry." He barked that order . . . to be met with more of that quivering mouth, entirely too soft for any boy or man to have.

"You can't make me stop," the insolent deckhand shot back with an arrogance only one born to a noble family might exhibit.

"Trust me," Nathaniel said brusquely. "I can, and I will."

"Is that a threat?" And this time, the lad's wasn't a challenge, but rather a curiosity-tinged question.

"No, it's not a threat, but a promise."

Cassius's mouth quavered, and more tears welled, even as the boat rolled sharply to the left.

And then, the boy gagged and—

"Bloody hell," Nathaniel muttered as his new cabin boy emptied the contents of his stomach right on his floor, and he jumped out of the way to avoid being splattered. What next?

"I-I'm s-siiiick."

Nathaniel cursed blackly and roundly. Everything about the young man was soft. There wasn't a person less capable of surviving on a ship.

He alternated a glower between his splattered floor and the deckhand responsible for it. "I see that," he said acidulously. "Get yourself cleaned up, and then get back here and see to this damned mess."

The green-looking lad stared, wide-eyed, back.

Nathaniel jabbed a finger at the doorway. "Go!"

His cabin boy jumped, already racing off, tripping over his feet in his haste to leave.

Letting himself inside his quarters, Nathaniel pushed the door shut, welcoming the quiet.

He shook his head wryly. His father had alternately pleaded with him and threatened him into giving up his seafaring ways. He'd been resolute in his refusal. Only to discover he'd prefer to cast himself overboard and swim himself back to merry old England than suffer a voyage with Cassius McQuoid.

His accidental deckhand forgotten, Nathaniel headed over to his desk, tugging free his shirt as he went. The single note that had been tucked inside his bag, as it invariably was, rested, sealed and untouched, upon the map that lay out.

He hesitated a moment, not wanting to read the letter.

Because he'd received enough before this to know the general idea of what would be written in those flowing, graceful strokes.

For through the years, his mother had made it her mission to attempt to create peace within her family.

To convince her six—now five—sons that the duke did, in fact, care—in his own way. And that they were loved by two parents, not just one, and . . . Well, it was all really irrelevant.

She may need to delude herself into believing the blustery duke was something other than a coldhearted peer driven by his reverence and love, first and foremost, for that title, but it was not an illusion that Nathaniel or his brothers had needed to maintain.

But then, in Nathaniel's case, he'd gotten away. He'd made a life for himself away from his family, and away from the duke.

And now, it was all about to be taken away.

Unless somehow, for the first time in the whole of her life, the duchess had managed to reason her husband out of his unswerving focus on controlling Nathaniel the same way he'd overseen Marcus.

Picking up the note, Nathaniel grabbed the emerald-encrusted steel dagger that rested on his desk and made quick work of the seal.

Unfolding the page, he skimmed the handful of paragraphs written.

My dearest son,
Each time you leave, my heart is full from knowing the
joy you find in your travels, and yet it weeps because

you are gone, and because of the dangers you face out there. Even with my fear for you, however, I've never sought to intervene or interfere, because I know the love you find in your seafaring ways.

You believe, following your last meeting with your dear father, that his threatening to end your seafaring ventures if you do not marry is driven by his need to be in control. It isn't.

Nathaniel froze. "The hell it isn't," he muttered.

I will confess, selfishly, that I've longed for you to give up your time at sea. I've lived with fear that you will one day lose your life on those waters that you so love, and that in so doing, you will never know what it is to have the love of a wife and a family of your own. I worry I will lose you as I lost Marcus. There has always been an understanding between Lady Angela's family and ours, one that was cemented with your late brother's engagement to the young lady . . . but this is about far more than just that connection. I *know* . . . she will make you a good wife. She is all things good and clever. If you are to be angry and carry resentment at the requirements your father put to you, then I'd have you place blame where blame is owed. We *both* want you to come home.

Nathaniel's jaw worked. Yes, both of his parents might wish for his return, but they did so for entirely different reasons.

A curse escaped his lips, and he crushed the pages in one fist, wrinkling the scrap and attempting to calm his riotous emotions.

It had been one thing when the order had come from his father. It had been expected of the cold, heartless bastard, who, despite the duchess's incorrect insistence otherwise, loved nothing and no one beyond his title.

But to know his tenderhearted mother wished it . . . and the reasons that motivated her?

Both his crew and the Crown depended upon Nathaniel's work as a privateer, and now all that continued only if he married and produced an heir as his parents expected. For he *also* had a duty to the title. It was a rank he'd never wanted nor desired, but one he'd been saddled with all the same. The bitter sting of regret left an acerbic bite on his tongue.

He forced himself to lighten his grip on the page and scanned the remaining sentences there.

> Please know, it is not just a fear of losing you to
> the seas that resulted in my interference. I truly believe
> you need more than a life of work, my son. You need
> a love like I have with your fath—

Crumpling the letter into a ball, he slammed it down on the desk.

If he were to continue to sail, they'd make him marry Marcus's intended, Angela. And he'd do it. Because there was only one thing he truly loved in this life, and that was the *Flying Dragon* and the freedom it represented.

Bloody hell.

Chapter 5

This wasn't so bad.

Later that afternoon, after Cassia had tidied herself, she'd sought out the captain's chambers and proceeded to straighten them.

In fact, all things considered, her situation could have been a good deal worse.

If the surly captain had discovered Cassia was, in fact, a female, it would have been disastrous.

But he hadn't.

And she found some solace in that not-insignificant spot of luck.

Yet it could be a good deal better . . . if her stomach weren't fighting every miserable back-and-forth sway of the boat.

"Ship," she said acridly, concentrating on speaking and breathing and her new work so that she didn't think about the bile continuing to creep up her throat.

Ship. Boat.

They were really the same thing.

Only a man would get so very hung up on the semantics of it all.

Alas, having brothers and many male cousins and kin, Cassia well understood they were all peculiar creatures who liked to pretend they were tough, and who presented a shell to the world, but ultimately, there was something soft inside. One just had to look close enough to see it.

As such, she didn't think it was a coincidence the assignment he'd given her was one that kept her close and safe from the rest of the crew, and also saw her given the shelter and security provided by his chambers.

The ship swayed violently, and tightening her fingers reflexively around the brush she clutched in a death grip, she closed her eyes a moment and willed her stomach to settle.

"'Quarters,' not 'chambers,'" she whispered aloud, focusing on that other difference he'd pointed out, in her edification of life aboard a boat.

A *ship*.

Think of the differences and the new lessons, to keep from thinking about the fact that she was stuck at sea with a ship full of strangers and a stomach that wouldn't quit.

If she survived this, it would be a tale her children and children's children would one day tell, a legend that lived on in the McQuoid family for years to come. How Cassia had set out on her own to see the world, as only men were permitted, and not only made her way but also lived amongst the toughest, nastiest sailors and their menacing captain.

Unbidden thoughts of the captain traipsed in. His skin golden from the sun. His noble jaw was too square and his aquiline nose too straight, and his cheeks were entirely too chiseled for him to ever be considered classically handsome.

But with his also-too-long golden hair tugged back into a queue, he may as well have been a Norse god, a Viking warrior of old, in full command of his ship and the lesser men—and lone woman—who answered to him.

Yes, if she survived his wrath, it would be a wonder.

What would such a man say, were he to discover he'd had his precious ship boarded by . . . a woman?

Cassia's stomach roiled, and this time the vicious churning had absolutely nothing to do with the boat—well, a little bit, it did—and most everything to do with the thought of just what would happen were she to be found out.

Dead . . . She'd be dead. Or worse . . .

And suddenly, all those gothic tales she'd read—books of ravished ladies and dashing pirates—proved a whole lot less romantic and more terror-inducing for how those suddenly authentic-looking scripts played out in real life.

With hands that trembled, Cassia cleaned the black bristles of her narrow brush. She dipped them in a glass of water she'd helped herself to from the kitchens, and the red paint turned the clear liquid crimson, like small drops of blood expanding and filling the glass. And also conjuring new, unwanted imaginings—of being found out and left at the mercy of a ruthless lot.

"Do not think of that . . . Do not think of it," she whispered into the quiet of Nathaniel's rooms, opting to use his Christian name to make him more human. More real. "Think of what you will see, and what stories you'll have to tell . . ." A story of grit and strength and—

A low whistle cut through the talk she gave herself, and she spun to face the person, whose arrival she'd failed to note.

"What in 'ell . . . ," the young lad whispered to himself.

Timothy. Painfully thin and lanky, he'd the look of a colt still not comfortable on his own legs. He'd also proven the least mean toward her of all the deckhands. Which was not, however, saying much.

"Do you like it?" she asked, reassessing the art she'd spent the better part of the day creating, taking it in with a critical eye. He'd said no fruit or country scenes . . . which, given they were on a ship, made complete sense. "I do believe I've quite admirably captured the waters," she remarked, motioning with the tip of the brush to those white-capped waves of deep sapphires and aquas. It'd been a remarkable feat, creating those many shades of blues from the paint afforded her. At the stunned silence of the fellow cabin boy beside her, she angled her head to the left and then to the right, eyeing her work all the more critically. "It is not my finest sky. I fear I may have leaned too much into the pinks for the sunset. I might have been better served mixing the red and blue to create a soft purple, and then from that, added my red." Cassia chewed at the thin end of her wooden paintbrush. "Are you thinking it is a bit . . . lazy . . . to have gone to pinks? Because I can see that," she allowed.

At the protracted silence, she looked over and found the boy's horror-filled sea-green gaze locked not on the painting, but rather on her. "Gor, yer stupid as shite."

She frowned. "I'd hardly say I'm stupid," she said defensively. "I know how to make orange. It's just that I opted not to."

"What in Satan's fiery hell is this?"

That thunderous shout brought Cassia and Timothy jumping.

"You painted my walls!"

That horror-filled, fury-laced shout reverberated off entirely too-low ceilings, and swallowing rhythmically, Cassia looked to the source of that rage.

Captain Nathaniel.

Her stomach sank. For in this instant, with rage rolling off him with the same ease of the waves undulating in the waters, the menacing figure before her was no mere "Nathaniel" and absolutely and only "Captain."

"Is something wrong with both your head *and* your ears?" he asked, in a low, gravelly tone that proved somehow more sinister than his previous shout.

She automatically took a step closer to Timothy.

"Timothy." The captain managed to bite out the three syllables into a clear order.

Timothy, who proved remarkably without mercy that day, bowed and quickly quit Cassia's side. He headed for the door and scurried around the captain.

The captain, who made no attempt to move out of the boy's way.

"You know, it really is quite rude of you to make him squeeze around you," Cassia said archly, cleaning some of the excess paint from her brush. "It would have been far more polite to step aside."

Effectively silenced, the captain gawked.

Having grown up amidst a large brood of siblings, Cassia had long ago learned the art of conflict. More specifically, the art of dealing with it. As such, at the moment, she methodically cleaned her brush. "Furthermore, shouting is also quite rude and, I'll add, in this instance, quite unnecessary. My work is hardly complete. I'm not so arrogant as to be above critique or criticism and certainly understand the reason for your upset."

"You understand the reason for my upset," he repeated, his tone peculiarly flat.

He really did have a habit of echoing her words.

Even so, Cassia nodded.

"You understand the reason for my upset," he said again, and this time she offered a more hesitant nod. "You—"

"I believe we've confirmed I certainly understand the reason for your upset. Yes." Cassia motioned with the now thoroughly cleaned bristles of her brush at the crux of his discontent. "This, right here. The pink." She frowned. "I really should have figured, with the way my own brothers feel about the color, that you'd react the way you did." Though in fairness to Arran and Dallin, they'd never been so over the top in their disdain as the captain and Timothy had.

Shipmen were a peculiar lot.

"I can lighten the pink, you know. As you see, I've more reds here." She motioned to that color in question, bringing his focus to the more pleasing portion of the sky she'd created upon the canvas he'd charged her with covering. "I . . ." Cassia's words trailed off, her eyes locking on the vein pulsing at the corner of his right eye. A bulging, throbbing vein that bespoke a man with a thin control of his rage.

She lowered her brush. "You're not happy."

Ever so slowly, he shook his head; that queue of blond strands flopped back and forth with the side-to-side movement.

No words.

He spoke not a single one.

Cassia bit the inside of her cheek.

Alas, survival was becoming increasingly unlikely at this point.

Oh, dear. This was very bad, indeed.

—————— ❧❧❧ ——————

Nathaniel wasn't one to lose his temper.

He'd been raised and reared in a household where any and all shows of emotion were not only discouraged but also instructed out of the boys who lived there by stern tutors who'd answered to an even sterner duke.

Only his mother had been permitted displays of emotion, and that had been only because she was of the fairer sex and Nathaniel's father had clear expectations of how women carried themselves as opposed to men.

There was even less a place for emotion aboard a ship. At sea, sailing a privateer ship during wartime and potentially facing enemy vessels at any moment, a man had to be in full and complete control—of his temper, his wits, and every other last part of himself.

But God help him, Nathaniel was being tested.

In this instant, with the chatterbox rambling on and on in that voice that hadn't fully changed, Nathaniel fought to retain every last lesson he'd learned, and it was all he could do to keep from shouting him down for a second time.

For Nathaniel saw red.

Nor was it just the thick blanket of dark red that had fallen over his eyes.

It was . . . red.

61

His walls.

His once plain-as-they-ought-to-be walls bore streaks of red and blue and—

A low growl started in his chest and worked its way up his throat and stuck there.

Pink. The lad had painted his room . . . pink.

"You really don't like it?" The tentatively spoken question emerged hesitantly from the boy, who'd fast made a menace of himself. "I . . . don't think it's as bad as all that."

"Oh, it is not bad," Nathaniel whispered, and the lad's face brightened. "It is a good deal fucking worse."

He may as well have kicked the boy's pup for the look he gave Nathaniel. Perhaps if he had been someone else, Nathaniel would have cared more. Or at all.

"You are done in here." Nathaniel didn't even bother to hide his grimness.

"I . . . but I'm not," Cassius said, gesturing with the tip of his brush and pointing at that damned atrocity upon his wall. "Mayhap once I finish, you'll be less harsh in your opinion. Mayhap, if you let me finish my work, you'll even like it?"

"Like it?" he echoed dumbly. *"Like it . . . ?"* And then it hit Nathaniel with all the force of a cannonball to the chest. The lad actually thought it was the scene he took affront with, and not the fact that he'd painted a scene, at all. "I asked you to paint my walls," he said, taking a step forward.

The young man immediately backed up. "A-and I did."

Just like that, that thin, tightly stretched nerve snapped like a fiddle string that'd been plucked too taut. "White," he bellowed, sending the lad jumping for a second time. "I asked you to paint my walls white."

Cassius was already shaking his head. "No, you didn't. You most certainly did not."

"Are you challenging me?" he barked.

"No."

Good, the boy wasn't completely dicked in the nob.

"I . . ." The lad paused. "Yes, I am."

Apparently, he *was* completely dicked, after all.

"But it is more that I am pointing out your directives. You said . . ." Then the boy dropped his voice, deepening it in a hideously bad but clear impersonation of Nathaniel's own voice. "You can begin by cleaning my quarters and then applying fresh paint to my walls. I'm not looking for bowls of fruit, baskets of flowers. Country scenes. This is a sea vessel. It's a ship. A *ship*. It's not the pleasure boat you thought you were getting yourself on."

So there wasn't something so wrong with the dandy's head that he remained incapable of memorizing those very specific, those very *exact* orders Nathaniel had doled out earlier that afternoon.

Nathaniel's nostrils flared, and he inhaled slowly through his nose and silently recited a shanty.

> "In Amsterdam there lived a maid,
> Mark well what I do say,
> In Amsterdam there lived a maid,
> And she was mistress of her trade,
> I'll go no more a-roving with you, fair maid."

"Are you . . . talking to yourself?" Cassius ventured in halting tones.

> "A-roving, a-roving, since roving's been my ruin,
> I'll go no more a-roving with you, fair maid."

And when those verses didn't prove near enough to temper his rage, he silently mouthed the remaining lyrics of that verse.

It was futile. "Hayes," he bellowed, and Cassius jumped an impressive foot in the air. "I want Hayes."

There were several long beats of silence, and then the quartermaster was there.

"Cap . . . ?" Hayes's greeting and question trailed off as his gaze landed on the newest addition to Nathaniel's chambers.

"Get him out of my sight for now. Put him in the galley." *Except, wait. No. Strike that.* "Not the kitchens. The lad'll burn my damned ship down. Assign him to the surgeon." *Only . . .* "No." Not the ship's doctor. The boy would somehow cut someone's limb off or spread scurvy. "Something . . . anything, where he's not getting himself into trouble. And keep on him." Because the good Lord knew the menace needed looking after.

Hayes nodded. "Aye, captain." He motioned for Cassius.

Cassius, whose eyes glimmered and glistened like enormous pools of despair, and—

Nathaniel grimaced. *Good God.* "No tears," he said sharply. "Absolutely no tears."

"I-I'm not c-crying." A bit fat drop tumbled down a ridiculously soft, plump, pale-white cheek, making an absolute liar of Cassius McQuoid and his assurance of the contrary.

Nathaniel dragged a hand down his face. The boy was going to get himself mocked mercilessly. He'd never survive. And yet, perhaps that was what he needed to put some hair on his chest and some strength in his spine. What failure was it on Nathaniel's part that he couldn't bring himself to do what needed to be done?

"This way," Hayes said with a gentleness Nathaniel had certainly never been capable of. But then Hayes had four sisters and was better at dealing with people who leant to the emotional side.

Cassius headed to Nathaniel's desk, and Nathaniel took in that detail to previously escape his notice—the jars and bottles he'd commandeered and turned into a makeshift art space.

"What are you doing?" he snapped.

"Cleaning—"

"Get out," he interrupted, startling the boy into dropping the brush with a soft little clatter. Nathaniel tried again. "That'll be . . . all for now."

And this time, Cassius raced past, joining Hayes and quitting Nathaniel's chambers.

The moment he'd gone, Nathaniel closed his eyes and shook his head.

Keep him out of trouble, and keep him away from me . . .

That's precisely what Nathaniel needed the other man to do.

It would be a miracle if Hayes succeeded in the impossible task.

Chapter 6

Cassia had once believed there could be nothing worse than being invisible to the world.

Just a handful of days into her sea voyage, she realized how wrong she'd been.

How very wrong.

There was something a good deal worse—being the object of ridicule and mockery. It was discovering one *deserved* to be the object of ridicule and mockery.

As the sun set over the vast expanse of ocean as far as the eye could see, Cassia scrubbed the decks as part of her latest assignment. She could think of just one thing—the captain hated her work. It was why he'd had Little Ron give her new orders, this time to clean the deck instead of the captain's cabin.

Nay, not only did the captain hate what she'd done, he despised it with a passion, a vitriolic loathing so great he'd rather she clean his ship and . . .

Cassia paused midscrub and stared blankly at the foamy suds upon the deck. Only, it hadn't so much been her painting the captain had despised. Rather, he'd been disgusted at how slow she'd been to grasp just what it was he'd expected of her. *Of course* he'd not wanted her to paint a scene upon his walls. How naive and incompetent she'd proven herself—time and time again.

And . . . that was so much of how she was and, worse, *who* she was. A ball of misery and humiliation lodged in her throat. It was why her clever and sophisticated sister Myrtle had been sent away to finishing school and Cassia left behind, with only the expectation that she'd wed and become some man's arm ornament. Because even her own parents hadn't believed she was capable of doing or being anything more.

With her continual fumbling of what the captain of this ship demanded of her, she proved her parents had been right. That the *world* was, in fact, right. She was hopelessly naive and . . . silly, so much so that she didn't have a husband and hadn't even had so much as a suitor.

Cassia made herself resume scrubbing, applying greater pressure to her work.

Before now, people didn't *hate* her.

Only, neither did people really . . . like her, either.

Not truly.

Oh, her parents absolutely loved her.

But it hadn't been until they'd chosen to send her younger sister off to finishing school that she'd gathered . . . that she was not special. At least, not the manner of special that resulted in special friendships and relationships. Like the one her sister had always had with their mother.

Or Myrtle now had with her husband, the Duke of Aragon.

And then there was Cassia.

Cassia, who'd an entire ship of men and boys hating her in like measure.

Or, rather, in some manner of competition to see who could hate her most.

A particularly powerful swell rocked the ship.

Not for the first time since she'd been assigned to cleaning the floors of the main deck, Cassia dropped her brush, staggering to her feet. She rushed to the railing, gripped it tight, and threw up.

Again.

Clinging to the side, she stared miserably out at the violent waves battering the side of the vessel. Seawater slapped her in the face, and even as she blinked against its salty sting, she welcomed the soothing cool of it upon her clammy skin.

How much did the stomach hold? And what happened when there was nothing left inside? Because surely she was fast reaching that point.

With a miserable moan, she wiped the back of her left hand over her mouth, sank against the railing, and rested her cheek along the smooth, cool wood.

"Ye finally takin' yerself a rest?" someone barked from behind. The man snorted. "An' 'ere we didn't think ye capable of it. 'Ere we didn't think ye were capable of anything but makin' the rest of us look bad."

Carlisle, she thought. It was always Carlisle plaguing her.

First, it had been because she'd not known the way and made endless mistakes at her chores. Then, when she'd finally flung herself fully into her responsibilities, determined to not bring any more attention to herself, she'd ended up earning his ire for making the rest of the men look bad.

Forcing herself upright, Cassia resumed scrubbing the floor.

She'd lost track of the number of sailors she'd met, each of whom despised her in like measure and never wasted a moment to threaten or mock her, but this man was her greatest detractor of all.

The wind whipped against Cassia's face, and she welcomed the salty air filling her nostrils and lungs, and then she made herself straighten and face the cruel sailor.

Or, in this case . . . sailors.

At some point, Carlisle had been joined by three of the impressionable deckhands. With scarves knotted around their heads, they had the look of pirates she and her siblings had played at during their younger years.

But everyone could be reasoned with. Surely they had . . . some decency to see she was ill?

"I'm not resting," Cassia said, her voice weak from her bouts of seasickness. "I'm sick."

Carlisle let out a sharp bark of laughter. "See that, we do."

"And smell it, too," Oliver added, his words met with another round of raucous amusement as his friends tossed him supportive elbows.

Oliver, who'd been so very nice . . . until the captain had relieved him of his duties cleaning his cabin and turned that responsibility over to Cassia instead.

No, there'd be no mercy from any of them. Refusing to engage, Cassia dropped to her knees and, keeping her head down, resumed cleaning the already immaculate deck.

"Greener he is than any sea I've ever sailed," one of the sailors called over.

"Easy, Carlisle, or you're going to have him casting up his biscuits again," someone shouted in return.

And like he'd told the most hilarious of jests, the lads and Carlisle all chortled with laughter.

Cassia gripped the brush in her hand hard. *Ignore them.*

Just as you would Fleur or Quillon or any of your bothersome brothers and sisters. And cousins. Why, given the sheer size of the McQuoids' wont to teasing, one would think she'd be accustomed to this.

But then, her family didn't say outrageously wicked things. Not like this. Not naughty words, melded with cruel ones. They told silly jokes and played harmless pranks.

"Wot say ye, McQuoid? Ye going to be sick again?" Carlisle taunted Cassia.

Putting her elbow into her work, Cassia concentrated on the mindless chore.

ScrubScrubStop.

ScrubScrubStop.

And then, the louts began to collectively make gagging sounds.

Cassia stilled her back-and-forth brushstrokes, glaring down at the deck.

Do not give them the satisfaction.

Do not . . .

"A pathetic excuse for a sailor is what 'e is," Carlisle jeered. "Afraid of the ocean as ye are, why, we'd be better tossing ye over and being done with ye once and for all."

A shiver traipsed along her spine—terror, it licked away at her. For what this man suggested . . . She believed he'd do it, too, and that he'd enjoy ending her mightily. Bullies found their power in the weakness of others. Determined to disabuse him of the idea she was a coward to be preyed upon, Cassia tamped down her fear and, jumping to her feet, wheeled to face Carlisle and the deckhands he'd gathered around her for the express purpose of making her miserable.

"I am not afraid of the ocean," she shouted, deepening her voice to a low growl. "I'm afraid of dying in it." Surely, with the way the violent waves battered the ship and swelled around them, the boys would at least understand that and leave her be.

The crew erupted with their hilarity, howling their mirth loud enough that it swelled over even the rough seas.

Carlisle gave her a little nudge. "Well, get on with it, will ye? Side of the ship needs scrubbing, it do, and yer the newest crew member . . ."

Yes, yes. She knew the remainder of that. Newest crew members saw to it. As in all manner of suspect, miserable assignments no other person ought, or would ever, want. And yet, she wasn't so gullible as to believe any person would be hung over the side of a ship to clean it. This was only more of his bullying.

A knot of fear formed in her throat, and she tried to swallow that along with the bile that was already threatening.

Her efforts proved to be in vain.

Retching for what was surely the thousandth time on this miserable voyage, Cassia turned in time to cast the little that sat in her stomach over the side; her shoulders and chest heaved, along with her belly.

Her moans of misery were lost to the laughter her seasickness invariably inspired in the merciless crew.

Sinking against the railing, she closed her eyes and gripped the wood beam hard.

Perhaps death would be preferable.

Someone shoved her hard between the shoulder blades, and Cassia dug her fingers into the railing.

"Well?" Oliver shouted. "Get on with it. A fresh wave of vomit for ye to clean off the wood."

Someone struck her sharply on the back, this time harder and with greater power, and she cried out.

"Off with ye, lad!"

And Cassia snapped.

She whipped around.

"Do not put your hands on me one more time, or I'll show you precisely what you can do with those rough hands of yours, Carlisle," she shouted, and the man's jaw slackened.

But she'd quieted him, and she took advantage of that unexpected silence. She turned on his mean fellow in arms, glowering at him with the same anger she'd trained on her younger siblings, Quillon and Fleur, when they'd put ink in Cassia's tea and she'd stained her teeth quite terribly. Once. And only once.

"You know what you are?" She didn't give him a chance to answer. "You are a nasty bully." She looked to the young deckhands, Oliver, Jameson, and Timothy, who flanked Carlisle's side. "The lads here look up to you, but instead of using your power for good, you bring them down, making them mean like you."

Another deckhand joined them—Little Rob, aptly named because of his painfully slender and small size. He took in the scene before him with wary eyes, and Cassia looked hopefully to the new lad for rescue.

He cleared his throat. "The captain be needing his bath drawn."

Never more grateful for that reprieve, Cassia made to step forward, but Carlisle stepped into her path. "The lad's busy. Tell 'im that."

The other deckhands exchanged nervous glances.

"I'm not really busy," Cassia explained calmly. "I'm being waylaid by Mr. Carlisle." *Tell the captain that,* she silently pleaded with her eyes.

Tension crackled around her, and she knew she'd gone too far with that appeal for help.

"Ye tell the captain that, and I'll make yer life miserable . . ." *Too.* It hung there in Carlisle's steely tones. "Is that understood?"

The little boy nodded, his throat bobbing wildly.

An idea took root. Cassia gave a toss of her head. "Either way, I don't draw baths." Which wasn't untrue. She didn't know a thing about that particular chore. "I *take* them."

The lads gawked at her.

"I have a message you can deliver to the captain," Cassia said, staying Little Ron before he could go. "You can tell Captain Surly-Breeches to draw his own bath. Why, even if I had the energy and inclination to quit my work on the main deck and draw him a bath, well, then I'd have done so two days ago for myself." Cassia waved an exaggerated hand about. "But here we are."

Silence met her response, and then . . . Carlisle erupted. Tossing his head back, he roared with hilarity, and Cassia glanced about nervously before joining him and the other deckhands.

Suddenly, Carlisle stopped and fixed a glacial look on her that, even with the sun beating down on the deck, managed to leave her cold inside. "Ain't that just like a nobleman. Always thinking of yer own pleasures. Expecting people to wait on ye, and all too happy to take yer comforts without a thought for others."

As if he'd read the tension and sought to escape, Little Ron backed away, tripping over himself in his haste, and Cassia well understood and envied him his flight.

A cold smile formed on Carlisle's hard lips, and the puckered scar just above the right corner of his unforgiving mouth twitched. "Ye ain't going to find any help here, ye ain't. Used to ye fancy kind in London, are ye?" He cracked his knuckles. "Ye want people to fawn over ye and drop ye bows, ye should have stayed in your parlor with the rest of the fine lords."

So that's what this was about. He'd rightly identified her as nobility and was determined to make her pay because of her birthright.

Not for the first time, unease swirled in her breast. "Let me be." She infused as much calm as she could into her voice. "I don't want trouble with you."

"Should 'ave thought of that before ye boarded a ship ye don't belong on," he jeered.

There'd be no help on this score. Giving up her attempts to reason with a man who couldn't be reasoned with, she spoke to the deckhands. "Captain Ellsby is a fair man." Hadn't he shown her more leniency than she deserved over her repeated blunders? "Do you truly think he'd want you to engage in bullying a fellow crew member?"

As one, the boys dropped their gazes to the deck and shuffled their feet.

Carlisle glared at Cassia. "Don't listen to 'im, lads. Ye know their kind. Use to orderin' people about, 'e is. 'e ain't one of us." With that, the brutish sailor made a fist and thumped it against his opposite open palm.

Her stomach churned, a product of the seasickness and terror.

And then he was on her.

———— ❧ ————

Nathaniel wasn't a man given to softness.

He'd grown up in a household with one miserable sire, as one of six brothers; the only speck of softness and light within the bunch had been their mother.

She'd been slight and quiet and often demure, deferring to her bear of a husband and drowned out by her brood of large sons, a brood given to wrestling and sparring and quarreling with their father.

As such, he'd personally say, thus far, he'd handled rather well the accidental deckhand aboard his ship.

When the lad had attempted to paint murals on his corridor walls, he'd assigned him a different task—his cabin—and the boy had proceeded to paint a damned scene there, too.

And when he'd cast the contents of his stomach up near Nathaniel's boots, he'd forgiven that affront.

The McQuoid lad had since proven himself quite competent. He'd flung himself vigorously into his work. But the line . . . it had to be drawn . . . somewhere.

It was a lesson Nathaniel well knew as captain of this ship, and a lesson he'd gathered even long ago, before he'd had his shipping company.

"What do you mean he's not there?" he asked, his voice a low growl.

One of his younger deckhands, Little Ron glanced down for a long time at his feet. "Said 'e's busy and wasn't of a mind to draw you a bath," he said weakly.

Nathaniel narrowed his eyes. "He said that."

"A-aye." Little Ron paused, then added something under his breath that sounded a good deal like, "And more."

Nathaniel tuned his ears to that latter statement. "What was that?" Because surely, he was hearing things. Surely—

The deckhand cleared his throat. "Oi said 'an' more,' Captain."

"And this . . . 'and more'?" he asked when it became apparent Little Ron had no intention of continuing.

"Called ye 'Captain Surly-Breeches' and said even if he had the energy and inclination to quit his work on the main deck and draw ye a bath, well, then, he'd have done so two days ago for himself. But here we are . . ." And Little Ron swept his arms wide and then closed as if repeating a gesture that Nathaniel would wager his entire shipping line he'd witnessed from the damned recalcitrant stowaway.

An unwanted deckhand who spoke in fine tones befitting his lofty station.

Nathaniel steeled his jaw. "Let it be clear to McQuoid that I'm expecting my bath filled, and if he's going to gainsay an order, I'll be more than happy to toss him overboard and give him the bath he desperately craves."

Little Ron gulped, and snapping the heels of his boots together smartly, he bowed. "Aye, aye. I'll try again . . ."

"Problems with the cabin boy?"

Nathaniel glanced over at the issuer of that sardonic question and scowled.

His friend promptly burst out laughing.

And it was only the history of friendship between them, the fact that Hayes had been like another brother to him over the years, that made him pardon that offense.

"What is it?" An unspoken "now" hung on the end of Hayes's query.

Nathaniel rolled his shoulders. "What *isn't* it now?" he mumbled. From painting his damned halls blue to painting an ocean scene in his chambers and now defying his orders.

"We were all young lords once, looking to escape. Luckily we had your uncle and his ship," the other man reminded him. Needlessly.

He'd heard the McQuoid name but had no real knowledge of the family. Just knew they were good *ton*. And Nathaniel well knew he'd his mother's brother, Lord Eric Holbrook, to thank for helping set him on his feet following his time in the navy. His uncle, who took great delight in riling Nathaniel's father, had been all too happy to turn over one of his ships so that Nathaniel could begin his own shipping venture.

"The fact that I understand very well what it is to need to escape that damned life is the *only* reason I've not locked him up or tossed him overboard," Nathaniel muttered, earning another round of laughter from Hayes.

He glared at his lifelong friend.

"Oh, come," the other man said. "You've never tossed a fellow overboard in your career."

"No." Nathaniel hadn't. But if anyone was going to push him to that point, it was decidedly the accidental deckhand he'd been saddled with.

Or perhaps the Captain Jeremy of some ridiculously named ship had known precisely what a menace the boy was and had given him some made-up name, saddling some other poor bugger—Nathaniel—with him instead.

"What is it you really want?" he asked, knowing intuitively that there was more to this line of questioning and discussion.

Hayes grunted. "The other lads are giving the boy a . . . difficult time."

"As they do every new member aboard the ship," Nathaniel pointed out. "Protecting him isn't helping him. The crew is going to see you're providing deferential treatment, and that's only going to make it go worse for him."

"I remember how miserable it was on my first voyage, Captain. The boy is constantly emptying the contents of his stomach and weak from being sick, and when he's not ill, the other lads are particularly cruel. Tying the laces of his boots together and lying about weevils in his bread and"—Nathaniel heard something in the other man's voice—"this is different."

Nathaniel snapped his brows together. "Different how?"

"The boy is younger and more naive and . . . and . . . not accustomed to the ribbing . . . and Carlisle, one of the men we were forced to hire . . . He is leading the charge."

Tension snapped through him. With the exception of Nathaniel, Hayes, and Albion, all the men who served aboard the *Flying Dragon* were born outside the lofty ranks of Polite Society. They were men from some of the harshest streets of East London, some of whom had found themselves jailed for one minor offense or another in Newgate, all of whom were former sailors or soldiers in the King's Army. The ones who'd been with him since the beginning, he knew and trusted with his life . . . but when one took on new crew members, well, one never knew what one was getting.

Impatient, Nathaniel cut into Hayes's lengthy list. "What do you propose?"

"I'm suggesting you tell the crew you've named him your new cabin boy. If they know he's directly responsible to you, that he has a position of privilege, then it'll go easier for him."

Just then, across-the-deck sniggering caught his attention, and Nathaniel glanced over to find the cause of his crew's amusement.

Oliver had flung a rope ladder over the side of the ship and was motioning for one of the deckhands.

A perpetually green Cassius stared in wide-eyed horror, and then, his enormous eyes bulging, the boy shook his head frantically and stepped back.

Immediately two other boys were there, gripping him by the shoulders and steering him forward, pushing him until he reached the railing.

Cassius shot his palms out, gripping the wood.

Nathaniel narrowed his eyes. "What in hell . . . ?"

"I believe they are intending to tell the boy he has to climb over and clean the side of the ship."

Surely the boy knows better than that.

"Surely he does not," Hayes drawled, confirming Nathaniel had spoken aloud.

Meanwhile, the crowd around the gathering of boys continued to swell, as more of the *Flying Dragon*'s crew rushed to take in the latest penalty.

Hayes stood, his hands clasped behind him, his gaze directed forward.

"Over with ye, boy," one of the crew shouted.

Just then, two of the men grabbed the boy and lifted him by his shirtfront so that his feet danced and dangled in midair.

Bloody hell.

Nathaniel took off running.

———— ✎ ————

It was funny the thoughts a person had when she was about to die.

Given the fact that Cassia had stolen away from home and, in boarding the wrong vessel, would leave her family wondering for all time just where their eldest daughter had gone, one would think she'd be mourning the life not lived and the family left behind.

Funnily, there'd been any number of times since the *Flying Dragon* had sailed, and Cassia along with it, that she'd thought death preferable to her eternally sick stomach.

Only to discover at the hands of merciless men how very wrong she'd been.

"Wants a fancy bath, do ye!" Carlisle taunted. "Well, 'ow's about a dip in the ocean instead, to clean yerself off?"

"No!" she rasped, thrashing and twisting, kicking her legs out—in vain. "Please."

Only her efforts here were met with laughter, as Carlisle grabbed her on either side of her arms, and hoisted her—

Oh, God.

Over.

"That is—"

Cassia screamed, screamed loud and shrill enough to drown out whatever words the equally merciless captain of this vessel was saying to his men.

She screamed for all she was worth and all she had. Even as she told herself to be still so the hands that held her didn't let go, she kicked her legs back and forth, and she clung to both sets of equally enormous arms about to hold her over the side of the ship.

Cassia stole a glance over her shoulder at the ocean below.

So this was how she was to die.

On occasion, Cassia had thought of the day she'd draw her last breath.

She'd had a macabre wonder about what that moment would be like and had always envisioned being an old woman with snow-white hair, tucked in her bed, wearing a soft smile as she, surrounded by a gathering of the many children she'd one day have, slipped from this earth, content in knowing her life had been full.

Never once in any of those many wonderings had she imagined dying before her twenty-second birthday.

Though in fairness, it wasn't just that she was going to die this day.

They were going to murder her.

Cause of death: drowning.

Drowned by a cruel sailor and the young, impressionable boys he'd gathered who quite despised her, which was rather peculiar, as children tended to like her.

Not these.

These nasty buggers, whooping and laughing and dancing about, were ruthless savages who'd not be content until they killed her.

She forced her eyes open and took in the churning waters below, whitecaps forming atop the peaks of waves that would swallow her whole. Dread sluiced through her.

She'd been so very wrong this voyage. Death was not preferable.

At least, not this death.

Perhaps another one.

Like . . . like . . .

Only, as her panicky mind raced, she couldn't drag forth a single pleasant-seeming death. That was, aside from the one she'd imagined as an old woman in her bed. But then, mayhap this was the Lord's punishment. Perhaps this was how she was to be repaid for sneaking off to see the world aboard Jeremy's ship, and pretending to be a lad, all in the name of exploring. Tears pricked her lashes.

Yet, why should she be punished? Why, when she was doing something no different from what any other man was allowed to do? And from the bowels of despair came the stirrings of a safer, welcome fury.

How dare the world?

And how dare this man?

Still, she was at their mercy.

"Please," she cried, pleading, begging.

A large wave crested against the side of the ship, spraying her face and slapping her body with icy seawater that easily penetrated her garments. She gasped as the chill of it seeped into her skin and sucked the breath from her lungs.

"Never tell me yer afraid of the ocean?" Carlisle guffawed, and not waiting for an answer, he directed his next words at the audience around them. "A deckhand afraid of the sea. Wot's next? A cook afraid of the kitchen?"

Laughter met the man's question.

"Please," she begged a third time, because, well, she wasn't really so proud as to not plead for her life.

"That is enough!" the captain thundered.

And there was a God, and surprisingly, there was also some mercy within the leader of this crew. For he managed to do what Cassia in all her begging and threatening hadn't—he silenced the fun they'd been having at her expense and called for them to save her.

The men holding her remained frozen. Horror wreathed their sun-weathered features, their eyes bulged, one man's grip went slack, and Cassia screamed as she slipped from his loosened hold, even as the other fellow now holding her tightened his hands on her.

And she wrapped her arms about those bulky muscles, attempting to claw herself free.

Then he dropped her.

Gasping for air, Cassia collapsed atop the deck, and her cap, knocked loose by Carlisle, fell over her eyes. She pushed it back into place, attempting to still her thunderous heart, sucked in desperate breaths, and laid her cheek against the deck surface, never more grateful for another person's arrival than she was Captain Ellsby's.

Mayhap she was going to survive this, after all.

The crew around her had gone silent, the sharp rasps of air she sucked into her lungs and the waves lapping against the side of the ship inordinately loud in that sudden, unearthly quiet left by these men who hated her. These men who'd attempted to kill her.

All the fury and rage and frustration bottled inside exploded from her.

Leveraging herself with her elbows, Cassia pushed herself upright and glared at the gaping men. "You are nothing but nasty, horrific, monstrous people," she said, jabbing her finger at Carlisle and the boys who'd done his bidding as she spoke. She paused. "Not you," she said to Little Ron, the one kindly deckhand. "I've got nothing bad to say about you, other than the fact that you could have tried to stop th-them." Her teeth chattered from the cold left by the wind's chill and the leftover fear she was certain she'd take with her to her eventual death. But it wouldn't be this day, and as the group parted and the captain stepped forward, she found herself enlivened just by the very nature of being alive. Perhaps any other time she would have been besieged with the suitable dread he always inspired. Not this time. Not with him and his callous crew and harsh words. She looked to the captain. He dared her with that flinty gaze to speak even a word. She wavered. Only for a moment. After all, she was a McQuoid who'd faced down a bevy of terrifying siblings and cousins. "You have a problem with your crew," she seethed.

A large gust of wind ripped across the deck, knocking the air from her lungs.

Tension snapped in the salt-filled air around them.

She'd gone too far—*again.*

She knew it in the unnatural quiet that descended over the vessel, with only that howling wind and the slap of the ocean waves against the ship filling the air.

Hayes tensed and looked from Cassia to the captain.

She shivered, dread skittering along her spine, and then the ship pitched under her, rolling violently back and forth and taking her stomach, along with her pride. And for the second time since she'd met the piteous man, Cassia opened her mouth and vomited at his feet.

A miserable moan escaped her, and she wiped at her lips, fighting the desperate need to cry again. Not that she'd done so publicly. That she knew she couldn't do if she expected to survive however long this godforsaken journey, in fact, was.

When she forced her eyes open, she found the captain's harsh, unforgiving eyes locked with hers.

Nay, not her eyes. Rather, her shoulder.

Cassia stilled, then registered her exposed plait. *No. Oh, God.* With dread mounting, she touched those tresses.

She swallowed hard.

This was not good.

This was not good. At all.

Chapter 7

He was a woman.

Nay, more specifically, *she* was a woman.

Lord of Lords, his deckhand, a dandy who blubbered like a woman and had soft cheeks like a woman did so because he was, in fact . . . a woman.

She was a dainty, delicate, lithe-figured minx.

Nathaniel attempted to wrap his sluggish mind around the implications of this discovery.

Christ in hell.

"We can always strip her naked," his seven-foot-tall sailor Shorty ventured. The young woman's cheeks went pale, and she retreated a step, shooting a swift, desperate glance over her shoulder to the seas, as if she were considering a jump. "To appease the gods of the seas, of course," the gentle giant of a man said on a rush, reminding them all of that seafaring belief. Shorty yanked at the kerchief at his throat. "Like . . . the mermaid at the front of the ship?" he croaked, reiterating that lore well known by all sailors about women on ships.

Women, who were notoriously bad luck for a ship and its crew.

"That's a block of wood, ye nobhead," Robinson whispered loudly to the sailor. "This one is an *actual* woman."

As one, they looked to the cowering lady.

And then Nathaniel's crew came alive in their outrage and immense superstition. They erupted in a flurry of shouting, shaking their fists at the young woman.

Nathaniel waded forward, and the men who'd converged upon her gave way.

The lady—she couldn't be more than eighteen or nineteen—eyed Nathaniel warily through those expressive greenish-blue eyes.

Good. She should be bloody scared. Terrified out of her damned mind.

"To your positions," he barked, and his crew instantly dispersed, scattering back to the jobs they'd abandoned.

Shorty lingered. Snatching the kerchief from his bald head, he twisted the crimson fabric back and forth in his enormous hands. "Didn't know, Oi did, Captain," Shorty said desperately.

"To your position, Shorty," he said tersely. The last thing he had time to attend to in this instant was the distraught, experienced sailor. He'd deal with him later.

Marching over, Nathaniel reached down, plucked the woman up, clasped her by the elbow in his firm grip, and steered her along the deck.

She emitted a little yelp. "I'm more than capable of walking myself. You needn't go steering me—"

"Silence," he boomed. "Are you capable of that?" Because that was all he needed from her in this moment.

"Of course I am," she scoffed, her breath slightly uneven. From the pace he'd set for them? Or fear?

If she were smart, it'd be the latter. Alas, the troublesome minx had proven herself anything but possessed of a brain. When it came to the art of annoying a man, well, she possessed that in spades.

"I expect you have questions for me," she said as they cut a speedy path along the main decks. "In which case, you'll likely want me to speak so that I might explain—"

"I don't." He bit out each curt syllable between his teeth as they reached the stairway leading below deck. He brought them to a stop and pointed downward. "Now, go."

She hesitated, then opened her mouth to speak, but must have seen something in his gaze, for she swallowed noisily and scurried down those steps.

Nathaniel followed quickly after her, passing those ridiculous walls she'd painted a damned vase of flowers upon.

Flowers.

Tears.

Prattling.

Lots of tears.

Of course.

Now it all made sense.

Nathaniel followed close behind the surprisingly fleet-of-foot stowaway. All the while, he sought to wrap his brain around the discovery and the implications of having a damned woman aboard his ship. With ships and the men who sailed upon them superstitious by nature, the last thing Nathaniel could afford on this, his last mission until he oversaw his damned responsibilities, was to play nursemaid to a young woman who wouldn't know how to avoid trouble if she'd been handed a map.

She would get blamed for every ill wind that blew their way. Crews were known to mutiny for less. His men were loyal, but these weren't all his men. The last-minute need to hire additional crew had left him with sailors whom he didn't know. Carlisle's treatment of the lass he'd thought was a lad was proof enough of that. The mission would be fraught with danger, and having a young miss in the mix went from dangerous to outright deadly.

By God, anything could happen at sea. He knew that. Hell, his ship had been docked near a vessel in port for routine repairs when it had exploded without warning. Even years later, the screams of agony and terror of all those innocent souls haunted him.

And that didn't include the risks during a voyage.

Violent storms that drove ships into sandbars.

Ships ramming other ships.

Cannon fire blowing up men and parts of the vessels.

The lady stopped so suddenly, he crashed into her back.

She emitted a mouselike squeak and pitched forward.

Nathaniel shot his hands out. Gripping her by the shoulders, he caught her before she landed on her face.

Add walking. Walking is apparently another hazard for a lady at sea.

"You know, you haven't said where you are taking me?" she said, wetting her lips. "It's the brig. Isn't i-it?" she stammered. And then . . . tears welled. Enormous crystalline drops materialized in her eyes.

"It'd serve you right," he snapped. This was too much. He wasn't in a frame of mind to speak to her. Not without losing his temper. "Hayes!" he thundered.

His quartermaster was there in an instant. "Captain?"

"Escort her to my cabin."

"This way," Hayes was saying, and in the young woman's usual fashion, she proceeded to rattle on a whole discourse that didn't require much from the quartermaster at all.

After the pair had gone, Nathaniel remained there, reining in his temper, because he did not lose his temper. Ever.

Not even when his father had stated Nathaniel's seafaring days were to be put on an unforgivable pause. Being calm had served him in life and battle. But this? This was too much.

To calm himself, he drew in a deep breath.

It didn't help.

There is a woman on my ship.

There is a woman on my ship.

There is a woman here.

Nay, a lady.

There is a lady on my ship.

Standing there, Nathaniel made himself repeat those words over and over in his mind.

To calm himself.

To keep from flying into a rage.

To keep from tossing her overboard.

Nay, he'd not toss her overboard.

He might want to, and she might have committed an offense worthy of it, but . . . he'd enough restraint.

Nathaniel was a master of restraint.

He never failed to exercise it. It was why he was on minute twelve now, outside his cabin and not inside, screaming down the lady's bloody head. The chit had absolutely no idea the danger she'd put herself in. The sea was dangerous enough. But by God, she was a lone woman on board a ship headed for hostile waters. He was sailing to intercept French war plans with the safety of a damned lady to now worry about. If it were an ordinary privateering mission, he'd have steered the vessel back around. But this voyage was vital to the war effort, and there wasn't a nearby port that was safe to leave her in.

Nathaniel jammed his fingertips hard against his temple.

"Do you want me to open the door for you, Captain?" That question brought Nathaniel's focus flying over to his quartermaster.

His damned grinning quartermaster, who was alone. He'd managed to detach himself from the prattling chit and gotten her to stay in Nathaniel's cabin. There was something to be said for that triumph this day.

"Do you find this amusing?" he snapped. Because undoubtedly there was absolutely nothing amusing about this.

"About the fact we've got a lady aboard our vessel?" Hayes chuckled. "Nothing good about that. Better an evil spirit than a woman."

An evil spirit.

With the way he'd last seen her, all pale and green from nothing more than the casual rolling of the waves, she'd had the look of the dead here to haunt.

Nathaniel caught the other man's look.

"What?" he demanded, because clearly his quartermaster wished to say something more.

"Well, it's just the lady may have been pretty desperate to climb aboard a ship. Must be running away from something . . . fairly dangerous."

That gave Nathaniel pause.

Yes, only a greater peril would send a young lady sneaking aboard a ship, and yet . . . A thought slipped in, and Nathaniel froze. "Or something else." *Someone else.*

Hayes stilled. "Surely you don't think the duke would send her."

As in, put a lady at risk so that Nathaniel would feel obligated to turn around, even if it meant abandoning his mission and leaving the lives of British soldiers to hang in the balance? Yes, he absolutely did believe his father capable of that ruthlessness. He believed the duke thought of nothing but his own wants.

"Wait outside my cabin until I'm . . . done interrogating the lady." He'd neither the patience nor inclination to worry about why the minx had colluded with his father. What he cared about, the only things he'd ever care about, were this vessel, his work for the Crown, and the people reliant upon him.

With that, Nathaniel dismissed the other man and, setting his jaw, made his way inside his cabin. He did a sweep of the room.

Gone.

At some point the bloody minx had slipped free, and—

A low, misery-laced groan echoed around the room, and Nathaniel whipped his gaze over to the owner of that suffering someone.

He narrowed his eyes.

Nay, at some point, she'd commandeered his bed. She'd not fully gained her sea legs yet.

Her cheeks pale and her eyes clenched shut, the lady clung to the side of the mattress—his mattress.

And if he'd been another man, any other man, he'd have felt a scrap of pity at the sight of her suffering.

Nathaniel, however, was all out of patience with his *deckhand*.

He slammed the door shut so hard the panel shook behind him, and the *thwack* thundered around the room. The young woman's eyes went flying open. "You," she said with the same dread that had previously been reserved to only the captains and commanders of vessels he boarded and commandeered.

"Were you expecting another?" he asked, imbuing as much ice and fury as he could within that query. "Prinny? Mad King George."

She cocked her head, the long auburn plait bouncing at her side as she pushed to unsteady feet. "Whyever would Prinny or King George be here? Do they sail?" Before he could answer, she added, "I did not know that. Even so, if they did, I'd not be looking to meet them."

Nathaniel opened his mouth to get a word in.

"Not because I'm disloyal to the Crown," she rushed to assure him. "I'm very much loyal. However, I'm not looking to meet the king."

And to keep from losing his bloody mind, and raging her down, he silently sang the shanty ditty called out by the men at the pumps and windlass.

> "I'll go no more a-roving with thee, fair maid.
> A-roving, a-roving, since roving's been my ruin,
> I'll go no more a-roving with thee, fair maid."

The lady's hesitant tones forced him away from that place of calm in which he sought to plant himself. "Unless . . . they're here," she ventured cautiously. "In which case, I'd not be rude and pay my respects."

Pay her respects? To Mad King George and Prinny? *Here?*

"You think I have King George and Prinny on my ship?" he clipped out.

"Do . . . you?"

"No," he snapped.

"No. No, that makes sense. It is just . . . my mind is all over the place since I discovered this isn't Jeremy's ship." She laughed, covering her face with her hands. "But imagine if Prinny *was* here? That would certainly make all of this awkward."

"Which part?" he snapped. "The lack of proper tea and biscuits for a high tea? Or your being unchaperoned, in the middle of the ocean, with a ship full of ruthless men."

Several lines creased her high-noble brow. "Well . . . the latter." Though with this one, that slight hesitation was hardly indicative of a woman fully committed to that answer. "And . . . they don't seem ruthless. Not all of them. The ones who hung me over the side of the boat. A couple, however, have been very patient and kindly toward me. Little Ron, for one . . . though they are all a little coarse in their speech."

"That was before," he said coldly, disabusing her of any notion of cheerful and, as she put it, kindly sailors.

She frowned. "Before *what?*"

He took another step closer to her, and the lady toppled onto the mattress, landing on her buttocks. As he leaned forward, snarling at her, she craned her head back. "Before they knew you were a damned woman who'd sneaked away on their vessel."

She blinked.

Hers were the biggest eyes he'd ever seen, and a mesmerizing shade, bluer and vaster than the Caribbean waters he'd sailed through. They were an azure green that distracted a fellow. He steeled his jaw. The last thing he could afford at sea was a distraction. Nathaniel got to the heart of it.

"What the hell are you doing here?" he demanded in steel-coated tones, scraping a gaze over her. "Who sent you?" he asked, even as he already knew the answer to his question.

His damned father had also anticipated Nathaniel's plans to leave early and, unable to snag a favor from Prinny quickly enough, had saddled him with a lady to worry about.

Except . . . would he have done that? Risked putting Nathaniel with another lady when he expected him to wed Lady Angela?

Confusion wreathed the young woman's high cheeks. "I sent myself. You see, I thought your boat—"

"*Ship.*"

"Was the *Waltzing Dragon.*"

"A bloody ridiculous name for a ship," he muttered.

"*I* think it is rather clever," she said defensively. "In fact, one might even say your *Flying Dragon* is rather cliché."

Cliché?

"*All* dragons fly. That is, the legends have them as flying. But waltzing is a forbidden dance, and it conjures—"

"Do you ever shut up?"

"Yes." She paused. "When the situation calls for it. This situation, however, does not seem t—"

"Trust me," he snapped. "It does."

The young woman pursed plump lips that he hated himself for suddenly noticing. Alas, for the first time in his career, he found himself in the presence of a person without a suitable unease around him. "As I was saying, I thought your b—*ship* belonged to my brother's friend Jeremy."

And then it hit him. "You were running away with the fellow." The poor man had undoubtedly come to his senses before committing himself to marriage and provided the minx the wrong ship name on purpose.

The woman cocked her head. "Marry *Jeremy?*" she echoed, her befuddlement worn in her words and in her eyes. She laughed. "Running away with . . . *No.* Jeremy is my brother's best friend. Not that I could not marry my brother's best friend, just that he isn't the sort I would harbor any romantic feelings for. I've known him since we were both pudgy, small babes and were playing at pirates. But Jeremy owns his own boat, and I was sneaking off"—she paused, her gaze growing distant, and when she spoke, her voice was sad—"to see the world."

To see the world. "Well, you've certainly seen it, haven't you?"

And as soon as he spoke those cold words, he wished he could call them back, only because more of those tears glimmered, and the last thing he wanted to deal with, the last thing he cared to deal with, was more of her bloody tears. *Any* woman's. They made him deuced uncomfortable—women *and* tears.

"What is your name?" he asked grudgingly, a safer question.

"Cassia McQuoid, of the McQuoid family." *God, she was a lady, after all.* "I gave you my family's name."

And then he blanched as she stood and dipped a neat little curtsy.

"You're a lady," he said, his tone accusing to his own ears.

The lady inclined her dainty chin as only a young woman could. "Well, I'm certainly not a gentleman."

"I mean of the peerage," he snapped. "You're the daughter of a peer."

"An earl."

He cursed darkly and roundly, and the lady widened her eyes. "I've never heard that one before," she said, an appreciative quality to her voice.

"Good. You can add it to your book."

"I don't have a book with curses." Her thin reddish eyebrows went flying up, along with a finger she shot toward the ceiling. "My journal . . . for my travels is for sketching, though I suppose I can add it to the pages. Do you think you would be so good as to fetch—"

The ship listed left, and the lady went sliding.

Nathaniel caught her to him and instantly regretted the decision, for it brought him flush with her small, soft breasts, and the flat of her belly and curve of her hips pressed against him.

Desire hit him. Aye, how had he failed to note that his new deckhand was, in fact, purely woman? Why, it was as plain as the freckled nose on her face.

The lady traced the seam of her lips once more, bringing his focus back to that flesh, and he did a sweep of her features.

With the high lines of her cheeks and narrow, pert nose, she'd not the soft, plump quality he tended to favor in women, and yet, from those angles of her face and the cream-white quality of her skin, she put him in mind of a perfectly sculpted statue, made real only by that dusting of freckles at the bridge of her nose.

"You're bad luck," he snapped.

The lady cocked her head. "I most certainly am n—"

"All women." He cut off what was undoubtedly about to be a meandering argument. "On board ships."

She gasped. "We most certainly are *not*."

The ship rolled slightly, and the lady's eyes slid shut, and her tone went as weak as her argument.

Alas, he was all out of pity for her.

Though in fairness, he'd not had it even to begin with.

"And just where does your knowledge of seaside cultures and customs come from, my lady?" he taunted. "All your years spent away at sea with Captain *Jeremy*?" With her green countenance and lack of footing since they'd set sail, he'd venture she hadn't so much as rowed a boat across whatever lake whichever family she belonged to owned.

"Oh, no," she said, when the ship listed gently once more. "This was to be my first time sailing with Jeremy." She leaned in and whispered conspiratorially, "I expect this will come to something of a surprise to you, but I've never set sail before."

Nathaniel folded his arms at his chest. "You don't say?" he drawled, keeping his features absolutely even.

She nodded. "Not even on a skiff on my family's Loch Allt na h-Airbhe."

Loch Allt na h-Airbhe? "You've made that up."

"No," she said with a solemn shake of her head. "I've not once been aboard—"

"The name of that damned loch."

"Oh, I assure you, not. My father's family is from Scotland." She was Scottish, then. Of course she was. "And my mother is part Scottish. We have a home there. In fact, you should sail your boat through the loch. They are quite lovely waters."

He went motionless. He couldn't even manage so much as to blink his eyes. For damned if there wasn't a ton to unpack within that handful of bat-shite-crazy statements. And if he were one of those lighthearted, cheerful fellows, he'd have tossed his head back and managed a laugh at the fact that she (1) thought to sail his ship through a damned loch and (2) seemed to think his boat—as she called it—was some kind of pleasure vessel.

"Oh, dear," the lady murmured. She peered up at him, and concern filled her eyes. "You've gone all queer in the face. Your stomach is unsettled, too. I would recognize—"

"My stomach is *not* unsettled." That avowal exploded vehemently from him. In fact, Nathaniel's *stomach* was the one damned steady thing about him at the moment.

"Of course not." The lady patted his hand and, as if a sea of observers had crowded around them, lowered her voice to a whisper so low even he had to strain to hear. "I have several brothers and know that gentlemen oft have a difficult time admitting a weakness."

But he wasn't a lighthearted, cheerful fellow. He was the captain of a ship, on a privateer mission, now saddled with a damned woman.

God, she was either obstinate or absent of anything between her two ears.

"Do you have a brain in your head?" he asked flatly.

"I do," she whispered, her voice miserable. "I wish, however, that I did not have a stomach. It is my stomach that is the real source of my woes."

Nathaniel gawked.

He couldn't help it.

"What in hell were you thinking?" he demanded. "That society wouldn't notice a damned lady has gone missing? That your parents won't?" Fury and panic made his voice pitch upward. And good God, what in hell did that mean of him, were they to find out she'd been with him—he, a marquess and a duke's son?

"Well, they didn't notice *Myrtle* went missing at Christmas for some several days or so, and by the time they did . . ." She prattled, and as she did, Nathaniel stared at her lips. The lady was a chatterbox. Because of course she was. "Well, you can imagine, they did everything possible to get back to Myrtle as quickly as they were able, but Myrtle was—"

And then it happened. He, a master of patience and self-control aboard his ship, snapped. "Who in hell is Myrtle?" he thundered.

The lady paused, her lips opening and closing like the trout dinner Jeremy fished them faithfully from the sea each night.

He'd stunned her.

Scared her, even.

And he couldn't care ten damns on Tuesday. Because he wasn't a man who cared either way about presenting himself as something he was not. Even for a lady's sake. It was why—

"Myrtle," the lady said patiently. "As in my *sister*."

"Oh, Myrtle," he said, with a false dawning understanding.

Only, by her smile and pleased nod, she was about as good at spotting sarcasm as she was at navigating aboard a sea vessel.

"You see, my family left Myrtle behind last winter when we departed for the Christmastide celebrations at Quagamore."

If Myrtle was anything like Cassia, well, Nathaniel was hard-pressed to believe all this "forgetting their daughters" business was a coincidence.

"Myrtle was resourceful and even managed to fall in love and find a husband." Amidst the misery swirling in her expressive eyes, a new, clear emotion came filtering forward: envy.

"Never tell me you set out aboard my damned ship for love and a husband?" he asked curtly, because if that was the foolish hope she'd carried, well, then she'd a better chance of starting a mutiny.

The lady blinked several times, and slid her gaze back over his way, as if she'd only just remembered his presence.

"Oh, no. Not at all. After two London Seasons, I've quite accepted I'm not the manner of lady to inspire love and prompt a declaration for marriage," she said pragmatically.

"I cannot even begin to imagine why," he said snarkily, and then wonder of wonders, coupled with horrors of horrors, the lady's eyes lit from within, and she clasped her long fingers together in a joined fist, and held them to her breast.

Adoration?

Nathaniel recoiled.

"Thank you," she whispered. "That is quite lovely of you, considering the fact that I boarded your boat upon false pretenses."

Nathaniel opened his mouth to disabuse her of the idea of that emotion, and also to point out for the flighty lady hopeless against identifying sarcasm that his had been nothing more than just that. But he stopped. Something held him back.

"It's a ship," he said, flustered.

"Yes, yes. But I've been thinking a good deal about that, and well, I'm fairly certain boats and ships are the same thing."

And she spoke with the absolute confidence of someone on whom it was entirely a waste of his actual breath to convince otherwise. And yet—

"It is entirely different."

"I don't see—"

"A ship is a large seagoing vessel and possesses a bowsprit and usually three masts, each composed of a lower mast, a topmast, and a topgallant mast. A boat is a small vessel—shorter than one hundred and twenty feet, for travel on water." As he spoke, the horror and panic of having a woman aboard his ship and on his latest—and if his father would have it, his last—mission, brought Nathaniel's voice climbing. "As in a vessel that, say, some empty-headed lady would, in fact, take to travel wherever in hell it is she wants to go," he finished on a thunderous boom.

Cassia McQuoid's perfectly arched auburn eyebrows inched up. "You're . . . speaking about me?"

He opened his mouth to snap her head off.

And stopped himself.

> "In Amsterdam there lived a maid,
> Mark well what I do say,
> In Amsterdam there lived a maid,
> And she was mistress of her trade."

When reciting those lyrics did nothing to lessen or lighten the volatile fury roiling within him, he silently moved on to the next in that song.

"I'll go no more a-roving with thee, fair maid.

A-roving, a-roving, since roving's been my ruin,

I'll go no more a-roving with thee, fair maid . . ."

His efforts proved futile. "What in hell are you doing here, then?" he bellowed.

The lady jumped a fraction, and damned if he didn't feel like he'd transformed into the blasted Duke of Roxburghe, blustering around servants and offspring alike. Nathaniel had grown well accustomed to his mother always darting off and keeping a distance when his father was in a temper. And the last thing he'd ever wanted to be or become was—

"You are angry," Cassia said simply, as if she'd herself made the discovery that the earth was a damned sphere, and without any of the hint of fear. She wilted not at all, and . . . well, damn him, but it was impossible to not admire the scatterbrain a small bit.

He growled. "Damned right I am."

"If you are upset, imagine me? I don't even want to be on your ship."

"Lady—"

"Cassia," she corrected, interrupting Nathaniel mid-lecture.

He stared back.

"It is just, given we're going to become friends over the next several weeks—"

"We aren't."

"And that I'm going to be on your ship all that time."

"Barring I don't throw you overboard?" he grumbled.

"Then it might make more sense if you call me by my given name, Cassia." He was across the room in a moment and reaching for the door handle. He needed to get the hell away from her before he lost his damned mind. "And that I call you—" Nathaniel shut the panel hard.

He stood there and stared at the opposite wood wall before shutting his eyes.

What a bloody fucking day—

The door hinges behind him squeaked, and he whipped around.

Hanging on to the solid oak panel, Lady Cassia ducked her head out. "May I call you Nath—"

"No. It's 'Captain.' Now shut the damned—" The lady slammed the door on the remainder of his voluminous shout, a shout whose echo mingled with the rattling of that panel.

A grinning Hayes stood in wait.

Nathaniel gnashed his teeth. He was glad one of them could find humor in this.

"Well?"

"Well, what?" Nathaniel asked brusquely.

"Oh, I don't know," the other man drawled. "I just thought you might have something to say about the fact we have a woman on board our ship."

Not just a woman. A lady. A damned fine-spoken, innocent lady.

Christ in hell. This was bad.

Nathaniel clenched his jaw. "There needs to be a guard stationed outside her door."

Hayes nodded. "Shorty."

Shorty had a softer side, having rescued injured gulls, and had once turned a ship rat into a damned pet. Perhaps he'd react the same toward a woman, who on a ship was a foreign animal in her own right.

"I take it the mission is being cut short?" his quartermaster asked.

Nathaniel slanted him a look. "Why would you think that?"

The other man's lips moved, but no words came out.

"Because a woman sneaked aboard my ship?" Nathaniel flexed his jaw. "I'm expected to turn it around and forsake my mission? I've not quit a single assignment, and I certainly don't intend to begin now because the lady confused our ship for a family friend's passenger boat."

"Is that what she did?" Hayes asked curiously.

"What she did is make a mess of my plans. I don't intend to let her muck anything up any more than she already has."

His quartermaster rested a hand on Nathaniel's shoulder.

He glared at the other man. "What?"

"The woman was hung over the side of the ship."

His gut clenched as he recalled the sight. The sailor who'd held her could have lost his grip. Wriggling as she'd been, she could have gone tumbling into the heart of the ocean. But she hadn't. "Deal with Shorty, and the other men involved." Shorty hadn't known Cassia was, in fact, a woman. Neither, however, were they allowed to be reckless with the lives of any members of his crew.

Hayes nodded. "And?"

"And what?" he asked tightly.

"And the lady is going to be terrified out of her mind."

The chatterbox in his cabin didn't have sense to be scared of anything. "What are you suggesting? That I coddle her?" When he spoke, however, his tone emerged tetchy to his own ears. "I'm not a nursemaid, Hayes." He'd no experience with innocent young women, what to do with them, how to treat them. He'd even less experience with dealing with those sorts in London, let alone ones who stowed away on his blasted ship.

"No. I'm merely suggesting when you deal with her, you . . . take into consideration the fact that she is young and obviously scared."

He recalled the wan pallor of her heart-shaped visage.

Scared . . . and sick.

"Tell Shorty she is not to leave her rooms," he said once more.

The other man bowed. "Aye, Captain."

And as Hayes rushed off, Nathaniel shook his head.

Given the circumstances he had run into thus far with this sailing, and crew, it was decidedly an ominous sign for their mission.

Nathaniel had not, however, failed once in his days at sea, and he didn't intend to stop now because some bored, reckless minx in London had taken it upon herself to *see the world*.

Chapter 8

Cassia had not been thrown into the brig, which she took comfort in.

Rather, she'd been made a prisoner in the captain's cabin.

Which in fairness was fine.

If she were going to die, she'd prefer to do so in the comfort of his surprisingly soft mattress rather than in the cold, merciless sea.

The waves pitched, and the ship rolled, and along with it, so did her stomach.

Sick as she was, she expected the better, more comfortable place to get on with dying of seasickness was in fact the captain's quarters, and not a jail.

Not that she'd ever visited a prison—a boating prison or a land one.

"Ship." She exhaled that word slowly through her teeth, attempting to breathe, attempting to think of anything but the fact that her stomach was revolting once more.

Her efforts proved in vain.

Gagging, Cassia stretched her fingers toward the white porcelain chamber pot and dragged it close. Hanging her head over the side of the bed, she threw up.

Dying.

She was certainly dying.

She'd been wrong yesterday.

Death might be a preferable state to the precarious situation she'd found herself in.

Nay, not precarious.

"Precarious" suggested she'd gone and done something like danced a third set with a rake or sampled oysters that had a slight smell.

Dangerous.

What she'd done in her error was land herself in a dangerous situation, finding herself lost at sea.

Though in fairness, they weren't lost. The captain and his angry crew knew precisely where they were going. And Captain Ellsby had been abundantly clear that he'd no intention of turning the ship around.

Which meant she was stuck. Reliant upon an unpredictable lot, at the mercy of men who—with the exception of a handful—had already proven themselves without mercy.

Unbidden, the thought slipped in, that sensation of being grabbed by Carlisle, the painful hold of his grip upon her as he'd wrenched her high in the air.

She squeezed her eyes shut, fighting desperately to ward off the memory, but her efforts proved futile as the same hopelessness and terror came rushing back.

But that was before they knew you were a woman, a voice at the back of her mind pointed out.

Now they know and . . .

Women, away at sea with a ship full of men, were invariably ravished.

A little moan of misery escaped, one that had absolutely nothing to do with the ship's violent sway and everything to do with the dark images flitting about.

Had she truly thought those gothic tales romantic?

Well, as a lady who now found herself living out one of those fantastical stories, Cassia could say the subject of those books was anything but romantic.

Footfalls echoed outside the chambers, and her heart thudded in a sickeningly slow beat against her rib cage.

These were his rooms . . . quarters. Whatever. It was the place where he slept and bathed.

That reminder didn't help dim that rapidly escalating dread.

The ship swayed, and gagging, she spit bile—all there was left for her stomach to give—into the captain's chamber pot.

The door opened, and she stiffened; hunching her shoulders, she curled into herself.

It was him—Captain Ellsby.

He stood, framed in the entryway. His sharp gaze cut across the room, doused in darkness, and penetrated it . . . and her.

Broad-shouldered. Big arms. Even bigger tree-trunk thighs. There was nothing soft about the captain.

That was, with the exception of those unfashionably long, golden strands he'd gathered into a queue at the back of his thick neck. The color of spun gold and sunshine, they were the flaxen hue a lady would have traded her English soul for. They put a person in mind of the all-powerful Zeus, in full control of all the mere mortals who moved amongst him.

And as he came forward, unlike Cassia, who'd climbed into his bed and commandeered it as her own for these past few hours, lying there miserable, he moved with the ease of a gentleman who had a solid marble floor under his foot.

And it was petty, but she resented him for being in full control of everything—including his stomach, while she could only muster enough energy to spit into a chamber pot.

"I'll have you know, you needn't worry much longer about me being on your ship. I expect to die soon, and then you can just cast me over."

The wood planks of the floor groaned, and then there came a slight *thwack* as he set something down beside her bed.

His bed.

This big oak bed with its cane-hinged sides was very much tailor-made to the captain of this ship.

The feather mattress dipped, and she closed her eyes. "If you've come to ravish me, like in some gothic novel, I'll warn you now you might get spewed on."

"I've decided to save my ravishment until you're feeling better."

Cassia opened her eyes, staring at the oak bedframe. Had she detected . . . a smile in his voice? Surely not. She was becoming delusional. Desperate for some hint of kindness. "Well, if that is the case, you may as well get on with it, as I'm never getting b-better." As if on cue, her body complied, and she rolled quickly over.

Only, before she could push herself upright, Nathaniel had slipped a hand under her, guiding her up and then helping her hang her head over, into the pot.

She retched, gagging, her throat burning, but alas, there was nothing left for her stomach to give.

Gasping, she collapsed, but he continued to hold her until the latest set of spasms seizing her frame had eased, and then he gently lowered her back down.

Coming to his feet, he crossed back over to the door, and she gave no small thanks to God for the captain's leaving, so that she might be spared this humiliation.

Only he opened the panel, ducked his head out, and exchanged words with someone who'd been stationed outside.

A moment later, Nathaniel shut the door and headed back over to the bed.

Pushing herself upright so that her back rested against the carved headboard, she watched him through wary eyes.

"You probably think I deserve this," she said tiredly, her shoulders sagging, and the strands that had escaped her plaited hair tickled her face.

Cassia closed her eyes. She couldn't so much as muster the energy to push them back.

Nathaniel brushed those strands from her cheek, and her eyes went flying open. There was a surprising tenderness to the large hand that now touched her.

Her breath caught in a funny way within her chest.

"I don't think anyone deserves to be riddled with seasickness," he countered with such a solemnity that it would be impossible to not believe his sincerity.

"Not even young ladies who stow away?"

"Not the accidental ones," he said gruffly. "Mayhap the intentional stowaways."

And for the first time since she'd learned of the grave mistake she'd made, a smile tugged at her lips. His lips, however, as unforgiving as the harsh planes of his face, gave no outward hint of mirth, as if carved of steel and stone. "You're . . . jesting."

"I don't jest." He paused. "Not *usually*. But then, this particular situation calls for it."

She was glad one of them might make light.

KnockKnockKn—

"Enter," Nathaniel barked in his no-nonsense captain's voice, instantly returning to the all-powerful, unapproachable leader of this vessel.

The door opened, and a moment later, Timothy entered, carrying a tray. Avoiding the captain's gaze and Cassia's as he went, it was a wonder the boy didn't overturn the items he carried. He set the burden down on the captain's desk. "Anything else you'll be needing, Captain?"

"That is all."

The lad beat a hasty retreat and shut the door quickly behind him.

The moment he'd gone, Nathaniel headed over to that tray.

Food.

"I'm not hungry." Closing her eyes, Cassia curled tightly into herself. Perhaps this was what he'd landed on to torture her. "I'm never eating again."

"Oh, you'll eat again," he said in a matter-of-fact way that made her believe that she might survive this after all and one day actually look forward to eating. "Not today, and not tomorrow, I suspect. But one day soon."

What had she done? What mess had she landed herself in?

How could she be such a failure when her younger sister had proven so competent on her own?

The boards groaned again, and the mattress dipped, and this time, she could not bring herself to look at him.

"Here," he said gruffly, and she forced her heavy lashes up. Nathaniel thrust a white, sturdy-looking cup under her nose, and she immediately inhaled the slight but noticeable aroma of ginger.

"I did not take you for one who kept regular teas," she said tiredly.

"Undoubtedly, I honor high teas, even in the roughest seas." His harsh features were even as he spoke.

She studied him with a new interest. "Indeed? I'd have thought you would—"

"I'm being—"

"Sarcastic," Cassia supplied for him, and then sighed. She really was deuced bad at spotting that. When she returned to London's shores—if she returned—she expected to have with her a healthy dose of sarcasm-spotting. "Well, I thank you for the offering. I'm not thirsty, Captain . . . ?" She left a question hanging there, searching for his name once more.

"It is just 'Captain,'" he said curtly.

And yet, he was determined to deny her that intimacy, one that would make him real and less terrifying, and was also no doubt why he insisted upon that formality.

Cassia angled her head back, and held his gaze. "It may be, but I'm not calling you Captain." No matter how angry it made him, she'd not do it.

———— ⁓⊙⌇⁓ ————

I'm not calling you Captain . . .

It was a first in his career or, for that matter, lifetime.

People—and certainly his crew—never defied him.

As such, he rocked back in his seat, flummoxed by the show of obstinance. At that, from a lady who'd sneaked herself on board his ship.

A muscle twitched at the edge of his mouth. She was as proud as she was bullheaded. "Every man aboard this ship calls me—"

"I'm not a man." Fire flashed in her sea-green eyes, setting them a-sparkle with an unexpected strength, and the passion in those entrancing depths momentarily knocked the rest of the words, and his well-articulated argument, square from his head. He wasn't a man to note a woman's eyes. Other parts of her? Decidedly so. But it was . . . those eyes. They were a thousand different shades of blue and green with little flecks of silver and even gold and—

"Did you hear me?" she asked, and then worry flitted through those expressive irises that put true meaning to the idea that eyes were the soul's windows. "Oh, dear. Have you been hit by seasickness, too? That is why you know so much—"

"I'm not seasick," he said swiftly, crashing to the present. "I've . . ." He opened his mouth to assure her that he'd ceased to be sick long, long ago, before remembering he didn't share those intimate details about himself—with anyone. He grunted. "I've known a number of men who've . . . had the ailment. Some . . . for years." Him. It'd been him.

Horror rounded out those large pools of her eyes. "Never tell me it will take me that long to overcome it, Nathan."

Nathan. Not Nathaniel. Not even his mother or brothers had been permitted to shorten his name in that way, or any way. The duke would have never permitted anything so informal. "Captain," he snapped back. "I've already told you. You'll call me Captain."

"But that makes you the terrifying man in charge of an equally terrifying crew."

"I don't understand." Anything where this one was concerned.

"If I refer to you by your given name, then you're just a man, and an approachable one, and I . . . I need that." Fire flared in her eyes once more. "So you can throw me in your brig for defying you, or hang me over your boat like Carlisle intended to do, but I'm not changing my mind." Just then, the ship pitched right, and she paled once more. She dropped back onto the mattress, and rolled onto her opposite side, giving him her back.

She was . . . refusing to call him Captain.

The lady—Cassia—was miserable.

Forlorn.

And it really didn't matter to him. Or it certainly shouldn't.

She was suffering from a misery of her own making.

Mayhap it was that he'd never been near a woman so small, and certainly not this innocent.

Mayhap it was that he didn't want to give her the opportunity to dissolve into yet another blubbering mess.

"Fine," he relented, and if he'd been a better man, or a different one, he'd have managed gentler tones than the snappy ones he currently gave her. As it was, however, he'd already made more concessions for Cassia McQuoid than he'd any other person to come before her, and any who would come after her. "When we're alone," he added.

The lady stilled, then rolled slowly back over, facing him. "What are you saying?" she whispered, searching his face.

"I'm saying you can refer to me as Nathani—*Nathan*." He tripped over that unfamiliar substitution. "Just not in the presence of the crew."

Which he'd no intention of allowing her to be, for that matter. Given her show of defiance over his form of address, he thought better than to say as much given this moment.

Tears flooded her eyes and he blanched. "Why in hell are you crying *now*?"

"Because I'm happy." With that outlandish admission, she sniffed, then dabbed at the corners of her eyes.

"That doesn't make a lick of sense. You don't *cry* when you're happy."

In fact, the people in his life didn't cry at all. The closest he'd come to it had been just prior to his departure from London, when tears had welled in his mother's eyes. But even then, she'd not let them fall.

"I do," Cassia said. "Lots of people do."

"Who?" he shot back before he thought better of it.

"Well, I do, for one."

"We've already ascertained as much."

What in hell was happening to him? He, a laconic man who valued silence above most anything else, found himself bickering *and* bantering with her?

"And my mother."

God help him, madness must be contagious, and he'd caught it from this one. "That's two."

"My sister Myrtle."

But he was hopeless and helpless to stop himself. "We've confirmed all the McQuoid females are given to tears."

"That's not all the McQuoid females. There's my other sister, Fleur."

Oh, Lord in heaven, and his was a prayer—there were more of her.

Only, she wasn't done. "And my aunt Leslie, cousins Andromena and Meghan." She paused. "And Linnie, too."

"Aren't those *all* McQuoids?"

Cassia pointed her eyes skyward. "I know what you're suggesting."

"Do you?" Because he rather thought if he pointed her on her way with a map, she'd not a clue. About *anything*.

"You're thinking *only* female members of *my* family cry."

She'd pieced it all together, then.

"But I'm absolutely certain if there are *eight* McQuoid women who do when happy that there are many other *non*-McQuoids who do, as well."

Eight.

There was a lot of eight chattering, troublesome, given-to-tears-even-when-happy women running all around London. It was enough to make a seafaring captain consider docking his ship in some distant harbor and never returning to rainy old England.

If Nathaniel had the use of both his hands, he'd have happily jammed them against his temples. Which only brought his attention back to the entire reason he'd come to visit.

He glanced down at the likely now lukewarm drink in his hands. "Here," he said, thrusting it at her. "It's laced with peppermint and honey, and it's been known to help those who fare poorly with the motion of the sea."

Tears again shimmered. "You brought this for me?" she whispered.

Nathaniel resisted the urge to scratch at his suddenly tight collar. She was making more of his actions than there was. Wasn't she? Why . . . he didn't do things, any things an innocent lady would ever consider even remotely romantic. "Please, do not cry again," he begged, because at this point, well, even he wasn't above begging.

He pushed the cup into her fingers, and this time, she took it.

Cassia edged herself backward until she rested against the solid back of his bedding. And this time, she didn't defend those drops or debate him; she just sipped at the tea. "Thank you, Nathan," she said softly.

There it was, again.

Nathan.

Nothing more than a form of his name, but wrapped in her euphonious voice. Slightly musical, and even more slightly husky, hers were the inviting tones all sailors were long taught to steer their galleons far away from.

And Nathaniel—*Nathan*—proved as weak as those poor-fated fellows, for he remained rooted to the edge of the mattress as she drank. She sipped, and while she did, she looked about his rooms the way a patron of London's premier museums might, taking in the details with a curious eye. She lingered her focus on the row of swords fixed to the wall.

"Better?" he asked, incapable of anything more than the usual graveled quality.

Cassia pulled her gaze away and shifted that wide-eyed stare back over to him. "No, but I thank you for caring."

Thanked him for caring? Disquieted, Nathaniel shifted on the bed. He didn't care. Not about people's comforts. Why, he didn't even *think* about them.

That was, aside from his mother, and much of that came from a place of love and maternal pity for the miserable man she found herself hopelessly devoted to, a man as incapable of loving as Nathaniel himself.

Thrusting aside those unnerving thoughts, he brought himself back to the reason for this exchange. "I have Cook boiling lentils. They've also been known to help with the ailment. The oceans, however, are rough. You'll find your stomach settling some when the seas do."

The boat leaned to the right, then rapidly straightened.

Tea sloshed over the side of Cassia's cup, and she held it out. "I don't think I can drink any more."

Nay, she sounded one more word away from heaving what little lingered in her stomach back up.

Nathaniel collected her cup, bringing it back to the tray, and returned.

"Let me see your arm," he said as he reclaimed his seat.

She didn't fight him or launch into a thousand questions about her arm and what the uses of the appendage were, as he would have expected from her.

Only, the moment he'd her small wrist in his larger hand, his mind went blank. The slender, snowy-white limb, soft as satin, bore a hint of faded freckles, as if the lady were a woodland nymph afforded only a short time in the sun, but who'd been marked forever by her love of that light.

"What are you doing?" she asked softly in an entirely too trusting, and certainly more trusting than he deserved, voice.

What was he doing, indeed? Nathaniel swallowed hard. Losing his bloody mind. *That* was what he was doing.

"The people in ancient China use a technique for healing and relieving the human body of pain. There are different points," he explained, shifting his fingers into position.

Under his touch, he felt the telltale beat of her pulse.

"This is the Nei guan," he explained, making himself speak aloud those details about the points and what he did, to keep from focusing on the satiny-soft texture of her cream-white skin.

This was why women weren't permitted aboard ships. Because they made a man forget all reason and muddied his senses and conjured all manner of wicked thoughts that made even the most self-possessed and in-control man weak with want.

Nathaniel rested his three middle fingers across her wrist.

"How did you learn of such things?"

"In my voyages to Asia. I like to learn about the places I travel to. Their customs. Their way of life."

"Do you still sail there?" She scrambled upright, excitement lighting her eyes. "Is that where we are going?"

"Not anymore."

When he said nothing more than that, Cassia pressed him. "Where *are* we going?"

He avoided her eyes. "The coast of Italy," he said. "The Adriatic."

She released a long, dreamy sigh. *"Italy,"* she repeated.

If she knew they were pursuing a French frigate, boarding that vessel, and commandeering their provisions, supplies, and future military plans in a battle to assert British dominance over the Adriatic, she'd not wear that same dreamy look. And for the first time, the reality of what they would do, and the potential harm she faced, left him cold inside.

"My brother travels," she announced into the quiet, fortunately not pressing him for further information. "Every time he leaves, I await his return because he always has some stories of what he did and what he's seen. He describes a world so different from the one in London, and one day I just . . . tired of my colorless existence. Why should only he join Jeremy? Why could I not, too? And now? Now, I will."

She'd not see what she thought she would see, the great cathedrals and museums filled with the masterpieces of Renaissance artists. She'd see the waters turn grey and black with the smoke of cannon fire, and the ocean waves slamming against the windows in his quarters as the battle raged. She . . .

"Jeremy?" He paused in his probing of her hand.

Before recalling—

"My brother's friend, Captain Jeremy." She spoke in a tone that suggested Nathaniel, by the very nature of his work, should have an inkling about some proper peer who sailed a ship.

"Captain Jeremy?" he drawled. "So *Jeremy* gets the courtesy of a title?"

"Well, he is *Jeremy*. And he's not at all intimidating. He's gone by Captain Jeremy since we were children playing pirates, and as such, it's nigh impossible to be afraid of someone one used to brandish a toy wooden sword . . ." Her gaze crept over to his row of weapons. She paused. "Not that you are necessarily scary," she said. More to herself? Or to him? It was hard to distinguish. "You *did* bring me tea, and you are concerned about me being ill and—"

"Do you ever stop talking?" he asked without inflection, his question prompted by curiosity, more than meanness.

"No. My father always said I was a magpie, and my mother said I should not care to be with people who did not wish to hear the sound of my speaking voice. And . . ."

He glanced up from his task, strangely wanting to hear the rest of those details about her.

Her cheeks reddened. "As you were."

And Nathaniel found himself oddly . . . regretful when she didn't complete those thoughts. He stiffened.

What in hell?

He wanted to know more about her? Preposterous. Nathaniel released her abruptly, and jumping up, he made to take his leave.

"Please," she called out, staying him in his tracks. "I . . . My family is big."

When she blurted that and only that peculiar detail, Nathaniel turned around slowly.

"It's just . . . there's always noise, Nathan."

"I . . ." He had no clue what she was saying.

"There is always happy noise, Nathan. My younger siblings playing and squealing as they run about. My other brothers visiting with their friends and telling ribald jokes and laughing loudly over them. And Myrtle . . . my sister. She prattles on and on and on."

"That appears to be a family trait," he said dryly.

She gave no indication she'd heard that droll response. "Now she has a dog who is always barking. And my mother. She loves to sing and she's always singing, and my papa joins in and . . . Unless you have a big family, you can't understand."

"I have a big family." And he still didn't understand.

She looked at him with surprise rounding her eyes. "You have a close family, too, then?" she said, her voice eager and excited, as if she were delighted in having found something that made them in some way similar.

He shook his head. "We aren't close . . . at least, not in the way you are describing." Were they in any way, really?

Mayhap that's why he was so fascinated by this woman before him. Mayhap that was why he found himself crossing back over and joining her at the table. He didn't know people were like her.

Cassia scoffed. "I can't believe that."

"It's not that we don't care about one another. We do. We just . . . live our separate lives . . ." His lips quirked in a wry grin. "Attempting to escape a father who is entirely too controlling."

"How many siblings do you have?"

"There's six of . . ." He paused. "Five," he amended quietly. "I have four brothers. My eldest died. He fell from his horse." Where had that come from? Marcus's death was something he never spoke of. With anyone. It was something he didn't tend to let himself think about, because nothing came in thinking of his death. It didn't bring Marcus back. It didn't ease the loss . . . or the regret.

Cassia's eyes brimmed with tears, and she covered his hand with her own. "I'm so sorry," she whispered.

Unable to meet her gaze, and more, the emotion there, he gave his shoulders a slight shrug. "It is . . . life."

"It is tragic."

He stared at the top of her head. It *was* tragic. That was precisely what it was. So much of it. That he and his brothers hadn't known the closeness this woman now spoke of. That Marcus had died, and he'd never come to know him. Disquieted by the maudlin regrets, Nathaniel made to stand.

Cassia gripped his fingers more tightly, staying him. "I don't want to be alone." Her voice emerged threadbare and miserable, and damned if he suddenly found himself powerless to grab that door handle and let himself out.

What in hell was wrong with him?

Briefly squeezing his eyes shut, Nathaniel headed across his quarters and stopped before his desk. He felt Cassia's eyes upon him as he tugged free a handful of books from the shelf there. Small leather volumes in hand, he headed over to the side of the bed, pausing only long enough to grab a chair.

Those big eyes of hers grew even larger in her face as he set up a place beside her.

Nathaniel snapped the book open. *"We depart for Europe—a misunderstanding arises between the captain and surgeon, though the scandalous aspersions of Crampley—the captain d—"*

"What are you doing?" Her whisper cut across his reading, and Nathaniel looked up.

"Reading." It had been a ridiculous, impulsive idea; he didn't even know where it had come from. Actually yes, yes, he knew. It was because she'd been so *sad* when speaking about the happy din of her family that he'd wanted to vanquish her misery. Nathaniel frowned. "Unless you'd rather I stop." He made to snap the book shut, but Cassia shot a hand out, touching her fingers to his.

"Don't! Please? I . . . I would like it very much if you read."

And said like that, for reasons he didn't understand, he was loath to deny her anything in that instant. He resumed reading.

"Crampley tyrannizes over the surgeon, who falls a victim to his cruelty—I am also ill used—the ship strikes—the behavior of Crampley and the seamen on that occasion—I get on shore, challenge the captain to a single combat—am treacherously knocked down, wounded, and robbed."

Nathaniel peeked over the top of the book.

Cassia had closed her eyes; a soft, wistful smile played on her full mouth. He may as well have been reading her poetry for the faraway, dreamy expression she wore.

It would be wise to leave . . .

Eventually, he'd send his ship's doctor to care after and occupy the lady. After all, that was the man's role. Nathaniel had more pressing responsibilities than playing nursemaid.

That would be wiser.

Glancing down at his copy of *The Adventures of Roderick Random* once more, he resumed reading.

Chapter 9

Time ceased to exist.

As one day turned into the next, the seas would settle, then rapidly churn, and along with them, Cassia's stomach. She was certain that the fates—or God, rather—had set out to punish her for her great act of disobedience. She was being taught a lesson, and one that she'd not soon forget.

For nothing else could account for the misery she endured.

And yet, through the misery, and the ofttimes-silent thought that death might be preferable to this, *he* was there.

Nathan.

Her use of his Christian name had ceased to be a mechanism to ease her fears of the powerful gentleman and had absolutely everything to do with the fact that it was humanly impossible to be as close and vulnerable as she now found herself to a person and not find one's relationship with him completely altered. Even though he could have slept somewhere else on his ship, he'd brusquely stated that he'd stay close to ensure protection. And she may have fallen more than a little bit in love with him for that concern.

Nay, weak as a babe, and lost and alone, and sharing quarters with one caring after her, and he the sole person speaking to her, their relationship had become intimate in ways she'd never before experienced with a man—not even her brothers, father, or male cousins. When he joined her in his cabin, he'd alternately look after Cassia and read to her. He'd read in his deep, low baritone . . . when she'd never thought a man would read to her. Granted, it wasn't poetry or romantic prose, and yet, somehow the subjects he read to her were even more beautiful because of the realness in his selection—nautical-themed books, like *The Adventures of Roderick Random* and *A General History of Pyrates*. And they talked about things that mattered. Their families. He had a large one, too.

Oh, Nathan was still crabby and surly and curt, but she'd come to realize those were just ways the gentleman also carried himself.

And there was no doubting he was a gentleman. Not just because of his refined tones, but also because during those fleeting moments when the ship ceased rocking and her stomach stopped churning, boredom had led her to explore his quarters. Rummaging through his shelving and things, she'd discovered an elaborate, though unfamiliar, signet ring and notes from King George himself, and nay, there could be absolutely no doubting that a man with letters from the king was anything but a peer.

Not a peer whom she'd ever seen in her London Seasons, per se. Nay, she'd not ever met any gentleman like him.

Though in fairness, if she were being truthful with herself, it had not been boredom that compelled her search of his private space and belongings, but . . . a need to know about this man who was so gruff and yet tender as he cared for her, massaging his enormous hand over the expanse of her back as she moaned in misery. Wiping her brow with cool water. And then abandoning his bed and sleeping on the floor so that she might have the comfort of his mattress.

Why, he'd even been so considerate as to bring her a brush of the softest horsehair and betel nut powder for her mouth.

Pausing in the act of brushing her mouth, she stared at her still pale, though noticeably less wan, visage reflected back.

At last, she'd stopped feeling as though she were going to die, or for that matter, wishing for death over this plague of seasickness, and she sat with her legs drawn up to her chest, staring with a breathless anticipation at the doorway.

Her ears pricked up as she caught the footfalls, and she quickly spat into the basin one of the cabin boys had brought at the captain's request for her to use solely for her brushing.

Cassia dashed back over to the bed and dived under the coverlet, positioning herself against the headboard, breathless. Those steps were sure and steady, and very clearly his.

Cassia quickly tucked the loose curls that had fallen about her shoulders back behind her ears and pinched her cheeks in a bid to bring color into their wan pallor.

There came a sharp, perfunctory knock.

His knock.

"E-enter," she called out, her voice uneven.

The door opened. Only, neither had it been Nathan's footfalls nor his knock. Rather, a familiar gentleman in fawn breeches, a white shirt, and a black jacket appeared.

You silly ninny. Thinking you can pick out the gentleman's footsteps. You're not so familiar with him.

Disappointment washed over her. "Oh," she said dumbly.

Mr. Hayes arched a dark eyebrow.

"Forgive me," she said on a rush, jumping to her feet. "I was . . ." *Thinking you were someone else. Hoping you were.*

"The captain sent me," he explained. Unlike the rough, coarse speech of the other crew she'd worked with, Mr. Hayes spoke with a measured quality that marked him as a gentleman. "Were you expecting I was the captain?" he asked with a knowingness that sent mortified heat rushing to her cheeks.

"I . . . yes. *Only* because he's been looking after me these past days, and only because he hasn't sent anyone else, and only because . . ." *I'm rambling.* She made herself stop talking.

Another hint of a smile played at Mr. Hayes's narrow lips. "Yes, he has been looking after you, hasn't he?" There was more of that hint of knowing and . . . curiosity. Fortunately, he did not press her, but rather shifted them to the reason for his presence. "The captain asked that I join you when your evening meal is brought in."

He wouldn't be taking supper with her this time? Disappointment swelled in her breast, and she forced a smile to avoid offending the kindly quartermaster. She was grateful when a pair of deckhands came in, bearing trays.

After they'd gone, Mr. Hayes made to leave, but Cassia motioned to the table. "Won't you join me?"

He hesitated, and then with a nod, he pulled out a chair for her like they were in a London dining room and, after she'd sat, claimed the spot across from her. Picking up a glass of claret, he eyed her from over the rim while she carved her cod. "Are you feeling better than you have been?"

Did she imagine there was a less-than-medical and different quality to that probing question? "Immensely so. The captain is a most excellent caregiver," she said. The kindest, gentlest. Cassia's gaze drifted past the quartermaster's shoulder, and she proceeded to provide him with an enumeration of all the ways in which Nathan had looked after her, taking care to omit the details about the pressure points he'd placed his strong fingertips upon and the massages he'd given, instead focusing on the foods he'd had brought to her rooms and the tea he'd poured and insisted she drink. "He's been ever so good to . . ." She found Mr. Hayes sharpening his gaze on her face, and she stopped. Clearing her throat, Cassia made herself take a bite of the fish and swallowed it before continuing. "He . . . has been very patient . . . given the circumstances."

She'd never known a large, powerful, callus-stained palm could be so tender.

In fairness, neither had she ever known a large, powerful, callus-stained palm in *any* way.

Cassia carved another piece from her meal, and then froze as horror crept in. She'd said too much. As it was, her reputation—

"I would never betray your confidence or the captain's," Hayes murmured, anticipating that worry, and some of the tension left her. "Captain Ellsby would not see your reputation harmed, and he'll ensure his men will not breathe word of the presence of a woman aboard his ship. He is fair and he is honorable, and they respect him."

Nathan was all those things. And he'd protect her reputation . . . if he could. Being a man accustomed to commanding others and having everyone obey his orders on board was one thing. Even if they did not breathe a word about her being here, her absence would still be noted, and Nathan couldn't truly protect her in this way. Tears pricked her lashes.

The handsome quartermaster instantly rescued a kerchief from the front of his jacket, and doffing that immaculate white fabric, he handed it over.

"I s-suppose it is s-silly, w-worrying about my reputation now," she whispered, her voice breaking.

"Yes," he murmured, his sharp features perfectly even. "I expect that ship has sailed."

Cassia froze, then caught the twinkle of mirth in his expressive eyes and promptly burst out laughing, with the quartermaster joining in. It felt so very good to laugh.

How much easier his smiles came than Nathan's. And yet, even with that, she found herself appreciating Nathan's elusive ones as not-so-very-small treasures. He was reserved, and yet even with that, he'd opened up to her in ways she'd never expected he would, talking about his brothers and his family.

Mr. Hayes reclined in his chair and, cradling his drink between his hands, continued to study her in that unnerving way. "From my talks with the captain regarding your health, and given my assessment of you now, I feel it is safe to say you've turned a corner."

"I do feel less like I'm dying and more like I might survive, but live somewhat miserably while I do," she finished, pulling another smile from the quartermaster.

He winked. "The ocean does have that effect on most."

"Did you suffer similarly when you first sailed?" she asked.

"No. I was fortunate as to never suffer from the malady. The captain, on the other hand . . ."

She widened her eyes. "Never tell me *the captain* suffered from seasickness."

"The captain suffered from the worst I've ever seen."

Her mind raced. He'd mentioned men who'd been besieged by that malady. He'd not, however, indicated he was, in fact, amongst those ranks. Cassia rocked on her heels, trying to imagine the strong, seemingly indomitable, man who'd cared after her laid low as she'd been, and yet, in her mind, she couldn't reconcile that imagery with the all-powerful captain of this ship. The fact Hayes possessed that intimate detail of Nathan also meant . . . *Be breezy.* "You've known him a long while then," she remarked, feigning casualness.

"Since we were boys at Eton. Back when I was smaller, painfully thin, and terribly awkward, and he was just as powerful and confident and strong as he is now."

She drew back. "I cannot believe you were ever so small."

He gave her another wink. "Kind of you to say, but I was freckle-faced and easy prey for the bigger, meaner kids. A handful cornered me one day when I was leaving my rooms and were roughing me up. The captain came upon them and . . . singlehandedly dealt with the lot."

An image slipped in of a younger Nathan, fierce and ferocious, and taking on a group of bullies in defense of a weaker, smaller boy. "He came to your rescue," she whispered.

He nodded.

Dropping her chin atop her hand, Cassia sighed softly.

"After that, we were fast friends. Both second sons looking to explore the world and find our place. We joined the navy and have been together since. I've been with him since the beginning and knew him when he was emptying his stomach into a chamber pot, praying for death when he was too sick to notice I'd come to check on him."

Cassia attempted to draw forth an image of the one Mr. Hayes painted . . . of Nathan, weakened by illness as she'd been, and found it nigh impossible when presented with the man who was so steady and in control of himself. "What is he like?" she asked, unable to help herself, wanting to know from this man who clearly knew him so well. "That is to say, is he always . . ."

"This cold and hard?" He grinned. "Always." His smile faded, and his expression grew serious. "But there isn't a kinder, more fair man than the captain. In my prior dealings with the English before him, and in my experiences with most men after him, they pass judgment on people in other places and other lands. The captain has always shown a genuine interest in them, however. He doesn't look down upon anyone . . . as you can probably gather from the manner of men he's hired to man his ship."

Yes, they weren't fancy lords and lofty gentlemen; they were men with rough accents and jagged scars. "How did he find his crew?"

"They are men who find themselves facing prison for petty crimes, stealing a loaf of bread to feed their families, poaching off a lord's property because they were hungry." In other words, Nathan had proven himself a champion of those in need.

As if realizing he'd shared too much of an intimate nature about Nathan, Mr. Hayes took a drink, then set his glass down. "It will be helpful for you to have fresh air, as that and the wind on a person's face often helps with the symptoms, and I expect between that, the more time you spend on the ship, and the methods the captain has been employing to help you, soon you will not even notice you are aboard a ship."

She'd been consigned to Nathan's cabin and told on that first day he'd discovered her identity that she was not to leave his rooms. "Unfortunately, I do not expect Nathan will prove accommodating of that request."

"Oh, he's pigheaded, but he's also more reasonable than one might think," the quartermaster said. "In fact"—he dropped his voice to a whisper and leaned down, shrinking the handful of spaces between them—"he's very tolerant and empathetic of those given to bouts of seasickness, given he still on occasion suffers the malady."

Cassia widened her eyes and pressed a palm to her mouth. "Surely not?"

Merriment and devilry sparkled in his brown eyes. "Only when the seas are rough. Don't tell him I—"

"What is going on?"

At that sharp query, Cassia swung her startled gaze over to the entrance of Nathan's cabin.

Mr. Hayes, however, straightened with a greater casualness, an ease of one who'd been completely unstartled, and he moved his focus over to the broad, muscle-hewn figure filling the entrance of the suddenly very small cabin. "Captain."

He'd resolved to stay away.

The last thing Nathaniel needed on this latest voyage was a distraction, particularly one posed by a garrulous minx who alternated between rambling, crying, and retching with disturbingly equal frequency.

It was why that morning he'd sought out Hayes amidst his usual mainmast duties and advised him to pay a visit to Cassia's side while her meal was being delivered. He'd told his damned quartermaster to see it delivered, not to sit and sip goddamned claret with her while she ate.

And yet, after Nathaniel had sworn to stay away, to eat his meal with his crew as he should, he'd thought about Cassia . . . and ultimately, he'd decided to join her so she wasn't alone. Not having known or expected that she wouldn't be. That she'd be smiling and conversing so easily with Hayes.

Hayes, who was affable and charming and everything Nathaniel wasn't, and hadn't really *cared* that he wasn't. Until now.

"You're needed at starboard, Hayes," he snarled, knowing he was being deuced unreasonable, unable to contain the biting fury in his voice and unable to explain why.

Nay, he knew. It was because the lady was a distraction to all who crossed her path. She'd made nothing but a headache of herself. Granted, a headache Hayes seemed to mind not at all.

The other man stood, and then dropping a bow, he said some quiet words intended for Cassia's ears, words that Nathaniel strained to hear.

She nodded, that little movement sending the bountiful curls that had escaped her plait these past days bouncing about her small shoulders.

When his tall, *charming* quartermaster swept past, Nathaniel pushed the door panel shut with a firm click.

"I'm not looking to have you distract my crew," he said the moment he and Cassia were alone.

"I'm not a distraction."

"You painted my ship," he said, taking a step forward.

"That was before I realized what you expected of me." She paused. "And I really feel those paintings were an improvement, Nathan."

"You were nearly killed." And that had been before the crew had learned she was, in fact, a female.

A scowl fell over her heart-shaped face. "I think it should be pointed out that your *crew* nearly killed me."

All his muscles coiled, tensed, and contracted at the memory of that day she'd been grabbed by Carlisle and lifted high above the deck . . . and how very close she'd come to . . . Nathaniel forcibly thrust those torturous musings to the furthest corner of his mind. There was no point or good in thinking of what had almost happened. He steeled his jaw. It was far more important to think about why it had almost happened.

"I don't want you speaking to the crew."

"This might be a poor time to bring up Mr. Hayes's suggestion that I—"

"No."

Cassia stamped her foot. "You don't even know what I was going to say."

"You were going to say he advised you to walk the deck and receive fresh air."

She wrinkled that freckled, pert nose of hers. "Very well, you do know. You are being unreasonable." He opened his mouth, but she didn't so much as draw a breath to allow him that word edgewise. "There is absolutely no reason—"

"*Every* reason." He managed to squeeze just two words in.

"—for you to make a prisoner of me."

In a bid to make himself heard, Nathaniel raised his voice. "There is *every* reason for that, too."

Alas, the chit spoke even louder, over him. "Unless it is your explicit plan to punish me for my clear accident by confining me to your dark rooms."

Good God, she was unshakable. Nathaniel gritted his teeth and tried again. "There are windows."

"And forbid me from speaking to anyone."

"They are working, and they do not have the time to be distracted with talks of the English weather."

"Why do you think I'm going to speak with them about the English weather?" Exasperation lent her words an upward pitch. "It always rains."

"I know that. But it's what the proper English sorts talk about."

"Nathan." Cassia gave him a look. "I sneaked off, stowed away on what I thought was my brother's best friend's ship. Do you truly take me as 'the proper English sort'?"

She had her first valid point there. "No." That changed nothing, however. Instead, Nathaniel clung to one not-so-very-small detail of what she'd said. "I don't want you to speak to them about anything, and I don't trust for one moment that you are capable of even a moment's silence or peace." His booming voice echoed off the walls of his "dark rooms," as she'd called them.

Cassia glared mutinously at him, and he saw the visible restraint she showed. In the taut lines her plump rosebud mouth made in the corners as she flattened her lips. The effort she made to say absolutely nothing. And she didn't.

For a moment.

"I am absolutely capable of moments of silence," she said on a rush, as if in getting the words out as quickly as possible, the speed of saying them somehow negated her losing the point.

"That is the thing, Cassia: you are not." He raised his voice to a near shout, and frustration coursed hot through him at that lack of restraint on his part when he was always restrained. Just not around this troublesome woman, and because of her. "You cannot *not* say anything. You talk to yourself when you're suffering through seasickness."

"It made me feel better."

"By God, you can't even be silent when you sleep. You mutter to yourself the whole night through."

Cassia swept over in a glorious display of defiance and fury and stopped the moment her bare toes touched the tips of his shoes. She tipped her head back and, angling her hands upon her gently flared hips, glared an impressively black look at him.

"If I'm *soo* miserable to be around, Nathan, then do not force me to force you to keep me here," she said, flicking both hands in his direction, as if she'd found his company contemptible.

"Force me to force you to keep me here," he mouthed. "That doesn't make sense."

"It makes perfect sense," she cried, throwing those expressive hands which, just as her words, she wielded like rapiers. "I certainly don't want to inflict my company on anyone who does not want it."

"Well, it seems that's precisely what you did when you stowed away on my blasted ship," he bellowed, knowing he was being a beast but unable to contain that shout. She was, in short, the first and only person who'd ever made him lose his damned head. Or distracted him. He dragged a hand through his hair. And yet, neither did he want to be a bully who made her cry, and he braced for the materialization of those crystalline drops.

Instead, this time, for the first time, there was only a fiery blaze of fury to match his own. "Well, you may rest assured, Nathan, we are well matched in one thing, for you are the absolute last person whose company I would ever seek out."

And as she prattled on in her outrage, in her show of bold defiance, it transformed her from interesting beauty to mesmerizing goddess of fire and fury. And he found himself annoyed for being the manner of weak fool to be captivated by the bright rush of color in her radiant cheeks. "And your boat the last one I'd have ever climbed aboard, had I known—"

"It is a ship," he said, wrapping an arm about her waist and drawing her close.

And it was impossible to say who was more stunned by that tender hold.

Cassia's eyes reflected back his own surprise and more: a like passion glittered in her eyes that revealed oh so much.

He immediately released her, unfurling his fingers, flexing them. "Forgive me. I . . ." *Nearly lost control. Had a momentary lapse where all I wanted was to kiss—*

As though she'd heard the unfinished thought inside his head, Cassia fluttered her lashes closed, then tilted her head up to receive his mouth.

And he was lost.

With a growl, Nathaniel kissed her as he'd longed to do these past days, and like a kitten who'd become a cat, Cassia curled her long fingers into the fabric of his shirt, and clutching it close, she drew herself against the wall of his chest.

Nathaniel filled his hands with her buttocks; scooping that delectably rounded flesh, he pulled her even nearer, pressing her to the hard ridge of his shaft.

She kissed with the same abandon that she gave to the words she spoke, free and unfettered. The brief hesitation and uncertainty that bespoke a woman who'd never been kissed faded, replaced in an instant with one who welcomed each slant of his mouth over hers.

He flicked his tongue along that seam, tracing that plump flesh, and a little moan whispered from her lips, fanning his own with that breathy heat made by the sound of her yearning.

Lust thickened in his veins. This was why women were not permitted aboard ships. This right here. Even as the voice of reason and logic and restraint hammered his head with that reminder and the urging to set her away, Nathaniel remained hopelessly bound, as unable to set her from him and end this embrace as any of those sailors lured out by the sirens at sea.

He slipped his tongue inside, and swirled it around the contours, tasting all of her, and she delicately prodded his, at first, and then matched him in a bold thrust and parry.

This was madness.

And yet, he, a master of control, found himself completely without any this time.

Chapter 10

Cassia had never been kissed.

Until now.

Oh, she'd *practiced* it a good deal.

She'd been so certain there'd be a kiss one day that she'd not wanted to not have some experience.

First, she'd done so in her pillow, and then courtesy of Sir Lance of Lot, the stuffed toy knight her youngest sister had been given as a babe and made a de facto friend and additional sibling. Cassia had confiscated that most realistic looking of dolls and practiced in preparation of the time when she'd have her first embrace.

An embrace that had never come.

Not from a stable boy.

And certainly not from any passionate lord when she'd made her Come Out.

In fact, she'd come to believe she was destined to die kissless.

Only to know this moment of grand passion and glorious heat and hunger.

Nothing, however, in all the books she'd read, or in her imaginings or dreams, could have prepared her for *this*.

This was what drove poets to prose and bards to song.

She whimpered, sliding her fingers along the contours of his chest, slab after slab of hard muscle, each ridge defined, and they rippled under her touch.

Nathan cupped her nape in one large hand that dwarfed her head and angled her, better positioning her to receive his kiss, and she gladly tipped and went, following where he led.

His other hand went on a busy search of her that should have shocked her with its boldness, and one that she should have pushed away because of it, and yet, her entire body threatened to go up in flames, and she was content to burn, desperate to know more of the feel of that possessive, powerful hand on her. He teased it down the side of her waist, and then brought his fingers climbing up once more to cup her breast.

Cassia moaned as, through the thin, loose fabric of her lawn shirt, he teased her, tweaking the nipple, bringing it to a hard pebble with the pad of his thumb. And then he cupped her again.

Her lashes fluttered and her legs sagged, but he was immediately there to catch her. Moving his hand from her breast, he slid it swiftly under her buttocks, drawing her to the long ridge of flesh tenting the front of his trousers.

Instinctively, she rubbed against him with an intuition as old as Eve, her body knowing it needed to stretch and move against that steel-hard flesh.

Nathan groaned, that low, desperate rumble, a remarkable display of wanting . . . for her. This big, powerful man, so restrained except in his fury, brought to the point of dissolved speech and frantic touches, because of her.

And it left her gloriously heady as heat pooled low in her belly . . . and even lower. In that place she'd previously only cleaned herself and never dared touch beyond that . . . even when she'd been curious.

In all the books she'd read, not a single one of them had mentioned the hunger or that wicked, forbidden ache that throbbed between her legs.

The manner of pressure that made a lady press them together in a bid to get some relief and—

Nathan ripped his mouth from hers, and she reflexively cried out at the sudden loss.

And in all her imaginings of how her first kiss would end, she'd never foreseen this.

Horror.

It was etched in every harsh plane of his sun-bronzed face.

That emotion even reached his bluish-black irises, and she dug her toes sharply into the planks of the floor.

"I didn't mean to do that," he said, his voice harsh. With his earlier desire? Or with disgust?

Nay, nothing could have prepared her for this.

"If you are blaming m-me," she rejoined, proud when her voice trembled only slightly, "then you—"

"No," he interrupted. "I am to blame. It was . . ." And for the first time since she'd met Captain Nathan, he floundered. With his words. His lips moving and his eyes relaying confusion as he sought to find his way. "I would never . . ."

Cassia tensed and braced herself. Waiting for him to say more. But not wanting him to.

Because she knew what he'd reveal.

Disgust with her.

Because ultimately, men did not want her.

Her own family did not want her. Not truly.

She was the daughter who'd been underfoot, but not the cherished one. From their father always finding time to speak with Myrtle about his collection of antiquities to Arran always returning from his travels with some knickknack or other he'd thought Myrtle would appreciate, Cassia's own company had never been so sought the same way by her kin.

Nathan blanched. "You're going to cry." He sounded desperate. For her not to, and that made it all the more difficult to stop those drops from welling in her eyes.

"I'm not," she lied, blinking, and one rolled down her cheek, making an absolute liar of her.

She wasn't even good at lying.

There came a flurry of footfalls, and a rap at the door.

Nathan positioned himself in front of her. "Enter," he barked, and his almost-too-deep-to-be-considered-a-baritone voice bore no hint of quavering or the weakness or desire of before. In fact, she may as well have imagined the kiss between them.

Of their own will, her fingers came up, and she touched that swollen flesh that still tingled with the remembrance of it.

The panel opened, and several deckhands streamed in, carrying two buckets each of steaming water.

And for all the misery and shame of rejection, warmth unfurled in her breast. He'd thought of her, again. Surely, with this latest consideration for her and her needs, he could not truly hold her in disdain.

"You need a bath," he said gruffly, sticking a knife blade into the ridiculously hopeful musings she'd allowed free rein in her brain.

A blush turned her entire body hot, and she glanced down at her toes, at the wall, at anywhere except him. Yes, she did. It was entirely different, having a hip bath. One could not properly—

Nathan brushed his knuckles over the curve of her jaw, gently angling her gaze up to his. "That is . . . I thought you would like one."

And in that moment, at that distinction he made, delivered in that gruff, slightly halting way, a moment where this always confident, powerful man proved uncertain, Nathan snagged another corner of her heart . . . for that consideration. For thinking of her in this way. "Thank you," she said softly, running her gaze over his face. "I would like it very much." She liked *him* very much.

A light flush dulled his cheeks, and he instantly dropped his hand. Reaching inside his jacket he withdrew something and pressed it into her hand.

Cassia stared at the cool metal key.

"Uh . . . er . . . yes, well, see that you lock the door when I leave." And then, turning on his heel, Nathan stalked off. He grabbed the door handle, and she waited for him to go. Wanting him to stay. Wanting him to resume that—their—embrace.

Only, he remained with his fingers frozen as they were. "Cassia . . . that . . . thing that happened? Our embrace?"

Her heart pounded, and she nodded before recalling he could not see her. "Y-yes?" she said, her voice tremulous.

"That should not have happened. It cannot happen again. I . . . My apologies."

His apologies?

Shame scorched her all the way to her toes, and she curled them sharply to escape it. "You needn't apologize," she murmured, wishing she'd been capable of calling forth a breeziness. "It was . . ." Just the most singularly magical moment of her life thus far. "Just a kiss."

He nodded jerkily and, with that, let himself out.

Cassia stood there, frozen, her heart pounding, trapped by an alternate want and need to either sigh or call him back, and then her whole body sagged.

He'd kissed her.

And then been horrified by it.

Never had she known something could be like that, that the simple brush of a man's mouth over hers could be pure magic. Though there'd been nothing simple about his embrace.

To her, it had been wondrous and gloriously splendorous and rapturous and, well, every other "-ous" word that indicated something life-altering.

To him?

To Nathan it had been a horrific experience that could not be repeated. He'd been so mortified by her and it that he'd fled her side like she'd set fire to his cabin.

He—

The door opened suddenly, and Cassia's heart doubled its beat as Nathan's broad form filled the doorway. She arched forward on the balls of her feet. He'd returned, after all. He—

"I told you to make sure you lock it," he said gruffly and jabbed a finger at the door. "Do it."

Her jaw worked. That was what he'd returned to say. "This is why you returned?"

"Yes. No."

She stared at him.

Muttering to himself, Nathan stomped across the room, over to the mahogany dresser there. Yanking a drawer out, he fished something from within and crossed over to her. "Here."

She stared down at his outstretched hand.

"It's . . . soap," he said, shaking his palm.

"I see that," she whispered. It was a blend of sandalwood and bergamot and smelled just like him, and he'd returned because he'd share it with her. Cassia made herself take it, and she drew it close.

"And I've a change of garments for you there." He pointed to the bottom drawer. "They're garments I've borrowed from Oliver. They should fit you well enough."

And a change of clothes? Her heart trembled. "Thank you, Nathan," she said softly.

He grunted. "Why wasn't the door locked?" he asked, as if he were unnerved by his own thoughtfulness and eager to shift the subject away from it.

"I was going to," she explained. "You needn't worry—"

"I think the only wise thing to do where you are concerned is worry," he muttered.

Once again she was caught between sighing at the evidence of his concern or stamping her foot in frustration that he believed her incapable.

He grunted. "Why are you looking at me like that?"

Setting aside the soap, she rested her palms upon his chest. The corded muscles jumped under her touch. "Because you care, and I think it is touching that you do."

She waited for him to deny it.

He only grew more flushed.

Blushing.

Captain Nathaniel Ellsby blushed. Another piece of her heart fell away and into his hands.

"What now?" he said gruffly.

"You are blushing, and I think it is very"—he recoiled—"endearing."

"I am *not*"—he dropped his voice to a furious whisper—"blushing!" His color rose once more, making an adorable liar of him.

Cassia touched his cheek. "Of course you aren't," she said in the soothing, placating tones she adopted when her youngest siblings were in a temper.

He thinned his eyes all the more, until his irises disappeared behind those slits of fury. "Are you talking to me like a babe?"

There was a warning there.

"Of course not," she scoffed, and some of the tension left his taut frame. "More like a young child. I find it helpful when dealing with my younger siblings and cousins, and—"

Nathan growled.

She smiled serenely up.

"Lock the blasted door," he blustered.

"As you wish, Nathan."

He paused, some peculiar emotion parading across his oft-opaque gaze, one that she couldn't identify from the brooding man before her. And then he nodded. "The—"

"I know, lock the door," she muttered as Nathan stormed off for a second time, following after him and then pushing the heavy wood panel shut.

"Now—"

She'd already slid the lock into place. "Happy?" she called out.

"I haven't been happy since I discovered you on my damned ship." Not even the heavy panel between them could have muffled that clear admission.

Cassia wrinkled her nose. "Well," she muttered. "I don't think you mean that," she called in louder tones to make herself heard. Cassia pressed her ear against the heavy oak panel, attempting to make out his response, and detected none.

And here she'd been waxing poetic in her mind about him and his kiss and every dizzying emotion she'd felt as he'd pulled her into his arms. Which was silly. As she'd said to him . . . it had been just a kiss. Only a kiss.

Why, it was so commonplace and so gross that even her entirely-more-affectionate-than-a-child-could-ever-wish mother and father engaged in the practice.

She closed her eyes.

Only, she knew she deluded herself.

For it hadn't been just a kiss.

But rather, *his* kiss.

When she'd both imagined and practiced kissing, she'd been certain it would be gross. After all, her elder cousin had shared one with one of Uncle Frank's stable hands when she'd been sixteen, and the young woman had described it in great detail to her twin and Cassia.

"Gross" had been a word to come to mind. "Awkward."

A man sticking his tongue in her mouth?

No, thank you.

Still, she'd practiced because her cousin had proven a kiss could come at the most unexpected of times, and Cassia hadn't wanted to be caught with her mouth open and her lips clueless as to what to do when it had.

Cassia opened her eyes and pressed her back against the door, borrowing support from the solid structure behind her, and she released a long sigh.

Sighing had always made her feel better.

A swift inhale and exhale.

Even a slow one.

This time, neither helped.

Her gaze slid to the bath he'd arranged; steam poured off the surface, and she wandered over to the serviceable brown furnishing, perfect for a man of Nathan's sheer size and breadth. Just like his having cared for her himself when he could have sent the ship's doctor early on, or reading to her or procuring her a bath, and now . . . entrusting her with a key to his cabin. He'd not locked her in but laid the key in her hand and trusted her to do that herself. Granted, he'd hammered home the point, but that was neither here nor there.

She sailed onto her knees and rested her arms along the narrow edge.

Her rumpled reflection stared mockingly back, and she assessed her visage.

Since she'd been presented before the Queen and officially made her debut before Polite Society, Cassia hadn't known the interest of so much as a single suitor. It had left her with a good deal of time to ponder . . . why.

She didn't possess the soft golden ringlets favored by the *ton*, but neither had she thought her auburn curls were so revolting as to dissuade all potential suitors. She was neither short nor tall . . . just somewhere stuck in between. She didn't have the bookish knowledge and clever skills of her younger sister Myrtle. Cassia was fine enough on the pianoforte, never stumbling awkwardly through recitals, but also not in possession of the fluidity and dexterity of the Bell sisters, whose performances people not only looked forward to attending—a rarity for London Seasons—but also clamored for an invitation to. Her eyes slid over to the burlap bag Nathan had set out beside the door that contained the items she'd taken with her when she'd run away, including her sketch pad and charcoals.

My art, Cassia thought as she shucked her garments and climbed into the bath.

Now, that had been the one area where she'd had *some* competence. Oh, she'd never be called an artist, per se, but she was skilled *enough.* Even so, it hadn't been as though a lady could walk about London ballrooms and attend dinner parties with a sketch pad in hand and turn that work around and display the one talent she did have to the world.

The one time she'd been permitted to paint outside her family's home was aboard this ship, and look at the disdain that had met her skills. Granted, she understood why. This was a ship, not a parlor. There was no place for art here. Just as it so often seemed there was no place in this world where she fit.

Tears blurred her eyes, and she blinked furiously to keep them from falling. She hated herself for this self-pity, and hated even more that she was hopeless to stop.

But mayhap that was what it came down to. Mayhap it wasn't that Cassia wasn't beautiful. Rather, it was that she was, in fact, unremarkable. She was no grand beauty, no virtuoso, no cleverest of ladies. She was something remarkably worse—*average.*

And the world never, ever noticed a person who was mediocre in every way, from looks on down to skills possessed.

"Nay, Nathan noticed you," she whispered miserably. "He noticed that he does not want to kiss you again." Sticking her tongue out at her reflected self, Cassia flicked her middle finger, swatting the water and sending droplets sailing and then falling back to the bath like so many raindrops falling from the sky.

And she shouldn't care that the entirely too-surly, brooding captain, who looked more like a pirate than a sailor, found her kiss too unbearable to wish to repeat.

And yet, she knew she lied to herself.

She liked him.

She liked his blunt directness and that he didn't speak to her in the grating manner most men—including, sometimes, her brothers—often spoke to women. Treating them as though they were a breed of creatures different from humans. She liked that he employed men and boys of all different stations and backgrounds, and that he wasn't so arrogant and small-minded as most members of the *ton*, who shunned anyone born outside their vaunted stations.

And she wanted him to like her in return.

Cassia drew her knees up to her chest and folded her arms around those limbs; her movements sent the tub water sloshing, rocking back and forth precariously at the edges.

The sooner this journey ended, the better off she would be . . . so that she could be far away from Nathan and these feelings he inspired— that she had no desire to feel for him.

Chapter 11

Later that night, his arms clasped behind his back, Nathaniel restlessly prowled the main deck of his ship, his legs, long accustomed to the motions of the ship, moving in perfect time to the vessel's gentle up-and-down sway.

The rush of the ocean waves slapped against the front and sides of the *Flying Dragon* as it sluiced through the calmer waters. The nearly full moon, unimpeded by clouds and joined only by a skyful of stars, left a luminescent glow upon the sea, that orb casting a bright light over the deck.

Nothing had the power to calm as the ocean waters did.

The powerful aroma of the salt-laden air, crisp and clean and so unlike the suffocating, heavy fog that hung over the crowded streets of London, had the power to fill a man's lungs and drive out the darkness. It cleared a man's head, and never failed to calm.

Or he'd believed that was the case.

Since Nathaniel had taken his leave of Cassia earlier that afternoon, nothing had been right.

In his head.

He'd been distracted, his thoughts locked firmly on her.

A minx of a woman with a tart tongue and a penchant for both prattling and crying, but who, by donning a disguise and setting out on her own to sail the seas, had proven herself brave and bold in ways that most grown men were not. Yes, he'd say it was dangerous and ill thought out, but only because he knew the perils for a woman aboard a ship. But Cassia hadn't just railed at a world where women were expected to grace ballrooms and parlors; she'd taken control of her life and set out to explore. And his appreciation of her, and her spirit, seemed even more dangerous than their embrace.

Nathaniel briefly closed his eyes.

He'd kissed her.

Nay, he'd not just kissed her. He'd bloody consumed her.

He'd made love to her mouth and traced every curve of her gently rounded body until he was driven nearly mad at the thought of ripping those garments from her and feeling that supple flesh, bared, under his naked palms.

She'd be satiny softness all over, and heat inside. And tight. Kissing as she had, timid at first and then unrestrained in her passion, there was no doubting Cassia McQuoid was innocent in all the ways there were for a woman to be innocent.

It was why he'd raced from her rooms and never looked back, even when his shift had ended. And it was why he'd avoided his quarters, even after Albion came to relieve him at the wheel.

And he'd been hopeless to focus at the wheel; even when the seas proved calming and steadying, he'd thought only of her sinking her supple body under those steaming waters, the heat of them leaving her skin flushed.

Never had he met a woman like her. Nay, never had he met a *person* like her.

One who was absolutely fearless of him, boldly commandeering his name the way he'd taken over lesser men's vessels. Cassia was as bold as brass, all spitting fury one instant; the next, her eyes wider than the big moon that hung overhead and filled with tears, which made him want to plead with her to stop, and not out of sheer annoyance—which it should be—but rather because the sight of her hurt was something he didn't know what to do with. He just knew he didn't like it, and it left his chest feeling a way it had never felt before.

And she was even so brave as to challenge him on his own ship.

Or stupid.

She could be that, too.

Nathaniel stopped at the bow of the ship, and gripping the gleaming wood rail, he stared out at the whitecaps breaking on the sea.

Only, she wasn't stupid.

Cassia McQuoid was a fine lady, one who didn't get the workings of a privateer ship. And why should she? With even finer manners and refined speech, she was the type of woman a respectable gentleman married, and certainly not the manner of woman who sneaked aboard a ship with a crew full of men.

He didn't know what to make of her.

She left him all tangled up in knots when he was never so twisted up, not even by his bloody interfering, all-powerful father.

A figure sidled up to him. "A bout of seasickness?"

Nathaniel stiffened. Hayes's entirely-too-amused-for-Nathaniel's-liking query came just beyond his shoulder.

Aye, he was seized by some malady. It was one inflicted not by the sea this time, but rather by the woman upon those waters with him.

He straightened. "I'm fine," he bit out.

"Is that why you are out here after putting Albion at the helm?" the other man asked with his unwelcome, sportive sense of humor.

"Is that what you've sought me out for?" Nathaniel scowled. "To play at nursemaid and order me abed?"

"I've come to speak about your passenger."

"I don't have a passenger," he muttered. "I have a stowaway."

"She's an English lady who speaks as refined as you and me," the other man said with his usual bluntness. That directness was one of the traits Nathaniel had always appreciated in the quartermaster, since the moment he and Nathaniel had worked alongside each other on their first naval ship. "So that tends to set her apart from the normal stowaway."

"It doesn't," he said tersely. Only, as Hayes shot him a look, he knew the inherent lie in the words he spoke. "Say what it is you want to say, Hayes."

"The lady needs fresh air." Nathaniel was already shaking his head. "It's been more than a week. You can't keep her locked in your cabin for the length of the voyage."

That was precisely what he intended to do.

He looked incredulously back at the other man. "Surely you aren't suggesting I grant her the freedom to walk the decks?" Why, the minx couldn't stay out of trouble if the good Lord had given her a book with instructions on how to do so. She'd cause a mutiny in a minute.

"She is suffering from seasickness."

"She's much improved," he said grudgingly. "Is she not?" he asked, suddenly concerned. "Did she seem like she's taken another turn—"

"No. She is much better, but she'll be that much more improved if she's able to use her legs and accustom herself to the roll of the ship and breathe the fresh air and feel the sun."

An image flitted forward. Of Cassia, the ocean breeze tugging at those auburn curls of hers, looser than a corkscrew and relaxed as the lady herself as she strolled the decks. The wind plastering the fabric of that white lawn shirt to her supple form.

He flexed his jaw. "No."

"You're being unreasonable," Hayes said in an infuriatingly calm tone. The affable quartermaster, who'd looked altogether too comfortable with the lady.

And that same niggling of annoyance that had hit Nathaniel when he'd seen the pair playfully chatting seized him once more. Nathaniel slanted a sharp glance at the other man, who'd become as close as any brother to him. "Why are *you* so concerned with her?" he snapped.

Good God on Sunday. What in hell was wrong with him? He dragged a shaky hand through his hair, and then midway through that gesture registered that disquieted motion. Nathaniel forcibly lowered his arm to his side.

"The better question is, Why aren't *you*?" Hayes asked quietly, and Nathaniel felt heat climb his neck.

"I am concerned. That is why I want the lady to stay below deck and out of sight, because . . ." Nathaniel bunched his hands at his sides and forcibly buried the unwanted thoughts swirling of all manner of harm Cassia could and would find herself out at sea.

"Never say you don't trust the crew to honor your word that harming the lady in any way is forbidden?"

"They aren't all my usual crew. You know that," Nathaniel said curtly, reminding the other man of the circumstances that saw them with a skeleton crew. "There are many who are new, men who we have only just hired for this mission, and as such, I cannot say definitively that she'll be safe with them, as I could about our usual crew." That much was true. It was also safer than admitting his desire for the lady and the inexplicable pleasure he found in her company. He tried again. "Anything can happen to her above deck. She could land herself in any manner of danger, falling over the side, getting washed over the side, hell, jumping over the side to follow a damned dolphin"—for all he knew about the troublesome magpie—"and then there *is* the matter of the crew's superstition about women on board ships, and there is the matter of the lady's reputation to consider. Not that I think a single man would say a word about her being here, gainsaying that order and . . ." He caught the knowing glint that emanated from Hayes's eyes, and Nathaniel made himself stop. But he blanched. Good God, the chit's ramblings were contagious. "I will take your advisement into consideration," he said tersely.

Hayes inclined his head, but by his expression, there was more he wished to say.

"What else, Hayes?" Nathaniel asked impatiently.

"You might try to show the young woman more compassion. She's found herself alone, at sea, away from everything that is familiar—"

"A choice she made on her own." And for it, nothing had been the same for Nathaniel. He'd not share the truth, that he read to her or sat and discussed their families. It was better the other man not know those truths, ones that discomfited Nathaniel.

The other man persisted. "Her decision doesn't erase the fact that she is eighteen or nine—"

"Twenty-one."

Hayes stared.

Shite.

"That is, I . . . suspect she's twenty or twenty-one," Nathaniel mumbled. He knew it. But he'd be goddamned if he said as much.

"Regardless," Hayes went on, "she's far from her family and comfortable life, and with a ship full of men who are nothing less than terrifying to most grown men."

Nay, Hayes was correct on that score. Cassia had believed she was boarding her brother's best friend's passenger ship and instead had found herself on one of the most notorious privateer vessels, made up of a sea of crew members from all walks of life, men who were more pirates than commonplace sailors.

He felt the quartermaster's eyes on him.

"You are not incorrect. Which is why asking her to remain in my cabin is better for her," Nathaniel said.

"*Better* for her?" There was a shade of incredulity in Hayes's tone, and a challenge there, too. "Is it *also* better for her that she be sailed into the middle of a sea battle against the French?"

Unwanted images slipped in of Cassia being dragged from his ship, taken prisoner . . . Nathaniel growled as a vicious vise squeezed around his gut. "I haven't ever lost a battle." Was that reminder for him? Or

Hayes? Ultimately, however, Nathaniel had never before had a young, innocent lady aboard his ship. Now he did.

His quartermaster proved tenacious. "But if you *do?*"

"What would you have me do?" he snapped. "Put an end to the mission? As it is, England is battling France for supremacy in the Adriatic. We are in a position where we can intercept their latest plans for the war and end this tug-of-war in that region."

"I don't . . . know the answer to that. We can leave her in a port . . . and then resume—"

"Leave her in a port?" he asked incredulously. "Drop an innocent English lady in an unfamiliar port—"

"Well, that has to be safer than sailing her into a match with the French."

"It won't be a match." They were chasing the ship, which was unaware. "We have the element of surprise—"

"What about this existence at sea is predictable, Ellsby?" Hayes exploded.

Tension crackled and sizzled like the sea right before a battle. "I've never compromised a mission." Nathaniel flexed his jaw. "And I don't intend to do so now, all because a young woman confused my ship with someone else's." He layered an edge of finality in that pronouncement, one intended to put an end to Hayes's challenge.

Hayes lowered his voice. "And when we return . . . there is the matter of fact that the lady will be ruined."

"*If* it's discovered she was in our company," Nathaniel pointed out, placing a slight emphasis on that distinctly important word. "The crew will say nothing." His was a confident avowal. "My men are loyal." Were they not, they wouldn't be with him. They'd proven their fealty and honor to him and this ship, and to one another, countless times.

Hayes winged a dark brow up. "But as you yourself pointed out, these aren't all your men. Do you also trust the lady's family servants will say nothing? That whispers won't start the moment her family discovers where she's been?"

And Cassia would tell them . . . something. The garrulous minx wouldn't be able to keep herself to complete silence were she handed a rag and urged to wrap it about her mouth, all in the name of saving her life.

He firmed his mouth. "What her family's faithless staff says or does not say is not my affair." Except, even before that pronouncement had fully left his lips, an image slipped in of a Cassia who'd traded her trousers and shirt for a satin gown, walking amidst a ballroom, filled with ladies whispering behind their fans, while the gentlemen at their sides talked around their hands about her. His gut clenched again. "It is not my responsibility what happens after this," he repeated in a different way, through tightly compressed teeth, unsure whether he sought to convince himself or Hayes.

Not for the first time since the other man had joined him, Hayes's look turned disappointed and disapproving, and *bloody hell*, if Nathaniel didn't feel that same shame somewhere deep inside.

"Given all of that," the other man said quietly, "you might attempt to be a bit more kind toward her."

"I *am* kind," Nathaniel protested.

"You were deuced rude earlier in your cabin." At Hayes's look, he felt his neck go hot.

"I'm as kind as I am able," he grudgingly conceded. "Now, are there any other topics you wish to cover about our *passenger*?"

Hayes inclined his head. "No, that is all."

"I was being sarcastic."

A smile ghosted the quartermaster's mouth. "I know."

Nathaniel, eager to end this discussion about Cassia with the other man, proved more of a coward than he'd ever believed himself to be, and with a brief word of good night, he headed for his cabin.

His cabin, where Cassia McQuoid remained.

Now it was surely safe, though.

He'd kept his distance for the whole of the day, joining his crew for dinner and having a tray sent 'round for the lady to enjoy by herself.

As he walked the familiar path he could make blindfolded and in his sleep, Nathaniel fished out his watch fob and consulted the time-piece there. *Midnight.*

Yea, the lady would definitely be asleep—likely for several hours now.

As such, it was perfectly fine to return, and to do so with the confidence that he didn't have to face the temptation of having her awake.

"Captain," Shorty greeted when he approached.

"Any problems from the lady?" he asked in hushed tones so as to not awaken the lady and put himself through more of that torturous wanting of her.

"Speaks to herself, she does."

Well, that came as no surprise.

"Pretty inventive with her curses, she is, too. Knows some good sailing ones in there."

There was a flash of appreciation and admiration in the seasoned sailor's wizened face.

Shorty, too?

Nathaniel frowned.

Bloody hell. A mutiny, indeed.

"That'll be all, Shorty," he said tightly.

After Shorty had gone, Nathaniel removed the key from his pocket and let himself inside his rooms.

He pushed the door quietly shut behind him and locked it once more, and then turned.

His gaze immediately found her.

Not lying in his bed as she'd been prior nights, with the blankets pulled up over her ears.

Instead, she remained upright, seated on the side of the bed, wearing . . .

He swallowed hard.

Or he tried to.

Basic functions like swallowing and thinking and moving so much as a muscle proved impossible tasks.

Cassia wore a shirt.

And only a shirt.

She'd availed herself to one of his, and the giant, crisp-white garment dwarfed her slender frame and hung just above her knees, leaving on display her bared lower limbs, from her knobby knees to surprisingly muscled calves, and lower to her bare, graceful feet. His body heated as he imagined all manner of pleasures to be had with such legs wrapped tight around his waist.

Her hair hung in a tangle about her narrow hips, a gloriously messy waterfall of silken auburn locks that looked sleek still from the bath she'd taken . . . which only conjured fantasies of a different sort.

"All the garments I arrived with needed washing," she explained, misunderstanding the reason for his study. "I see you looking at me," she said archly. "And I know what you are thinking."

She had no idea. Absolutely none.

For if she knew the manner of wicked thoughts he entertained about her—about them—she'd have bolted past him and tossed herself overboard and taken her chances with the sea.

Cassia sniffled, and Nathaniel recoiled. There wasn't a greater slayer of desire than tears.

"Just say it."

"Say *what?*"

"I'm hopeless," she whispered, and with that whispery-soft wail, she threw her arms wide, and flung herself back onto his mattress, her slight form bouncing amongst the feathered top. Reclined as she was, the shirt she'd pilfered from his belongings climbed several inches higher. And all the self-control he'd prided himself on before meeting his unruly stowaway proved absent once more, and his gaze went to the slight part in her shapely legs. His blood heated, and his body instantly stirred.

Nathaniel swallowed several times and forcibly wrenched his gaze away. He needn't have worried about her noticing his lecherous study. At some point while he'd been staring at the expanse of her cream-white limbs, she'd dragged a pillow over her head.

Reining in that rampant hungering, Nathaniel sighed and started over. "Be kind," he muttered. "Be kind . . ."

"Are you talking to me or yourself?" she called, her voice muted by the feather pillow.

God, she had sharp ears.

"I don't talk to myself," Nathaniel said when he reached his—her—bed.

Cassia shifted the feather article and angled her head a fraction so she might look at him. "So you were talking to me, then?"

"No."

She puzzled her high, proud brow.

"I didn't talk to myself . . . until you." He mumbled that last part under his breath.

Cassia made to return the pillow to her head, but Nathaniel caught it and set the article aside.

"What's your problem?" he asked with the same bluntness he reserved for all his exchanges with his father and crew and brothers, before recalling Hayes's earlier urgings. "That is . . ." Nathaniel cleared his throat. "Why are you . . . Why are you . . . ?"

The lady stared expectantly at him.

"Sad." He forced the word out.

"I'm not s-sad." The slight tremor to her voice made a complete lie of that false assurance.

"You're a terrible liar." If he'd been an affable, charming sort, like his ship surgeon, Nathaniel would have mustered some gentleness to that statement.

Tears welled anew in her eyes, and his gut muscles clenched. "Don't cry," he said roughly, and not solely because he had absolutely no idea what to do with those drops, but rather because the sight of her suffering was having the oddest effect on his chest, leaving it all tight with a vise gripping at his heart.

"You can't order me not to c-cry." A drop fell, and the sight of this hit him like a blow to the belly. "O-or, I suppose you can because you just did, but you can't make me not cry." With that, she curled herself up tightly, and presenting him with her back, she stared at the wall.

Nathaniel sat there, helpless. For in this, Cassia was correct. He couldn't make those tears stop. And he hated that for reasons the lady would never believe, because, hell, Nathaniel didn't believe it himself. The sight of her suffering struck like a blade he'd taken to his arm in a sea battle two years earlier.

"Y-you're right, you know," she said, her voice smaller than he'd ever heard, even when she'd been at her sickest, pleading with him to cast her overboard to end her misery.

Nathaniel shook his head, before recalling she couldn't see that gesture. "I . . ."

The lady rolled back onto her other side. "I am a terrible liar." Cassia's full bottom lip trembled.

"And?" he entreated, because he had no idea why that should make her cry, too.

"And I'm terrible at everything, Nathan. I can't even plait my own hair."

Ah.

"I don't have a lady's maid, Cassia," he said gruffly, but also without inflection.

"I know that." She struggled up onto her elbows, then pushed herself upright so she sat beside him in a matched pose. "I didn't even consider that when I left."

"That you should bring your lady's maid with you?"

"No," she said in exasperated tones as she threw her hands up. And then she stopped, her jaw slackened, as she looked over. "You're making a jest."

Nathaniel winked. "Don't tell the crew."

Something passed through Cassia's eyes in an instant, a shimmery light, as those green-blue pools the color of Caribbean waters went all soft—a faraway, dreamy glimmer that terrified the hell out of him.

He scrambled away, putting several inches between them on the bed.

Cassia blinked as if coming to from a stupor, and when she did, she sighed, that sadness returning in the form of her soft exhalation and in her eyes and damned if Nathaniel didn't yearn to see that happy glitter once more.

And then, silent when she was never silent, Cassia reached for a brush he'd not noted beside her until her fingers were upon the silver handle, and wordlessly, she dragged it through her waist-long tresses.

Each and every upward and then downward stroke brought the fabric of his shirt stretching and pulling against her chest, and unbidden, his eyes locked on the shadowy outline of her breasts, the dusky hint of those tips pebbled by the cold. His breathing grew shallow as he took air in slowly through his nose and exhaled out his tightly closed lips. He was an absolute scoundrel. A blasted fellow as weak as Adam, lusting after a woman so innocent and vulnerable.

"Here," he said gruffly.

Cassia paused midstroke and stared questioningly over at him.

Nathaniel flicked four fingers of his right hand against his palm, motioning for the silver brush.

She hesitated, then held it out.

As he closed his palm around it, his gaze snagged on the three letters there: *CDM*.

Cassia . . . C . . . McQuoid.

And Nathaniel was beset by the unlikeliest of needs to know the mystery behind that unknown-to-him letter. Knowing it changed nothing and served no purpose—that was, other than to learn more about Cassia-with-the-Mysterious-Middle-Initial McQuoid. Despite knowing all that, Nathaniel found himself asking, "What is the *C* for?"

She stared quizzically at him.

Nathaniel touched his index finger to the elaborately curved letter. "On your brush."

"Oh. It is my middle initial."

He stared, waiting for her to say more, and when he was still waiting several moments more, a grin pulled at the corners of his lips. "I gathered as much. What is your middle name?"

Her mouth pulled. "Cora."

Nathaniel froze. *"Cora."*

"I know," she said, mistaking the reason for his response. "Cassia Cora."

"It's a fine name."

She snorted. "You aren't the charming sort, so you needn't try and pretend on my behalf. They sound quite ridiculous together."

Nathaniel opened his mouth to defend the sincerity of his admission, and then frowned. Not the charming sort? Of course, he knew he wasn't charming. He'd long known his quartermaster, Hayes, was invariably the fellow who knew how to charm a lady into a smile, or out of her slippers. But something in hearing Cassia acknowledge his lack of charm . . . grated.

"I'm not pretending. Just like I don't charm, I also don't *pretend* on anyone's behalf," he said gruffly. "Cora. It comes from the name Persephone. She was the Greek goddess of the sirens." That queen perfectly embodied everything Cassia was. "It suits you," he settled for.

Squinting in a comical way that tugged another reluctant grin from him, Cassia leaned up and peered at his face. With a slow nod, she sat back down. "Very well. I believe you, Nathan . . . ?" She added an up-tilt to her lilting voice that transformed it into the question it was.

"Nathaniel. The Marquess of Winfield."

Her perfectly formed eyebrows shot up. "You are a *marquess*."

He gave a curt nod. A marquess, destined to be a duke. He was well accustomed to the fawning and obsequiousness met with that revelation.

"And you are a captain of a ship . . ."

Only this woman would gloss over that lofty title and go dreamy-eyed over the fact that he sailed, and not the rank he was born to. And that realization left him with an odd sensation in his chest.

"See?" Cassia plucked the brush from his fingers and ran it through those tresses as she spoke. "That is the problem with the world," she said, pausing to jab her brush at him, punctuating her statement.

He cocked his head. "That I'm a marquess?"

"No," she said, rolling her eyes up to the ceiling. "That you're a nobleman and you are permitted to have your own ship and sail the seas and live a life outside of Polite Society."

"Is that what you want?" he asked quietly, compelled once more by this unexplainable need to know more about Cassia Doris McQuoid. "To live a life outside of Polite Society?"

"I don't want to live a life, either in it or out of it. I just want to have the freedom to choose to move between whatever it is I want to do."

"And what is that?" he murmured. Moving closer, he settled his fingers on hers, which had resumed those strokes. "What is it you want to do?"

———— ⟨⟩ ————

What is it you want to do?

No one had ever asked that question of her.

158

No one had because it had always been expected what her future would be: she would be the wife of some perfectly acceptable, affable nobleman . . . which meant she would be an arm ornament . . . and . . . not much more.

Whereas her sister had been sent away to Mrs. Belden's Finishing School and lived outside of the same walls they'd always known and learned what it was to survive on one's own.

But Cassia had learned, in this moment with this man beside her, that she didn't want to just survive. "I want to live," she whispered, staring at the table covered with Nathan's colorful maps. "But . . . I don't even know what that means," she said, and then as the realization hit her, all those truths came rapidly tumbling out, spilling from her lips. "I want to know what it is to do something more than curtsy or work at needlepoint. I hate needlepoint." But she'd learned it and perfected it. "I want to know how people outside of London and Scotland live. What foods they eat and how they dress, and feel the sun on my face, because the sun . . . it is a rarity in London, you know," she said needlessly. Of course, everyone knew rain and clouds and fog competed for the greatest time spent in the English sky.

The energy drained from her. "But . . . the problem is . . . I can't. Because the extent of the skills and lessons imparted me over the years were those reserved for a lady. Because it was *always* accepted that I'd never leave and never be anything more than . . . than . . . some good-enough gentleman's wife."

"Don't you dare settle," Nathan said sharply, and she blinked slowly and looked up. "Don't you dare settle for some good-enough gentleman. Find a damned fellow who treats you like you are the sun the English sky needs, and treasures you for that light."

Cassia's breath caught, as in that moment she fell, hard and fast and forever, in love with Nathan Ellsby, the Marquess of Winfield. This gruff, rough, and altogether tough ship's captain who cursed and grunted, and who was very real for those emotions.

As if on cue, he grunted, then plucked the brush from her fingers and resumed brushing the back of her head, those almost dry locks that she'd been unable to reach.

"Do you think we'll meet across a London ballroom?" she asked softly, and he paused a moment.

"I . . ."

"We'll, of course, pretend we do not know one another." A sad smile pulled at the corners of her mouth. "It'll be a secret only known by you and me." And she'd mourn that until she drew her last breath. "One that my husband, of course, cannot know."

He growled. "Don't marry a man who'd find fault with you for how you lived your life before him."

"You're charging me with an impossible task, Nathan. Gentlemen are very specific in what they expect of their wives and future wives."

"Then marry a man with less specific expectations," he snapped.

"Will you discuss me with your wife?" she asked, angling a glance over her shoulder, and then promptly wished she hadn't.

He froze.

She wished she hadn't, because she'd unwittingly conjured images of the fortunate woman who'd one day be the Marchioness of Winfield.

"I thought so," she said, the smile she plastered on her lips straining her cheek muscles.

Nathan resumed, a second time, brushing her hair, and this time, she didn't speak. This time, when the silence fell, it was comfortable and companionable, and she took that gift.

Over the course of Cassia's lifetime, all manner of people, from her lady's maid on to her mother and younger sisters and cousins, had brushed her hair.

Not a single one of those times had felt like this one.

How could such a simple, routine task also prove so . . . intimate.

And there was no doubting, this was intimate.

From the way he filled his hands with a portion of her curls and then brought that brush gently through her hair.

Cassia closed her eyes and surrendered fully to the moment. Then, after a long while of running those bristles through her drying tresses, he set it aside, and she bit her lip, filled with an aching regret at the end of that intimate moment.

Only, he set the brush down on the mattress and filled his hands with her hair, ever so gently separating the mass of her loose tresses in one hand, and then with the other, he layered them over the partition he'd made.

And then it hit her, and so much warmth flooded her heart and spread through her entire person. She angled a slight look back over her shoulder.

He grunted. "Keep your head straight. Please." He tacked that last word on grudgingly, as if it pained him to do so, and she smiled, directing her gaze forward as he braided her hair.

As he expertly braided her hair.

In all the times she'd imagined the man she would one day wed, she'd thought about what her relationship might be with that man. Ofttimes in her imaginings, she and that unknown someone would settle into a familiar, comfortable union known by Cassia's own parents. They'd read together and be part of their children's lives together. But never could she have imagined the intimate end of what that marriage would be. Not in the bedchambers, but rather a greater intimacy that came from those before-now-imagined exchanges.

Now that Nathan cared for her in this way, she could not think of settling into a future with a man who did not carry out this same role.

Nathan's fingers worked rapidly, like a man who'd overseen the task thousands of times before this one.

Like one who'd overseen the task thousands of times . . .

That reminder played over and over in her mind like a stale ball-room orchestra's use of the quadrille strains. Unwittingly, she'd conjured thoughts she didn't want to have.

Of Nathan with . . . other women before her.

And worse, the women who'd come after her.

She scowled.

"You have experience plaiting." She couldn't keep the arch tone from her voice.

"Aye."

He didn't even seek to deny it. Jealousy, her color was green, but felt red and slipped around a person's veins. "From your many lovers?"

"Boat lines."

She angled another glance over her shoulder at him.

"I had to plait certain lines of the ship," he explained, and she couldn't help the giddy rush of relief that filled her. "And I've had many lovers, too."

She scowled.

Nathan gave one of her curls a playful tug. "Whose hair I've not braided."

And then it hit her. She widened her eyes. "You are teasing."

"Don't tell my crew. Though they wouldn't believe you if you did. I also plaited my dog's hair."

A snorting bark of laughter slipped from her lips. "You jest."

"Not on the latter. A bearded collie," he added.

Something in that detail he shared was intimate, but in a different way from the act he now performed on her hair. Not only did he have a dog, but he'd braided the animal's coat.

Oh, my. For if there was a man a woman could love, it was one who loved dogs.

"You have a dog," she whispered.

"I had one. He passed on two voyages ago. I've not . . . come 'round to having a second."

There was an aching sadness in that admission, and Nathan cleared his throat, as if embarrassed by that show of emotion, and she ached to turn and take him in her arms.

"I am so very sorry," she said softly.

He grunted. "Loss is part of life."

"Yes, it is, but the truth of that doesn't make the reality of it any less painful."

"What of you, Cassia McQuoid? Do you have pups of your own?" He put that question to her, and she'd have waged her left littlest finger he did so in an attempt to move them to topics safer and less painful. "Pugs? Terriers?"

"My family never had dogs. At least, not the faithful-family-pet sort. There's only ever been hunting ones, who were always my father's and brothers'. I've tried bribing them with treats." She sighed. To no avail. The family dogs, just like her family and men everywhere, were wholly unmoved by her.

Unlike Myrtle . . . "Myrtle and the duke have one," she added.

He paused mid-winding of the plait he now made.

"My sister and her husband," she explained. "Surely I have mentioned them before. The duke has an enormous dog. More of a wolf, really." In fact, when her mother had the idea to drag her next door to meet that lofty lord and attempt to arrange a match, Myrtle had been more excited at the prospect of having that dog, and not so much the duke. "He was our neighbor. Is." She tacked on that reminder. Even all this time later, the shame and humiliation of that first meeting with her sister's now husband coursed hot and fresh as it had yesterday. So why did she continue talking? Why did she continue to bare those most humiliating details to this man, who, for the length of time they'd known one another, was a stranger more than anything? "I paid a visit with my family, but he wouldn't even open the door."

"Ah." There was a wealth of knowing contained within that slight exhalation, and she looked back, once again staying his efforts.

"What?"

"You were in love with your sister's husband first, and that is why you ran away."

Cassia scrunched up her nose. "Why must it be when a woman runs away to the sea that she is rushing to meet a man or running from heartbreak?"

"I . . ." He shook his head. "It's not?"

She shook her head. "I'll have you know, women, just like men, wish to see the world. We, however, aren't afforded those same opportunities." Cassia paused, her eyes lingering on the circular glass panels overlooking the ocean waters. The moon shone on the sea, bathing it in a bright-white light. "Except Myrtle," she said softly to herself, as he resumed pulling the brush through her hair. "My parents sent Myrtle away to school so that she might have an education."

Whereas Cassia? In Cassia, they'd not seen a daughter worth sending away to grow on her own. They'd not believed her capable.

And with every fiber of her being, she hated that, with the latest quandary she'd landed herself in, she'd proven them right.

———— ❧ ————

This wasn't a conversation he wished to have.

Or it was one he shouldn't find himself wishing to have.

Just as he shouldn't be brushing her hair, and yet, oddly, he found himself wanting to do both.

"And I take it you weren't sent away to finishing school?"

Cassia hesitated. "Me? No."

"And that's something you would have wanted?" Even as he asked it, he already knew the answer, because he knew this inquisitive woman with a penchant for exploring would have only welcomed the opportunity.

"Yes," she said softly, and then she propped her right fist under her chin, and even in silhouette as she was, he detected the wistful quality of that positioning. "They wouldn't have ever sent me away. No one really has a high opinion of me. Including my parents. They always thought me flighty. You'd probably agree with them."

Two days ago, he would have answered in an immediate affirmative.

Hell, even one day ago, his response would have been a resounding yes.

He could not, however, bring himself to utter that harsh concurrence.

"No, to my parents . . . They only ever saw me capable of one thing."

Nathaniel paused midstroke.

"Marriage," she explained. "And in the end, I couldn't even manage that." That sadly spoken pronouncement came so soft he had to strain to hear it, and when he did, the sound of her suffering kicked him squarely in the chest.

"The men in London are fools," he growled. The lot of them dandies or rakes or scoundrels who all perceived themselves as larger-than-life figures.

"Yes," she said bleakly. "Well, then, what does it say about me if even a fool won't marry me? My brother-in-law isn't a fool," she added, raising her brother-in-law's name once more.

This illustrious brother-in-law whom she insisted she hadn't held a tendre for, and yet, if she didn't, she sure spoke enough of the damned clod. Why did annoyance slither and twist inside?

"He didn't marry you, though, did he?" he snapped, his tone harsher than he intended.

Cassia tipped her head in that endearingly confused way of hers. "No. I said as much. He married—"

"No," he said impatiently. "I'm saying he's a damned fool. For not marrying you and marrying your sister, instead."

She laughed, that merriment as clear as the bell that, on occasion, rang on his ship, only shades lovelier for the slightly husky quality to it.

He bristled. "What?"

"I'd not imagine you of all people issuing platitudes to anyone."

"Because I don't. I don't waste my time with them," he said bluntly.

"Oh," Cassia said softly, and her eyes glittered and sparkled in a way he'd not known eyes could. In that way the poets whose works his former tutors had insisted Nathaniel read had written of, and in a way that Nathaniel had believed was utter rubbish because eyes didn't shine. Only to be proven wrong in this moment, by this woman. For her eyes did. They glittered like a thousand stars within the vast night sky. "But I have no illusions of who I am. I'm a woman who's been sheltered"—aye, she was correct on that score—"and who desperately wanted to see the world, and my family knows precisely what I am. Myrtle is clever and capable." And there was clearly sisterly pride in her tone.

Surely she saw that, whatever her sister was, Cassia was a thousand-fold more capable. "*You're* clever and capable, too," he said gruffly as he finished up her plait.

Cassia gave her head a wag, toying distractedly with the ends of the ribbon he'd made in her hair. "No, I'm not," she said matter-of-factly, and it grated. "You think it, too."

He'd thought it, but he now knew that wasn't really true. "You're just a woman who is out of her element, Cassia."

"My one passable skill is painting, and you see the mess I made of that when you had me paint." His gaze went over to the unfinished nautical scene, and now, knowing the identity and the source of confusion that had brought that work about, Nathaniel studied it and saw it in a new light.

"You really are very good with a brush," he said bluntly.

"Thank you. I did think I was, if not good, passable."

"You paint, but that isn't all. You're curious and interested in people and experiencing life, and those are skills, too. You *are* clever and capable, and I'll not debate you further on the point."

He should have recalled she was the one person who'd not simply take the nail he put in the end of a point or discussion as the end it, in fact, was.

"If I were so clever and capable, you'd not keep me shut away, afraid I'm going to land myself in trouble, Nathan."

If she were anyone else, he'd have thought she was angling to get herself out of hiding. "You will . . ." Nay, not "will." That wasn't an option. "You would land yourself in trouble." Keeping her in his cabin was for her own good, even if she was too innocent to see it.

"First complimenting my painting, then calling me clever and capable. Well, if I were"—she flicked him on the arm with her middle finger—"if you were confident in my abilities, you certainly wouldn't have to shut me away the whole voyage."

"It's not a voyage. It's a . . ." *Mission.*

She stared at him through the biggest, widest, most innocent eyes. "Yes?"

Cassia, who spoke too much and said even more, was the last person he could afford to have discover his wartime efforts for the Crown. Those were details not even his own parents were in full possession of. "Fine—it's a voyage," he settled for. "And it's not *you* I don't trust."

"It's your crew then?" She batted her eyes, those long lashes fluttering too innocently to ever be coy or pretend.

"No." He tensed his jaw. "Yes." *Bloody hell.* "It is complicated." He'd trust his crew with his life, and yet . . . these weren't all his men. "Men at sea are a superstitious lot, and there are . . ."

She stared expectantly back. "Yes?"

"Enough superstitions about women at sea that it's safer if we don't . . . test my crew." Because he'd never had a woman aboard his ship before Cassia, and he'd never have one aboard his ship after her.

Odd, that it should leave him strangely . . . sad at the thought.

"What kind of superstitions?" she asked, her patent curiosity tingeing that question.

"Women are a distraction to sailors, and the seas seek to punish the crew for their behaviors."

Cassia laughed. "What rot! And if that is the case, then why do you have a carved, painted, painted . . ." Her cheeks flared a crimson berry red.

She was adorable when she was embarrassed. If he were a true gentleman, he'd have let her leave that sentence unfinished. Alas, he was no gentleman in truth, only in name, and it was deuced enjoyable teasing her. "Yes?"

"Naked woman"—she dropped her voice to a scandalized whisper—"on the front of your ship."

"Because naked women calm the seas."

Cassia burst out laughing before registering his expression. "You're serious."

"Deadly. A woman's bared breasts are said to shame the unruly seas into a calm, and sailors are clear-eyed and able to safely guide the ship."

"La," she said with a roll of her eyes. "If that's the case, then I should just go without a shirt and there'd be no problem."

Except her playful response conjured an image of Cassia, naked, prancing and prowling about with her breasts bared, and lust coursed through him, his shaft rising uncomfortably large, straining the front of his breeches at the image she painted. His breathing grew shallow and labored.

"Nathan?" Cassia's voice called across the storm. "I'm just teasing. I would, of course, not go naked about—"

With a growl, he reached over and drew her onto his lap. He had his mouth on hers in a moment.

And she was all softness and warmth and surrender in his arms as she sighed and tangled her hands about his nape.

"I like your kiss," she admitted, breathless, between each angry, bold slant of his lips over hers. Each angry, bold slant that she met with a like vigor.

"I'm so glad you approve," he grunted, angling her nape to better avail himself of her mouth.

"Love it," she whispered against his mouth. God, she was a chatterbox even in moments of passion. Oddly, that only fueled his wanting for her. "'Like' is hardly a strong enough word to capture my feelings on the—" Nathaniel slipped his tongue inside and tasted of her once more. Drank of her, as he'd longed to do since that first, and earlier, kiss.

This. This right here was why women had no place aboard a ship. Because he was hopeless to think rationally or to think anything but of how damned good it felt to have her in his arms.

Nathaniel swirled his tongue around hers, lightly sucking at the end, and she whimpered, her body moving rhythmically against his. Her hips lifted in slow undulations that redoubled his hungering.

In one fluid motion, Nathaniel guided her back and downward, and never breaking contact with her mouth, he positioned himself over her. Anchoring himself on one elbow, he brought his other hand up to cup the gentle swell of one of her breasts.

The enormous fabric of his lawn shirt hung loose about her, and taking advantage of that gift, he shoved the article down and bared her breasts to his touch.

Nathaniel palmed the pillow-soft mound and then shifted his attentions to the pebbled peak, closing his lips around it and suckling of the pink tip.

Cassia cried out, her hands automatically coming up and twining in his hair as she anchored him close to that space where her heart beat.

Nathaniel growled, his breath coming harsh and fast as he reached his hand down between her legs and then rested his palm at that apex.

Moaning, Cassia lifted her hips into his touch, moving restlessly against his palm.

She was passionate and perfectly free as she made love. As a woman ought to be, and as he knew she would be. And yet—

Nathaniel froze, hating that honor reared its ugly, unwelcome, but ever-present head.

And with a pained groan, he ripped his hand away and forcibly rolled himself off her, falling onto his back beside Cassia with their shoulders touching.

Bloody, bloody hell.

He squeezed his eyes shut tightly and concentrated on calming a raging desire for this woman that wouldn't quit.

The mattress dipped, and he felt Cassia straighten, and coward as he was, he prayed she'd get up and get herself to the other side of the cabin. To move away from him, because Lord knew he couldn't trust himself around her. She touched a tentative hand to his shoulder, and her touch was like a firebrand.

Knowing a glimpse of the chore that had led Adam to commit that ultimate sin in the name of all mankind, Nathaniel swung his legs over the side of the bed.

Cassia instantly scrambled up onto her knees; his shirt slithered down about her lithe frame.

"You're leaving," she remarked, and he felt her gaze following him as he headed over to the chest under the wide set of windows at the back of the room.

Nathaniel fetched himself several blankets and a pillow, and then carrying them to the far corner of the room, as far away as he could get, because that distance proved essential, he dropped them down. "I'm sleeping here."

"You don't . . . have to."

Was she mad? "I do," he said, his voice strangled. He'd not leave her alone. He trusted *his* men, but temptation could be hard, and with their leave cut short—

"We can sleep together."

Satan was real, and the sin of lust and temptation came not in the form of an apple, but in the innocent words of Cassia McQuoid. "We cannot sleep together," he said, his tone harsher than he intended, but also better that way for the distance he desperately, desperately, needed from this woman.

She immediately went quiet, and he used the time to put together the makeshift bedding he'd had for himself these past several days.

That silence proved as short-lived as all the lady's other attempts at it.

"I can sleep on the floor."

"Cassia, you're not sleeping on the floor," he said impatiently as he dropped to the floor and pounded away at his pillow several times. "Now, would you just go to sleep?" With a quiet curse, he flopped himself back and lay there.

Her quiet sniffling reached him.

The sound of her tears, a lance to his chest.

Nathaniel squeezed his eyes tightly shut. "What?"

She sniffed again. "I've disgusted you again."

That's what she thought. That he'd stopped their embrace because he was disgusted by her?

Let her think that.

Let her hold on to that alternately foolish and innocent conclusion she'd come to, because that was better, and safer. It would allow him the distance he needed from her. And yet, even knowing that, he couldn't let her to that incorrect opinion. One that would put him with the likes of her deuced stupid brother-in-law, who'd chosen the inherently less-worthy sister.

Nathaniel's eyes went flying open, and he stared at the slats overhead. "You've not disgusted me," he said harshly. And then registered that other—important—word she'd spoken. "Again?"

"That's why you left before," she whispered, her voice achingly soft and painful, and it wrenched all the way through to a heart that wasn't as hard as he'd previously taken it for.

Nathaniel swiped a hand over his face. "I left because I want you, Cassia," he said bluntly. "Despite knowing you are a lady." And that she'd wed another, and when this voyage was over, he'd be tied to the bride his father had chosen for him. "I want to make love to you." He turned his head, facing her across the room.

The moon's glow cast such an ethereal, bright light over the room, it put Cassia's face on full, vivid display. Her rosebud mouth formed a small moue of surprise, and it hit him that she had absolutely no idea how damned desirable she was or how badly he wanted her.

"I . . . would like that, too?" There was an up-tilt to her words that turned them into a question, and a strained chuckle rumbled in his chest and made its way up his throat, sticking there.

"Good night, Cassia."

There came the rustle of sheets and coverlets as she shimmied back under the bedding, and he closed his eyes once more as his mind drew forth a tempting image of her slender, muscled legs exposed and his shirt rucked high about her waist.

Which only conjured thoughts of her bare thatch, and the sprig of colors between her legs; they'd be downy soft and—

His breathing grew labored.

Cassia's whisper cut across the quiet. "Nathan?"

Do not answer . . . Do not answer . . . She'll stop . . .

Engaging her any further was dangerous.

"Are you sleeping?"

Bloody hell. She would not stop.

"Yes," he snapped, his voice tight and sharp.

"I . . ." Cassia's words emerged haltingly. "I don't believe you are. If you were, you'd not be talking. Unless you talk in your sleep—"

"You talk in your sleep," he said gruffly, not sure where that pronouncement came from.

The sheets rustled. "I do? I don't think I've ever done that before. Not that I'm privy to what I say or don't say in my sleep. But my lady's maid never said as much, and I do think—"

"Cassia," he said warningly. "What do you want?"

"Oh, yes. Forgive me. That is right. Before I left you to sweet dreams"—*sweet dreams?*—"I really would ask that you consider not keeping me a prisoner in here. I really would like to see some of the world before we return and go our separate ways, because . . ."

Go our separate ways . . .

As she chattered on with no end in sight, his mind lingered on that handful of words.

Their time together was finite.

In fact, every day that brought him closer to the upcoming confrontation with the French brought him one day closer to being done with Cassia McQuoid.

Except, where he'd expect a vast rush of relief at being freed of her mischievous ways and endless blathering, he found himself oddly . . . melancholy.

"I know you are concerned about me, and I am very touched by that concern," Cassia was saying.

Off his head. The lady was driving him absolutely insane.

Or mayhap he was already there. "Fine," he spat, anything to get her to cease her jabbering for the night so he might get some well-needed rest.

Cassia stopped midsentence and, squirming out from under the bedding, jumped up onto her knees. "Truly," she exclaimed, clasping joined fists close to her chest.

"Mr. Hayes believes it will be good for you," he said, already regretting his own capitulation on the matter. "But you need to stay out of trouble," he added, the warning not even going unfinished before she was talking over him.

"You have my solemn vow that I won't do anything. I'm generally quite accident-prone, you know—"

"Cassia . . ."

"Oh, yes. Right. Right. I'm so excited. How am I expected to sleep? I do believe I'll sketch. Not now, of course. Now, we need to sl—"

"Cassia," he said for a second time, his tone the firm one he used with his deckhands when their work was too sloppy.

"Right. Right. Or should I say, 'Aye, aye, Captain'?"

"Nothing. You say nothing." He bit each syllable through his teeth, and at last, the lady went silent.

There came the rustle of more blankets. Despite her worries to the contrary, Cassia's breath fell into a slow, even rhythm. A moment later, her soft little snores cut across the quiet.

Nathaniel lay there, staring up at the ceiling, waiting for it. Waiting. Sure enough, Cassia, the lady with a million words, found her voice in her sleep. Her slumberous musings came with every other word coherent, and some in between inaudible.

"Pomegranate . . . grapefruit . . . apples . . . grapes . . ."

And as she resumed this night's rambling discourse, the hint of a smile dragged at the corners of his mouth.

Chapter 12

Last night had been a dream.

The moment Cassia struggled to lift her heavy lashes and greet the new day, all of her prior exchange with Nathan had danced at the corners of her consciousness.

For surely a dream accounted for that powerful embrace and wondrous moment of passion between them? And his gruff decision to let her out of his chambers and onto the main deck.

Only, as she popped out of bed . . . his bed . . . and found a tray of crusty bread and a bowl of boiled lentils had been brought and thoughtfully set out, her heart tripled its rhythm.

It hadn't been a dream. Humming softly to herself, Cassia jumped up and padded across Nathan's cabin, the hardwood floors cold under her feet.

A note sat propped against a pitcher of water. Scrawled on the front was her name, done in bold, confident strokes, which could only belong to a man as powerful and no-nonsense as Nathan himself.

Her heart hammering, Cassia picked it up and unfolded the page. *Stay out of trouble.*

Cassia paused midreading and wrinkled her nose in annoyance. "What? Did you expect he'd wax some kind of poetic about you?" she muttered to herself. That he'd been captivated by her kiss? If that'd been the case, he'd have not fled his bed for a spot on the floor. Giving her head a shake, she resumed scanning the handful of terse sentences he'd penned.

Do not talk to the men while they're working. Do not go near the edge of the ship. Find a quiet spot, and just . . . sit . . .

"Well, I never," she exclaimed, her chest hot with indignation.

I've brought you water to freshen up.

Just like that, her annoyance faded away as she looked up and over to the porcelain bowl on the washstand across Nathan's chambers, and she melted inside that he should think of her.

If you have any concerns, Hayes will be there to answer your questions.

Cassia's fingers tightened on the corners of his pages.

He'd passed her off onto other members of his ship.

She tried not to let that hurt.

She tried desperately to be only grateful that he'd agreed to allow her to walk about the ship's deck, and it really shouldn't matter at all that he didn't intend to have any dealing with her.

She tried.

And failed.

Her lower lip trembled, and recalling Nathan's opinion on tears, she instantly sank her teeth into the bottom of that flesh. "You ninny. He's been abundantly clear in his opinion of you." And in his expectation for their future.

They didn't have one.

They weren't even to acknowledge one another across a ballroom when he was one day wed to some other woman and she was married to some other man, and blast it. Tears blurred her vision and made it nigh impossible to see.

Cassia blinked rapidly so that she might clear her vision and read the remainder of Nathan's note.

Postscript.

Stay. Out. Of. Trouble.

The great dunderhead.

Her tears instantly receded.

"Twice," she mumbled. Refolding the letter, she set it down. "He really felt he needed to say it *twice*?"

Well, she would show him. He'd see that he'd absolutely nothing at all to fear, and that she could be trusted with free rein to move about his ship.

A short while later, after Cassia had gone through her morning ablutions and seen to her wrapping, she exchanged his nightshirt for the clean pair of trousers and fresh shirt he'd set out. Cassia grabbed the ancient hat that had been in her family for generations, and as she headed over to where her bag rested in the corner, she jammed the cap on her head.

Dropping to her knees, she rummaged through the sack until her fingers collided with the heavy, cool leather of her sketch pad. She drew out the beloved article, along with one of the boxes of charcoals, paused, and then grabbed for the red and black chalks.

Humming to herself, Cassia popped up, headed across the room, and gripped the long brass door handle carved in the likeness of a dragon, its long teeth made for the part of that intricate piece a person was to grab.

Cassia let herself out and found Shorty there, on alert as he'd been all prior days since Nathan had sent her below deck. "Good morning, Mr. Shorty," she said with a cheerful wave.

He grunted. "Miss." That greeting emerged gruff and brusque, spoken in the tones of thick Cockneys that wrapped the meaning of his words in a haze of confusion she had to sort through.

"Oh, you may call me Cassia," she offered, and then with her spare hand, Cassia patted the top of his enormous, weathered, suntanned hand. "And you needn't worry about hanging me overboard. I know you did not know that I was a woman. Though in fairness," she felt compelled to add, "you really shouldn't go about hanging *anyone* over the side of a ship. Not that you aren't perfectly strong and capable of hanging two grown men in each hand overboard," she hurried to assure him. "Just that it's in bad form to do so, and I trust you would feel terribly if you accidentally lost your hold and dropped a person to the ocean."

The big, bald-headed man with a red kerchief wrapped about his neck opened and closed his mouth like a giant trout who'd landed itself ashore. "Ye talk a lot," he blurted.

"Your captain said as much, too," Cassia muttered, and then brightening, she smiled. "Though I suspect it's really just more that you're all too busy working to note what is, in fact, a very normal discourse." Cassia gave a jaunty wave. *"À tout à l'heure."* She hurried down the narrow corridors and made it nearly three paces before registering the shadowy presence close at her heels.

She stopped so abruptly, Mr. Shorty nearly came crashing into her. He caught himself just before that collision. "Are you *following* me, Mr. Shorty?"

"Guarding you. The captain asked me to watch you."

Annoyance stirred. Nathan had assigned her a governess or nursemaid, like she was a child. It was precisely how everyone had treated her. Her parents, unwilling to send her away to school. Her brothers, endlessly lamenting her tendency to land herself in various scrapes.

Only, on the heels of that came a softening inside.

Nathan was *worried* about her.

And it was better to focus on that than the fact that he didn't trust her to not land herself in mischief. Well, she'd show him he had absolutely nothing to worry about where she was concerned. She was *entirely* capable.

Cassia resumed her walk, stretching her arms out slightly to steady herself as the boat pitched and rolled under her feet.

Only, unlike the violent upheaval it had wrought in her stomach those first days of her sailing, this time her belly churned only slightly.

Grabbing the railing, Cassia made the climb above deck. With every step that brought her closer, the morning sun grew increasingly bright, and she squinted until she reached the deck, emerging to an onslaught of blinding brightness. Instantly tearing up, she kept her eyes narrowed and lifted her sketch pad and pencil above her brow, using it as a shield.

Shut away these past days with her only exposure to light being that which had streamed through the row of windows in Nathan's cabin, Cassia had to blink several times, accustoming herself to it.

She carefully lowered her book and then opened her eyes, testing her vision, and then all the air exploded from her lips on an awestruck exhalation.

Cassia remained rooted to the deck, her gaze locked on the vast, cloudless sky, a shade of azure the likes of which she'd never known, even on the longest summer day at her family's country seat in Scotland, far away from London.

"It is beautiful," she whispered.

"Aye, a sight, isn't it," Shorty said behind her with all the pride of a new papa looking upon his babe for the first time.

And a sight it was.

Beckoned by the majesty of that endless scape of vibrant blue, Cassia wandered over, making her way to the railing.

"Good day, miss!"

She jumped at that boisterous greeting and looked toward the owner of that deep baritone, a shade less deep than Nathan's and also a good deal friendlier.

The navigator, Lieutenant Albion.

"Lieutenant Albion," she greeted as he approached. Cassia dropped a curtsy, but he waved off that deferential dip. "It is so very good to see you again."

"No need for formalities," he called in a jovial voice.

He smiled where Nathan scowled. He was as polite with discourse as Nathan was blunt.

And certainly, with his close crop of wind-tousled chestnut curls, his perfectly chiseled features, and aquiline nose, he was a good deal more classically handsome than Nathan with his slightly squarer, broader features. And yet, oddly, she found herself preferring Nathan's gruff, bluntly direct, harsher handsomeness.

The navigator reached her, and she smiled up at him.

"The captain asked I show you to a spot he's designated for you." He held an elbow out, and she slipped her spare fingers atop his sleeve, allowing him to lead her onward.

As they walked, Shorty followed at a discreet distance behind them.

"You are feeling better?" he asked.

"I am much improved. Na—the captain was ever so attentive and helpful," she said.

The navigator slid her a curious glance. "Was he?"

Cassia frowned. Did the other man not believe Nathan capable of possessing those qualities?

"Oh, yes. I promise you, he is quite competent as a nursemaid. He is ever so skilled on the methods he learned abroad, and he supplied me with teas that helped tremendously, and he was very considerate of my circumstances." Unbidden, a memory slipped in of his tender touch upon her wrist and then . . . the more recent kiss that had followed. And he'd kissed her in places she'd not known a man kissed a woman. Her breath hitched and—

"You don't say," Albion marveled, snapping Cassia to the present.

Her cheeks burnt hot, and from the corner of her eye, she caught the navigator's full-fledged grin.

At that continued naysaying where Nathan was concerned, Cassia frowned. "I *do* say," she confirmed. "*In fact*, I just did."

The moment they reached a place near the front of the ship, Lieutenant Albion guided them to a stop. "The captain arranged this place for you."

Cassia followed the navigator's gesture to several crates that had been set out and positioned as makeshift seating, with a checkered blanket carefully folded over those articles and tucked under the bottoms to keep the wind from pulling that covering away.

Touched once more by that consideration, she felt her heart go soft all over again. He'd done this . . . for her. Nathan was touchy as a surly bear she'd found particularly fascinating in the queen's menagerie. But time and time again, he'd proven himself endearingly considerate from the way he cared for Cassia when she'd been seasick. Or the drinks he'd brought her, and now . . . *this*.

Cassia stole a discreet look about, searching for . . . and then finding him.

Her gaze collided with him. In full control, he gripped the ship's wheel, speaking in clear, distinctive, and commanding tones to a sailor whom she did not recall having met in her brief time working as a deckhand.

Cassia's pulse fluttered.

Someday, when she was old and her auburn hair had faded to white and her face was aged by life and time, she'd forever recall Nathan as he was now.

She drank in the sight of him.

Those unfashionably long, golden strands drawn into a tight queue at his nape, with several locks having pulled free. His broad back and shoulders proudly straight, each muscle clearly defined against that crisp white lawn garment. The black fabric of his trousers hugging thighs bigger than any of the many tree trunks she'd ever scaled in the course of her life.

He was nothing short of male perfection.

Muscled, where the men in London were soft.

Bold and powerful, where every last lord was deferential and polite to the point of dullness.

And she wanted to know absolutely everything there was to know about him.

Feeling Lieutenant Albion's stare as she studied Nathan, it still took a concerted effort to pull her gaze from his person. "What kind of business does the captain do?" Whenever she asked him that question, he'd proven . . . evasive, turning a question on Cassia, instead, about herself.

Behind her, she caught a slightly strangled sound from Mr. Shorty, and the quelling look his superior, Lieutenant Albion, gave him. "The captain deals in various goods of value to the British kingdom and its people."

A frown teased the corners of her lips. That was . . . vague.

When it appeared that was all the navigator intended to say, she prodded him. "What *kind* of goods?"

Lieutenant Albion's expression grew shuttered. "The crew does not speak about the specifics of the captain's business. If you have further questions beyond that, then you should put them to him." From anyone else, that advisement would have been taken as a sharp rebuke. Albion, however, spoke in a gentling way that did little to dissuade.

"Have you sailed with him long?" she asked, desperate to know so much more about Nathan.

"Since his first day in the navy," the other man answered automatically. "We served alongside one another. We, the captain, me, and Hayes," he clarified, "were all second-born sons who'd been forgotten by our fathers. Eventually the captain had the idea to establish his own line and did so with the help of his uncle, who'd his own shipping business."

Despite her best attempts, Cassia found her eyes creeping back over to Nathan. How many men born to the peerage would ever do something so enterprising? When most second-born sons entered the clergy or lived a comfortable, privileged life, Nathan had joined the navy and then created a business of his own. This, when men in the peerage were dissuaded from doing anything considered menial. And her awe and appreciation redoubled.

She caught the look Lieutenant Albion cast over the top of her head and followed his stare.

Nathan had a dark glower fixed on his navigator. He shifted that disapproving glance briefly over to Cassia, and then swung it back to the navigator once more.

"Oh, you needn't worry," she assured him. "His bluster is far worse than his bite."

The big, chestnut-haired fellow with suntanned skin chuckled. "Never let the captain hear you say that, Miss MacKay."

Miss MacKay?

She puzzled her brow. And then it hit her. They wished to conceal that she was, in fact, a McQuoid.

As it is, your chances of your reputation surviving this mishap are slim indeed.

And yet, strangely, at this moment, with the warmth of the sun kissing her face and the light breeze a balm upon her skin, she could not bring herself to muster sufficient regret.

Cassia leaned up and in and whispered, "It cannot be MacKay. The MacKays are engaged in an ancient feud with my family. I can be anything but Ma—"

The gentleman brought his hands flying up. "*Ohhhh,* the captain said it is," he interrupted on a rush, and Cassia stopped herself. "If you have problems with it, you will have to take it up with him."

As one, Cassia and the navigator looked toward the gentleman in question.

Chapter 13

What the hell was Albion speaking with Cassia about?

What had the other man said that had been responsible for her damned smile and then laughter? And worse, what had he said to cause her to frown so, and for sadness to enter her eyes?

Nathaniel wasn't sure which sent fury rippling through him more.

Even so, he made himself wrench his focus back from the pair, who'd returned to smiling at one another, looking at each other, and speaking with their heads angled close, like they were the only two souls in the world.

Nathaniel set his jaw.

It was fine.

As long as Albion was entertaining Cassia, the lady was occupied, and she was out of trouble and out of Nathaniel's hair.

Why did that realization not bring with it the rush of relief it should?

Because his navigator had responsibilities on this ship, ones that decidedly did not include playing nursemaid to Cassia McQuoid. Nay, that task had fallen to big, intimidating-to-all Shorty.

That was the *only* reason he cared.

Nathaniel stole a glance at the bald-headed crew member he'd fetched from the gallows years earlier, who'd been only loyal to Nathaniel for that rescue.

The damned fellow wore the same silly grin as Albion did and Hayes *had*, looking just as gratingly besotted.

Shorty? Besotted?

What in hell power did the minx possess?

You know . . . It's why you struggle to sleep long after Cassia drifts into her noisy, sleep-talking slumber, and why, against all reason and better judgment, you find yourself wearing that same damned grin when she is rambling on about . . . whatever matter she chooses to ramble on about at that particular moment.

A gust of wind tore across the ocean, and he welcomed the calming feel of it against his flushed skin.

"And I said . . . why . . . it is only . . ."

Those gusts of wind carried every other word Cassia now gaily spoke over to Nathaniel.

Boisterous laughter went up from her captivated audience of two.

He gritted his teeth. *Bloody hell.*

That was more than enough.

"Albion," he bellowed, and the laughter down deck immediately died, and Cassia went silent, and damned if didn't make Nathaniel feel somehow *worse*.

A moment later the navigator appeared beside him, issuing a respectful salute. "Capt—"

"What the hell do you think you're doing?" Nathaniel snapped, interrupting that deferential greeting.

Lieutenant Albion puzzled his brow. "I . . ." He shook his head.

"You have a job on this ship."

Anyone else would have quaked, and certainly wouldn't have challenged Nathaniel on the point. "You advised me to escort the lady, and to show her to where—"

"Yes, I did. I didn't ask you to join her for goddamned tea and biscuits."

"The lady doesn't eat biscuits. That is, unless they're dipped in chocolate or marshmallow cream."

He stared incredulously back at the other man. "You obtained all that in the time you were with the lady?"

"I offered her . . ." Color heightened in the other man's cheeks, and Nathaniel strained to hear the remainder of Albion's mumblings.

"What was that?" Nathaniel asked, cupping a hand around his ear. "It sounded as though you said . . ."

"I offered her refreshments."

It'd been the considerate thing to do. The gentlemanly one. And Nathaniel should be grateful the other man had seen to it when Nathaniel himself had not. Lord knew he certainly didn't have the time or inclination to be bothered watching after the sea sprite who'd invaded his ship.

Only, that relief didn't come. Only more of this red-hot annoyance consumed him, knowing Albion should be spending time alone with Cassia.

You are losing your damned mind.

"You should have your head about you. We've a mission to complete," he reminded his navigator.

The other man held his gaze. "That mission is still happening, then?"

First Hayes and now him. Nathaniel bristled. "Why wouldn't it?" By his calculations, they were less than two days away from catching the French ship and overtaking the war plans they were transporting.

Albion looked pointedly toward Cassia, who watched them both intently. Cassia, who was innocent and garrulous, and who'd be thrust into the middle of a battle.

His gut clenched.

Nathaniel wrenched his gaze from hers. "It is happening," he gritted out. He'd never abandoned a mission, and he didn't intend to start now because—

"The lady will be in danger."

Thoughts slipped in. Of a smoky, fiery sea battle. Of ruthless French sailors boarding the *Flying Dragon* and dragging Cassia from below deck.

Despite the warmth of the full sun overhead, cold sweat broke out on his brow and slicked his palms. "Nothing is going to happen to her, because nothing is going to happen to the ship."

"But it . . . could," Albion said quietly.

Nathaniel gnashed his teeth. Both his quartermaster and his navigator thought of her well-being before their mission. What was it about Cassia McQuoid that made a man lose his mind?

"Is there a problem, Nathan?"

Nathaniel whipped his gaze over to Cassia, who was making a march toward him and Albion.

He narrowed his eyes and welcomed the diversion from a discussion he'd not wanted to have with either his quartermaster *or* navigator. As Nathaniel saw it, there were any *number* of problems. All of which led back to her. The latest of which now included the minx who'd quit her previous place on the ship and joined him and Albion—Albion, whom she'd been smiling and laughing with. And who'd also had several of his crew thinking about quitting the mission over.

Cassia reached him and, dropping her hands on her hips, stared up at him with an impressively governess-like, stern stare. This, when she'd been all smiles and blushes for the navigator.

"Well?" she dared.

He firmed his jaw. "I assure you my navigator certainly does not require defense from you."

"Were you *yelling* at him?"

"I do not yell." Nathaniel didn't need to rely on those outbursts, though in fairness, this minx challenged every last bit of restraint he'd prided himself on carrying. "To your station, Albion," Nathaniel instructed through his clenched teeth, which, with this much gritting, he was destined to chip or lose on this latest voyage. Taking Cassia gently but also firmly by the arm, Nathaniel proceeded to guide her back to the spot he'd designated as hers.

"Why are you scowling at Lieutenant Albion?" she demanded as they went.

"I assure you, it is not your business."

Halfway across the deck, and only halfway closer to depositing her in that spot on her own, Cassia dug her feet in so that Nathaniel was forced to either stop or continue on and drag her.

Bloody hell.

Nathaniel stopped. "What?"

"Was it because of me?" she asked doggedly, wholly unperturbed by his attempt to put a nail in the coffin of this conversation he decidedly did not wish to have.

"It is because he has other duties on this ship, and entertaining you is not one of them." Nathaniel again reached for her arm, but she drew the slender limb back.

The lady danced away from him. "He was *being* polite."

Nathaniel kept his features blank. "Well, given that, on future sailings, I'll strip him of his responsibilities as navigator and put him in charge of the important task of schooling the crew on manners and decorum."

Her brow scrunched up endearingly. "Surely that isn't a role on a *ship*?" Her eyes lit. "But if it *is*—"

"No, Cassia." He briefly closed his eyes. "It is not."

She pursed her lips. "You're being sarcastic again?"

"I'm being sarcastic again."

"What is it with men and sarcasm?" she muttered to herself. "You. My brothers. My brother-in-law. Jeremy." Jeremy, the soft, dough-faced *boat* owner she'd put him in a column with. My God, Nathaniel's fall had been fast and ignoble. "Do you know how much time is wasted in discourse, simply having to sort out what a man truly means—"

"Cassia, I don't doubt for a damned moment if I told you what I truly meant, it wouldn't lead you in the same circles you manage to bring us whenever you talk."

She inclined her head and smiled at him. "Why, thank you."

And damned if that sunny smile on her full red lips didn't leave him with a greater warmth than the bright morning sun beating down on them.

"Furthermore, I have a bone to pick with you." Cassia's expression instantly turned glowering.

"This I have to—"

"I am a *McQuoid*," she whispered.

"Yes, I believe we've ascertained as—"

"As such, I cannot be a *MacKay*."

The spitfire would challenge him . . . even in this? He closed his eyes and summoned a familiar sea ditty.

> "In Amsterdam there lived a maid,
> Mark well what I do say,
> In Amsterdam there lived a maid,
> And she was mistress of her—"

"Nathan." She tugged at his sleeve. "Are you singing again? That is really a rude . . ." Her eyes went all soft. "Though also an endearingly adorable habit, I confess."

His mind came to a screeching halt mid-verse.

Endearingly adorable?

His eyes flew open, and he schooled his features into a harsh mask meant to dissuade her from further nonsense and disabuse her of the notion that she had any say over setting the terms for her being above deck. "For the purpose of this trip, you are, in fact, a MacKay."

Alas, he should have known better than to think he had a shot at schooling her.

"The MacKays are notorious thieves who've been raiding from the McQuoids as long as our families have inhabited the Highlands. First, they stole the bride of Laird Lachlan of the McQuoids, then continued to pillage. Their cattle. Their tartans. Even their hay."

"Not their hay?" He kept a completely straight face . . . that also went *completely* undetected by her untried ears.

She gave her head an equally solemn nod. "Even their hay. As I said, I can't be a MacKay," she insisted. "Surely you see that now?"

"Well, not because of the bride-stealing or cattle-raiding, but the hay? The hay absolutely did it for me."

Cassia opened her mouth, then frowned. "Sarcasm?"

He touched the brim of an imagined hat. "Indeed."

She doffed her hat and used it to shield her eyes.

With a curse, he grabbed for the article to cover up that auburn braid of a thousand shades of red, but she held it out of his reach. "Cassia, you need to cover your—"

"Well, I'll have you know"—her frown deepened as she masterfully interrupted and ignored him—"it wasn't *just* the cattle. They also snatched the McQuoid clan's pigs and—"

"*Ehhhh.*" Nathaniel raised his voice over hers, instantly clamping his hands over his ears.

Bloody hell.

Cassia stamped her foot. "What now?"

"You have to cover your hair."

She drew back. "With a hat? Whyever would I do—"

"Because red hair is bad luck."

Cassia scoffed. "That is nonsense." She gave the locks in question a toss. "Furthermore, the shade is more *auburn* than red."

"It's the same thing," he muttered. Tugging free her cap, he placed it gently but firmly atop her head. "And don't mention that word on a ship," he said tightly.

"Which one? 'Hair' or 'hat'?"

"Cassia," he warned.

The lady eyed him with suspicious eyes. "You're funning me."

"I assure you, I'm not." He kept his features deadly serious. "I don't *fun* anybody."

"That I can believe," she mumbled under her breath.

He cupped a hand around his ear. "What was that?"

She threw her arms up, an exasperated little sputter escaping her tempting rosebud mouth. "You are infuriating, Nathaniel . . ." She paused. "I don't know your *entire* name."

"And that matters?"

The lady nodded, sending the too-big-for-her-head cap slipping over her brow. "Well, you know mine is Cassia Cora McQuoid, and furthermore, if one wishes to provide a proper rebuke, one most certainly requires a person's *entire* name."

"You want to know my full name so you can dress me down?"

She gave another exuberant bob of her head.

"I'm going to have to decline," he said.

Bright crimson splotches flared in her cheeks, and her enormous eyes went several degrees bigger. "You are *insufferable*, Nathaniel *MacKay*!"

He opened his mouth and closed it. He tried again. "*MacKay?* You know my surname."

"Yes, well, if you're going to saddle *me* with the name MacKay, then you shall wear that horrible one, *too*," she vowed.

Saints on Sunday, she'd managed to circle them all the way back to their latest—earlier—argument.

Do not engage her. Do not engage her. He fell back on more lyrics.

> "I'll go no more a-roving with you, fair maid,
> A-roving, a-roving, since roving's been my ruin,
> I'll go no more a-roving with you, fair maid."

"If you're a MacKay and I'm a MacKay," he said, after he'd calmed his mind, "it would mean we were relations, and we are decidedly not related." Because men didn't kiss family members the way Nathaniel had, and desperately, against all better judgment, still wished to kiss the infuriatingly tempting woman before him.

"Well, then." Cassia looked at him with a stricken gaze, and the pain in her eyes hit him square in the stomach.

What in hell had he said *this* time?

Cassia drew into herself. "I will leave you to your very important responsibilities, then, Nathaniel, and see to entertaining myself. I'd ask you to go kindly on Lieutenant Albion. He was just being nice." With that, Cassia turned and stormed off.

Mayhap it was the briskness of that movement, coupled with the sharp gust of wind that ripped across the deck, but the lady's cap went flying.

Nathaniel made a frantic dive at the same moment Cassia did—colliding with the lady's smaller, slender frame, and he shot his hands out reflexively, catching her just as they went crashing to the floor of the ship. In one swift motion, he rolled, reversing their positions so he took the brunt of the fall.

Only, he didn't feel any of it.

Her.

He felt only her.

Her soft, supple frame perfectly molded to his body.

She was a mermaid. A sea nymph. A siren. A veritable Amphitrite.

And every last thought fled as desire raged through him.

"Nathan," she whispered, her voice breathless. "You are quite crushing me." Laying her palms on his chest, she gave him a slight shove, also managing to push back the desirous musings he had no place having, and certainly not *here* of all places.

Silently cursing, he jumped up, and even as he helped her back on her feet, Nathaniel frantically searched the deck for that article.

Alas . . .

Near a half dozen of his crew formed a line near him, their eyes concentrated over the side of the ship. His stomach sinking, Nathaniel followed those stares to the distant scrap of black bobbing in the water.

Cassia moved past him and gripped the rail, leaning over. "My cap," she bemoaned. "I loved that article. It was my lucky"—Nathaniel instantly slapped a palm over her mouth, muffling the remainder of that pronouncement—"hapf." She still managed to squeeze a close iteration out.

Catching her by the arm once again, Nathaniel proceeded to tug her along, pausing only long enough to grab the art supplies she'd come with before guiding her down the deck. "Here." He stuffed the pad into her spare hand and held her charcoal in his.

"Will you slow down?"

No, he absolutely would not.

He could not.

He felt her annoyance. It was as real and as palpable as the joy she so often wore.

He didn't stop until they reached the station he'd set up for her.

Nathaniel pointed to the makeshift seating. "Sit."

"Sit," she mumbled. "I'm not a dog, you know. And you needn't be so annoyed at my losing my cap. Why, imagine how I feel. That cap has been in my family for some time. It belonged to a stable master from the MacKay clan, who absconded with it and came to join my family because he'd fallen in love with—"

"It's bad luck."

"Falling in love with a McQuoid?" she scoffed. "I assure you, it's not."

He briefly closed his eyes. "Losing a hat over the side of a ship. It signifies that the voyage will be a long one."

"And that is a bad thing?"

"It is when . . ." He immediately closed his mouth.

Cassia cocked her head. "When?" she prodded, urging him to finish his thought.

The last thing he could afford, however, was to reveal the precise manner of shipping venture he ran. The day they closed in on the French vessel, the *Renard*, he'd see her below deck and . . .

And do you really think she isn't going to have more questions for you?

"Nathan?" she urged a second time, her perfectly formed, reddish eyebrows coming together.

"It is a bad thing when one is overseeing business." There. He'd keep it as vague as possible for—

"What kind of shipping venture *do* you run?"

Christ. His was a prayer. "A lucrative one."

She wrinkled her nose. "Well, that is vague. First Lieutenant Albion, and now you."

"If you want to remain above deck, then I suggest you sit, now." Nathaniel jammed a finger to the spot he'd had the quartermaster set for her. "And just . . . stay away from the side of the ship, and don't . . . do anything else that's going to cause trouble."

"Do you truly think I wanted to lose my lucky cap?" The tenacious minx slipped her hands onto her hips and scowled. "Because I assure you, I didn't. I could have asked you to try to return for it. But I did not."

"Casssia," he said warningly, squeezing an extra syllable into her name.

"Fine. I'm sitting, I'm sitting." And with an impressive toss of her head, her braid whipping him on the arm, she sailed onto the seat the way a queen might take a place at her throne.

She looked up, the sun bathing her face in a soft glow, the sight of her briefly stealing the breath from his lungs and the thoughts from his head.

"Are you going to join me?" she asked, her voice hopeful.

And through the dazed state she'd put him in, it hit Nathaniel: she actually wanted him about . . . It was unfathomable and unfamiliar. Most feared him, and certainly the ladies in London dropped their gazes when he passed. And oddly, Nathaniel found his chest rather light at her response. It made him wish he might stay. Which was, of course, utter madness. "I am on duty," he said, and the way her entire expressive face fell, damned if he didn't wish he could call back that admission.

He shot a hand up, and Shorty immediately moved over into position beside Cassia.

"Do not let her out of your sight," Nathaniel instructed the other man.

"Aye, Captain."

And before he did something utterly ridiculous, like surrender his duties for the day and remain with her, Nathaniel turned on his heel to go—

When she started to whistle.

He stopped midstride and closed his eyes.

Bloody hell.

Nathaniel turned, and instantly shifted course.

Cassia had already turned her attentions on her sketch pad. All the while, she whistled a cheerful tune he couldn't name.

With a growl, he stomped over the remaining way. "What the hell do you think you're doing?" he asked, his tone surlier than he intended, but the one he adopted with all.

Cassia glanced back up. "Nathan!" she exclaimed as if they'd only just met after a long time apart. "You've b—*eep*!" Her voice dissolved into a high-pitched squeak as he plucked her up and set her on her feet. "What are you doing?" she demanded, jumping out of his reach when he attempted to take her by the arm.

"Whistling, ye be," Shorty said behind her, and she cast a confused glance back at the big guard assigned her.

"And there is something wrong with my whistling?"

And hell if she didn't sound a wrong word away from crying.

Shorty widened his eyes. "No. Perfectly lovely, it is," he said in a rush, and she smiled as if he'd grabbed her a star from the sky.

The toughest member of Nathaniel's crew went all soft, his eyes stupidly dazed.

She'd even charmed the terror-inducing-to-all Shorty. This was enough.

Growling, Nathaniel took her gently but firmly by the arm. "Let's go." He steered her the length of the way, this time not stopping until he reached his cabin. When he reached the door, he pressed the handle, and motioned her to enter.

Cassia dug her heels in, remaining rooted to her spot. "What are you doing?"

"I think it should be clear. We tried. We'll try again tomorrow. You are done above deck." As it was, more of his men had gathered the moment they'd heard her break out whistling.

"Yes," she said calmly. "I'd like to know—"

"Because you were whistling."

She stared back. *"Annnd?"*

"And sailors believe whistling aboard will bring bad weather. That it challenges the wind and causes it to increase, which will usher in a storm."

Cassia snorted. "You sailing men and your hair colors and words, and surely you don't believe *that*."

Nathaniel wasn't sure what he believed or didn't believe. What he did know, however, was that the men who comprised his crew feared whistling and feared her.

He felt the stare Cassia moved over his face. "You do believe it," she remarked with all the wonder in her voice as the first sailor who'd discovered the earth was not, in fact, flat. "You are superstitious, Nathan?"

His neck went hot. "I believe sailors by nature are a superstitious lot, and as we are now, I've got you, a female, on board"—he shot a finger up—"which is one sign of bad luck. I've got you, a redhead—"

"I've already said, my hair is more auburn."

"Losing a hat over the side of the ship." He added a third digit, and then promptly a fourth finger. "And you lost it on a Friday." When she opened her mouth, he intercepted her next line of questioning. "When Friday is a notoriously unlucky day of the week."

"Are you telling me sailors *never* sail on Fridays?" she drawled. "Why, that must make it rather difficult to travel."

Alas, the minx had perfected irony, then. Ignoring her droll response, he lifted his palm and waved it about. "That's plenty of omens to scare the crew, and the last thing I can afford is to have them . . ." Seeing her as a threat to be disposed of. These were not all men he ordinarily traveled with. As such, they were unpredictable, and he could not ensure they'd not attempt to harm Cassia.

He went cold inside.

Cassia batted crimson lashes that went on forever. "Yes?"

She'd absolutely no idea the peril she might face, and that in itself ravaged his mind and soul. "Distracted," he settled for. "I can't have them *distracted* any more than you've already distracted them. My crew is a well-oiled machine," he said. "Some of them are old sailors who've been with me, and others are new." Men he didn't yet know how well he could trust. "One thing they all have in common is that they are very superstitious. This mission is very important; I don't want to do anything to rock the boat."

Cassia hugged herself and the art supplies in her hands close to her chest in a sad little embrace. "You are locking me away again?" she whispered, her voice so aching and full of so much hurt and regret he'd have rather plucked a sword from his wall and run himself through if it would stop her pain.

Nathaniel recoiled. He'd never felt that way . . . about anyone. What in hell sorcery had Cassia woven that accounted for . . . *this*?

He forced himself to draw in a slow, even breath. "For today, Cassia," he said quietly. "Tomorrow, you can . . . try again."

Her face brightened, and she threw herself at him with such a suddenness that even her slight, slender frame nearly knocked him over.

He braced his feet and caught her to him.

"Thank you," she exclaimed, breathless. "I promise you will not regret it."

And yet, as he reluctantly set her from him and quit his cabin, he already found himself doing just that.

Chapter 14

The following morning, Cassia made her way starboard, greeted by an almost eerie quiet and calm.

There was that, too.

And also, silence.

The usual jovial laughter that rang out around the deck had at some point faded.

Something was . . . *different.*

The sky was still its usual vibrant azure, dotted with a handful of clouds as if the Lord had put them there to break up the perfection of that otherwise flawless horizon.

And then, she felt it.

Or rather . . . she didn't feel it. That was, anything. She didn't feel *anything.* Tucking her sketch pad under her arm, with Shorty following closely behind, she paused and did a sweep of the deck.

"We're not moving, Shorty," she remarked, and did a search for the nearby wharf they'd surely arrived at.

"No, miss. Indeed, we aren't."

Hearing something foreboding in his always deep voice, she glanced back. "Why have we stopped?"

The big man assigned to guard her twisted his cap back and forth in his large hands. "Can't say," he croaked.

What in blazes?

With a frown, Cassia glanced about.

Searching.

Looking.

And then finding . . . *him*.

All the air slipped from her lungs at the sheer sight of Nathan, muscular and masculine, and in full control.

He stood, with his arms on his narrow hips, assessing the seas below, all the while firing off words that sent the crew assembled around him nodding and scurrying off.

When the last of that small contingent of men had hastened on to whatever duties he'd called out, Nathan's body tensed. It was as if he'd felt her watching, for he turned slowly.

Cassia shot her spare hand up and waved it at him.

Even with the length of the deck separating them, she caught something move in his eyes; something in the heated intensity with which he looked at her unleashed a swarm of a thousand butterflies within her chest, and those creatures danced within.

And then he was moving toward her, striding with long, purposeful strides that easily ate away the distance between them, and with every step that brought him closer, a breathless anticipation built. "Natha—"

"You have to go below deck," he said flatly, cutting her off.

And just like that, all those butterflies within stopped their flight and plummeted. "'Good morning,' Nathan, is the proper greeting," she gently chastised. "To which I'll say, 'It is a very good morning, indeed. The boat has stopped swaying, and I don't even feel a hint of seasickness.'"

"Because the ship has stopped moving."

"Yes, I just said that," she said, exasperated.

"The men believe it's because you were whistling," he said tightly.

She laughed.

She couldn't help it.

Nor did she attempt to try.

"You're jesting," she said between her mirth.

Alas, Nathan's face remained a mask of somber seriousness.

She threw her arms up. "I'll never understand you sailors. You said whistling increased the winds. Not that it stopped them."

"Bad luck, it be," Shorty whispered, interjecting on his captain's behalf.

Nathan nodded and pointed at the other man. "Take her back below."

"Nathan," she entreated, sidling away from Shorty and closer to Nathan. "I'll stay out of trouble."

"I don't think you could help yourself from finding it with a direct appeal to God himself for assistance with the task," he muttered.

"Well, that is rude." Cassia rested a palm on his chest, and tipping her head back so she could meet his gaze, she held those most mesmerizing of blue eyes. "Please."

Unblinking, he shifted his eyes over her face, then unleashed an inventive curse she took care to note for future use.

"Fine," he snapped, and she clapped her hands excitedly, albeit awkwardly with the burden she held in her arms. Dismissing her outright, he looked to Shorty once more. "See that she stays out of trouble."

"I resent that, Nathan," Cassia said, setting her jaw. "I'm quite—"

"Will do, Captain." Shorty's avowal drowned out the remainder of her words.

Oh, blast and damn men. They are insufferable, the lot of them.

Someone down deck called out for Nathan, and he glanced off in that direction before returning his focus briefly back to Cassia. "Just—"

"I know. I know. Stay out of trouble," she exclaimed, and it was as though she were forgotten a moment later as Nathan stalked off with those long, powerful strides. And she was helpless to do anything but stare after him, watching him in all his might, leading the men around him.

Never, in all her Seasons or any of the times before them, had she witnessed a more virile, compelling figure than Nathan Ellsby. And as he stalked the length of the lines, calling out orders as he went, and as those lesser men around him rushed to do his bidding, she knew she never would meet another like him as long as she lived, and that certainty left her bereft.

"Miss?" Shorty's hesitant query pulled her back, and she forced herself to resume walking to the spot that Nathan had designated as hers. After she'd seated herself and set out her pencils, Cassia flipped through her sketchbook until she landed on the incomplete rendering of Nathan.

"It's a good likeness of the captain."

She glanced up to find Shorty's stare on her work.

It was also the first time in the days she'd been assigned him that he'd specifically addressed her. Usually, conversation with the big sailor had come reluctantly, and always from discussions she'd dragged him into. "Do you think?"

"Aye. Mayhap ye can draw one o' me?" Color flared on his cheeks. "Never 'ad me likeness done."

And touched by that humble request, she offered Shorty a gentle smile and waved four fingers on her left hand. "As you were," she instructed. "Just . . . pretend I am not sketching you."

"Kinda 'ard not to when yer looking roight at me, drawing me."

"Fair enough," she allowed. "I always felt that way, too, when I was having my portrait done." It was why all the framed family portraits including Cassia revealed a girl and then young woman with eyes like a deer that had been trapped. The portraitists had always been too snobbish or too engrossed to engage her, ultimately shushing her to silence as they worked.

And then she began to sketch. "How long have you known the captain?" she asked, her questioning aimed at relaxing the sailor, somewhat self-serving.

"Since 'e began sailing his own ship. Sprung me from the gallows, he did."

Her fingers wavered, and she glanced briefly up before returning her attention to her efforts. "What . . . ?"

"What crime did Oi commit? Stole some apples from a London vendor."

Hunger had driven him to it. "And you were nearly hanged for it?" she whispered, horrified at the world which would imprison a man and end his life for the crime of simply being hungry. Cassia made herself resume her strokes on the page.

"Aye. The captain interrupted it himself, he did." Old, rheumy eyes lit with admiration and wonder. "Marched through the crowd and exchanged some words with the gaoler."

She paused briefly again. "What did he say?"

"Said as a son of Duke of Roxburghe, and godson to the king, he demanded to know the crimes of the six men present."

"What were they?"

"Thefts of purses, goods. One man killed his wife." He added that last part more like a casual afterthought.

"And then?" she asked, completely engrossed in his telling, and this time, she had to force her fingers to continue the task.

"And then, he had our sentences commuted. That is, aside from the fellow who killed his wife. The rest of us he set free, and himself saved us from swinging. When it was done, he offered us the opportunity to have a new life aboard the *Flying Dragon*."

He'd offered them the opportunity. As in, he'd not expected they return a favor for commuting their sentences and sparing their lives.

"How many of you decided to join him?"

"Every single one: Lorde, Winters, Waxhaw, MacGregor, and meself."

All five whose names she recalled and were crew members she'd met at various points.

203

"Each of them is loyal to the captain. Would give our lives for him, we would."

As Cassia worked in silence, she considered all Shorty had shared.

She could certainly see why he and the others had proven faithful to their captain. It wasn't just the case of a title commanding respect, but rather the man himself. In a world where people who did for others expected something—anything—in return, Nathan had given Shorty and those other men a new lease of life.

Reaching for the blue, she proceeded to color in that crisp, blue sky that she knew she would see in her dreams long after she disembarked from the *Flying Dragon*, found herself ensconced safely in her home, and returned to her tedious life.

Cassia finished her rendering and studied the likeness a moment before looking up.

"Finished, are ye?"

She nodded. "Would you like to see it?"

The big man nodded, his bald head bobbing enthusiastically, putting her in mind of Horace, her sister's enormous wolfdog.

Cassia set her pastels aside and then turned the book around for Shorty's inspection.

His face remained a perfectly frozen, completely undecipherable mask.

And then he touched a hand to his barrel-size chest. "Never thought to see me in a painting before."

Cassia angled her head around the page, and studying it with him, she chewed at her lower lip. "I do believe I've captured parts of your likeness well." She continued to worry her lip. "Though I suspect I might have—"

"It's perfect, it is."

She beamed. "Do you think so?"

"I know so."

Cassia carefully tore the page out along the seam and handed it over. "Then it is yours."

"Mine," he whispered, his always deep voice made all the deeper for the emotion in it.

"Well, well, well. Look wot we've 'ere. Yer playing nursemaid to the damned witch."

She and Shorty looked up as a small gathering of the crew formed a half circle around them. Carlisle, the deckhand Oliver, and Turner, each of a varying height, thickness, and age. They looked back, their equally hard stares locked on Cassia.

She shivered, and despite herself hunched back in her makeshift seat. "Gentlemen," she greeted, forcing that word out in a chipper voice she certainly did not feel.

Shorty frowned. "Get on with ye now. Yer new to the crew, but ye already know the captain doesn't take to his men bullying anyone, especially not a lady. So just leave the lass alone." And then, balling a meaty fist, the old sailor beat it against his opposite, open palm.

Carlisle locked his gaze in a silent battle with Shorty. "Don't think we will."

To give her trembling fingers a task, Cassia closed the pad and set it down behind her.

She hopped to her feet. "Is there something I might help you with?"

Carlisle glared at her. "Ye and yer fancy talk and fancy ways. Ye've been nothing but trouble since ye stepped on this ship."

The way she saw it, in her excelling at her chores when she'd been disguised as a deckhand, he'd been the one responsible for all the problems. Cassia, however, knew better than to say as much.

"What do you want, Mr. Carlisle?" she said calmly, in coolly composed tones she did not feel.

He narrowed his eyes. "For ye to leave."

"I intend to," she promised, using a cadence of speech that had never failed to calm even her youngest siblings and cousins. These men, however, remained completely unmoved. She forced a small laugh. "Given our current location, I can't very well leave *now*."

Except, instead of ushering in any amused chuckles, the trio of men stared blackly back.

Only the small deckhand, Oliver, shifted and swallowed loudly, his gaze falling to the deck.

"Get ye gone now," Shorty snarled, and positioned himself directly in front of Cassia, and never had she been gladder that Nathan had assigned her the old sailor's protection. "Before ye get yerself into trouble with the captain." He trained his focus on Oliver. "Ye know the captain won't like what yer up to here, boy."

Oliver swallowed wildly, but his jaw remained resolute.

Carlisle chuckled, a cool, mirthless laugh that, despite the warmth of the sun, sent gooseflesh rising on Cassia's arms. "The captain's dealing with a problem below."

She shivered. They'd orchestrated a diversion. They'd deliberately seen Nathan leave his post at the deck.

Shorty took a step forward, and Carlisle matched his movements, jutting his chin out at the bigger, bulkier sailor. "Whose side are ye on?" Carlisle demanded.

Shorty glared. "She's just a wee lass."

"Ye've only ever been on the side of the crew, and now even ye'll be swayed. She's a witch, she is," Carlisle snapped.

"Yer just angry because Captain punished ye good for harassing the lady when ye thought he was a lad."

"Lad or lady, she's still a fancy sort, living her comfortable life while the rest of us toil. They're all the same." He shot another glare Cassia's way.

Shorty scoffed. "The captain hisself is a nobleman. Ye've got a problem with 'im, too?"

The protracted silence and lack of a reply were the only answers necessary. Carlisle was a man who'd a problem with the peerage, and after hearing the tales Nathan and Shorty had both shared of men who'd nearly hanged because of their hunger, she could understand why.

Carlisle jerked his chin Cassia's way. "Brought nothing but trouble to us, she has. We'll die out here."

"Och, it's a single day without wind," Shorty protested. "Hardly reason enough to go get yer craw up."

As they debated, Cassia swung her gaze between the two men.

"She's a damned fancy lady who don't give a shite about anything or anyone but herself, and worse?" The other man jabbed a finger at Cassia. "She's a jinx, and she's a distraction the captain doesn't need."

"Like ye know what the captain needs!" Shorty growled. "Ye've been 'ere for not even a whole voyage, and Oi can tell ye, after this, ye won't be 'ere for a second one. The captain expects loyalty from his crew."

Before they came to blows, Cassia hurriedly inserted herself between them. "Oh, I assure you, I'm not a distraction," she swiftly interjected. "Nathan is quite capable of seeing to multiple tasks, and we—"

Several sets of angry stares swung her way, and she made herself stop talking.

Shorty grunted. "Let's get ye below deck, lass," he said, sidling left, and she matched his steps, keeping herself close to the big sailor.

And then the men converged, three of them, one bashing a pan over the old sailor's head, and Shorty went completely still, and then his eyes rolled to the back of his head.

His body hit the deck, hard.

Cassia widened her eyes, momentarily stunned into silence, and then she quickly fell to her knees. "Shorty!" she exclaimed, tapping his cheeks firmly. Alas, he remained completely motionless.

Then . . . she registered the complete quiet.

Slowly, Cassia picked her gaze up from Shorty's prone form, and she found three sets of hard eyes trained on her.

She dampened her mouth. "G-gentlemen," she said with another forced smile, climbing to her feet, and at the lethal menace penetrating from their eyes, terror compelled her forward. With a scream, Cassia sprinted past the angry lot of sailors.

She made it no more than four paces before one wrenched her back and slapped a beefy palm over her mouth, stifling the remainder of her cry. Her heart hammering away with terror, she bit at the hand suffocating her.

With a curse, the sailor holding her yanked his hand back.

She let fly another scream.

Her captor—Carlisle—stuffed a rag in her mouth and drew it tightly behind her head.

She glared at the wiry fellow, Turner.

The young man's enormous Adam's apple bobbed. "Get it done, quick," he urged in a frantic whisper.

Get it done? Oh, God on Sunday. Dread slithered around her insides. She thrashed her head back and forth, undulating wildly, her efforts in vain, as someone dragged her, kicking, over to the rail. In one effortless movement, he caught her about the waist.

Cassia jammed the heel of her right foot backward hard into the shin of the one holding her.

He grunted. "Stop fighting, you witch." And this time, he wrapped the arm around her middle more tightly, making it impossible to drag in a breath, and stars darted behind her eyes.

A thunderous roar went up around the ship, a primal shout belonging to a warrior of old and centuries past, and at the sound of it, her captor loosened his grip on her waist.

Her heart pumping with relief, Cassia whipped her head sideways. *Nathan.*

Nathan, but Nathan as she'd never before seen him.

Stalking forward like the all-powerful God Zeus come to life, to punish the mere mortals who'd thought to cross him.

A giddy relief filled her chest, and at the sight of him, she found herself smiling around the cloth like a lackwit.

Carlisle and Turner struck her hard between the shoulder blades, giving her a mighty push, and Cassia gasped as she pitched sideways. Then she was falling. Falling. And still falling.

And she hit the water, hard.

Chapter 15

Cassia McQuoid was dead.

Or she was going to die a swift death.

Briefly frozen midstride, Nathaniel's entire body jolted and jerked, and then a cry climbed his throat, and he set it free, finding movement once more.

As he bolted the remaining length of the deck, his men parted like that biblical Red Sea.

In one motion, Nathaniel climbed atop the railing and dived forward, his arms arced down.

The ocean rushed up to meet him, and as he cut through the surface, the seawater flooded his ears, muffling all sounds except for the thundering of his heart.

She is dead.

Agony sluiced through him even as he forced himself to the top, blinking back the salty sting of seawater. "Cassia," he thundered, frantically scanning the otherwise placid surface for any hint of the woman who'd so upended his world.

She'd driven him half-mad from the start, and yet . . . she'd made him laugh and smile more than he'd ever done in the whole of his miserably serious life.

And now she was dead because he'd failed her. He'd failed to protect her and keep her safe.

A painful moan started in his chest and got caught somewhere in his throat, choking him to death on his own misery, and he preferred it. He preferred death to losing her.

Diving back under, he forced his eyes open. Ignoring the brief sting, he propelled himself forward, searching for a hint of Cassia, searching so long that even when his lungs burnt, he continued swimming until his chest threatened to burst. And he forced himself above once more, gasping for breath as he continued his desperate search of the surface.

Panic and horror thundered away in his ears. It grew and doubled and then redoubled, and he dived under the waters once more.

Please, God.

Please, God.

It was a prayer.

It was a litany.

A mantra.

Two words that kept him from going completely mad.

Nathaniel's chest heaved from fear and his exertions.

He'd not survive this. The innocent minx, dead at sea. All her cheerful chattering, silenced forever, her body gone to the fishes—the end of her smile and laughter and dreams of exploration . . . and it was his fault. Because he'd not been watching after her. Because he'd allowed anything to happen to her.

A groan spilled from him, and he briefly closed his eyes.

For fuck's sake, man. Find her.

From aboard the ship, shouts went up amongst his crew.

It pulled Nathaniel from a rapidly spiraling quagmire of panic, and he opened his eyes. "Cassia!" he bellowed.

"Yes?"

That quietly spoken, as-always-happiness-filled answer briefly froze him and time altogether.

He'd merely imagined her and her dulcet tones. He—

Only, as Nathaniel turned to the sound of that cherished voice, Cassia smiled back, spreading her arms in perfect arcs as she treaded water.

She was here. Alive. Unharmed. Smiling as she always did.

"Cassia," he whispered, her name emerging harsh and raspy from his lips. *Dead. I am dead, and this is my heaven, being reunited with her.*

Cassia's already enormous smile widened, wreathing her full cheeks. It danced in her eyes, and something in his chest shifted at the sight of it. "Nathan," she returned as though they greeted from across a ball-room and not fifteen paces apart in the vast ocean.

The vast ocean filled with sharks and countless other predators of the sea who'd be happy to feast on the both of them.

With a curse, Nathaniel swam the remaining distance between them, even as Cassia matched his own powerful strokes, and they were meeting in the middle.

Nathaniel immediately had her in his arms, clutching her to him, sending water spraying as he drew her against his chest. "Cassia." Her name was a harsh, hoarse whisper wrenched from him as a prayer as he placed a hard kiss against her temple. And then, retaining his hold upon her, he edged back slightly so that he could verify with his own eyes the woman before him was real. That she'd, in fact, survived.

Smiling.

She was always smiling. *Still.*

Even with several of his crew members having tried to end her.

Coldness flooded him all over again.

Dead. They were dead, the three of them.

Her smile slipped and dipped and stole some of the light he'd managed to find in these moments. "You're angry. I'll have you know it was not my fault, Nathan."

"You're alive." He said it aloud because he needed to say it aloud. Because he needed to hear it spoken to believe it himself. To reassure himself. To remind himself.

She wrinkled her pert nose. "Well, that is quite rude. It was hardly my faul—*eek*." Her voice climbed to a high squeak as he anchored her closer to him.

"I'm not angry," he rasped. "Not at you. I could never." How had he ever been angry with her about anything?

She blinked her wide, innocent eyes quickly. "You aren't?" Cassia cocked her head. "Because you *look* as though—"

He kissed her, silencing what was sure to be a lengthy evaluation from the lady, desire commingling with the relief and jubilation of having her in his arms. In feeling her. In knowing she lived.

She sighed and twined her arms about his neck, nearly dragging them under.

Nathaniel broke that embrace, adjusting their bodies and sweeping his arm in smooth, steady arcs to keep them afloat. He touched his brow to hers. "Cassia."

Her long auburn lashes fluttered open. "Nathan?"

"You were wrong."

A frown tipped the corners of her plump lips.

"You do have another skill you failed to mention."

"Yes?"

He grinned slowly, the expression imbued with so much relief it felt stupid to his own muscles, and yet he was hopeless to help it. "You can swim."

She smiled again. "Yes, Nathan. I didn't mention that?"

"You did not." The most important of skills, a lifesaving one, was one she'd mastered. In fact, she'd a skill in the waters unmatched by most of his crew.

And then his shoulders shook, and a low laugh born of relief and dizzying joy lightened him, and Cassia joined in.

And because he needed to desperately remind himself that this moment was real, that he'd not conjured one last final meeting between them to hold on to forever, and that she'd not, in fact, perished at sea, he gripped her harder to him.

Cassia grunted, the bell-like ringing of her laughter instantly fading. "Are you *trying* to drown me, Nathan? Because that really would be quite rude of—"

Nathaniel kissed her to quiet once more, taking and tasting of those silky contours briefly, and then parting.

She blinked, dazed again, and then picked up precisely as she'd left off. "Because if you are—"

Nathaniel took her mouth a third time, and this time, she melted against him, opening her mouth and letting him in.

Dimly, he registered shouts from above, and a *splash* as a ladder hit the water.

"Come," he said gruffly. Making himself relinquish her proved, however, as hard a task as any battle he'd waged or fought on these seas.

And yet as she effortlessly kept pace with him, no easy task, given the height difference between them and the years of practice he'd had, Nathaniel's gaze continually went to her.

She flew through the waters, a mythical mermaid come alive in every way.

They reached the side of the ship, and with the same agility as she'd moved through those waters, she now climbed the rope ladder's rungs with the grace and ease of a lady winding her way up Italian marble steps to some grand ballroom.

Following close behind, Nathaniel's gaze took in her every moment, the sway of her hips and the way those trousers hugged her sinuous frame, highlighting the delectable curve of her derriere. Her garments, soaked from her dunking in the sea, clung to every inch of her. Every inch, from the white lawn shirt that left nothing to the imagination to her trousers that kissed each curve of her long, sinewy legs.

Lusting after her . . . in this moment?

You truly are a cad.

The moment she reached the top, Hayes was there to help her over. "You can swim," he remarked with the same veneration that had gripped Nathaniel.

"And"—Cassia shot a finger up to punctuate her point—"dive."

Hayes grinned. "And dive."

"In Lach Morar, the children have always gathered for annual Loch Games, we call them, in honor of the Greeks and the first Olympics. My father is an antiquarian who studies ancient civilizations and fashioned the events around them. There is racing, but I was not so very fast on land. I knew if I was to compete, my best chance at a victory was always in the water, and . . ."

And as she rattled on and Hayes drew up the rope ladder, Nathaniel was never more grateful to the other man for being the effortless talker and listener he was.

Until he took his last breath, Nathaniel would forever recall the moment she'd gone hurtling overboard, her delicate, willowy form there one moment and gone the next, and then the violent splash as she'd struck the waters below.

His breathing grew raspy and harsh in his own ears, and he had to remind himself to breathe again. More easily.

She was alive.

But she almost hadn't been . . .

Had she been any other woman, she'd have perished at sea, and it would have been Nathaniel's fault.

His fault for the end of that smile and—

"Nathan?" Cassia ventured hesitantly.

"I'm fine," he said roughly, and she immediately went quiet.

And he knew he was surly, but God help him, he'd always been hopelessly rough around the edges, and this moment was no exception, this moment with her alive only because of her tenacity years earlier and determination at winning a game amongst her siblings and cousins.

This was why he'd resolved to never let any woman in his life. Nathaniel was too much like his father, incapable of warmth and more comfortable with running his business. His shipping enterprise was something he understood, and even the seas were predictable with their unpredictability. Women, however? He'd no idea how to make them happy, and it'd never crossed his mind that he'd ever wed and bring a woman aboard his ship.

That brief—but also eternal—moment of terror where Cassia had almost perished because of him and the work he did and the people he'd dealings with. Only, in all his years as a privateer, he'd amassed any number of enemies whom he'd foreseen as threats; he had known threats against him and those he cared about, posed by those past foes. Never had he expected his own men to turn upon him.

Nathaniel firmed his jaw.

It was an essential lesson he could not forget.

It was a reminder he'd desperately needed.

He needed to return Cassia to the folds of her family, and then, once he knew she was safe and being looked after, he could resume sailing without the paralyzing fear that continued to grip him, even now.

At Hayes's side, Shorty dropped a blanket around Cassia's shoulders. "Ye lived." The older sailor's lower lip trembled, and tears filled his eyes.

"I can swim, Shorty," Cassia chirped happily. "Worry not about me. The better question is, How is your head?" she asked, patting Shorty's sun- and age-weathered hand.

And just like that, the tears vanished, and a lopsided grin formed on the other man's mouth. "Gonna take more than a knock on the 'ead to do me in, miss."

Aye, Nathaniel well knew that feeling. He'd felt that same smile on his lips just moments earlier, when Cassia had sluiced her way through the ocean waters to reach him. What lady who'd nearly been killed worried not about herself, but another? There was no one like her. He'd sailed nearly every end of the world, and there wasn't a person like her.

What if she hadn't known how to swim?

His mind shied away once more from that question as terror licked at the corners of his mind, and fueling the rage to drown out the mind-seizing fear, he looked to the one who'd nearly ended Cassia McQuoid.

Fury tightened in his gut as he turned all his focus on the subdued sailors caught between five other members of the crew.

The loyal lot restrained Carlisle and the others, their grips white-knuckled, indicating the strength of those holds. And yet, given the man's sag forward, and between his stooped shoulders and the lifeless quality of his arms, their efforts were unnecessary. Unnecessary, and yet also essential.

For there was no greater danger to a ship captain than to have a crew member who gainsaid orders. Failure to assert his role as commander and hold the other man accountable was the stuff mutinies were born of.

Icy tendrils of rage furled about Nathaniel's heart, spreading to every corner of his chest cavity, and he welcomed it, fed it. Fueled himself upon it.

"Escort the lady below deck," Nathaniel murmured, and strode the length of the deck toward a quaking, pale Carlisle, Turner, and Oliver.

The bastards had nearly killed her.

And they would pay the price for it.

Fingers settled on his sleeve, and he whipped his gaze sideways.

Cassia stared up at him, through those saucer-size round eyes. "What will you do to them?"

"It isn't your concern," he said tightly, motioning once more for Shorty.

Cassia stayed the giant of a man with nothing more than a single gentle look, and then she turned her focus back up to Nathaniel. "I say that it is," she insisted.

Murmurs went up from amongst his crew.

Silently cursing, Nathaniel looked to Hayes. "Attend the three while I escort the lady below." With that, he took her lightly by the arm and steered her away from the assembled crew members and below deck. The moment they were out of sight, he whispered sharply, "You cannot challenge me in front of my crew, Cassia. They'll mutiny." They'd already come damn close this day.

Her face grew stricken. "I didn't think . . . ," she whispered. "I'm sorry. I'd just thought, given I was the one tossed overboard, I had a right—"

"No."

"To know."

"Asking me is challenging me," he explained calmly. "Do you not know the only thing keeping you alive on this damned ship is me and my authority over them?"

Her lower lip trembled.

And in that moment, he discovered he was capable of more softness than he'd ever before believed of himself. She'd endured more today than most; no soft lord in London would have been so unshaken as this spirited, joy-filled woman before him. "Cassia, please go to my cabin."

And he'd even managed to say "please." Why, that was a single first for—

"No." This time, her challenge came in the form of a nearly silent whisper even he had to strain to hear. But he heard it. And he appreciated that this time, even away from the crew as they were, she'd offer that challenge so discreetly.

Nathaniel closed his eyes. God, if she wouldn't try the patience of every last saint and the good Lord himself. "Cassia," he entreated.

"What will you do to them, Nathan?" she pleaded, and he opened his eyes once more, the words freezing on his mouth as he took in the sight of her.

Bedraggled, with her drenched, plaited hair dripping water about the deck as she clutched the wool blanket that had been given her with a grip that had drained the blood from her knuckles.

"They'll be flogged and then put in the brig until we disembark, and then they'll be removed from service."

"Even Oliver?"

"Cassia, he was as much a part of it as—"

"But he is a boy," she pleaded. "Not even thirteen." Cassia rested her fingertips on his forearm. His muscles jumped under her delicate touch, and he dropped his arm to his side. "Please, don't," she whispered.

Please, don't?

What in blazes was she saying? Surely . . . and then it hit him.

He narrowed his eyes. "Oliver bullied you the moment you replaced him as cabin boy, and you'd now plead for him?"

"He lost his post because of me. Either way, he's a child, and I'd ask you to spare him."

There came a knock on the door. "Captain, they're bound and ready," Shorty called.

Nathaniel acknowledged that announcement. "I'll be along." After the loyal crew member had gone, Nathaniel trained his focus on the all-too-forgiving woman before him. "He deserves to be drawn and quartered for what he did to you, Cassia. All of them do," he said, remembered fear making his tone harsher and sharper than he intended, and yet God help him, the memory was still too fresh.

He suspected it might always be.

"I wasn't hurt, Nathan," she insisted.

Did she truly think he would weaken . . . *on this*?

She'd be wrong.

"They attempted to kill you," he said bluntly. "*That* is what they did." Fresh terror flared to life, and Nathaniel told his brain to tell his heart to slow and tried to recall how to breathe.

His efforts proved in vain.

Cassia rested her fingers on his wet sleeve and gently squeezed. "That's what Carlisle did. He's a grown man. *Not* Oliver. Oliver is a boy." She guided his hand to her chest, laying his palm atop the place where her heart beat. Fast but steady. "And I am alive, Nathaniel," she reminded him, giving much important life to those words he struggled to let sink in. "I am alive."

She lived. That was the important part.

Keeping her alive was just as vital, and doing so required he mete out deserved punishment to the ones who'd put hands upon her.

He took her gently by the shoulders and bent his head so their eyes met. "At his age, on the sea and the streets of London, Oliver is a man," he said, willing her to understand. "Cassia, if I do not do this, I send a message that I am weak in how I run my ship. It puts you, him, and the entire crew at risk." Nathaniel gave her a light squeeze. "But if I do this, he will *learn*, and he can prove himself loyal once more and remain part of the crew, instead of facing a life on the streets of London." Carlisle and Turner, on the other hand—they were done. New to his crew, they'd proven themselves disloyal and dishonorable and would be cut loose.

Cassia dropped his arm and grabbed the other end of the blanket she'd been given, and she hugged herself. "I understand." Her fingers trembled slightly on the fabric she clutched about her, the only indication of her disquiet.

Releasing her, Nathaniel turned to go.

Cassia dug in. "I'm going with you."

He whipped back to face her. "Cassia, you don't know what you—"

"I know precisely what I'm saying, and what you intend to do, and if I'm the reason for it, then I'd see as every other member of the crew will."

She'd not been the reason for it.

Carlisle had been the one responsible for his own actions this day.

Nathaniel warred with himself. The idea of whipping a man in front of an innocent Cassia McQuoid left him more than slightly queasy.

She insisted on watching.

Nothing short of physically tossing her over his shoulder and locking her in his cabin would see her gone. The same way he knew she chatted like a magpie and swam and excelled in art, he now knew she'd a stubborn streak as bold and big as her Scottish namesake and spirit. "Very well," he said quietly.

They didn't speak again as they made their way back to the main deck. As he made the march, he was aware of Cassia's silence. For the first time in all the time he'd known her, she wasn't prattling or garrulous or smiling. Hell, even when she'd been tossed overboard, she'd had a smile as she'd swum over to meet him. After she'd joined Shorty, Nathaniel turned his attention on his crew.

Carlisle, Turner, and Oliver had been strung up. The three sailors' shirts had been removed; Carlisle's bared back revealed faint white marks left by a previous whipping.

Not in Nathaniel's employ.

Nathaniel had never been forced to whip a single man in his crew.

Never had there been reason to. They'd always been loyal and obedient.

Until now.

Now there was reason to whip *three* men.

Flexing his jaw, Nathaniel held out his right hand.

Hayes immediately came forward with the cat-o'-nine-tails.

Albion joined them; he dropped his voice to a nearly inaudible whisper. "Surely you aren't allowing her to remain for this?"

Had those tones been spoken for the crew, it would have been another challenge Nathaniel could not ignore, and yet this was a man who'd saved his life scores more than he'd deserved, and who was a friend beyond this ship, too.

Nathaniel looked over to where Cassia stood alongside Shorty. The pair made up the middle of the gathered crew; her cheeks, previously flushed from her dousing in the sea, had gone pale, making her crimson mouth a stark flash of red within her face. "She stays."

The other man looked as though he wished to say more in protest, and Nathaniel narrowed his eyes warningly.

He'd allowed that earlier questioning, but there was a limit to what Nathaniel would permit.

Albion nodded once and stepped aside.

"Carlisle, Turner, Oliver," Nathaniel called out loudly as he headed for the men tied to the mast.

Clasping his hands at his back, Nathaniel centered himself before the three offenders and read aloud from the Articles of War. "If any officer, mariner, soldier, or other person in the fleet shall strike any of his superior officers, or draw, or offer to draw, or lift up any weapon against him, being in the execution of his office, on any pretense whatsoever, every such person being convicted of any such offense, by the sentence of a court martial, shall suffer death"—Oliver's face grew several shades whiter as tears brimmed in his eyes—"and if any officer, mariner, soldier, or other person in the fleet shall presume to quarrel with any of his superior officers, being in the execution of his office, or shall disobey any lawful command of any of his superior officers, every such person being convicted of any such offense by the sentence of a court martial, shall suffer death or such other punishment as shall, according to the nature and degree of his offense, be inflicted upon him by the sentence of a court martial." He paused, letting those rules of the ship ring out before continuing on. "If any person in the fleet shall quarrel or fight with any other person in the fleet, or use reproachful or provoking speeches or gestures, tending to make any quarrel or disturbance, he shall, upon being convicted thereof, suffer such punishment as the offense shall deserve and a court martial shall impose." Nathaniel passed his gaze amongst the three men. "For your crimes, Oliver, you are sentenced to four lashes."

More tears fell from the boy, but he merely nodded in acquiescence.

"Carlisle, Turner, you shall each receive the maximum lash count of twelve strokes for each offense." From the corner of his eye, he caught the way Cassia briefly closed her eyes, and he steeled himself, forcing himself to focus on the trial before him. "Do you have anything to say against your sentence?"

Oliver shook his head. "No, C-captain." His voice emerged threadbare.

Carlisle and Turner, on the other hand, stared mutinously out, maintaining their silence.

Nathaniel looked to his quartermaster.

Hayes stepped forward and waited for his command.

Nathaniel nodded.

The quartermaster let the cat-o'-nine-tails fly. The whip hissed and then landed, the sickening sound of it as it slashed through Carlisle's flesh splitting the quiet.

Carlisle's entire body jerked; the ropes strained under that shifting, but otherwise, there was silence. He released not so much as a moan or whimper or cry.

Hayes paused after each lash, to run his fingers through the cat-o'-nine-tails to wipe the blood and sweat. Through each blow that left the already scarred flesh tattered like a slab of massacred meat on the butcher's table, Nathaniel remained stoic, stony-faced.

When Hayes concluded the twelve lashes, he called over Albion. A fresh whip in hand, his navigator waited for the command. At Nathaniel's nod, the lieutenant launched into the next set of lashes. Carlisle's legs gave out, and this time, with each strike landed by the navigator, the sailor groaned.

And then he was done.

Nathaniel moved next to Turner, and when he'd concluded, he looked to Oliver.

Oliver, who was four stones lighter and more than a foot shorter than the sailor who'd led him on this path. And despite his role this day, Nathaniel's stomach churned. For this was no new member of his crew. This was his former cabin boy.

Hayes gave a slight nod, one indicating he'd see to the horrific task, that he knew the struggle Nathaniel faced.

It would be the coward's way to let another member of his crew dole out the boy's punishment—no matter how deserved it was.

Taking in a slow breath, Nathaniel kept his features even, and forced himself to administer each lash of Oliver's punishment. Through it, he forced himself to not look at Cassia. Knowing he couldn't face her in this moment.

The boy cried out, and Nathaniel's chest seized at the suffering he was inflicting. Knowing he had to do this did not make it easier.

She remained silent. And yet, it was that silence from an always garrulous Cassia McQuoid which was somehow all the worse.

Don't look at her.

Don't look at her . . .

Think of her elation at seeing you, just moments before Carlisle shoved her, mouth gagged, off the side of the main deck, and into the sea.

Lash.

Imagine if there'd been a swarm of sharks there, hungry, and eager to feed on her delicate flesh.

He let the whip fly once more.

When it was done, silence reigned amongst the crew.

At last, he let himself look at her. Cassia stood there, wan and quiet, and then without a word, she left.

Chapter 16

Sketching always helped.

As did painting. Painting helped, too.

Whenever Cassia had been upset over the years, empty pages of sketch pads had been the source of comfort that had pulled her from her doldrums.

Except, those had been hurts over quarrels she couldn't even now remember with her siblings.

This?

That which haunted her today would haunt her forever.

The large, brawny sailor with his suntanned, already whip-scarred back, bearing fresh marks left by his flogging.

Because of her.

It had been because of her.

Seated on Nathan's bed, Cassia paused midstroke and stared unblinkingly, blankly, down at the rendering she'd made of Carlisle.

Even in her sketch, she'd managed to capture the volatile rage from his heavy, squared features and his eyes. Hatred had brimmed within.

Because he did not like her. Nay, that wasn't quite right. He hated her. Hated her enough that he'd attempted to kill her, and had it not been for Nathan, Cassia likely would have found herself on the losing end of a crew angry with her for her sex.

It was a reminder of the grave mistake she'd made.

All of it.

Because Carlisle and Turner wouldn't have gotten into the trouble they had, and Nathan wouldn't have had to inflict those lashes on Oliver . . . if it weren't for her.

And she didn't know how to face him or his crew after this. They'd already hated her. Now they had greater reason to do so. Nor could she blame them. Today, a boy had suffered at Nathan's hand for those mistakes.

Footfalls sounded in the hall, and unlike before, she now detected the difference between Nathan's tread and that of his strong, powerful, but slightly more fleet-footed quartermaster.

There came the murmur of words between Nathan and Shorty, and as he pressed the handle to let himself in, Cassia hastily dropped her gaze to her pages.

She felt his eyes land on her the moment he let himself inside, and as was his laconic way, he closed the panel behind them, locked it, and moved deeper into the room without saying anything.

Not a single word.

Why should he wish to speak with you? Why, after all the problems you've brought him?

And what did it say about her selfishness that even with that, even knowing she was not only unwanted by them but also a burden, she wished to be here anyway?

With him.

Tears smarted, and she blinked them back.

From the corner of her eye, she caught him moving methodically about his cabin.

Then he stopped before her. "You're awake."

His was a statement, and yet, Cassia nodded anyway.

The mattress dipped as he settled onto the side. "Is your stomach—"

"My stomach is fine," she interrupted, touched that he should ask, that even with what she'd done, he'd ask after her. "I hardly feel the roll of the ship anymore."

"That might be because the ship isn't rolling anymore," he said playfully, and it was the first in all the time she'd known him there'd been not a hard, satirical edge, but a gentle teasing instead.

Strangely, that only made her want to cry all the more.

"No," she murmured. "The ship isn't doing anything anymore."

That was right. The winds had ceased, and the ship stopped, as they still waited for the winds to pick up so they might resume their journey once more. It was also the reason for Carlisle and Turner's intent to drown her. Her fingers curled reflexively around the charcoal in her hand, so tightly she nearly snapped the piece.

So tightly, she would have.

But Nathan brought his hand up, covering her smaller, charcoal-stained one with his larger, callused palm.

"May I?"

It was a moment before she registered just what he was asking.

Cassia looked from her sketch pad to Nathan, and then handed it over.

He accepted the book in his larger, sure hands. Long fingers that had been forced to violence because of her . . .

As he silently flipped through the pages, beginning with those Scottish landscapes she'd captured and continuing on to more recent times—her time aboard his ship—she stared, riveted by his hands, unable to look away.

Seeing the twitch of those hands, as he'd brought that whip down across Oliver's small back.

Cassia bit her lower lip hard.

"You're good." His was a matter-of-fact statement that he directed at a rendering he'd paused upon, one of the main deck bustling with his crew, each man in profile, visible by nothing more than their backs.

"For all the good the skill does me," she murmured.

"Why do you sketch?" he asked suddenly, and she blinked slowly at the unexpectedness of that question.

"I enjoy it. It calms me."

"Then that is a skill that serves you well."

Only, this time, it didn't. She sank her teeth into her lower lip, biting hard on that soft flesh. This time, not even drawing had helped calm her frayed nerves or take away those haunting images of the vitriol Carlisle and Turner had unleashed on her, or the return fury Nathan had unleashed on them.

Nathan snapped the book closed with a quiet click.

"Are you all right?" he asked with a tenderness that matched his touch, with such a concern those blasted tears threatened once again.

A single tear falling, Cassia managed nothing more than a shaky nod.

Using his opposite hand, Nathan caught that drop with the pad of his rough thumb, brushing the moisture away.

Another was there, quickly taking its place.

Nathan collected that one, too.

Her mouth trembled as she fought for all she was worth to keep from dissolving into a watery puddle of misery and regret. "It is all right to cry, Cassia," he murmured, gently palming her cheek, and she leaned into that oh-so-tender touch.

"You hate tears," she whispered, her voice miserable.

"I'll make an exception this time," he said, and lightened those words with a light tug on the end of a lone curl that had escaped her plait.

And then it was too much.

The torrent opened.

With a great, gasping sob, Cassia released her grip on her sketch pad and pencil and flung herself into Nathan's arms.

He immediately folded her within that warm, solid, protective embrace.

And Cassia just wept. She cried so hard her body shook, and the strong expanse of his heavily muscled chest absorbed each tremble.

All the while she cried, Nathan continued to simply hold her, stroking smooth, soothing circles over the small of her back.

"I-it was s-so awful," she said as she wept.

Nathan's arms spasmed about her.

He groaned. "I didn't want you to see that."

Cassia pushed away. "I-it is not a-about me," she explained, willing him to understand. "I-it is about . . . those men."

"Those men?" he echoed, and instantly all hint of warmth receded as Nathan went completely hard, his harshly beautiful features freezing into a mask that had once terrified her. "They got precisely what they deserved." His voice emerged as a raspy, low growl. "Carlisle led an insurrection and attempted to kill you. He enlisted the aid of other men, and they would have done so." He paused. "And were they given another chance, they'd still do it, and yet you'd cry for them."

There was a wealth of confusion in that slightly pitched-up question.

"I don't like to see anyone hurt, Nathan."

"Not even men who'd kill you if they could?" he asked bluntly.

"No one, Nathan." She jumped up and began to pace. "I came between you and your crew."

"Their *actions* came between those men and me."

Cassia increased her frenzied pace, whipping back and forth. "I've brought problems by just being here."

"Well, that much is true," he said in his usual droll way, and she shot him a look.

Cassia resumed her march. "There is no place for me, Nathan. In London, I was invisible. Not interesting enough to court. Not clever enough to be sent on to school. And now I've found a place that I very dearly love to be . . ." *With him.* Tears filled her throat, briefly choking her and the remainder of that thought.

Nathan stood, coming closer but allowing her space with which she could still pace. "You love the sea?" he asked quietly. She felt his eyes examining her as she strode back and forth. "Even seeing the expanse of it, and how easily you could have perished in these waters? Had the ship been moving and had Turner chosen to act then, you would be . . . dead." Something dark flashed in his eyes, and was it the shadows of the room playing off his powerful frame, or had he shuddered?

Cassia nodded jerkily, and then stopped, facing him. "I never knew there could be a place like this," she said, lifting her palms up, trying to make him understand. "Like that fabled place traveled by Odysseus, come to life, and . . . it's a place I cannot be." But it was a place he would forever be. Her throat closed off once more. "It's one more place I'm not wanted."

"Is that what you think, Cassia? That I don't want you?"

"I know you don't." She tipped her chin up defiantly toward him.

He stared at her for a long while, and then with a groan, he lowered his head.

She was already tilting her mouth up to his, to offer herself to him.

Their mouths met in a fiery explosion.

And this kiss was unlike all the others to come before, but no less special, possessed of its own magic.

Nathan dusted his fingers along her jaw, urging her with his touch to open for him, and Cassia parted her lips, and he swept inside. He tasted of her.

And she tasted in return.

All the while he made love to her mouth, Nathan searched his hands over her, stroking her hips and then moving his quest higher, palming her breasts.

"I thought you were dead, Cassia," he said harshly, between kisses. "I went mad in that moment."

Because of her?

Odd, that such a simple pronouncement should leave her as dizzy as his embrace. "I thought you did not even like me," she said, breathless, between each slant of his mouth over hers.

"I like you," he growled. "I like you *too* much."

She moaned, her head falling back in supplication, and Nathan moved his trail of kisses elsewhere, licking and nipping at the corners of her mouth, and lower, worshipping her neck. "I-is there s-such a thing as l-liking someone too much?"

Because wasn't that putting a person . . . close to love, then?

"Oh, yes," he said in his usual rough manner that teased forth another smile.

"I hate to tell you that you're wrong, Nathan. There's no such thing as—" He took her mouth in a long, hard kiss that silenced her and left her dazed.

When he moved his mouth from hers, Cassia blinked several times. "I was saying . . . I was saying . . ." What had she been saying?

"You always chatter."

He touched his tongue to hers again.

"I do," she breathed after he'd swirled that flesh in a wicked little dance within her mouth.

"It wasn't a question."

Oddly, he didn't sound so very annoyed at that husky musing between kisses. He sounded . . . quite . . . endeared by it. Which was preposterous. Nathan wasn't the manner of man to be endeared by . . . anything or anyone. Certainly not her. And yet, she could almost believe it.

And mayhap it was only because she so very much wanted to believe that he hungered for her, as she did him.

At least, in one way.

Somewhere along the way, he'd come to matter more to her, and before she left, before her time here with him was done, she wanted to steal every last memory and moment she could with him.

Nathaniel needed to drown out the bloodcurdling images that had gripped him this day. Of Cassia, sailing over the side of his ship. Cassia nearly killed. He wrapped an arm around her waist, and even as he drew her close, she sighed and curved her body into his, like a bloom angling for the sun.

Nathaniel claimed her mouth, devouring it, devouring her. Hopeless and helpless to do anything in this moment other than to drink fully of her.

Gripping his shirtfront, Cassia leaned up and into the embrace.

Cupping one hand about her nape, he angled her, urging her to open for him, and as trusting as she'd been from the start and in every way with him, she opened her mouth and let Nathaniel inside. He swept in, lashing his tongue against hers, swirling it around that delicate flesh that dueled and danced in return. She'd the sweet, familiar taste of the apples she so loved, and he'd never not see or eat of that fruit again without thinking of her, the Eve to his fallen Adam.

And Nathaniel continued that descent harder and faster, plunging himself fully into that current of this hungering for her, letting himself be pulled and swept away.

Cassia tugged free the queue at the nape of his neck, and she tangled her fingers in his hair.

A primal growl shook his frame, and Nathaniel angled her head, tipping it slightly to avail himself of her neck. He suckled at the place where her pulse beat at a maddening pace for him.

With a growl, he shucked free his shirt and tossed it aside.

There was no danger in this moment. Now, Cassia was safe here with him. For now, there was just this.

There was just them.

And until then, Nathaniel was determined to have this pleasure and passion between them.

Lowering himself slowly, and carefully, framing her body between his elbows, he never broke their kiss. She kissed him with the same abandon and passion and boldness with which she lived her life.

And it was heady and enlivening, a manner of sorcery that charmed a man out of the all-consuming fear of loss and replaced it with the dazzling light of life's greatest perfection.

Nathaniel slid a questing palm down her side to that graceful curve of her hip that, from the moment he'd discovered she was a woman, he'd been hopeless to fail to note and dream of touching the way he did now.

She moaned, and Nathaniel parted her lips, engaging in that bold dance with their tongues. He swirled it around her mouth and suckled the tip of that pink flesh.

Cassia's hips moved rhythmically in a reflexive way, undulating against him, pressing her flat belly against the rigid line of his shaft.

He groaned and moved against her in return. Feeling like the green boy of his youth, finding that with this woman, he still was, because everything felt new. Everything was new with her. From the way he saw the sea and the world around him to the way it felt to kiss.

And now, making love with her.

Making love, which would, in turn, also change . . . everything.

Reality bucked its head, demanding Nathaniel's attention, and he fought back the incommodious intrusion.

He wrenched his mouth away, his breath raspy and harsh from the chore it took to stop, when every part within urged him to take her and this moment.

Cassia's long lashes flew open, revealing wide, startled irises where confusion melded with passion. "What—?"

"I cannot be landlocked," he said, his voice hoarse and rough.

Her brow furrowed with that adorable befuddlement that was so patently hers, and she looked left and then right. "We are still at sea."

A pained laugh rumbled against the walls of his chest, which still rose and fell fast and hard.

He touched his brow against Cassia's. "I meant . . . after this."

"After your voyage?"

After the battle.

"After we return to shore," he said, his tone sharper than he intended, only it wasn't frustration with her this time, but rather the kick of agony that came in thinking of that inevitable parting.

Understanding dawned in her eyes. "Oh." She paused, then lifted her right palm, stroking back the strands of hair that hung over his right eye. "I didn't think you would give up your ship for me, Nathan," she said so simply that it hit him like a kick to the gut, because . . . she didn't know just how much she'd come to mean to him? How could she not? How had she not gathered that she'd thoroughly, madly, and completely upended his entire neatly ordered existence and mind and every part of him?

She hadn't, though.

And it was better that way.

And in the greatest battle he'd ever fought in all his seafaring days, and matches with his father combined, he did the impossible: Nathaniel rolled himself off Cassia and lay on his back, their shoulders kissing in the way he longed to make love to her mouth still. The way he longed to just out and out make love to her. And his randy shaft, who cared not at all for right or wrong or honor or dishonor, throbbed hard within the confines of his trousers.

Cassia turned onto her side, propping herself up onto her dainty left elbow, and then distractedly slid her fingers through the light matting of hair upon his chest.

He winced, and she stopped.

"You don't want me," she whispered, and there was such a crushing ache of misery and regret and understanding in those four words that cut him to the core of a soul he'd not even known he'd been in possession of until her.

He should let her to that ridiculously off-the-mark conclusion she'd somehow drawn, and yet, God help him for being weak, he could not hurt her that way. He could not lie to her in this.

Nathaniel caught her fingers in his and dragged them to his chest, to the place where his heartbeat thudded wildly and erratically because of her touch. Because of her.

"I want you more than is good or safe, Cassia McQuoid," he said harshly, and then he drew her fingertips to his lips, pressing a kiss against her wrist, that delicate place where her arm met her hand. "I want you against all my better judgment. It is only honor that keeps me from doing that which I want to do now. Because you deserve more than a man who cannot give you less than—"

Cassia kissed him; it was a hard, fleeting kiss, and he opened his mouth to deepen it, to take more of her. To take all of her.

She drew back slightly, and his body shuddered at the loss. Only . . .

Cassia moved her gaze over his face. "Why do you not allow me the decision of what I want, Nathaniel?" She cupped the hard line of his jaw in her butterfly-soft touch and angled his face closer to hers so that his eyes met hers. "And what I want is you." She spoke unfalteringly, her passion-heavy tones rich with an age-old knowing that went back to the days of Eve and her avowal of the very fruit she intended to eat from.

Nathaniel stiffened. And God help him, he was helpless and hopeless to deny her—or himself—that gift. He slid his hands down her trim waist, gripped either side of her hips, and sank his fingers into that supple flesh.

And this time, as they made love, Nathaniel surrendered himself completely and fully to her and this moment.

Chapter 17

The winds resumed.

Following the night he'd made love to Cassia, they'd picked up once more to the jubilant cheers of the crew.

And with Carlisle and Turner in the brig, there'd not been a single incident since. An incident which Nathaniel couldn't even give more of a name to because of the memories it stirred, the ones that threatened to drive him mad.

Nay, there'd been no conflicts or trouble.

Everything had gone smoothly since.

By his navigational estimations, they were just a handful of days from the *Renard*, which was what all his attention and energy should be focused on. Every sea battle required a man to have his wits about him. Failure to do so saw a crew killed and a ship seized. Or worse, downed.

So what accounted for this restlessness?

Standing at the side of the ship, Nathaniel stared out at the vast azure skies that met the darker blue of an equally vast ocean. The rocking of the ship and the briny sea air didn't provide their usual calming effect.

This was the last of his journeys until he returned and saw to his father's bidding.

That's what he told himself anyway.

Only, he knew he lied to himself. Nathaniel couldn't go through with the arrangement the duke wished him to make.

He knew that.

Hell, he'd known that the minute he'd laid Cassia down in his bed and made love to her.

Each of the half dozen times he'd made love to her over these past three days.

Yes, in making love to Cassia McQuoid, honor dictated that Nathaniel do right by her. His father would be furious. Outraged. Outraged enough to finally put an end to Nathaniel's time at sea—as he'd been vowing for three years.

That was the source of his discontent.

Wasn't it?

The fact that he knew honor dictated he marry Cassia, and in so doing, the future he craved at sea would come to an official end at his father's hand.

Unbidden, his gaze moved over to that spot Cassia had settled into as hers. She sat while Shorty stood, and whatever she'd said to the big sailor caused him to bellow with laughter.

Cassia joined in, her mirth bathing her cheeks in a soft color, those cheeks which had developed a tannish hue in her time outside.

It suited her.

That color.

The sea.

Being here with him and his crew.

Goddamn it.

He cared about her. He'd known just how much the moment she went over the side of his ship and he saw her disappearing from his life forever.

But hell, he didn't *want* a woman in his life whom he could care about. Not when that could be used against him . . . and worse, against her. And more . . . there was the expectation his parents had for him, a requirement that he fulfill the familial duty and marry his late brother's betrothed.

A marriage of convenience to a woman he was linked to in name only, with the world knowing it was a match born of duty and necessity, would be forever different from a match he'd willingly entered into with a woman who held sway over his heart.

Sway over his heart?

His mind balked and shied, and he recoiled. And yet, there it was. He loved her. Against logic and reason and knowing the responsibilities and the expectations the duke had for him. And more, knowing that a failure to do as his father wished would result in the end of his career. Because his father would not countenance this disobedience. And all the men who depended upon him, the work he did for the Crown—

Everything inside seized up as the same sense of helplessness that had gripped him when Cassia had been flung overboard gripped him once more.

When his mind *should* be on overtaking the French squadron and intercepting Boney's plans in the Adriatic, Nathaniel could think of nothing but *her*.

As if she felt his stare, Cassia glanced over.

She smiled back widely, her cheeks dimpling.

She lifted those fingers holding the always-in-her-grip charcoal and gave a little wave before returning her attention to her drawing.

Nathaniel continued to watch her.

In the whole of his sailing career, he'd always been focused on his work.

It was how he'd convinced himself he could take on an enemy ship with Cassia aboard.

That was what he'd told himself.

And yet, standing at the rail of his ship, unable to look away from her, he made himself face truths he'd not acknowledged before now.

Out on the ocean, he'd faced any number of risks before.

In fact, before any and every battle, he'd found a thrill of anticipation. He'd never doubted his ability, and he'd also known not so much as an iota of hesitation over boarding those enemy vessels and relieving those captains of their spoils. At that, spoils which would not aid them in their quest of hurting the Crown. Nay, he'd never faltered or felt so much as a frisson of unease.

Until now.

The ship rolled gently under his feet, and yet, instead of finding any calm in that light, familiar rocking, his stomach continued to roil. Twisted up in a thousand knots, his gut churned worse than it had when he'd first climbed aboard a ship.

Fear.

It was a first for the whole of his damned life.

He was bloody afraid.

Nay, not just afraid. He was out of his mind with terror; it lapped against his mind and soul and chest with the same incessant beat of the waves that crashed against the *Flying Dragon*.

In the past, when he'd engaged in those sea battles, there'd been confidence in his ability to win and a lack of fear in what should happen to him if he lost. Oh, he'd thought of his crew. But he'd also known the best way to serve his crew was to develop an unwavering confidence in his own abilities.

Nor did he attempt to delude himself into not believing this new, unwanted, gripping emotion had anything to do with one thing.

That was, one person.

Cassia.

Because before there'd been no Cassia aboard to think about.

Cassia, with her bright sunny smile and her ability to prattle on from sunrise to sundown.

Had he ever really found it annoying? How could he have found it—and her—anything less than endearing?

A wistful smile stole across his lips . . . and then slowly faded as he looked out.

"Captain, you wished to see us?"

Nathaniel tensed as his two most loyal crew members joined him. He'd been expecting them. He'd called for them.

A ledger containing the ship's coordinates in hand, Albion didn't waste any time. "By my estimation, even with the delay in travel, we've made up nearly all the time between us and the French ship," his navigator said. "Traveling the same waters, they were undoubtedly impacted by the same wind and currents—"

"That isn't why I've called you," Nathaniel said quietly, interrupting the other man midsentence. Albion looked up from his notes, his expression more than slightly stunned.

Hayes, however, watched Nathaniel through hooded eyes.

"I"—Nathaniel lowered his voice—"wanted to discuss Cassia."

His navigator lowered his books, and both men stared solemnly back.

"If anything happens to me," he began quietly, "I'd ask that you look after her. That you see she is safe, and that you escort her back to her family." There was no one he trusted more. He knew either man would lay down his own life if it meant seeing her safe. "You'll . . . guard her well."

"With our lives," Hayes vowed. "And when we are all safely ashore," he asked Nathaniel, "what . . . then?"

In other words, what would happen between Nathaniel and Cassia? It was a question only one he was closer with than even his own brothers would dare ask. Nathaniel scraped a hand down his face. "I . . . don't . . . know." Because he didn't. If she were with babe, he'd marry her. Absolutely. That was not in question. He cared about her. More than he'd ever believed it possible he could care about anyone, but there were the expectations his family had for Nathaniel, ones that had direct implications on his future in sailing, and as a result, all those who relied upon him.

Nathaniel stared out at the sea, where the lap of the ocean waves had always brought solace and calm. Now there was none. "The duke is determined I . . . fulfill my duties as marquess." He proceeded to explain the circumstances that had led to their hasty departure, and the implications Nathaniel's marriage to Cassia would have on the ship and crew. When he'd finished, understanding dawned on Albion's face. "Ah."

There was a stretch of silence between them as they stood and stared out at the sea. A silence that Hayes broke. "You're a capable leader. I've fought with you in some of the bloodiest battles, faced some of the most ruthless pirates. And I do not doubt you can make your father see reason."

Nathaniel managed his first laugh of the day. His friend had more confidence in him than he deserved. "Even if he did not interfere and I was permitted to sail again, there is a w . . ." *Wife.* His mouth went dry, and he could not manage to squeeze the word out.

"A wife," Albion drawled. "I believe the word you are looking for is 'wife.'"

Only, she wouldn't be just any wife. It wouldn't be a formal arrangement with no feelings involved; there'd be genuine affection and real emotions, emotions like fear at what could happen to her, were she to become his wife. "Cassia," he whispered, willing them to understand those feelings he couldn't explain. Not even to these two closest friends. "There is . . . *her.*"

"And?" the other man asked. "She is comfortable on the sea. There is no reason she can't sail with us in the future," Albion pointed out. "Why does it have to be the end?"

Nathaniel frowned. "I'm risking her life now because there was no choice." Because there'd been no safe port in which to leave her and

Hayes. "I'll not do it in the future." Certainly not if they married. "Her security and well-being would fall to me."

Hayes chuckled. "The lady seems entirely resourceful. She found her sea legs, so much so that she passed herself off as a more-than-competent deckhand when she did, and was so good at what she did, she earned your appreciation and Carlisle's wrath." Nathaniel growled, and his quartermaster rushed to add another thought. "She can also swim better than even Albion here."

"Hey, now." The navigator tossed an elbow.

"Which is saying a good deal, as Albion is quite the skilled swimmer," Hayes said, blunting that slight. "I trust she'll be just fine at sea."

Nathaniel stared incredulously at his quartermaster. Did he not recall just how they'd discovered how skilled a swimmer Cassia was? She'd been tossed overboard by a damned sailor.

As if he'd read Nathaniel's thoughts, Hayes cleared his throat. "That is . . . with our usual crew, who is honorable and loyal, who would appreciate her presence as I, Shorty, Albion, Little Ron, and the others do. Either way," he went on, "I'm not suggesting you bring the lady on future missions. Wars don't last forever," he reminded him. "Eventually they end, and when there's peace, the allowances granted privateers, even those of a duke's son, come to an end. You can convert your shipping to new endeavors. Ones not fueled by war."

"Don't all shipping ventures ultimately involve war?" Nathaniel pointed out. If they weren't acquiring their enemies' resources at sea, they'd be waging battles in distant parts of the world, where England had exerted her control over unwilling peoples.

"There is no reason you can't deal in exports . . . wool and other textiles to the Americas . . ."

"The same America we are still at war with?" Nathaniel drawled.

Hayes smiled. "As I said . . ."

"I know," he muttered. "Wars do not last forever."

Marriage, however, did. Every muscle in his body coiled tight at the reminder. The only responsibility he'd ever foreseen, the only future he'd imagined, had been one at sea. Not . . . not . . . the prospect now before him. Nathaniel cursed. "You can say I'm a damned fool." Hayes and Albion could say it for the both of them.

"I wouldn't presume," Hayes said, his features even. "Women have driven any number of men to decisions that they wouldn't have ordinarily made."

A tinkling bell-like laugh rang out clear across the deck, the gentle sea breeze drawing that siren's sound closer, and like one of those hapless sailors, Nathaniel's gaze slid over to Cassia.

Whatever words Shorty had spoken had put a healthy bloom in her cheeks, and with the wind toying with the errant curls that had escaped the latest plait he'd made her, she was a sight he'd never forget, this slip of a woman who'd fit so effortlessly onto his ship and amongst his crew and into his life.

With a word of thanks, Nathaniel dismissed the two. After they'd gone, he shifted his focus back to the imp on his deck. At some point, she'd swapped out her charcoals for playing cards that Shorty, having sat beside her on the floor of the deck, dealt between them.

Engrossed in whatever the old sailor was saying, Cassia sat with her legs crossed, alternately nodding and stopping Shorty and putting a question to him.

Unlike his elder brother, Nathaniel had never much thought about the woman he'd one day marry. It hadn't been a thought he'd needed to have, and so he hadn't. Until he'd reached his twenty-eighth year and his brother had taken a fall from his horse. From that moment, Nathaniel had known everything had shifted. He'd known because his father hadn't even permitted Nathaniel the opportunity to mourn Marcus's passing before he was summoning Nathaniel and putting all manner of orders to him about his future and the ducal expectations that now fell to him.

Even when he'd known the duke would not relent until Nathaniel committed himself fully to the Roxburghe title, he'd still not considered the unknown lady who'd ultimately become his wife.

Now, he found his gaze drawn to the woman with her legs crossed before her, and like it were the most natural thing in the world, she chatted amicably with the burly old sailor Nathaniel had rescued from the gallows almost a decade to the date ago.

He'd not imagined a wife who'd sneak aboard ships to see the world, or don trousers, or challenge him at every turn. For the simple reason . . . he'd not known there was or could be a woman like her.

And he certainly didn't know what to do with a wife who was innocent and sweet, and incapable of anything more than a laugh or smile, and who prattled on as long as the longest summer's day at sea.

But he also knew what honor dictated.

That was absolutely the only reason he found his legs moving so effortlessly over, and why he joined her even now at middeck.

The moment his shadow fell over the pair, Shorty jumped to his feet.

Cassia glanced up, holding her hand of cards over her brow to shield the sun that beamed from behind him. "Nathan!" she greeted happily. "I mean, Captain!" she quickly amended.

Had anyone ever greeted him so? Not even his own mother, who dearly loved him, had ever found that level of exuberance and warmth at his arrival. Alternately, it unnerved him and left him with a peculiar warmth inside.

"Won't you join us?" Cassia patted the spot beside her. "Shorty was just teaching me the rules of écarté." She motioned for Shorty to join her on the floor once more, but the sailor remained standing at attention beside Nathaniel. "Have you played it?" Cassia didn't allow him a chance to answer. "I've only played whist, which I confess I'm not very good at, but—"

"Leave us."

Shorty instantly dropped a bow and took himself off.

Cassia followed the sailor with her gaze, and then frowned. "Nathan. I am not happy with you for sending Shorty away. We are—"

"We're getting married."

"You . . ." She puzzled her brow. "And Mr. Shorty are getting married?"

He cocked his head. "What? No. Not . . . Shorty and me." He slashed a hand between them. "You and me. We will marry."

Chapter 18

For a good portion of her girlhood years and then all of her adult life thus far, Cassia had imagined the day some suitor would swoop into her life. He'd be hopelessly and helplessly and madly, deeply in love with her.

And the day he professed his love, he'd also drop to a knee and ask her to be his wife.

In all her dreaming, that moment, that day, those words he'd have spoken, *all of it*, had been romantic in nature. The man she'd imagined would be unfailingly romantic, penning sonnets and snipping strands of her hair to tuck close to his heart.

That man she'd dreamed of had never been anything like Nathan.

And yet she'd come to appreciate that she didn't need sonnets or love songs or poems written in her honor. She wanted a man who treated her as an equal and who saw her worth as a person and who didn't stifle her, but rather supported her, allowing her to grow as a woman.

As such, Nathan's words, spoken in that gruff and rough and unromantic way, she would have joyously accepted—if it had been a question. Not this statement of fact born of his gentlemanly sense of honor.

"Well?" he barked. "Do you have nothing to say?"

Feeling his hard, unwavering stare upon her, Cassia exchanged the deck of cards for the more familiar comfort of her sketch pad. She opened the book once more, turning to her latest drawing.

"You know, Nathan"—she added several lines to her latest rendering, one of Hayes—"'Good afternoon' is generally the more traditional greeting," she said, imbuing as much sarcasm as she'd learned from this man himself into her words, words she intended as flippant.

He blinked slowly. "I beg your pardon?"

She brightened. "You are excused." Cassia resumed her sketching. "It was hardly an amusing jest."

A low growl echoed above her, and she kept her focus on her book. "I was not apologizing."

Her heart jumped. "Oh." She paused and glanced up, craning her neck all the way back so she could meet his fierce stare. "Well, you should be."

"I'm telling you that we'll marry," he said, his tone angrier than she'd ever heard it. That was, with the exception of when he'd dealt with Carlisle, Turner, and Oliver. Not many days ago, the sound of it would have stirred terror. No longer.

Cassia set aside her book and climbed to her feet. "You don't tell someone you will marry them, Nathan," she said patiently, thinking she was perhaps more a saint than her family had ever credited for mustering that sentiment.

A frown formed between his eyebrows. "I just did."

"Yes," she said, her calm slipping. "Yes, you did." She tapped his arm. "You're supposed to *ask*."

Understanding filled his dark-blue eyes. "Marry me?"

Only the slight up-tilt managed to transform those same two words into a question. And she realized in this moment it was everything she wanted. He was everything she wanted. If that question had been real. If it had come as something more than an order and were spoken from a place of longing and love. Her heart squeezed painfully so that her entire chest ached. She didn't want Nathan this way.

She inclined her head. "No."

His brows dipped. "No?" he growled.

"No . . . thank you?" she ventured, and before she tossed aside her pride and took what he offered, and a mere scrap of all she wanted from him, Cassia bent, retrieved her things, and headed back to his cabin.

She made it all the way to the stairs before she registered his footfalls following close behind her.

"No?" he repeated, his voice tinged with shock and annoyance.

Cassia wrinkled her brow. Leave it to Captain Nathaniel Ellsby to be the annoyed one in this.

"I said, 'No, thank you,'" Cassia repeated as she reached below deck. "I was perfectly polite in my rejection."

"Is that what you think I am upset about?" he demanded, his footfalls close to hers. "Your *manners?*"

"No?"

They reached his cabin. "No." That syllable emerged as a low growl.

"I believe we've already ascertained that my answer"—to his nonquestion that he'd only reluctantly transformed into one at her correction—"was, in fact, a decided no." With that, she clasped the handle of his door and let herself in.

Nathan followed behind her, and then with the heel of his boot, he shoved the panel shut. Hard.

It shook, reverberating in its frame.

"You are rejecting me." He sounded so truly incredulous and hurt and shocked that she took mercy on him.

"I'm sorry, Nathan. Fear not. There are other fish in the sea." She brightened. "Do you like that? My ocean reference? Jeremy taught me that phrase after I told him of the duke's rejection, and I rather liked it. Given your seafaring ways, it does suit, doesn't it?" When he continued to stare slack-jawed, she frowned. *"Doesn't it?"*

Alas, that sea reference did not seem to mollify him. Not one bit. Splotches of angry color filled his rugged cheeks.

"We made love," he snapped.

And despite herself, despite all the ways—the very many ways—in which they had been intimate, she felt a blush steal over her body from the tips of her hair on down to her toes.

"Why?" she asked softly.

The frown lines at the corners of his mouth deepened. "Because we desire one another—"

"Not *why* did we make love," she said, taking a step toward him. Cassia tipped her chin back so she could meet his eyes. "Why did you ask to marry me?"

He tugged at his shirt collar. "Because it is the honorable thing to do . . . and I . . ."

Cassia held her breath.

"I care about you," he finished, deflating that great hope in her heart.

He cared about her, and even that admission had been a reluctant one on his part.

Disappointment filled her breast, and she proved so very selfish and greedy because she wanted more.

Does it matter, though? a voice needled. *He cares about you.* He'd just said as much. That was enough. Or it should be.

Cassia lowered her eyes to his neck and fought to release a painful breath she'd not even realized she was holding. She'd thought there could be nothing worse than never finding a man to truly love her. There was. It was finding a man whom she loved so desperately and discovering that he only cared for her.

"Cassia?" he said gruffly.

She forced herself to meet his gaze. "Would you have offered to marry me if we hadn't made love?" she asked quietly, and she heard it, a palpable hesitation from him that hung in the air between them. "I thought so, Nathan."

He flexed his jaw. "But we did make love. Furthermore, you should have considered that before." He lowered his voice. "You'll be ruined if society learns you've been aboard my ship, alone with me and my crew."

Not for the first time, she allowed herself to think precisely what would happen if the world discovered where she'd been these past days. Her siblings would be ruined, and while she hurt inside at the idea that she might inadvertently have brought pain to her family, she could not bring herself to regret the freedom she'd known, and she was staggered by the realization that she'd change nothing. She'd not give up these experiences, and all she'd seen . . . or the time she'd had with Nathan.

Cassia lifted her gaze to Nathan's, only to find his eyes searingly on her.

"Your crew will not say anything, Nathan," she said softly. "No one knows I'm here." She turned her palms up. "Why, no one even knows my real name. I am a MacKay." She paused, chewing at the tip of her finger. "Though I suppose I should consider what might happen if the world believes a MacKay was alone at sea. I suspect the feud between our clans would only further intensify, and—"

"Cassia," Nathan warned in his low, deep baritone.

"Don't you see," she cried softly. "I don't want you because you feel obligated. And it may seem silly and immature and naive, but . . . but I always wanted a man who wanted to be with me not out of any sense of duty."

"Why can't it be both?"

She willed him to understand. "I want romance, Nathan." She moved her eyes over each angle of his beloved face. "I want a man so moved by his feelings for me that he'll write me verses or sing me songs or . . . or . . . snip a lock of my hair to keep close . . . or brings flowers."

He stared at her with stricken eyes. Or mayhap that was her own expression reflected in his deep sapphire irises?

Cassia drew in a slow, uneven breath. "I do thank you for worrying after me and my reputation." She placed her palms on his chest and smoothed them over the soft fabric of his lawn shirt. "However, you needn't. I'd resigned myself to being a spinster prior to this voyage. I won't marry . . ." She paused, and her fingers stilled, resting against the hard, muscled contours of his chest. "Unless it is for love."

The muscles under her palm jumped in the only indication he'd heard her.

He stared back, his expression unreadable, his gaze opaque, and for a long, long minute, Cassia held her breath and waited. Waited for him to speak the words she so desperately wished for him to speak. Waited for him to offer meager assurances of his affections.

And yet, as only silence continued on, hope withered and died and fell like a thousand little charred scraps to her lower belly.

At last, he nodded, slowly. "If you change your mind . . ."

Oh, God. Why does this hurt so very badly? "I won't," she said, her voice thick to her own ears.

Nathan searched his gaze over her face. "Why are you so damned obstinate, Cassia McQuoid?"

"La, Nathan. I might even think you *want* to marry me," she teased. Only her voice trembled, for her words weren't in jest; they were those of a woman who desperately wanted them to be true.

Nathan lingered, looking as if he were about to say more, and Lord help her for being a fool, hope came roaring back to life, and her heart lifted. Then, lowering his brow, he touched it to hers.

Shouts went up around the ship, cutting into whatever he was about to say.

A moment later footsteps thundered; the men and cabin boys in the lower deck streamed past, their feet having the sound of one of those thunderous stampedes her brother Arran had regaled Cassia and her siblings with the tales of some years earlier.

Nathan was already striding across the room, reaching for the handle.

KnockKnockKnock.

He yanked the panel open, interrupting Hayes mid-pounding of the door.

"What—?"

"The *Renard*," Hayes interrupted. "He is putting us on the defensive."

Nathan released a black curse that sent heat to her cheeks and, without a backward look, stormed from the cabin. His quartermaster followed closely behind him.

Cassia hurried after them. "*Renard* . . . You have a fox at sea?" she asked.

Both men ignored her.

"He'd the wind on his side," Hayes was saying.

Cassia quickened her steps. "I'm really quite good at giving animals a chase. My sister once had a rabbit who was really quite speedy, and he took flight . . . not the actual flight. He's not a bird, however—"

At last, she was seen. Nathan and Mr. Hayes paused briefly and stared at her incredulously a moment before resuming their talks, as Cassia found herself instantly forgotten for a second time.

And as Nathan fired off a series of questions, barking orders as crew members rushed past, she lengthened her strides, hurrying to keep up as Nathan and his second-in-command took the stairs quickly.

"Can we outrun him?" Nathan asked.

Outrun him?

Cassia paused on one of the rungs. Her brow dipped. *What in blazes . . . ?*

One of the cabin boys—Little Ron—brushed by, knocking her back to the moment, and Cassia resumed her climb, doing a sweep of the bustling main deck.

"See to the breechings!" Nathan shouted as one of his men came near, and a pair hastened in the opposite direction.

All hands had assembled, each man frantically rushing about, with shiny sabers fastened to their sides.

Sabers?

As Cassia hurried to join Nathan at the helm, she scanned the horizon, her eyes immediately landing on the outline of a large vessel. Even without their elucidation, Nathan and Hayes's peculiar conversation began to make more sense. Suddenly, years of tales her brother and Jeremy had regaled Cassia and her siblings with came to her, of pirates, great scourges of the sea.

Cassia gripped the railing. "It's not an *actual* fox, is it?" she whispered. "Fox . . . isn't a person." She made herself say it aloud. "A ship. It's a ship."

Nathan jerked his gaze over to her, looking at Cassia as though he'd only just recalled her presence. "Get her below."

Stunned, Cassia widened her eyes . . . and then it hit her, all the questions she'd asked him about his shipping company, his evasive responses. His crew's evasive responses. "Nathan, are *you* a pirate, too?"

"A privateer," he grated. "This isn't the time."

"What is the difference?"

"Cassia," he said tightly, and looked again to his second-in-command. "Get her below deck. Stay there with her."

Stay with her?

"Every hand will be needed on deck," Hayes protested, pausing long enough to sluice a black look her way.

"Those are orders, Hayes," Nathan barked, and the menacing ice in his eyes managed to chill even Cassia.

Nathan would remain here and face a crew of ruthless pirates. Images darkened her mind, of him taking a blade through the heart. Her insides twisted, and she gripped his arm. "I don't want to leave . . ." *You. I don't want to leave you. Or lose you.*

He slid his gaze over her face, moving it like the softest of physical touches. "I will be fine," he said gruffly.

Her eyes smarted. "You don't know that." He hated tears, and she hated for him to see them. Especially now. Cassia looked away, back out over the horizon, to that increasingly larger ship bearing down on them.

Nathan cupped her cheek, angling her face back to his. He traced the winding trail left by her teardrops with the rough pad of his thumb.

She sniffed. "You hate tears."

"I hate to see *you* cry," he corrected, and the unexpected tenderness in that clarification only made more tears well. "I need you to go below, Cassia," he said quietly. "Having you above deck is a distraction. Knowing you are here, that you are here even now, prevents me from being clearheaded, and I need to be focused."

And she needed him in her life. She knew that now. She loved him so hopelessly and so desperately, she'd take him in the only way she could have him. It didn't matter that he'd felt obligated to offer for her. He loved her and she loved him, and that was what mattered most.

Cassia gave a shaky nod. "Nathan, I . . . will."

"Good."

"No . . . that is . . . I will." She wetted her lips.

He pinned that intense stare on her.

"Marry you," she clarified. "When this is over. That is, if you still—"

He leaned down and swallowed the rest of that pronouncement with his kiss, robbing her of those words of love she'd speak and of the very air in her lungs.

It was over too quickly, done before it had begun.

Dazed, her lashes fluttered.

Nathan looked over to a stony-faced Hayes.

And reluctantly, she allowed that other man to escort her back to Nathan's rooms. They reached the stairs, and she paused to look back.

Nathan stood at the center of the ship, shouting orders to every sailor. He was a breathtaking sight of a man in full command, a towering figure who, with his tone and quick orders, inspired confidence, and it was impossible to imagine anyone defeating such a raw, powerful figure . . .

Only, despite that strength, he was real and human and flesh and blood, and flesh could be pierced, and blood spilled.

A tortured moan slipped from her lips.

"Cassia?"

Hayes's impatient query startled her back to the present, and Cassia yanked her attention forward and followed him.

When they'd reached Nathan's cabin, he pressed the handle and motioned for her to enter, following in close behind.

Once inside, Hayes locked the door, blotting out the din from the activity above.

There was an unnaturalness to the quiet, a hum of silence which mingled ominously with the muffled shouts and clatter of footfalls overhead.

Restless, Cassia stared out the back window. Within the lead panes she caught sight of Hayes, pacing restlessly back and forth. Disquieted when she'd only ever seen him calm, and the sight of him so sent panic swirling inside her breast.

"You were much calmer at our first meeting," she remarked, needing to fill the void of their silence.

"That's when I thought you were a green boy, new to sailing, and before I discovered you are, in fact, a lady out to explore the world." He smiled, and that grin felt strained, distracted.

Shouts went up from above deck, the men's voices so clear and loud, as if they were right outside, they brought her attention to the ceiling.

"It will be fine, Cassia," Hayes said quietly. "This is . . . normal."

She managed a nod. It was a normal she didn't like or know. "I trust Nathan and the men."

Cannon fire exploded over the waters, and the ship swayed violently. Hayes managed to keep standing, even as Cassia was knocked from her feet, landing hard on the floor. The force of that fall pulled a sharp cry from her lips as pain shot from her hip up to her right shoulder. All around them, Nathan's papers and maps went flying, his always orderly desk thrown into a chaos to match the tumult outside. Ivory vellum rained about the cabin like the stream of fire trailing from the sky painted black in battle.

With a curse, Hayes marched over, as easily as if he were striding across a ballroom, and extended a hand to help her up. "Are you—?"

"I'm all right," she interrupted. She'd suffered a small fall. The men outside, however, shouting and crying, were battling for their very lives.

Another explosion sent the ship rocking, this time knocking Hayes onto his buttocks beside her.

"Are *you* all right?" she asked, glancing over.

His mouth twisted wryly. "I'd feel eminently better if I were out there."

As one, they looked to the opposite window; the rectangular windows framed a horrific tableau unfolding on those waters, and Cassia's stomach pitched again.

Nathan was out there. While cannonballs exploded and shots were fired, he was in the midst of it.

Squeezing her eyes shut, Cassia bit the inside of her cheek hard, focusing on the pain, searching for a distraction and finding none. Because in this instant she imagined a world without Nathan in it. She saw him being cut down and his life ended. Her breathing grew raspy in her ears.

"Fiiire," someone shouted, and more shots were fired, staccato reports of muskets and pistols that went on forever, so different from the times she'd used one of those weapons while hunting with her brothers and Jeremy. She'd never hunt again. Not with now knowing the terror the animals had faced in those moments.

She dimly registered Hayes sliding over to take up a place alongside her on the floor.

"Cassia," Hayes said again, this time with a firm insistence that forced her to open her eyes. "He will be fine. I've fought alongside the captain since we were just boys out of Oxford. There isn't a more skilled, capable sailor than he."

"I believe that," she whispered. And yet, she might be naive and innocent in the ways of life and war, but she was wise enough to know that war was unpredictable. That anything could happen. "Nor is it just Nathan," she confessed. So many men on this crew mattered to her. "Shorty is out there and Little Ron and Lieutenant Albion and—"

"Do you know what I always find helpful during a battle?"

She glanced over. "Fighting?"

He snorted. "Fair enough. Yes, well, on the eve of a battle, then. A sailor is always prepared, and yet in the days or night leading up, the mind can have a tendency to wander to the darkest end of what's to come. But worrying? It doesn't fix anything, Cassia," he said, his voice earnest. "It doesn't lessen the danger or end the battle any quicker."

"What helps, then?" she whispered, her gaze locked on the ominous scene out on the seas. The enemy ship had drawn nearer, so close she could now make out the distinct outline of each detail of the vessel, from its massive sails to the bold, bright colors of the French flag it flew to the uniformed men aboard . . . and the cylindrical heads of their cannon pointed at the *Flying Dragon*.

"A distraction," Hayes said, and blinking back a dazed confusion, Cassia glanced over.

A distraction? A distraction. Yes, of course.

Cassia glanced about Nathan's upended cabin; his quarters, always so neat, were now in disarray. His important papers were strewn about the room. She couldn't be of any help to him out there, but here, she could do something.

Pushing onto her knees, Cassia proceeded to gather up the ledgers.

"That's better," Hayes said, climbing to his feet, and as she stooped, picking up those leather books, the quartermaster headed to the row of weapons hung at the opposite wall. Removing a bayonet, he studied the weapon and practiced aiming that muzzle.

"They are getting closer," she whispered.

"Aye," Hayes said quietly, confirming she'd spoken aloud.

Cassia tore her gaze from the horrifyingly entrancing tableau of that vessel sailing ever closer. *You wanted to experience the world, and now you are experiencing it . . . in all its horror.*

"I-is that normal?"

"Aye."

"Will they . . . make it on board?"

"No one has before," Hayes said, pride tingeing that pronouncement.

Setting Nathan's books back upon his desk, she knelt and started collecting his maps. "How long are battles at sea?"

"It varies. Some have taken an hour. Others all day. Some last days."

Cassia paused in her cleaning. "Days?" she whispered.

"This one won't be that long," he rushed to assure her. "Find comfort in the fact that the British are more successful because of our higher rates of accuracy and fire. We are a naval nation. The French? They aren't as skilled. They are notorious for standing off downward at twice pistol shot, and they fire upward at their opponent's rigging to take out their rival's masts. It's a bold move, trying to maneuver astern, but it has proven ineffectual, too."

It was a logical argument he gave, one grounded in naval facts and experience, reminding her that Mr. Hayes was not just a gentleman; he was a skilled naval officer. She'd cost Nathan a reliable fighter in his quartermaster. Just as her presence had wrought problems with Carlisle and Turner and Oliver and the other men who'd served on Nathan's ship and taken exception to her being here.

She was a distraction that none of them could afford.

Her heart spasmed.

Cassia went back to tidying Nathan's space. As she did, Hayes continued his examination of different weapons affixed to the wall. And her mind shied away from the reasons he was testing those guns, what that evaluation meant. Why he occasionally paused to point a gun or musket at the doorway . . . knowing he prepared for the possibility of the enemy overtaking the ship and storming Nathan's cabin. There was only one reason they'd storm the captain's quarters, because—

Mmm. Mmm.

Her mind balked and shied away from what it meant, because she couldn't let her thoughts go there. She couldn't imagine a world without Nathan in it.

Cassia set the last of the maps down, and then set to gathering up the hundreds of sheets of parchment scattered throughout the room.

The cannon fired once more, and she stared with horrified eyes, unblinking as it sailed nearer, landing just a handful of paces from the *Flying Dragon*, and the ship rocked violently, again throwing her sideways.

Through this latest assault, Hayes remained unflustered, his legs not even faltering under that latest blast. Instead, he caught her, keeping her on her feet. After Cassia found her legs, Hayes released her and headed to stare out the windows at the fight unfolding.

As Cassia worked her chest heaved, and her body sweat . . . because of fear.

Yes, she was afraid.

Only, she wasn't afraid of dying.

Rather, she was afraid of not . . . living.

Odd, she'd lived twenty-one years, and never had she appreciated how little she'd experienced until she'd had a taste of it with Nathan.

And she wanted to. She wanted it so very desperately.

She'd set out to see the world, and she had . . . with Nathan, but this had just been a glimmer of a taste, and she wanted all of it with him.

The whole thing.

She didn't want to paint the same paintings or sketches of the same people and places she'd known forever.

She wanted to sail the waters and see where the other side of sailing brought them.

And she wanted all that to be with Nathan, too.

As she tidied the scattered papers, she skimmed her gaze over words inked in bold, strong strokes, a confident hand so very clearly that of Nathan, a powerful man who would be in possession of those sturdy letters.

Cassia reached for another; unlike the others, this was crumpled. She smoothed it out and made to set it with the others . . . and then stopped.

This one was different.

Written in a delicate hand.

> My dearest son,
> Each time you leave, my heart is full from knowing the joy you find in your travels, and yet it weeps because you are gone, and because of the dangers you face out there. Even with my fear for you, however, I've never sought to intervene or interfere, because I know the love you find in your seafaring ways . . .

She paused.

Those tender words were ones conferred from a mother to her son. They were intimate and private, and she'd no place reading them.

And yet . . . she stole a glimpse at Hayes, who continued to examine his gun.

Unbidden, her gaze slipped down once more.

> You believe, following your last meeting with your dear father, that his threatening to end your seafaring

ventures if you do not marry is driven by his need to be in control. It isn't.

I will confess, selfishly, that I've longed for you to give up your time at sea. I've lived with fear that you will one day lose your life on those waters that you so love, and that in so doing, you will never know what it is to have the love of a wife and a family of your own. I worry I will lose you as I lost Marcus. There has always been an understanding between Lady Angela's family and ours, one that was cemented with your late brother's engagement to Angela . . . but this is about far more than just that connection. I *know* . . . she will make you a good wife. She is all things good and clever. If you are to be angry and carry resentment at the requirements your father put to you, then I'd have you place blame where blame is owed. We *both* want you to come home.

Cassia stopped reading, her gaze locked on that single word, and her heart ceased to beat, too.

What was Nathan's mother saying?

Only, Cassia knew. It was stated clearly there; even so, her mind shuttered and her soul balked. And because she was a glutton, Cassia glanced down at the note a second time and made herself read every last word written there, again.

Please know, it is not just a fear of losing you to the seas that resulted in my interference. I truly believe you need more than a life of work, my son. You need a love like I have with your father. Angela understands the future that awaits her as a duchess, but she'll also become a friend to you, as your father and I are friends. Yes, I know you probably don't believe either of these possible, but—

Cassia's heart remembered its function; this time, it beat a slow, sickening rhythm against her rib cage.

Nathan was . . . to be betrothed.

And worse . . . it was to his late brother's former fiancée, a young lady who was intelligent and kind and closely linked to Nathan's family. In short, a woman who was everything Cassia was not.

And even worse than that, Nathan's sailing career was reliant upon his marrying the woman his father and mother had selected for him, which meant—

Cassia yanked her fingers back, away from those hated pages. In having agreed to be Nathan's wife and allowing him to do right by her, she'd ultimately prevent him from doing the one thing he loved most, something that his crew relied upon him to do for their own security.

And it would all . . . stop.

Because of me.

"Oh, G-god," she whispered, her voice cracking.

"Cassia?" Hayes asked, concern filling his voice.

Cassia's lower lip trembled. "I'm f-fine," she said, her shaky response proving she was the worst sort of liar. "I-I am worried, is all."

It wasn't all. She was worried, of course. But her heart was breaking, too. This was why a person didn't go snooping. This right here. Because ultimately one always came upon things they didn't *really* want to know.

Doing so, however, did not change the words on that note.

It didn't change what was to be.

"I promise, it is going to be all—"

"You can't promise that, Hayes," she cried. "You cannot tell me that any of this is going to be all right." As soon as the words left her lips, she wanted to call them back, only feeling worse. "I'm—"

"Don't apologize," he said solemnly. "You are facing things most grown men don't even know of."

Cassia folded her arms at her middle. She didn't deserve that grace. Not when her being here and Nathan's promise to marry her would result in Hayes and all the crew of the *Flying Dragon* losing their livelihoods. For she'd no doubt that Nathan would marry her—he was a man of honor. But in doing so, he'd grow to resent her for costing him what he wanted most in life.

Tears scorched her eyes, and she wiped a hand angrily over her cheeks.

Silly was what it was. Crying like this. Crying, when her life and the lives of Nathan and his crew hung in the balance, all dependent upon the outcome of this sea battle.

Boom.

A violent explosion rocked the ship, and the floor moved out from under her, the suddenness of that blast knocking away the damning note, and Cassia went flying through the air.

A pained hiss exploded from her lips as she crashed onto the floor, landing hard on her side; a vicious throbbing shot from her hip up to her arms.

Breathless from the force of her fall, Cassia lay there dazed and motionless, her cheek pressed against the floor, and her gaze locked on the water rushing into Nathan's cabin.

A loud ringing filled her ears, and through the din of the battle, she tried to sort out what had happened . . . and what was happening?

Water.

Which meant there was a hole . . .

They were taking on water.

Cursing blackly, Hayes grabbed up weapons. "Do you know how to shoot?" he asked loudly over the noise of it all.

Cassia managed a nod. He thrust a pistol into her hand, and she stared at his mouth as it moved, but like this moment, it was moving entirely too fast, and she was struggling to sort out what was happening. "In case you . . ." Taking her by the elbow, he steered her to the door. "We have to get out."

She glanced back to the shattered window.

Another ship had entered the fray, the massive, white-masted vessel appearing amidst the smoke left by the cannon's fire. It towered over the horizon, so that even where she stood, Cassia had to tip her head back.

Even as they made a hasty retreat from Nathan's cabin, crew members were streaming in with buckets and tools, and it was pandemonium as they set to work repairing the damaged ship.

Chapter 19

Starboard, his hand clenching on the hilt of his bayonet, Nathaniel watched as the enemy ship drew closer.

At his side, Albion matched Nathaniel's movements and, with an equally intense gaze, followed the approach.

"I know," Nathaniel grumped.

"I didn't say anything," the other man reminded him.

"You didn't need to."

Never in all the years Nathaniel had operated as the Scourge of the Seas had he lost a sea battle.

In fact, with each one he'd fought, he'd been as empowered and energized as he'd been eager before those fights.

In the more than two dozen skirmishes he and his crew had engaged in, they'd always emerged triumphant. There'd never been a doubt as to the outcome, and a certainty of anything other than the demise of a French vessel.

That was, until now.

Now should prove the first time they would fall.

The *Flying Dragon* was to be overtaken.

And God help him, as he shouted orders to the men manning the cannons and the crew around him scurried into position, it was only Cassia he could think about.

Restless, Nathaniel squinted, attempting to make out the shadowy outline through the smoke.

At his side, Albion stared through the bring 'em near against his eye. Wordlessly, he handed it over to Nathaniel.

Accepting the telescope, he adjusted the lens, bringing the distance into better focus, and his muscles instantly coiled tightly.

He cursed.

"A second," Albion said needlessly, holding aloft two fingers.

This one wasn't flying French flags. It was a privateer that had come to feast on the French navy's efforts.

One ship, one crew, they might triumph over.

A second?

Panic. It was a foreign sentiment he'd never known in the heart of battle. In the past, he'd always been enlivened by the fight. Never had he known this numbing dread that spread like a poison within.

Lowering the telescope, Nathaniel looked to Albion. "I need your assurance . . . if something happens to me, you and Hayes will look after her."

"You'll live because you're too damned stubborn to die," his navigator murmured, and then Albion inclined his head slightly. "But you have my word that I will defend her this day with my life."

And after this.

Nathaniel's chest constricted painfully.

But if Nathaniel died, and she somehow managed to survive . . .

Innocent Cassia, with her smile that went on for days and her adorable tendency to chatter, would find herself at the mercy of a rival ship. The fact that those men operated for the French government, whereas Nathaniel did only with special permission from the king, meant nothing.

In the game of war, all rules ceased to exist; the honor that dictated ways in the ballrooms and Polite Society was a world away, which meant any courtesies afforded Cassia in London, or even in foreign courts abroad, should she have attended them, ceased to be here.

His stomach revolting, Nathaniel fought back those images rapidly threatening to overtake him.

He could not let those thoughts in. Not when in so doing, he cost himself a clear head, when a clear head was what he desperately needed to protect Cassia.

Nathaniel firmed his jaw and turned to face his crew, assembling them with a single word. When they were before him, quiet and pale as he'd never seen them, Nathaniel proceeded to walk back and forth amongst them.

"We have fought twenty-six sea battles," he called, stalking up and down the decks. "And in how many of those battles have we emerged triumphant?"

"Twenty-six," came a unifying shout amongst the men and boys assembled.

"How many lives have we lost?" Nathaniel followed with that question.

"None!" That echo rose high and powerful from his crew.

Their shoulders drew back and higher with every reminder his words served as.

"None," Nathaniel repeated. "The *Flying Dragon* has never been defeated. It has never been taken. Let that record remain." Brandishing his sword, he pointed it at the smoke-filled sky that had blotted out all hint of blue and ushered in a false night. "Fight," he thundered. "Fight for your crew. Fight for your freedom. Fight for your lives."

His men hefted their swords overhead as, a moment later, the French frigate used pull arms to snag the rigging of the ship to bring it alongside, and those uniformed men in their tidy blue wool scrambled over.

And with a shout, Nathaniel threw himself into the fight.

—⁓⁂⁓—

Hell.

They said there were seven layers to that underworld, and standing at the back of the ship, Cassia believed she'd stumbled upon an eighth.

Acrid smoke stung her nostrils and clogged her lungs, making it a chore to get a proper breath.

A pistol in one hand and a small sword in the other, Cassia paused at the top of the stairs leading out to the battle unfolding, and coward that she was, she wanted to flee.

She wanted to rush headfirst back in the direction she'd just come, hide herself away in Nathan's cabin, and even with the water rushing in, barricade the door yet again.

Only . . . Her heart spasmed. Nathan was there.

Amidst those incoherent wartime shouts and cries was Nathan's voice somewhere.

Or what if it isn't?

Her body trembled, and her eyes slid shut under the heavy weight of grief and despair brought at the mere thought of a life without him in it.

She'd already resolved there wouldn't be a future the way she'd wanted with him, but even the thought of losing him to another woman—of him marrying a lady who'd been hand-selected for him by his family and giving that same woman children and the life Cassia yearned to have with him—was nothing compared with the pain of losing him on this day forever.

Cassia forced her eyes open.

She and Hayes had sought refuge down a corridor. He'd positioned himself before her, his musket at the ready.

He paused, turning back, and shouted, making himself heard over the sounds of gunfire and the cries of battle. "Are you—"

At that moment, a tall, bewigged fellow in a blue uniform stepped into the corridor.

Cassia lunged forward on the balls of her feet. "Hayes!" she cried. Lifting her pistol, she fired.

A cloud of smoke immediately filled the air before her; when it cleared, she found Hayes's would-be assassin sprawled on the floor. Unconscious. Or . . . dead.

Oh, God.

The quartermaster jerked and turned quickly back, his gaze landing on the felled sailor, and then Hayes turned that stunned stare to Cassia. And then he found his voice. "We have to get you out of here," he bellowed.

Only, as he took her by the hand and steered her through the ship, overrun with enemy sailors now sparring with Nathan's men, there was no shelter. There was no place that was safe.

Then, she and Hayes were parted. Cassia cried out as a pair of strong, powerful arms grabbed her back.

She lashed out, flailing, before registering . . .

Gripping her hard by the shoulders, Nathan looked her over. "My God, Cassia. What in hell are you doing here?" he rasped, and then, as the world burned around them, he pulled her into his arms.

"The cabin has been damaged," Hayes bellowed. "It's taking in water. There are crew seeing to it."

"Nathan, I . . . shot a man."

Her voice was dazed, her gaze distant.

He groaned. "Cassia—"

Through the hell of the world falling down, there was still an odd calming and peace in just being here in his arms. She loved him. She always would. Whether she lived just a handful of minutes more—which appeared increasingly likely—or if she somehow survived to being an ancient woman of eighty-one, the memory of him and the love she carried for him would last with her until she drew her final breath, and then well into the beyond.

Nathan worked his gaze frantically over her face, and for an instant she believed all the emotion, all the love, she felt for this man glittered to life in his dark sapphire eyes.

"I need to find someplace safe for you," he said harshly, and he motioned with a hand.

Hayes was instantly there.

"Get her below deck. Back to my cabin and see she doesn't—" Nathan stopped midorder as his gaze went to the other ship that had pulled up close.

"Nathan." Cassia tugged at his sleeve. "What is it?"

"Get her out of here, Hayes!" he bellowed, and the quartermaster instantly wrapped a strong arm about her waist and hauled her off.

Cassia wrestled against him. "Hayes, please."

"You are making it worse, Cassia," he said against her ear.

She was making it worse. That was what she'd done at every turn where Nathan was concerned. Where even with the grave mistake she'd made in boarding the wrong ship and finding a grand adventure and joy and wonderment, she'd brought nothing but trouble to Nathan.

Cassia went limp and stared unblinkingly into nothing as she was hauled off to the kitchens.

And she remained there, with Hayes positioned in front of her, poised for battle, as time inched on with an agonizing slowness. In her mind, she saw it all play out, Nathan battling the enemy.

She loved him.

She loved him with all she was.

Whimpering, she buried her face against Hayes's back, the fabric and explosions drowning out the sounds of her misery.

If they survived, she would set him free. This was his life, and if he married her, she'd rob him and his crew of the work they did . . . that mattered so very much to him. She couldn't bear to be the one responsible for his unhappiness.

Except there was no certainty that either of them—any of them—would survive this day.

The battle raged on, leaving her with only the tumult of her thoughts and the threat of battle. She'd never again know Nathan's embrace. There'd be no future for them. She'd never again see her family.

Cries and shouts thundered over the clang of swords striking.

And then there was an eerie silence.

Cassia shivered. "What is it?" she whispered.

A moment later thunderous cheers went up, shouts of Englishmen, not French. Stomping feet, and then she heard it . . . Nathan's voice, loud and strong and powerful and alive.

She gripped Hayes by the arm. "Is it over?"

He grinned, dusting a hand over his sweaty brow. "It is."

With a cry, Cassia took off running. She needed to see Nathan.

"Cassia," the quartermaster shouted, charging after her.

Except . . . they'd survived, and the thrill of being alive and knowing Nathan was alive filled her. There was only one person she wished to see.

Jeremy.

Cassia jerked to a stop and furrowed her brow. *"Jeremy?"*

Hayes looked at her confusedly.

That voice mixed with the shouts above, so familiar, and yet—perhaps this was the end. Mayhap it was true when they said in a person's final moments on earth, everyone and everything to come before flashed before one's eyes.

"Impossible," she said.

Because how to account for the familiar sound of Jeremy's bellowing, that voice raised similarly to when she'd played at pirates with him.

"Cassia?"

Ignoring Hayes's worried tones, she trained her ears instead, listening for one voice amidst the crowd.

There it was again.

"Jeremy!" Cassia gasped and took off running.

"Cassia!" Nathan shouted after her.

Ignoring him, she continued her race across the deck.

———— ❧❧ ————

They'd been boarded.

Again.

Only, that other crew, also without uniforms, turned their efforts on the French, and it was as though a palpable energy had been breathed anew into Nathaniel's crew as those men joined them in the fight.

Through the years, Nathaniel's crew had easily overpowered their opponents. As such, the hand-to-hand combats had never been drawn out. The fights had been quick, and the spoils swiftly achieved. There'd never been a lengthy war between Nathaniel's vessel and others.

This new crew to join them fought with an ease and skill that bespoke of men who'd fought and fought often.

The clink of metal striking metal as swords met in a noisy clash, mingled with the thunderous boom of the ship's cannon fire that had become an assault on the French ship.

And then . . . there came that belated shout of surrender from the French commander, one that cut through the battle and brought an eerily abrupt cessation of cries and an errant clatter of sword clanging, as men registered at different times the significance of that cry.

His chest still heaving with the energy that came from fighting and surviving a battle, Nathaniel looked to an approaching figure, whose long, bold strides marked him as the captain of the ship who'd joined them in their fight against the French.

A cry went up.

Nathaniel's entire body jerked.

A woman's cry.

Cassia.

His heart pounding, Nathaniel looked frantically for her.

She came racing forward, and he stretched fingers out to reach for her, but like an elusive specter, she slipped past.

"Cassia," he shouted as she went hurtling by, and then he took chase after her.

Only—

Cassia flung herself forward . . . into a pair of waiting arms—those of the captain who'd boarded Nathaniel's ship and lent Nathaniel's crew his support. Large, powerful arms instantly folded her close, in an embrace that was all too familiar.

"Cassia?" Incredulity filled the man's greeting. "What in hell?"

Shock filled the other man's deep tones, a question that ricocheted as an echo of the very one knocking around Nathaniel's head.

Alternately laughing and sobbing, Cassia continued to cling to the other man, and red-hot rage fired through Nathaniel's veins, and a growl rumbled up his chest and stuck somewhere in his throat.

"What the hell is the meaning of this?" Nathaniel snapped, and Cassia turned radiant eyes back to him, eyes that shimmered with tears, not like the miserable ones he'd brought her to, or near to, all the times before this, but with joy, and damned if her joy wrought by a different man didn't have the same vicious searing impact on his heart.

"Nathan," Cassia said happily through her tears. "It is *Jeremy*."

"Jeremy?" he repeated dumbly.

Jeremy.

And then it hit him.

The man whose ship she'd intended to board hadn't been a pudgy, soft-faced Englishman with an equally soft middle and schooner. Rather, he was a man with two inches on Nathaniel's own impressive six feet four inches and equally muscled, and also . . .

Jeremy.

Captain Jeremy, who did not fly flags.

Captain Jeremy.

"The Terror of the Seas," Nathaniel muttered.

Cassia laughed and playfully swatted Nathaniel's arm. "Jeremy isn't a *terror*. He is . . ." And then she widened her eyes. Her words trailed off. "Arran," she whispered.

Nathaniel's brows shot together. Who—?

Cassia squirmed out of the other man's embrace and went flying in the opposite direction.

"Cassia!" There came a second man shouting her name, his voice filled with a like shock.

"Arran," Cassia cried as yet another held her close. The pair continued to hold one another.

Arran.

And then Nathaniel recalled the whisper of a story she'd shared . . . about her big family . . . and the brother who traveled.

Weeping happy-sounding tears, Cassia took the big man by the hand and tugged him on to Nathaniel. "Nathan," she said between laughter and sobs. "It is my brother."

Chapter 20

Her brother was here.

As was Jeremy.

Jeremy and her brother, who were both . . . apparently pirates. Or privateers. Either way, it was the same thing. That great secret they'd somehow managed to keep from Cassia and their family and the entire world. For surely had any of the McQuoids known, then all the McQuoids would have known. Because there weren't secrets in their family.

At least, not as long as it was a shared secret.

And another time she might have been riddled with resentment that her brother had kept such an important part of himself from Cassia, and yet, she could not be upset. Not this day anyway.

He'd helped Nathan. Together, he and Jeremy had lent Nathan and his crew their assistance and saved all their lives.

That was absolutely all she *should* care about.

Except, she found herself incapable of silently mourning and lamenting the . . . end.

For there could be no doubting . . . this was the end of her and Nathan and their time together.

Seated in Nathan's quarters at one of the dining tables, her elder brother occupied the chair next to her.

"Were you . . . hurt?" he finally asked, his voice hoarsened.

Cassia whipped her gaze up. "No! Nathan and his crew, they've treated me with respect and cared for me." There was no need for him to know what had transpired with Carlisle. It was in the past.

Arran narrowed his eyes. *"Nathan?"*

Staring into the teacup, Cassia gripped the edges a little too hard, sending several droplets over the side. *I will not survive this. How can I?*

She made herself lighten her hold and take a sip.

"Surely we are going to speak of it?" Arran gently said.

"Speak of . . . ?" Cassia lifted her gaze, and he pinned a look on her, stifling the rest of that flippant response.

"Oh, I don't know," he said in acerbic tones she'd never heard from him, and certainly never heard directed her way. "Just how you've come to be alone with one of England's most ruthless privateers?"

Cassia frowned. "He's not ruthless. He's good and kind and helped me when I was seasick. He even rubbed my ba—" The tic at the corner of her brother's eye revealed the volatility thrumming inside him, and she let that thought go unfinished.

"And that still doesn't answer how you are with him, Cassia," Arran repeated in harder tones than she'd ever heard from him.

"It was a mistake."

"Yes, I'd say it—"

"I was looking for Jeremy's ship."

That managed to silence her brother. A moment.

"Jeremy?" he asked slowly.

She nodded. "Jeremy." Cassia paused. "As in, your *friend*. The one who is even now talking to—"

"I know who Jeremy is," he snapped. "What in hell were you looking to do on Jeremy's ship?"

"See the world," she said. And it was precisely what she'd done. In so many ways. In every way possible. She'd tasted freedom and found love, and it would have to be enough to carry with her into the rest of her tomorrows.

Her brother fell back in his seat. *"See the world?"* he echoed dumbly.

And the shock in his voice tipped her from a place of misery of loss to annoyance at this world that she lived in where men were permitted dreams and the opportunity to travel while women were expected to be content with a tedious existence devoid of all adventure. A thread broke. "You'd fault *me, Arran?*" she shot back. "You, who've been practicing the greatest deception? You who, every time you returned, pretended that you were simply *traveling?* Why, perhaps if you'd been honest, I would have found a different ship."

He choked. "Found a *different* ship?"

Cassia gave a toss of her head. "I couldn't have very well plotted to board a pirate ship."

His voice rose a decibel. "Are we even sure *that* would have stopped you?"

"I . . ." Cassia narrowed her eyes. "You're being sarcastic."

"I . . . yes, I was, but . . . ," he stammered, "that is neither here nor there."

"No," she said, schooling her features into a mask *Nathan* would have been hard-pressed not to be impressed by. "Why should we speak of that when we could instead be discussing the fact that all these years, you've gone about playing at pirates with Jeremy?"

High color flooded his cheeks.

Good.

Given that deception, he should feel . . . something.

"You allowed me and every other McQuoid to believe there was nothing untoward about your sailings," she pressed. "While all along, you've been facing down French ships and, it appears, impressing men."

Her brother raked a hand through his hair, and then caught himself. "We're not *impressing* the French sailors," he muttered. "We just don't . . . let them go down with their sinking ships, and in turn, escort them to . . . ." The red of his cheeks deepened. "And this isn't about me,

Cassia. It's about you." He shoved back in his seat. "Cassia, what in hell were you thinking?"

"I'm thinking I've never gone anywhere or seen anything," she cried, and pent-up frustration brought her flying to her feet, the mahogany dining chair scraping noisily upon the planked wood flooring. "All my life, I've been the McQuoid who's gone nowhere, who has seen and done absolutely nothing. You. Father. Dallin. Even *Myrtle*." Her younger sister had been granted more experiences than Cassia ever had or, if her parents had their way, ever would. "Mama and Papa sent her away so that she might have an education beyond that which a family governess provides. But me?" Cassia pumped a fist against her chest. "It has always been expected that I'll remain in London, the arm ornament for some husband, and no one"—her voice climbed as she spoke, but God help her, she was hopeless to stifle it—"absolutely no one considered what was to happen if I never found even a properly dull husband to marry. Everyone would be content to let me remain as the unworldly, inexperienced-in-every-way McQuoid, and I don't want that, Arran," she entreated, desperate to make him understand. "I wanted a taste of freedom and exploration that is denied to women, and for a brief time"—for an all-too-brief time; the fight went out of her—"I had it," she whispered, her shoulders sagging.

And she had. She'd seen so much of it. With Nathan. And she'd carry each and every moment she'd had with him, forever. *Oh, God.* Cassia folded her arms around her middle. Why must losing him hurt so very badly?

The scratch of wood scraping wood filled the room as Arran pushed back his chair and climbed to his feet. He held his arms open, and in that instant, as Cassia threw herself against her brother, she felt very much the young girl who'd lost charades matches to every other McQuoid, back when it seemed like there was no greater pain than losing a child's game.

Arran simply held her, and she took the support and love and warmth he conferred. She took all of it, even as her heart and soul cried out for the comfort to be had with a gruff man who quite despised tears and—

Cassia blinked furiously.

"Do you want to talk about it?" he asked against the top of her head.

She shook her head furiously. Only . . .

And then the story came tumbling out. Cassia proceeded to tell her brother everything about how she'd come to be with Nathan, and how he'd cared for her, taking care to leave out only the intimate moments she'd shared with him.

"Oh, Cassia," he said, his voice pained.

When she finished, she felt her brother's eyes on her. Probing.

"You love him."

Cassia bit down on her lower lip, sinking her teeth hard against that flesh. She made herself step out of her brother's arms, and edging back several steps so she could meet his gaze more squarely, she said, "I can't marry him."

She braced for the fight.

That did not come.

"I wouldn't expect you to," her brother said in grave tones.

Cassia bristled. "You think he would not make me a good husband? Because I'll have you know, he's a good man and honorable and caring and—" And she loved him. She loved him with all she was.

Arran rested a hand on her shoulder and squeezed lightly, bringing her gaze up to his somber one. "I don't think he'd make you a good husband," he said gently, "because I don't believe any man is deserving of you, Cassia."

Tears filled her eyes once more, and this time, she didn't try to fight them. This time, Cassia gave in to the torrent and, with a great gasping sob, collapsed against her brother's chest and wept. She wept until her sides ached and her chest hurt as badly as her heart at losing Nathan.

Nay, not that badly. Nothing could compare with that agonizing, crushing weight bearing down on the organ.

"If you want to marry him, however, Cassia, and it is a matter of him not doing right by you—"

"He would," she cut him off, disabusing her brother of that erroneous conclusion. "He will . . . but I . . ." Cassia made herself draw in a slow, steadying breath. "I cannot have him that way."

"Why don't you let him decide?"

"If you'd been alone with a young woman, even if it was her fault, would you decide otherwise?" she countered, and yet as soon as she did, she immediately regretted the reminder of her reputation and the fact she'd likely gone and ruined herself.

He flexed his jaw.

"Furthermore, he would grow to resent me, and I . . ." Pain lanced her breast. "I could not have that, Arran," she whispered. "It would break my heart."

His features spasmed. "And I'd spare you a broken heart and any hurt if it were in my power," her elder brother said gruffly.

Going up on tiptoe, Cassia kissed Arran's cheek. "Thank you." She paused. "I need to speak to him."

"Of course—"

"Alone."

———— ⌘ ————

She'd been crying.

Pacing the narrow corridor outside his cabin, Nathaniel turned briskly and headed back past that panel.

Through the sound of her misery, her and her brother's murmurings had been heavily muffled by the solid oak, and it had taken Nathaniel all he was to keep from tearing it apart with his bare hands and clawing his way into the cabin to get to her.

And what do you think is the reason for her tears? a voice gibed in his head.

At some point, she'd stopped.

And yet, that did not ease the fiery pain in his chest.

For he knew the exact source of her misery: she'd witnessed the hell of a sea battle. She'd nearly perished, and it would have been Nathaniel's fault. His missions had always mattered most. The work he did for the Crown and his men . . . and since he was finally being honest—for himself. It had been his own pride and sense of accomplishment and the desire to be the best at sea which accounted for that decision. With Captain Tremaine's assistance, Nathaniel had intercepted the French plans in the Adriatic and also rescued British sailors who'd been imprisoned. Any other time, that would be enough. That would be all he was thinking about after a battle.

Nathaniel stopped several paces from his cabin doorway as images slithered forward, thoughts that would haunt him still when he was an old man with white hair and missing teeth and his ears failing to hear: Cassia as she'd been, running through the chaotic corridors because his cabin had suffered damage, her willowy form made murky by the cloud of cannon fire and smoke, a pistol in one hand and a small sword in the other.

How was it possible to feel equal parts awe and admiration and mind-numbing horror and regret?

Nathaniel squeezed his eyes shut, but it didn't help. The memories continued to come.

"Nathan . . . I . . . shot a man . . ."

The horror that had wreathed her voice and delicate features, and pain when the man she'd shot would have certainly not hesitated to inflict an even greater suffering upon her.

And it had been because of Nathaniel.

Nathaniel, who in all his arrogance and avarice, had jeopardized Cassia, a breath of light in a dark night sky, pure of spirit and even purer heart, and he'd subjected her to things that made grown men with battlefield experience shake.

He didn't deserve her.

Hell, no man did.

But certainly not him.

Click.

Nathaniel's eyes went flying open, and he spun toward the opening of his room.

Cassia's brother sized him up, and by the antipathy in the other man's gaze, a gaze that was so very much Cassia's, he'd found Nathaniel wanting.

And why shouldn't he?

Even so, Nathaniel narrowed his eyes and inched his chin up a fraction.

"My sister wishes to speak with you," her brother said in indecipherable tones, and he stepped aside, allowing Nathaniel to pass.

Nathaniel inclined his head slightly.

As he entered the cabin, he pushed the panel shut behind him and Cassia so that they were alone.

She stood there, barefoot, her lawn shirt, untucked as it was, hanging down about her slender limbs, dwarfing her form, and also an unwitting—and unnecessary—reminder of just how delicate she was.

The Dark Memories, as he'd now forever think of them, drifted in, and sweat beaded at his brow.

"You're well?" he demanded, his voice emerging sharper and harsher than he intended, and yet, the nightmare of the fate she'd nearly met made him helpless to gentle his tone.

"V-very," she replied with the strength and tenacity only Cassia McQuoid was capable of.

Some of the tension sapped from his frame, and a small smile pulled at his lips as he drifted over and cupped her cheek. Softer than silk or satin, Cassia possessed her own feel of perfection, and she leaned into his touch. Her lashes fluttered shut the way they did just before she reached her climax.

Those intimate details he now knew of this woman, and so many more he wanted to know.

He expected that should terrify him.

It did not.

It made him hungry in ways that moved beyond the mere desire stirred in his—

"My brother is here," she said softly, unexpectedly, and also effectively dousing that hungering.

Nathaniel made himself stop touching her and forced his hand back to his side.

"Yes, I believe we've ascertained as much." Her brother and his big, burly, strapping friend, *Captain Jeremy*. A handsome blighter.

Nathaniel hated him for all he was worth, a petty and ungrateful response, given he had possibly saved both Nathaniel's arse and his crew's.

"We've . . . spoken. Arran and I," Cassia continued. "I'm going to return with him."

Of course she would. It was logical and made sense, and he should be glad. He *should*. "That makes sense," he made himself say. His ship needed to be repaired, and Tremaine's ship hadn't suffered the same amount of damage. Even with that, Nathaniel wanted her here. "When we return, I'll visit your family and—"

Cassia interrupted him. "We don't have to marry, Nathan."

He frowned. "What are you saying?" he asked bluntly. What the *hell* was she saying?

She blinked those endlessly long auburn lashes. "Well, you see, before my brother and Jeremy"—Jeremy, again; that familiarity set his teeth on edge—"arrived, there was absolutely no accounting for my whereabouts, but now there is." And he gave thanks for her tendency to prattle on enough for the both of them.

Nathaniel should be grateful. Marrying her as he'd intended would have meant he could not fulfill the commitment his father would have him make to another woman. That commitment which would and did secure Nathaniel's future as a privateer. So why did that suddenly feel . . . not so very important? Why did it feel hollow and leave him this strange empty way inside?

"It will be explained that I was traveling with my brother," Cassia was saying, "and so my reputation will be spared, and we won't have to wed."

We won't have to wed.

There it was.

Once more, there came none of the relief that admission should usher in.

Especially as she sounded so . . . so . . . damned happy about it.

Cassia stared up at him through her always sunny eyes, and an even more effervescent smile. "Isn't that wonderful, Nathan?" she asked, joining her hands in a single fist and bringing them to her heart.

"Yes," he said dumbly. "Wonderful." His throat, thick, made that word emerge garbled and distorted to his own ears.

For a spark of an instant, he caught something flash in her eyes, a flicker of pain and regret and . . .

Pain and regret?

Why should she feel that? Why, when he'd put her life in jeopardy? She was better off without him. She knew that.

Even so . . .

"And what if his crew speaks?" he demanded furiously. "You're trusting your reputation to men you don't know."

"They're Jeremy and Arran's crew," she said with such trusting in those two other men that his teeth clanked sharply together and sent pain shooting up his jaw.

Good. Pain was good. Pain helped.

It was a distraction from . . . whatever this vicious sensation was, cleaving away at his heart.

Nathaniel lowered his voice to an angry whisper. "And if there is a babe?" he demanded. "What then?"

For an instant, Cassia's eyes glinted and glimmered with a preternatural light. "I . . . I did not think of that," she whispered.

And conjured of his own reminder for her came thoughts of Cassia, her belly, rounded with child—*his* child—and her cheeks flushed with happiness, and for a sinful second, he wanted that image to be real. He yearned for a babe with this woman—a tiny girl with reddish-brown curls and an equally impish smile that dimpled her cheeks, and his chest stirred, that longing growing, expanding like a soap bubble he'd once blown out of his tub as a boy, that white sphere had taken flight across the room, only to—

Pop.

"I will . . . notify you if anything changes," she vowed. "But if it doesn't . . . we're free, Nathan."

Cassia held his gaze with her own, her eyes a shade of blue to rival the purest clear sky on the best sailing day. And damned and hell, he knew from this moment forward, every time he stood at the helm of his ship, he'd see those cerulean pools.

"Cassia?" he murmured, and she drifted closer, angling her neck back.

"Nathan?" Hers was the throaty, husky voice that followed their energetic bouts of lovemaking, conjuring those dangerous-in-their-own-right memories, too.

He dipped his head a fraction, and she tilted hers back.

Her lashes drifted closed, and he stopped, his lips a hairbreadth from hers. "Be happy," he said gruffly, and her eyes went shooting wide. "You deserve it."

He didn't deserve her.

Hell, no man did.

But certainly not him.

And she'd realized it, too.

Chapter 21

Cassia had been home a single week.

Everything had changed, and yet at the same time, nothing had.

She was seated in the breakfast room with her boisterous younger siblings chasing one another about the table while Myrtle's dog, Horace, chased happily at their heels, yapping noisily after them. Her parents, engrossed in a discussion about something or other, paused periodically, only long enough to put in a halfhearted attempt at corralling their unruly offspring.

Cassia's elder brothers, Arran and Dallin, seated at the opposite end of the long, rectangular table, chattered on without a care for the melee around them.

Yes, everyone and everything was much the same.

It was one of the things she'd always loved about her family, their togetherness and closeness.

As Cassia toyed with the edges of her untouched eggs, her gaze snagged upon her younger sister seated beside her husband. The couple leaned intimately toward one another, young lovers who saw none of the racket around them. Myrtle and Val had eyes for only one another, and never had Cassia felt more miserable for what they had and she so desperately wanted.

No, that wasn't altogether true.

To give her fingers a purpose, Cassia shoveled a large spoonful of eggs into her mouth.

And promptly regretted it, as it was a chore to swallow around the tears which, since she'd parted ways with Nathan, had lodged permanently in her throat.

Upon the *Waltzing Dragon*'s arrival at the Brunswick Dock, she'd begun her menses and had been beset by the overwhelming urge to sob. For as pathetic and wrong as it had been, she'd yearned to have Nathan's babe—it would have been a piece and part of him, and it would have also meant that he'd be in her life still. That he would have married her.

The housekeeper hastened into the room with a paper for the countess, and Cassia turned her head.

There came the clatter of a fork striking the porcelain dish, and then a gasp.

Cassia looked to the sound.

Her mother had a hand pressed over her lips, her cheeks ashen as they'd only been when she'd discovered her oversight in forgetting her younger, then unmarried, daughter in London.

At present, Cassia's father scanned the same newspaper he'd relieved his wife of.

And so on, and so on, McQuoid after McQuoid read and then passed the pages on, elder siblings bypassing the grasping attempts of the youngest ones to read whatever had resulted in her family's horrified shock.

Cassia dropped her chin atop her hands and stared miserably down at her dessert plate.

It didn't matter.

There was nothing in those pages Cassia—

"Cassia is being gossiped about?"

That brought her head flying up, and she looked to Quillon, her eleven-year-old brother, who'd managed to snatch the newspaper from Arran's fingers. Their youngest sister, Fleur, dived for the pages, snatched them, and darted off, and pandemonium erupted at the table as parents and elder siblings alike attempted to confiscate that newspaper.

Horace lent his boisterous barking to the melee.

Cassia is being . . . gossiped about?

Cassia sat stunned, motionless for several moments. *What in blazes?*

As Fleur evaded her family, she read a different part of that article as she went: *"Little attention was paid the absence of Polite Society wallflower Lady C M, an absence explained as a visit to their family's Scottish estates. This author, however, has it on authority that it was not . . ."*

A dull humming pulled only every other word recited by her sister into focus.

"Scotland . . . rather . . . the lady was alone . . . at sea."

"You went to *seaaaaa*?" Quillon wailed. "That is outrageously unfair, as I wanted to be the next McQuoid who took to sailing."

Heart hammering, Cassia ignored her brother's lamentations, jumped up, and raced into the fray.

Fleur's flight had slowed as the younger girl continued to read the words written in the scandal sheets, and using that distraction to her advantage, Cassia rushed past Arran and plucked the newspaper.

"Heyyyy." Fleur's frustrated shout rang out over the din.

Ignoring it, ignoring her, and all her family wildly speaking over one another, Cassia frantically skimmed the front page, finding her own name there.

Scandal

It is only just recently learned the reason for the peculiar absence of a certain Lady C McQuoid. The young lady rushed off without the benefit of a female companion or chaperone. It was not, in fact, a visit to family estates in Scotland that accounted for her disappearance, but rather . . .

"An attempt to elope," she breathed, rocking back on her heels. Dazed, Cassia resumed reading the handful of sentences there. With . . . Lord Jeremy Tremaine. When she'd finished, Cassia turned the page over, front and back, searching for . . . something. Anything. A correction. An unnatural and first-of-its-kind silence swallowed the dining room, and she looked up. "I wasn't eloping with Jeremy," she said dumbly, needing to say something.

"That is good," Fleur piped in. "Because I would have been very cross with you, as I intend to marry him some—*ow.*" The younger girl glared at Quillon, who'd pinched her arm. "What was that for? I was merely—"

"Because you can't marry him now, as he's gone and ruined Cassia." The boy spoke with all the exasperation afforded a big brother dealing with a younger sister from the beginning of time. "Cassia has to marry Jeremy."

As if burnt, Cassia dropped the pages, and they hit the floor with a loud *thwack.*

Horace was there in an instant, claiming that hated newspaper in his big jowls and racing off to chew on his prize.

"I . . . it wasn't . . ." It hadn't been Jeremy whom she'd been alone with. It had been Nathan. And even so . . . "I didn't rush off to . . . elope. I went . . . to see the world." And she had. And she'd fallen in love with a man whom she'd been hopeless and helpless to do anything but think about since her return. A man whom she'd saved from marrying her, but now . . . instead, she'd been linked to Jeremy, which meant . . .

Her stomach revolted worse than it ever had while at sea, and she fought frantically against that nausea. She closed her eyes, but not before seeing the look exchanged by her parents and siblings.

All the life drained from her muscles, her legs going weak, and she caught the edge of the table to keep herself upright, and then fell into the nearest vacant chair.

Cassia dimly registered her mother dispelling her eerily quiet brood, the patter of footfalls, and then the quiet click as the door closed behind the last departing McQuoid.

When she found herself with a shrunken audience, Cassia looked up to find her parents, Myrtle, and Arran remained.

"I wasn't eloping," she said weakly.

"I know," Arran said quietly, and yet there was something more in that solemn admission. A sad note of regret and finality.

"I cannot marry him," she said, panic pitching her voice up an octave. "It would not be fair to Jeremy." Or her. She didn't love him, and he didn't love her. "I—"

"You do not have to marry Jeremy," Myrtle said quietly, earning a sharp look from their elder brother. "What?" she asked defensively. "She doesn't." Myrtle paused, her brow wrinkling. "Unless . . . she wants to?" There was an up-tilt that transformed those words into a question.

Cassia's mother spoke a handful of quiet words to her husband, who nodded, and then striding over to Arran, he gathered him by the arm in the same way he'd done when Arran was a troublesome boy and escorted him out of the room.

"I should be there as . . ."

The door panel and retreating footsteps swallowed whatever else Arran was saying.

Cassia sat on the edge of the chair, hugging her arms tightly around her middle.

"You were not in Scotland," Myrtle said into the quiet, a faint thread of hurt to that statement.

She managed to shake her head.

Say nothing. To anyone.

That had been the agreement she had come to with her parents and Arran and Jeremy. *Someone* had spoken. Only the story that had been told wasn't true. Nor did it really matter anyway. The *ton* had a scandal, and Cassia was at the heart of it.

Of course, it had been inevitable that someone would say something. Of course, it had been both naive and optimistic on her part, and on the part of her family, to believe where Cassia had gone and what she'd done could remain a secret amongst them forever.

"*Were* you running away with Jeremy?" Myrtle murmured.

Miserable, Cassia shook her head a second time.

"I was not even with Jeremy until Arran arrived," she said, her tongue heavy and her throat thick. And then the words and all the truth tumbled out for her younger sister, who had been granted the freedom to leave the family fold and attend school, gifts Cassia had not been offered, and which she'd shamefully resented her sister for, those things beyond her control. And now her younger sister had also managed to find love and happiness, and had everything Cassia yearned for.

When she finished, tears fell, and Cassia wiped them away furiously; a remembrance of Nathan in all his gruff ways and annoyance whispered forward, and she was hopeless to keep the thoughts of him and them together at bay.

"*Do not . . .*"

"*Do not 'what'?*" Cassia whispered.

"*Cry.*"

"*I cannot help it.*"

"*You can . . . You just aren't trying . . .*"

Her mother, seated on the other side of Cassia, touched her fingers, drawing Cassia out of her own miseries. "You are quiet," she remarked.

"I don't . . . really know what else there is to say," Cassia said, her voice hollow.

A smile teased at her mother's mouth. A smile? Most mothers would have been beset by tears of their own and screeching. Cassia should be grateful.

"I meant since you returned," her mother said in that gentle way of hers that only made Cassia cry all over again.

It was a wonder anyone had noticed, lost in one another as they always were.

Horace lowered his enormous head onto her lap, and Cassia hugged her arms around the dog, taking the comfort he conferred.

There came the scratch of wood striking wood as her mother dragged a chair over, and Myrtle pulled one onto Cassia's other side.

"I expect there was a man . . . one who is not Jeremy?" her mother ventured.

Cassia blinked slowly and picked her head up.

"My dear," her mother drawled. "There is always some man behind it."

Myrtle nodded in concurrence.

"There is," Cassia whispered, forlornly, her heart aching all the more. "Or . . . there was." And freed by that admission she'd promised Arran not to make, not even to their parents, she told her mother and sister everything. She poured out every detail about her time with Nathan, and their eventual parting.

When she'd finished, her mother was silent for a long while, and then she released a sigh. "Yes, well, we cannot have you marrying Jeremy, then. Not that I don't think he'd make you or any woman very, very happy. Just that he's a bit of a rogue and—"

"Mama," Myrtle said, cutting into their mother's ramblings.

"Uh, yes, right. As I was saying . . . you won't marry Jeremy. That is settled."

How many mothers would have allowed Cassia that decision? With a thoroughly ruined reputation and absolutely no marital prospects, any other peeress would have been adamant that the decision had already been made the moment Cassia had taken flight.

Her mother rested her hand atop Cassia's. "Now, there is the matter of *your* happiness."

"That is not something so easily settled," she whispered, her voice catching and breaking.

Horace gave a little whine and nudged her lap with his nose.

She patted the dog affectionately.

"You are . . . certain he does not love you?" Myrtle put forward hesitantly with the optimism only possessed by a woman who had been gifted with a love match.

Cassia let her head drop along the back of her chair and stared up at the ceiling. "He loves sailing."

And mayhap, one day, he'd love the woman his parents required him to wed in order to keep sailing without his father's interference.

Jealousy snaked through her, a vicious, searing blaze of heat that burnt like vinegar. And until Cassia drew her last breath, she would hate that faceless woman for having absolutely everything Cassia wanted in the world—Nathan.

"Very well, Cassia's love is . . . not in love with her, and we cannot have her marrying where his heart is not engaged," the countess said in her no-nonsense tones. "Therefore, there is nothing to do but hold our heads up."

Cassia stared incredulously at her. What was she saying?

"I'm saying, we act as though *nothing* has happened. We do not hide you away as if you've done anything wrong because, well, you haven't."

She and Myrtle gave their mother a look.

"That is . . . aside from the running away and disguising yourself as a deckhand so that you could sail with Jeremy, and—" Her mother cleared her throat. "But we shall not speak of that. Now, come." With a clap of her hands, the countess popped up from her seat. "There is your aunt's ball this evening, and we have to see you readied. I'd not have us attracting gossip for being missing at Aunt Leslie's grand fete."

"Yes, because our absence will definitely be what has the town talking," Myrtle drawled.

And perhaps another time, before she'd known Nathan, Cassia would have never detected that drollness, but now she did, and she even managed a smile. For a moment. Her lips slipped once more. "I don't want to attend Aunt Leslie's ball," she bemoaned. She wanted only to hide herself away and drag the coverlets over her head and forget . . . all of this.

"Of course you do," Mother chided, lightly rapping her knuckles. "You love Aunt Leslie's affairs because they are lively and merry, and tonight shan't be an exception. You will have fun, and in so doing, the world will see you've absolutely nothing to be ashamed of. It is settled."

It was settled, then.

Chapter 22

Nathaniel hated being on land.

When he had the solid ground under him, he found himself longing for the slow roll of the ocean under his feet, counting down the days until he was free to return.

He'd always hated London.

Never more, however, had he despised it as he did with this vitriolic intensity.

Seated at the mahogany desk in his Mayfair townhouse, Nathaniel absently spun the mounted globe, sticking his finger in a random spot in the same way he'd done since his parents had gifted him the German relic from the famed navigator Behaim.

When his finger stopped the turn, it landed Nathaniel, as it so often did, somewhere in the middle of the ocean.

As a boy, that truth had held a singular fascination for him, how vast the water was, and how limited the land. It had led him early on to want to explore those endless oceans that made up the globe. The sea had always beckoned. Land had always repelled him.

Nathaniel stared blankly at the faded black ink upon the pale-yellow globe.

Only, this time, for the first time, that searing sentiment had nothing to do with a longing to return to the sea.

Rather, it had everything to do . . . with her.

Lady Cassia McQuoid, the chattering lady who cried when she was happy and sad, and who swam like a mermaid and thought nothing of storming into battle with a pistol and sword drawn to save life-hardened men who'd been sprung from the gallows.

And after docking in London and returning to land, Nathaniel discovered there was something he missed even more than the ocean.

Her.

From the moment she'd been helped overboard onto another man's ship and stood at the railing, Nathaniel had watched her until she'd been nothing more than a faint speck upon the horizon, lifting a hand in a final wave before she'd faded altogether from sight . . . and his life.

His throat worked painfully, struggling with a motion that he'd only just discovered wasn't so very rhythmic, after all.

He . . . hard, cynical, coolly practical Nathaniel Ellsby, Marquess of Winfield and future Duke of Roxburghe, wasn't immune to hurt and loss.

He missed her. He missed her so damned bad it felt like he was dying the slowest of deaths inside, a cancer eating away at his soul and leaving him hollow and empty.

He missed her even more than he missed the bloody sea.

From the corridors, there came a thunderous boom.

"Where in hell is he?"

That question was met with an impressive calm from Nathaniel's butler. "His Lordship is not receiving guests."

The former sailor converted into head of Nathaniel's household in London deserved a raise.

"Not receiving guests? I'm not a damned guest. I'm the Duke of—"

The din reached a crescendo outside Nathaniel's office.

The heavy oak panel exploded open, and Nathaniel's father stormed in with the duchess trailing close behind, speaking quiet words to Nathaniel's head servant.

Bloody hell. The last person he cared to see or talk to was the man before him. "Father, Mother, to what do I owe this pleasure?" Nathaniel drawled, pushing away the globe and standing.

"Pleasure?" his father boomed. "Pleasure? If it was a damned pleasure, you would have paid me a visit when you arrived two days ago," he snapped.

"I was being sarcastic."

"I know," the duke said, even as Nathaniel's mother joined him and placed a kiss on his cheek. "I don't like it. So I ignored it." His father jabbed a long finger at him. "I've ignored a lot of your insolence these past years, but I've reached my limit. You have a responsibility, and you've dragged your heels long enough."

"What your father means is we are ever so glad you're back," the duchess murmured.

His Grace grunted. "No, it isn't." As the duke launched into a familiar lecture, Nathaniel's gaze drifted to the globe.

Responsibility.

That was all Nathaniel and his brothers had ever been or would ever be to the duke, a man who put his title first before anything and anyone. And Nathaniel . . . had only just discovered that, not unlike the duke who'd put that title before all, he'd done the same—with his career at sea. Having made something of nothing, unlike his father who'd had everything pass to him for no other reason than the blood flowing in his veins, Nathaniel had believed his focus on his shipping business had made him a better man. But being a better man was about knowing the people in your life, learning their fears and interests outside of the work they did for you. And family. It was about being a family.

It had taken him losing Cassia to see all the worst ways in which he'd become emotionally detached like his father. He'd had only his work for the Crown until she came into his life. Just as the duke had done with his title, Nathaniel had put his work above anything and everything.

The permanent ache that had settled around his heart since she'd gone throbbed once more.

"Nathaniel?" his mother murmured quietly. "What is it?"

Nathaniel couldn't get the words out.

God, how was it possible to have gone from not believing in the emotion called love to being its latest, greatest victim, ravaged inside by it?

Thump.

His father brought his fist down hard on the edge of Nathaniel's desk, setting the globe spinning and bringing Nathaniel's gaze back over to his fuming father.

"Are you listening to me, boy?" His Grace demanded.

No. But that didn't matter. Nathaniel well knew what this visit was about.

"I'm not marrying Lady Angela," he said quietly.

His father's jaw slackened and his mouth parted, and he looked with wide eyes over at his wife, Nathaniel's mother.

Yes, because it wasn't every day that someone subverted the powerful peer's wishes.

The duke found himself in an instant, recovering from his momentary shock. "What the hell do you mean, you aren't marrying her?" he thundered, and the duchess made soft, soothing tones, stroking his arm to calm him the way she might a skittish horse.

"Let us hear Nathaniel," she said.

"I heard him," the duke blustered. "I don't like what I heard."

"Darling," she said to her husband, that affectionate endearment that had made Nathaniel cringe over the years, and also one he could not understand. How could his kind, docile, sweet mother hold any affection for a miserable, blustery fellow like the duke? "Why don't we sit?" She looked to Nathaniel. "Don't you think it would be a good idea if we sit and speak?"

"I don't want to sit and speak. I want the boy to listen," the duke growled.

Even so, Nathaniel's father grabbed the chair and settled into it. Folding his arms at his barrel-size chest, he glared across at Nathaniel.

Nathaniel waited until his mother sat before reclaiming his chair. "I'm not marrying Lady Angela."

"You already said that," his father snapped. "Why not?"

Nathaniel opened his mouth, but the duke didn't allow him a word edgewise. "I'll tell you why," he said, his nostrils flaring like a bull Nathaniel had once watched in Spain giving chase to the fool with a crimson flag in the middle of a ring. "Because you are determined to make things difficult for me. You've never been able to do what is expected of a gentleman."

"And what, exactly, is that?" Nathaniel interjected dryly, folding his arms to match his father's pose. "Live a life of comfort off the backs of other men and women who've made me a fortune, while I spend my time frittering between sipping brandies at White's and dancing in London ballrooms?"

"Yes!" the duke exclaimed.

The duchess rested a palm on her husband's, silencing with that single touch whatever words he opened his mouth to speak.

Nathaniel knew that touch from another woman.

The kind that made his thoughts stop tracking and left him light inside, as he'd never known a person could be.

"Nathaniel, tell us why you don't wish to marry Angela?" his mother gently urged.

"I don't love her," he said flatly.

A resounding silence filled his offices.

His father recoiled in his chair, the deep buttoned back of that Chesterfield Chippendale seat all that kept the stunned lord from being knocked on his arse. "Love? *Looooove?*" he echoed dumbly, managing to squeeze three whole extra syllables into that single-word utterance, and earning a look from his wife for it.

"What is this, Henry, dearest?" she demanded, a warning in her voice. "Are you suggesting you don't believe in love?"

"No. Yes." The duke's high-chiseled cheeks went ruddy with color. He dropped his voice to a quiet whisper, angling his shoulder toward Nathaniel and facing his wife. "Of course I believe in love, lovey."

She arched an impressively imperious blonde eyebrow. "Only for yourself, then?"

"Yes. No. It's just . . ." Nathaniel's father slashed a hand his way. "This one . . . doesn't . . ."

"Believe in love?" the duchess supplied. "I daresay, given the fact he indicated it as an impediment to his future with Lady Angela, it is safe to assume he, in fact, does."

The duke found his footing. "It's safe to assume he's found a way to subvert my demands."

"*Demands*, Henry?"

The warning in his mother's tone was enough for Nathaniel to sit back in his seat and allow the duke to continue to flounder all on his own.

"You know what I mean, lambkin," His Grace said in high, sing-song tones, and Nathaniel winced.

Lambkin?

"Actually, I do not, Henry. Are you suggesting our son is using love as a way to evade marriage?"

"I . . ." The duke scratched his high, noble brow. "Didn't I just say as much?"

"If you were wise, dear, you'd not admit as much," his mother warned, and then, her features softening once more, she looked over at Nathaniel. "Is there anything else you wish to say . . . regarding your newfound appreciation of love?"

"I'm in it," he said, the admission falling clunkily from his tongue, and then a lightness filled him, leaving him buoyant and lifted. "I'm . . ." Nathaniel grinned.

In love.

I love Cassia McQuoid madly, deeply, truly, and every way in between.

The duke gesticulated wildly at Nathaniel. "The boy can't even say it, Ruth."

"You cannot even say it, dearest, but I daresay that does not mean you aren't, in fact, in love?" the duchess drawled, raising the color in her husband's cheeks once more.

"I'm in love," Nathaniel said quietly, and strangely, that admission didn't choke him or give him pause; it didn't feel awkward and wrong. It only felt right, and he only felt . . . freed by it.

"Who in hell did you fall in love with?" the duke wailed. "You've been on your ship for the past weeks." He paused, his brow dipping. "Haven't you? Or is all that sailing nonsense false, too, and you've just been—"

"I'm in love with a young lady, Lady Cassia McQuoid"—another grin tugged at Nathaniel's mouth as memories traipsed in of Cassia introducing herself to him aboard the *Flying Dragon*—"of the McQuoid family."

"Who the hell are the McQuoids?" his father barked. "I don't know the McQuoids, and I know every family of import."

"The Earl and Countess of Abington," the duchess supplied. "They are quite respectable."

"They are of Scottish descent," Nathaniel said, finding entirely too much glee in that announcement.

His mother gave him a look.

The duke may as well have sampled rancid venison. His facial muscles twisted and contorted. "Scott—"

"Oh, do stop baiting your father, Nathaniel," the duchess chided. "The McQuoids' younger daughter is recently a duchess. The former Duke of Aragon's eldest lad."

His Grace sat up straighter. "Oh?" he asked, his earlier upset replaced by a sudden interest.

"The poor boy was made a young widower and only recently remarried to the younger McQuoid sister, who, by my accounts, never had a London Season." As she launched into a lengthy summation of everything she knew about Cassia's family, Nathaniel's mind again drifted.

His mother knew so much of Cassia's family. It was singularly odd that she should have been in possession of those details and a vague knowing of Cassia, when before this she'd been a complete stranger to Nathaniel.

Now he wondered at what it might have been to have met Cassia across a ballroom.

She'd have been lively on her feet, and bright-eyed, and he'd have been hopeless to not notice her.

"And dare I ask how you came to know the lady?" his mother ventured, slashing into those musings and bringing Nathaniel back to the present.

He shook his head. Those details he'd not share even with his parents.

Puffing out his cheeks and pursing his lips, His Grace grunted, "Fine. I'll . . . allow the union."

"I wasn't asking permission," Nathaniel murmured, and then catching his father's narrowed eyes, he decided to concede some this day. "But I appreciate your supporting the match."

Leveraging himself up with the arms of the chair, the duke stood and jabbed that long finger his way. "Get on with it, already, before I change my mind and . . ." The glacial look Nathaniel's mother gave her husband managed to quell the rest of that warning. "Just do it." With that, he turned on his heel and stomped off.

Nathaniel's mother came to her feet, and he instantly jumped up. Coming around the desk, she reached up and patted him on his cheeks, framing them gently in her hands. "I am so very happy for you." She gave him a none-too-gentle pinch. "But like your father said, do not tarry. A gentleman must never take for granted a lady's love, or that she will be there waiting for you."

Bending down, Nathaniel dropped a kiss on her cheek. "I love you."

His mother's eyes grew misty, a teasing glimmer sparkling in them. "Well, if my boy has not learned to speak that word without blanching." She kissed his cheek. "I love you, too."

"Ruth!"

That thunderous shout from the corridor broke the moment, and mother and son glanced at the doorway. "Your father is cranky."

"He always is," Nathaniel said drolly.

"And he has a soft heart, under it."

"*Ruth!*"

Patting Nathaniel's cheek, the duchess turned and rushed off. "Coming, dear heart . . ."

As the couple's voices and footfalls receded, the tension eased from Nathaniel's shoulders. Now he could go to Cassia. He should have gone to her days earlier but had needed to close out the business of his latest sailing.

His butler ducked his head inside. "I know you said you aren't receiving guests, but these ones insisted you see them. Wouldn't be turned away."

Bloody hell. His father had changed his mind.

Gritting his teeth, Nathaniel turned a glare on the doorway. "I'm not changing my mind if—oh."

Hayes and, alongside him, Albion. Albion carried a newspaper in his hand. Hayes, who hovered in the doorway, twisted his Oxonian hat between his fingers. "Captain," he said quietly.

Nathaniel had only ever seen them this stoic before battle. "What is it? I have matters I—"

"I think you need to hear Hayes," Albion said, nodding at his quartermaster.

Both men entered, stopping when they reached the foot of Nathaniel's desk.

Hayes continued to toy with the brim of his high black hat and then stopped that distracted movement.

Albion spoke. "It . . . is about . . ." His navigator looked to Hayes, and something passed between them.

Unease skittered along Nathaniel's spine. "What is it?"

"During the battle, your papers were thrown about your cabin," Hayes blurted.

That's what this was about? The entire cabin was in disarray. With the damage they'd sustained, he'd been fortunate to salvage the ship and the room. When neither of them spoke, Nathaniel looked impatiently between them. "And?"

"And . . . I'd suggested Cassia find a distraction, and so she set to work collecting your papers, your maps, your ledgers . . ." Hayes paused. "Your letters."

His letters.

Nathaniel froze. And then all the air left his lungs. She'd seen the note from his mother. *Of course.* It was why before the battle she'd agreed to marry him and then had so suddenly changed her mind.

Or is it merely that you are wanting that to be the case?

Because ultimately, he intended to prove he was worthy of her, to give her all the romance she'd insisted she wanted. Even if he wasn't good at it. He would figure it out for her . . . because with her in his life, he could do anything and be anything.

He smiled. "I'm going to marry her. That is where I was going. If you'll excuse me—" Nathaniel stepped around them.

"You . . . don't know then?" Hayes hazarded, freezing him in his tracks once more.

His smile withered, and he faced the pair. "Know what?"

His two closest friends exchanged another glance.

His unease grew; it spiraled and fanned out. "What in hell is it?" Nathaniel snapped.

"Society is gossiping about Lady Cassia," Albion answered quietly.

Nathaniel's heart stopped its beat for a moment, then picked up a frantic rhythm.

With a curse, he reached across the desk and grabbed the paper from Albion's outstretched fingers, quickly scanning, and with every inked word read, that thick haze of red fell further over his vision. Blinding rage the likes of which he'd never before known seized his every sense, blinding, deafening, and sour to the tongue.

Scandal

It is only just recently learned the reason for the peculiar absence of a certain Lady C McQuoid. The young lady rushed off without the benefit of a female companion or chaperone. It was not, in fact, a visit to family estates in Scotland that accounted for her disappearance, but rather . . .

Nathaniel frantically read the remainder, then froze. Rage briefly blackened his vision. "Tremaine didn't ruin her," he thundered. *I did.*

"No. I know that," Hayes said. "We . . . we thought you should know . . ."

Nathaniel seethed. In that entire salacious story, there wasn't a single mention of him. Rather, Cassia's ruin had been written with another gentleman and another story, one that wasn't Nathaniel and Cassia's, but damned Tremaine and Cassia's, which erased Nathaniel from a picture he'd been the player in and put another man as the one to wed her.

He growled. It started low in his chest and climbed higher.

"Over my dead body," he seethed.

Albion nodded to Hayes.

"It was Carlisle," Hayes quietly explained. "He was bragging at the wharf about making it so that the woman you loved had to marry another."

Nathaniel cursed. He should have expected Carlisle wouldn't have taken well to being flogged, locked up, and discharged. And rightly, the bastard had accurately calculated that there would be a fate for Nathaniel worse than giving up his shipping line—losing Cassia to another.

Not breaking his stride, Nathaniel steeled his jaw.

He was going to win the heart of the woman he loved.

Chapter 23

Cassia had spent two and a half London Seasons being invisible to Polite Society.

Later that evening, on the sidelines of her aunt Leslie's ballroom floor, for the first time in the whole of her life, Cassia found herself the focus of the event.

For all the wrong reasons, of course.

Oh, Cassia had put on a brave show, a smile, and a stiff upper lip as her mother had instructed, but never had she been more miserable in the whole of her life.

And yet, the rub of it was, ruined with a false story that had substituted one man's name for the next in an otherwise accurate depiction of where she'd gone and what she'd done, it wasn't her lack of future marital prospects she mourned. Rather, it was the man she so desperately missed, still.

Her brother Arran, stationed at her side, cleared his throat. "Do you want to dance?"

"We've already danced, Arran," she muttered. "I've danced with both of you," she reminded Dallin, who'd set himself on Cassia's right. "Dancing with my brothers is hardly how I wish to spend my evening."

"I'm offended," Arran said, touching a hand to his chest in feigned hurt, and despite herself, she felt the beginnings of a smile. "I'll have you know my skill as a dancer is legendary."

Only—

Her smile slipped.

Did Nathan dance?

It was something she did not know about him. It was something they'd not covered in all the discussions they'd had. There was so *much* she didn't, and never would, know. Some other lady would find herself in possession of the answers to those questions.

Nathan, who hated cravats and Polite Society events and—

Her lower lip trembled, and she bit it hard to still that quiver.

Whispers went up around the ballroom.

Though in fairness, the room had existed in a perpetual buzz of whispers, occasionally ascending and descending in volume but always about her, and their stares always accompanying that chitter.

Except . . .

Cassia cocked her head.

Not . . . now.

The crowd had found someone else to stare at, someone more interesting than her and her scandal, and Cassia stretched up on tiptoe, searching for the poor soul, also her savior—and then froze, understanding in an instant the reason for the crowd's fascination and singular absorption.

Cassia's breath caught, and she touched her fingertips to her lips.

Because there could be no doubting the tall figure, cutting an incisive path through the gathering of her aunt and uncle's guests, was of a manner to inspire all the attention a person had to give.

And it had been that way for her, as well, from the moment they'd met.

He strode purposefully across the ballroom floor; guests parted, making a path, and Cassia followed him with her gaze, not blinking, afraid she'd merely conjured him of her own yearning and if she did not continue watching him, he'd disappear.

"Who in hell is *he*?" Dallin murmured. "The fellow is—"

"Perfect," she whispered soundlessly.

"A mess." Arran completed their eldest brother's words for him, and Cassia was briefly struck by the reminder that aside from Arran, her mother, and Myrtle, the rest of the McQuoids knew nothing of Nathan. Nathan, who'd been such an important part of her life.

"He is the Marquess of Winfield," Arran murmured, holding a glass of champagne out for Cassia.

She ignored that offer of fortitude, capable of seeing just one man, the same man she'd longed for since they'd parted ways.

Transfixed, Cassia followed Nathan's determined march, as in command of the room he'd silenced by his presence alone as he'd been of his ship.

Nathan, who'd traded his shirtsleeves for a formal jacket and cravat. He strode directly to the small orchestra upon the dais at the front and center of the room. The quartet of players sat with their string instruments poised as if to play, but suspended in the same stupefied state as the rest of the room.

Ladies craned their heads around the taller gentlemen next to them, as those same men stretched their necks to make sense of what exactly it was Nathan was doing.

Nathan stopped before the dais, where Cassia's aunt Leslie and uncle Francis stood. He said something to the pair, and the couple beamed, motioning—

Dallin whistled. "What in hell is he doing?"

Nay, what in hell had he *done*? In one fluid movement, Nathan leapt up onto the dais and positioned himself at the center, and the same way he'd scanned the horizon aboard his ship, he surveyed the ballroom, moving his gaze methodically, purposefully about—until it ultimately landed on Cassia.

He pointed a finger toward her, and even with the length of the room between them, his penetrating stare pierced hers. "I'm not romantic," he declared, his deep baritone thundering around a room quiet enough to allow for the echo of a pin drop.

"Is . . . he telling . . . me that?" Dallin asked from the corner of his mouth.

Me.

Cassia's heart hammered.

Nathan is . . . speaking to . . . me.

"I've never had an interest in being a romantic. I'm practical and logical and unemotional," Nathan continued, his voice a near bellow that continued to carry throughout. "I don't write poems, and I don't know ballads, Cassia McQuoid. You deserve ballads and a smiley fellow who sings them to you."

"I don't want ballads," she whispered. *You. I want you.*

"Why is that shouty fellow addressing my sister?" Dallin demanded of Cassia and Arran and their parents, who stood nearby.

They ignored him.

"But, Cassia," Nathan shouted into the crowd, and seeing not the audience of guests who swung their gazes back and forth between her and Nathan, she forgot the room. She forgot her family. She forgot all but Nathan.

"Yes?" she called, her voice ringing out loud and clear and with a steadiness that did not fit with the wild thump of her heart.

"I'm not a romantic fellow who writes verse, or sings songs"— Nathan's booming voice moved all the way through her—"but I want to do all those things anyway . . . because of you." He paused. "For you."

She gasped.

As did the sea of four hundred guests present.

Nathan opened his mouth and sang.

"As I was a-walking down Paradise Street
To me way-aye, blow the man down."

Two lyrics in, Aunt Leslie and Uncle Frank's orchestra commenced playing, a touch too slow for the slightly too-fast cadence of Nathan's singing.

"A pretty young damsel I chanced for to meet.
Give me some time to blow the man down!"

In fact, he sang quite badly, in an endearingly off-key way, his voice slightly too deep for the musicians desperately attempting to find—and failing to match—their unlikely singer's song.

"She was round in the counter and bluff in the
bow,
So I took in all sail and cried, 'Way enough now.'
A pretty young damsel I chanced for to meet.
Give me some time to blow the man down!"

"What in hell is that song, and why is this stranger singing it to my sister?" Dallin demanded of the army of McQuoids around him.

"A sea shanty," she whispered, her voice breaking, and then her family forgotten, Cassia started across the room toward Nathan.

"So I tailed her my flipper and took her in tow
And yardarm to yardarm away we did go."

And as he sang, Cassia lengthened her strides, and then it was as if her legs moved of their own volition, and she was flying past her family's guests.

Until she reached him.

"But as we were going, she said unto me . . ." Nathan's voice trailed off.

Breathless as much as from her race across the room as the dizzying effect he had upon her, she tipped her head back to meet his gaze. "You are here," she whispered.

He nodded. "Aye."

"Why are you here?"

"I needed something from you, Cassia," he murmured, and then in one fluid movement, he unsheathed a dagger.

Gasps went up.

"I never snipped one of your tresses, Cassia." Hovering his blade near the lone curl dangling at her shoulder, he lowered his voice. "May I?"

Incapable of words, breathing a chore, Cassia managed only a weak nod.

Wordlessly, Nathan clipped that curl, and then tucked it reverently in the front of his jacket, before resheathing his blade in his boot.

"Why?" she whispered.

His features softened in a way she'd never before seen. "You still have not figured it out? Why, I am here because I have missed you."

The raggedness of his voice wrenched her heart.

"I've been lost without you, Cassia McQuoid. I want to spend the rest of my days with you, learning real ballads to sing to you."

She searched her gaze over his face. "But . . . the arrangement to the woman your family wishes you to—"

"I would never marry her." Nathan cupped her cheek, that tender touch earning as many gasps as when he'd pulled out a knife. "Not when I love you so madly, deeply, and hopelessly, Cassia McQuoid."

Oh, God. Her heart quickened, that organ leaping in her breast. And yet . . .

"But you will have to give up the sea if you do not, Nath—"

"Oh, Cassia," he entreated. "I don't have to. I informed my father of my feelings for you. I made it clear I could never wed another woman."

Tears filled her eyes. He would have forsaken all he loved . . . for her?

At her silence, Nathan's brows stitched together in an angry line.

"Are you trying to dissuade me from my efforts?" he demanded, and a laugh bubbled past her lips. "Because I'll not be dissuaded."

A tear slipped down her cheek, and with a groan, Nathan caught it with his thumb, dusting it away. "I never want to make you cry, except for the happy tears."

"You said there was no such thing," she reminded him, her voice thick with emotion.

"I didn't know about them until you. You showed me everything I want, Cassia. A life. A family. With you." He held her stare. "I love you, and—*oomph.*" Nathan grunted as Cassia flung herself into his chest, and he immediately folded his strong, corded arms around her in the warmest of embraces.

"Don't you know, Nathan . . . I don't want ballads . . . ," she rasped between her tears.

"You don't?" he ventured, his voice so adorably befuddled it pulled a laugh from her.

"I want only sea shanties as we explore the seas together." Cassia edged back a fraction so she could hold his eyes with her own. "Will you spend all your days traveling with me, Nathan Ellsby, as both my captain and husband?"

He scowled. "Cassia McQuoid, did you just . . . propose to me?"

She smiled. "I did."

"That is my role," he grunted. "I—"

Stretching up, Cassia offered her mouth to his, dimly registering somewhere in the crowd the scandalized gasps and the furious shout of her eldest brother. "Is that a yes, then, Captain?"

Nathan's lips tipped up in a slow, crooked grin. "Aye, love. That is a yes."

About the Author

Photo © 2016 Kimberly Rocha

Christi Caldwell is the *USA Today* bestselling author of numerous series, including Wantons of Waverton, Lost Lords of London, Sinful Brides, Wicked Wallflowers, and Heart of a Duke. She blames novelist Judith McNaught for luring her into the world of historical romance. When Christi was at the University of Connecticut, she began writing her own tales of love—ones where even the most perfect heroes and heroines had imperfections. She learned to enjoy torturing her couples before they earned their well-deserved happily ever after. Christi lives in Charlotte, North Carolina, where she spends her time writing and baking with her twin girls and courageous son. For more information visit www.christicaldwell.com.